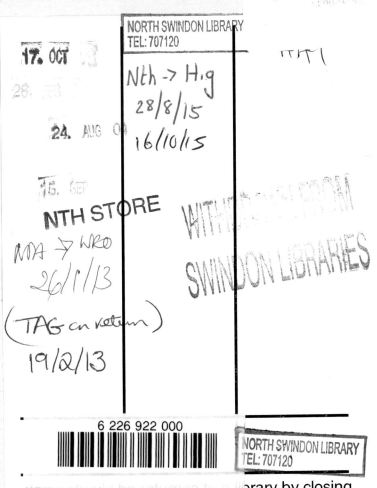

SILKS AND SADDLECLOTHS

BARRY WASS

JANUS PUBLISHING COMPANY
London, England

First published in Great Britain 2001
by Janus Publishing Company Limited,
76 Great Titchfield Street,
London W1P 7AF

www.januspublishing.co.uk

**A CIP catalogue record for this book
is available from the British Library.**

ISBN 1 85756 560 6

Typeset in 10pt Baskerville

Cover design Hamish Cooper

Printed and bound in Great Britain

Chapter One

It must have taken Victor's sleep-deprived and befuddled brain thirty seconds or more to realise that the incessant drone that he was hearing was, in fact, coming from the clock radio at the side of his bed. Eventually the message sank in and he reached out a weary arm and fumbled with the switches until he found the correct one. Thankfully, he turned it off. It was still dark and he had to screw his eyes up in order to focus on the green, illuminated figures that proclaimed the time: 4 a.m.! Shit, it was still the middle of the night! Then he remembered. He had wanted to get back to Melbourne before the Cup was run, so that he could watch it with Amanda and the twins – the Melbourne Cup – the race that brought the whole of Australia to a standstill and was now truly an international event. Horses were now coming from all over the world to compete. Ever since the Irish stayer, Vintage Crop, had won in 1994, owners and trainers from the United States, England, Europe and Japan had been leading the assault on one of the richest, handicap horse races in the world.

It had been really bad luck that had delayed Victor's departure from Canberra. A twenty-four hour virus, which he had picked up somewhere, had actually kept him confined to bed for three whole days and he was unfit to drive. The doctor had not given him the all clear until late yesterday evening and he had decided against a night drive back to Melbourne. Instead he had reluctantly settled for an early morning departure. He had intended on an early night, last night, but the company had insisted on him faxing his report on the deal with the Americans. His illness meant that he would not have been back in time to prepare for the shareholders' meeting. Victor was the company's chief negotiator and that was why he had been sent to Canberra to attend the exhibition in the first place.

It had been really quite a coup for Victor to have won the contract to supply video gaming machines to the Las Vegas Consortium. The competition had been very stiff, to say the least. Now he was looking forward to the week's leave that he had been promised should he manage to pull off the deal. He knew nothing about the technical side of the operation, but he was a born salesman and therein lay his strength.

The clock in the lobby had been showing 12.45 when Victor had finally made his way up the stairs to his room and bed. Remonstrating against himself this morning, he managed to drag his body from under the covers and into the shower. He spent the next fifteen minutes goading his aching and tired body into wakefulness. He had paid his bill the previous evening, when an apologetic, but unhelpful, night manager had told him that the kitchen staff did not come on duty until 5.30 a.m. He therefore was forced to make do with two cups of black coffee until he could find somewhere open on the way to Melbourne.

By now Victor was starting to regret his decision of having driven up instead of flying. When the company had told him that he was expected to ferry the Americans around to visit the local sights, not that there was much to see in Canberra, he had opted to take his own car. That way at least he was assured of collecting a nice expense cheque at the end of the month. All things considered, he was not really in the frame of mind for an eight-hour drive back home.

As he made his way out of the motel car park he pointed the nose of the Fairlane towards the Barton Highway; it was just striking five. Victor had to drive about twelve miles before he came across a truck stop that was open. Pulling in, he parked between a Mack and an International and made his way across the asphalt, towards his breakfast. Some thirty minutes later, feeling considerably more fortified by a meal of bacon and eggs, followed by a plate of pancakes washed down by strong black coffee, Victor was once again on his way.

He was about three miles from Yass when the CD player started to act up. In spite of today's technical advances, nobody as yet had perfected a CD player for a car that did not pick up some dust when travelling over long distances. Pulling in to the side of the road, Victor ejected the George Jones disc that he had been listening to, and inserted the laser cleaner. The cleaning cycle only took a couple of minutes but he preferred the player to be at a standstill when he used it. Satisfied that it would now play as it was designed to do, he re-inserted George Jones and, after checking that it was indeed performing correctly, he nosed the car back onto the highway and continued on his way.

The vehicle had only travelled about a further two hundred metres when, to his annoyance, Victor realised that his pulling over to the uneven shoulder of the road had resulted in him having a flat tyre. Somehow, this did not feel as though it was going to be his day. Little did he know what other horrors fate had in store for him, before this day would see its close. This was going to be one day that Victor Barnes would remember for the rest of his life.

He eventually changed the offending tyre and, after throwing the now useless one into the boot, drove off once more in the direction of Yass and a public toilet. His hands were black from the wheel and he needed to clean himself up. By the time that he had driven around the town a couple of times, he realised that there was no public convenience open at that hour. Finally he came across an inevitable McDonald's. He began to realise that any chance that he had of making Melbourne before the race was rapidly disappearing. He decided that he should telephone Amanda and let her know that he was going to be late. He knew that she would only panic if he did not arrive when he said that he would. He also knew that in spite of the money that he earned, she hated him being away from home so much.

In fact, if he was honest with himself, he was beginning to feel the same way himself. No amount of money could really compensate for being away from her and the twins so often. He had tried several times to land himself a job in the office, but Wainwright, the managing director, had just laughed at him. 'Barnes, you are one of the highest money earners of the company. In fact you take home almost as much as I do. Why on earth would you want to give that up? Tell your wife that she should check your bank balance whenever she is feeling lonely. That will soon change her mind, I can tell you!'

Victor could still hear the man's words ringing in his ears. No wonder Wainright had been married three times and was currently going through his third divorce. Oliver Wainwright thought far more of the money that he made than he ever cared for his wives.

Victor reached for his mobile phone which he normally carried on his belt, but then remembered that he had packed it in his suitcase, as the battery was flat. After the three-day confinement in bed it was currently useless. Inquiring of the hostess at the counter, she informed him that the closest public telephone was about a hundred metres down the road. Thanking her, he picked up his coffee and left. Upon reaching the call box, he discovered that his journey had been in vain. Staring at the vandalised telephone, he almost felt like crying. How many Chinamen had he run over, he mused, to have such a run of bad luck? He decided that the best thing was to return to his car and continue towards home. He could stop at the first telephone box that he reached on the way.

This time fate seemed to take pity on him as he soon saw a newsagent that was open. It had a yellow phone standing royally outside its door. Pulling up, he went in and purchased a slab of chocolate and the morning paper. He asked the proprietor for enough change to enable him to speak to Amanda for a while. He felt that he needed the calming influence of her voice to settle him down – he had earned the luxury after so much going wrong with the day. In fact, the way that his luck was running, he might not even have a bet on the Cup. That indeed would be a first for him. He had never missed laying a wager on the Melbourne Cup since he had arrived in Australia, some twelve years ago.

The number must have rung for almost thirty seconds before a somewhat breathless Amanda answered it. 'Hello, Amanda Barnes speaking, could you please hold the line for just a moment. Thank you.'

'Amanda. It's me. What on earth is going on?' His query went unanswered, however, and he had to wait a full three minutes before he could hear her coming back to the phone. 'Amanda, today is fast becoming a real bad hair day, to coin one of your favourite expressions. For goodness sake, tell me what is going on there?'

'Oh Victor, is that you darling? I am so sorry but it looks as though James has appendicitis. He has been complaining of severe pain in his side. He also has a temperature of 103 and has spent the last couple of hours vomiting. I was just getting him ready to take him into the children's hospital. I think that he is past seeing the local doctor.'

'Is he genuinely ill then? You know how he loves to put it on. I was ringing you to tell you that the way things are going I don't think that I shall be able to get back in time to go to Flemington for the race. I thought that I could meet you at your Mum's and we could all watch it with her.'

4

'If James has appendicitis, then I shan't see it at all.'

'Perhaps I should meet you at the hospital then. I would get there before I reached your Mum's.'

'OK then, let's do that. I am sorry darling, but I will have to go. I can hear James calling out.'

'Have you called an ambulance?'

'No, because I don't think that they would class him as serious enough to warrant one. I am going to drive in. See you later Victor. I love you.'

'I love you too Amanda.' Victor was just able to get the words out in time, before his wife replaced the receiver.

Replacing his telephone, Victor recovered his change and slowly walked back to his car. He could not remember any day when things had gone wrong so much in so short a time. Opening the car door, he sat there for about five minutes then, starting the engine once more, reversed the Fairlane and once again headed for the Hume Highway and home.

He was about two miles out of Gundagai, when the temperature gauge on the dashboard suddenly shot the needle into the red. At the same time he heard an ominous hissing coming from the direction of the bonnet. Another Victor immediately came to mind. The one from the popular British TV show *One Foot In The Grave* and his most famous saying 'I just don't believe it!' Pulling to the side of the road yet once again, he walked slowly around to the front, where he was met by the sight of a pool of hot water. It was running from underneath the bonnet of the car into the grass verge. Savagely, he kicked the front tyre in anger and let out a yell of despair to the sky. Morosely he then returned to his seat and slumped there with his head in his hands. Of all the times for his mobile to be out of action! Finally, he dragged himself to his feet once again, locking the car door, though it was hardly worth the bother. No one would be able to drive the car very far. He then set off to walk into town. The next time that the company sent him anywhere, he was going to fly, even if it meant having to pay his own fare.

For once the gods smiled on Victor. As he started to tramp somewhat wearily along the road, an elderly lady in an old, beat-up Dodge pulled up and offered him a lift. He accepted gratefully and for the next ten minutes nursed a far from docile Pekinese. His owner meanwhile chatted on about the unreliability of today's modern cars.

Dropping him off at the service station, the old lady wished him good fortune and pulled away in a thick cloud of blue smoke. After a few minutes' haggling, the owner agreed to his son driving Victor back to his car and fitting new hose for him. The $50 charge was exorbitant but by now Victor was past caring.

'I should really ring the hospital and see how James is,' he thought to himself, 'but the way that things are today, he most likely won't even have seen a doctor yet.' He decided that he would wait until he reached Albury/Wodonga. At least it would mean that he was back in Victoria and almost halfway home. Also, it would be about lunch time so he could grab a bite to eat there. Then he could drive non-stop to Melbourne. He could call in at the local tourist trap, The Ettamogah Pub, but he didn't think that he was really in the mood. To cope with busloads of Japanese tourists, all busily clicking away with their cameras; wanted something a bit more up market. He knew that he was kidding himself and would most likely end up in one of the golf club's bistros.

Victor surprised himself and discovered a more than passable French restaurant. He thoroughly enjoyed his *coquilles Saint-Jacques provençale* followed by strawberry crêpes. While drinking his coffee, his thoughts once again turned to Amanda and James. It was unusual for his son to be ill, though he had fooled his mother on more than one occasion, more often than not when it was his turn to do his share of the chores. Victor knew for a fact that James had faked high temperatures before, usually by running the thermometer under the hot water tap. However, Amanda had said that he was vomiting. Perhaps he really was sick this time. Leaving enough money on the table to cover the cost of his lunch, Victor crossed the restaurant to the blue phone in the corner.

When he finally managed to get through to the hospital, he had to wait almost fifteen minutes while someone checked for James' name. He was nearly at the end of his change when the receptionist got back to him. 'I am sorry Sir but there is no record of anyone by that name attending here so far today.' A little puzzled, Victor dialled again and asked the operator for his own number, reversed charges.

'I am sorry Sir, there is no reply from that number,' she told him.

Slowly he replaced the receiver. By now he was feeling more than a little mystified. 'Where on earth are you, Amanda? Even with all the traffic going to Flemington, you should have reached the hospital by now. Or did James make one of his miraculous recoveries?' He had a habit of that, if he thought his phoney sickness was going to stop him from doing something that he wanted to do. 'Maybe you have gone to your Mum's after all and...'

'Hey mate, that is one of the first signs you know.' A coarse voice broke into his thoughts. Victor looked up to see a young boy grinning at him. 'You are talking to yourself, mate. They lock you away for that.' The kid grinned at him again and then ran off down the street laughing. Victor smiled sheepishly as he realised that he must have been voicing his thoughts out loud as the boy had said. In fact, he was not even aware that he had left the restaurant and was standing outside. 'Well, standing here is not going to achieve anything. The best thing for me to do is to get back to Melbourne.' He spoke aloud to a startled bird that had perched momentarily on a rubbish bin. He then walked briskly back to his car.

Within minutes he had reached the freeway and was speeding towards Melbourne.' In a way it is a shame that the freeway cuts out all the small towns but when you are in a hurry like I am, it does save a lot of time,' Victor thought to himself. 'Now it is only a matter of three and a half hours' drive to Melbourne.' He switched off the CD player. 'Sorry George, but if I can't get to Flemington in time, at least I can listen to the races.' So saying, he switched on the racing station on the radio. There were still a couple of hours to the Cup, but the announcer would no doubt keep the general public up to date with the betting fluctuations.

'Damn it! I didn't have a bet then. Oh well if I don't make Melbourne in time, I will take it as an omen. The way that this day has gone my money is better off in my pocket. Any horse that I backed today would most likely fall and break its leg,' he reflected. 'Although I suppose that I could pull off into Wangaratta if I really wanted to. It is unlikely that I will pass a phone on this road. Nor have I enough change left to make a call if I did. I hate not having a bet though. God, I wish I knew what has happened to Amanda. She and the twins are most likely at her Mum's. I don't see where else they could be if they are not at the hospital. No, I think that the best thing would be to get home as quickly as possible.'

Having made his mind up Victor switched the CD player back on. The magnificent voice of George Jones boomed from the speakers as the Fairlane ate up the miles towards home.

7

Victor had been driving for about two hours when he spotted a dark saloon ahead. It was parked on the grassy, centre meridian strip. Almost automatically, he eased his foot off the accelerator. He lightly touched his brakes to reduce his speed. Not that he was speeding, but he always liked to be well within the speed limit, especially whenever he saw what he believed to be a police car. There were more and more unmarked cars on the road nowadays in an effort to cut the ever-climbing road toll. Victor passed the suspect car at a sedate fifty-six miles an hour and smiled to himself as he spotted the telltale camera, mounted on its dashboard. He was more than a little surprised and somewhat apprehensive when, in his rear view mirror, he saw the car move onto the road. It followed him, flashing its headlights and showing a blue light from its windscreen. Victor gently slowed, then pulled over to the side of the road and stopped. The police car pulled in behind him and its driver cut its engine. Victor got out of his car and walked slowly back to the squad car. As he neared the other car, he saw that its driver was on the two-way. He was no doubt checking that Victor was not driving a stolen vehicle, he supposed. He had no doubt that he had not been exceeding the speed limit, unless his speedo was at fault.

'Good afternoon officer. Is there a problem?' Victor asked. The policeman by now had finished his call and had got out of his car also. 'Good afternoon, sir, may I see your driver's licence please?' The man replied, stretching out his palm.

'Certainly officer.' Victor reached into his rear pocket, pulled out his wallet and after extracting his licence, handed it to the man. 'I am sure that I was not speeding though. I know that sometimes on these straight roads, one can travel too fast without realising it. I am quite certain that I was well within the limit.' The policeman did not answer him but instead looked firstly at his licence and then at the notebook that he had in his hand. He gazed at Victor for a few moments, then somewhat hesitantly asked him. 'That is your car, sir, and this is indeed your licence?'

'Of course it is my car and you can tell by my photograph that it is my licence,' he snapped. 'Just what is the problem? I am trying my best to get home. I have had a very trying day and this is not helping. Now, if I was speeding, which I don't admit for a minute, please write me a ticket and let me get on my way.' The other man looked decidedly uncomfortable, as he tried not to look Victor in the eye.

The latter however, held his gaze firmly and noted with mild amusement that the other man actually squirmed.

'Mr Barnes, I am truly sorry. I realise that this must be very annoying for you. If you could just bear with me for a few minutes, everything will be explained. I apologise for the inconvenience but if you would just go and sit in your car I promise that I won't detain you any longer than is absolutely necessary.'

'What do you mean detain me? What the hell is going on here? I demand an answer and I demand it right now. What am I supposed to have done?'

'Mr Barnes, you have done nothing illegal I can assure you. I have been instructed to detain you while someone is on their way from Wangaratta to see you. I am afraid that is all that I call tell you at this stage, so would you please be a little patient and go and sit in your car?'

'What if I decide to drive on? Would you arrest me?'

'No, sir, I would not do that. I do assure you that it is in your best interests to wait for the people that are coming from Wangaratta. They will be able to explain everything to you just as soon as they arrive and answer all your questions. So please, Mr Barnes, just go and sit in your car.'

By now, Victor was almost as intrigued by all this as he was annoyed at the delay. What on earth had he been stopped for? Also, who was this mystery person that was coming from Wang' to see him? 'Okay, I will do as you ask. Not that I have much choice I would imagine,' he said grudgingly. He almost had to laugh at the thankful look that swept over the policeman's face at his words. He wondered what kind of trouble the man would have been in if he had driven off. He walked back to his car but leaned up against the bonnet instead of getting back in.

It must have been about ten minutes later that Victor saw a regular patrol car approaching from the opposite direction. Its occupants must have been looking out for them because as they drew level the car slowed. Making an illegal turn across the centre strip it pulled up alongside the unmarked car. The officer, who had stopped Victor, spoke briefly to the driver of the second car. It then slowly drove towards him and came to a halt in front of the Fairlane. 'Well I couldn't drive away now even if I wanted to,' mused Victor to himself. 'What the devil is going on here? I've got a strange feeling that I am not going to like this, one little bit.'

The driver of the second car, Victor noticed, was a girl. She sat at the wheel as its other occupant, a man in his fifties and wearing a suit, got out of the car. He slowly walked over to where Victor was standing.

'Mr Barnes, I do apologise for keeping you. I am Inspector Edwards.' Victor shook the proffered hand. As he did so, a dreadful sense of foreboding, swept over him. 'Are you all right sir? You look a little pale.' Edwards asked him.

'Yes, I feel fine,' Victor replied testily. 'Just tell me what all this is about. I am in somewhat of a hurry to get home.'

'You are a hard man to find, Mr Barnes. Your mobile phone seems to be switched off and...'

'The battery is flat. Why would you be trying to get in touch with me anyway? Is there something wrong with James?' Victor suddenly started to feel tremors of alarm racing through his body. The inspector hesitated momentarily. Then he said softly and slowly, 'Mr Barnes, I am very sorry to have to tell you, but your family were involved in a very nasty accident, this morning.'

'An accident! How bad was it? Were they hurt very badly? Wait a minute, why would you be here unless they were?' Victor stopped, unable to say the words that sprang to his mind. He reeled and Edwards grabbed him and held him against the car.

'Your wife is in a very bad way, I am afraid. She is in the Alfred Hospital at present. She was taken there after it happened.'

'What about the twins? Are they okay? What happened anyway?'

'I am afraid that I don't have many details. We received a call from D24, asking us to locate you. They found one of your business cards in your wife's handbag. When they could not raise you on your mobile they telephoned your office. Luckily, your boss was there working. He told us that you were driving back from Canberra. We have had patrol cars looking for you everywhere. We had almost given up hope of spotting you when...'

'Do you know how the boys are? What actually happened?' Victor grabbed at the other man's arm desperately. Edwards gently eased Victor's clutching hands off him.

'I am sorry but we have no information on the boys' condition at this time. Your wife was driving through Camberwell Junction, when a transporter hit her car. Apparently, the driver was coming down Burke Road when he must have suffered a heart attack. The truck was fully loaded with cars. It met your wife's car in the centre of the junction.'

'Oh my god!' Victor felt physically sick. 'This is all my fault. If I had flown to Canberra as I normally do then I would have been home. Amanda wouldn't have had to drive James to the hospital. It's all my fault. My fault.' The inspector gently laid a hand on Victor's shoulder. 'You cannot blame yourself, sir. It was an accident and no one is to blame. If you would like to get into your car, sir, I will drive you to Melbourne. Constable Andrews will precede us and give us an escort. We will soon have you at your wife's bedside.' He tried to open the passenger door but it was locked. He went back to the driver's side, leaned in and unlocked the door. Walking back, he opened the door and gently pushed Victor towards the seat. After motioning to the girl in the other car to move out, he settled himself in the seat normally occupied by Victor. He started the engine. He was about to move off, when he remembered the unmarked car behind them. He signalled to the waiting patrolman who ran up at the summons.

'I am sorry son, you can return to your normal duty. Thank you. You have done well spotting Mr Barnes' car.' The young officer flushed with the praise. Saluting, he then walked back to his own car, ready to take on the world of speeding drivers once more.

Finally, Edwards eased the Fairlane back onto the highway and gunned the engine. True to his word, the police car escorting them turned on its siren. Victor watched the red and blue flashing lights, almost in a daze. They had driven for about three miles before he turned and spoke to Edwards. 'Why are you doing this for me?'

'In spite of what you might think of us Mr Barnes, we policemen do have hearts,' he said with a smile,' and besides I welcome the chance of going to the "Big City". I don't often get the opportunity.' Victor grunted, then slumped into his seat. His mind was racing with numerous thoughts of what he might find when they reached Melbourne. 'Oh please God, let them be okay.' What would he do if Amanda were crippled for life? She was so outgoing and full of life. What if she had been blinded? His over-active imagination raced with terrible thoughts of horrific injuries to his beloved wife.

'Don't you worry Mr Barnes, we will soon be there and you can see her for yourself.' Victor came back to reality with a start. 'God! He must have been talking aloud without realising it again. He must get a grip on himself. He had to show a brave face in front of Amanda.' He sat back in his seat and closed his eyes. He was aware that they must have been travelling well over the speed limit. He had a strange feeling that if he didn't look to see exactly how fast they were moving, then they would arrive there sooner.

When he finally opened his eyes again, Victor was more than a little surprised to discover that they were driving along St Kilda Road. The Alfred Hospital was only minutes away. Inspector Edwards drove into the car park reserved for doctors and parked neatly between a Mercedes and a Porsche. He turned to Victor. 'Would you like Constable Miller to come in with you? It might speed things up a little, finding the right doctor.'

'Thank you. That would be great. I really do appreciate your help. I know that I would never have gotten here so quickly on my own. I should have been pulled over for certain at the speed that we were travelling.' Edwards just grinned. Getting out of the car he went over to speak to the young policewoman who had been their escort. She had followed them in and was parked behind them. Victor saw her look in his direction and nod her head, then both she and the inspector walked back towards him.

'Mr Barnes, this is Constable Miller. She will look after you for the time being. I have to go into headquarters to see someone. I sincerely hope that your wife will be okay.' He shook Victor's hand and walked back to the now vacant police car. With a final wave he drove off.

'Perhaps we should go in Mr Barnes,' the policewoman said quietly. His stomach heaving, Victor nodded his head in agreement. He then followed her through the main door of the hospital. Once inside, Constable Miller went up to the reception desk and spoke to the receptionist. Victor saw her look towards him before picking up one of the telephones in front of her. She spoke briefly and then replaced the receiver. 'The doctor will be right down, Mr Barnes. Perhaps you would like to take a seat for a minute?' she called over to him. He shook his head and started to pace up and down. She said something to Miller but Victor was unable to hear. By now his stomach was in a tight knot and he realised that he was sweating, quite profusely. His mouth was completely dry and his heart was hammering so loudly in his chest that he was amazed that they could not hear it. Panic began to mount in him.

A man in a white coat walked down the corridor towards him. 'Mr

Barnes, I am Dr Wallace. Would you follow me please?'

'My wife! How is she? And the boys, how are the boys?'

Dr Wallace opened the door of a small room. He motioned Victor inside. 'After you Mr Barnes.' He then followed him in, quietly closing the door behind him. 'Perhaps you might like to sit down for a moment?'

'Hang it all, when is somebody going to give me a straight answer?'

'Mr Barnes, I am sorry but I am the bearer of some very bad news I am afraid. I am sure by now that you know that your family were involved in a very nasty accident this morning.'

'Yes I know. A truck hit them. How badly hurt are they? Can I see them?' The doctor hesitated for a moment. 'There is no easy way to say this, Mr Barnes. Your two sons were sitting in the back of the vehicle when the truck hit them. Unfortunately, the force of the impact dislodged one of the cars that it was carrying. The boys did not have a chance. The only thing that I can say, in the way of consolation, is that they would not have suffered. The falling car, well, it completely flattened the rear of your car. They would have died instantly.' The doctor's tone caused Victor to start trembling violently.

'And my wife, how is she?' he said slowly.

'I am so very sorry, Mr Barnes. Your wife passed away twenty minutes ago.'

It was at that moment that Victor's world came crashing down around him. His legs turned to jelly and waves of nausea swept over him. He fought to get his breath. Spasms of pain jagged across his tightening chest. His vision slowly dissolved into a murky, red mist. From his mouth emitted an anguished cry of 'Nooo'as he slowly crumpled into a sobbing heap on the floor. His body shook with involuntary jerks as though he was in the midst of a seizure. The doctor observed him sadly. He knew that for the time being, anyway, anything that he did would not penetrate through Victors grief. He turned and left the room leaving the door slightly ajar.

Crossing over to the desk, he motioned to Constable Miller. 'Do you know of anyone that you could contact to come and take him home? He is certainly in no fit state to go by himself. Neither do I think that he should be left on his own at the moment. The present mood that he is in, well he could do anything.'

'The poor man. What a tragedy this is. It is hard enough to come to terms with one member of your family being killed but when an entire family is wiped out... I know that I would be in an awful mess if it were me. Inspector Edwards left me here to take him home. He guessed that there was little hope of Mrs Barnes surviving. Perhaps if I were to telephone his boss, he might know where we could find a relation. Even a close friend, just someone to stay with him.' Miller herself found it very difficult to talk, just being aware of the facts. A couple of tears rolled down her cheeks and she wiped them away, angrily. 'I am sorry, doctor, we are supposed to be able to handle situations like this. When it is really bad though it still manages to get to you.'

'Don't apologise my dear. We all are affected from time to time. We would not be human if we weren't. If you would like to get in touch with his boss, I will get a nurse to help me with him.' Dr Wallace patted her sympathetically on the shoulder and walked off to the nurses' station. After speaking to one of the nurses there, they both returned to the room. They found Victor was still lying on the floor crying, his hands clasped tightly to his face.

'Mr Barnes, let us help you up and into this chair.' The doctor said softly. He motioned to the nurse to take Victor's arm. Together they gently managed to lift him and seat him in the chair. 'Can I get you anything Mr Barnes? A nice cup of tea or perhaps you would prefer coffee?' the nurse asked him. Victor shook his head but did not speak. He just sat there, slumped in the chair, his head bowed and his eyes closed. Eventually the tormented sobs that once wracked his body slowly subsided until they finally stopped.

There was a tap at the door and, walking over to it, Dr Wallace found Constable Miller standing there. 'I have managed to get in touch with his brother-in-law. He should be here in about thirty minutes. How is he?'

'Still in shock of course but he should be okay.' The doctor glanced at his watch. 'I know that this an imposition, but do you think that you can stay with him until his brother-in-law arrives? I have to get to a staff meeting. I will arrange with the desk that there are some sedatives left for him. I think that it is best if he takes them when he gets home. By rights he should go straight to bed.'

'Of course. The Inspector warned me that I might be here for a while. Actually, it suits me because I won't have to go back to Wangaratta until tomorrow now. I don't have the chance to spend the night in Melbourne very often so I shall make the most of it. I just wish that it were on a happier occasion, that's all.'

'Unfortunately we see far too much of this kind of thing here. They are not always as bad as this of course. I should have a very thick skin by now, but like you sometimes these things can still get to you. Thank you for your help Constable.' They shook hands and he left the room, leaving the two women to care for Victor.

Some forty minutes later, Victor's brother-in-law, Dan, arrived. He too was white-faced and finding it hard to contain his tears. Between the three of them they managed to get Victor into Dan's car. He was about to drive off when Miller remembered the tablets. Telling Dan to hold on she ran back inside. 'The doctor said to give him three of these when you get him home. The best thing for him right now is a good twelve hour's sleep.'

'I am taking him to my house. My wife has made up a bed for him in the spare room. We thought that it would be better than...'

'I am going home to my place.' Victor suddenly seemed to come to life. 'Take me to my place, Dan.'

'Don't you think that it would be better if you spent the night with us, old son? I can take you home tomorrow after you have had a rest.'

'You either take me home or I will drive myself,' Victor snapped testily and opened the car door.

'Okay Victor. I will take you home if that is really what you want right now.'

'I do so let's get on with it. Thank you for your help, Constable.'

'In view of the circumstances, I can't say that it has been a pleasure, sir. I am truly sorry about your family. In times like these it is very hard to know what to say.'

Victor nodded. 'That's okay, but thanks anyway.'

Constable Miller watched as the car drove out of the car park. Turning to the nurse she said, 'It's times like these that I hate my job.' Without waiting for an answer she made her way to her own car.

Upon reaching home Victor got out of the car. 'Thanks a lot Dan. I suppose that I shall have to go back and pick up my car tomorrow. That's providing that it is still there, of course. It could have been towed away by then.'

'Don't you worry about that. The hospital knows that it is yours. I will get one of the boys to drive me in to work tomorrow and I will collect it for you. I might ask my assistant Karl. I know that he is going to be in a good mood. He backed Major League six months ago at

15

100-1 to win the Cup. The thing romped in by five lengths.'

'Oh, the Cup. I had forgotten all about that. I didn't even have a bet this year. It must be the first time since I came out here that I haven't.'

'Well, you saved your money. I am sure that you wouldn't have backed Major League. Its form has been atrocious this year. It was a real boilover, the bookies would have been very happy. Now come on, enough about horses, let's get you inside and settled. I will ring Naomi and let her know that we are here. She has been busy making you up a bed at our place.'

'Thanks Dan but you can get off home. I shall be all right I assure you. I would rather be own my own for a while anyway.'

'No chance! If you won't come to our place then I am staying here. There is no way that I am going to leave you on your own tonight. I will ring Naomi and she can come over and cook us some tea. I am not going to take no for an answer, old son. Now get in there and get yourself up to bed.'

'How am I going to sleep at a time like this?'

'By taking those sedatives that the doctor gave you. Get some sleep and you will feel more able to cope with things after you have had some rest.' Sensing that it was going to be a lost cause arguing with Dan, Victor reluctantly walked up the drive. He opened the front door and just stood there. For a moment, a dreadful sense of desolation swept over him once again. He broke out in a cold sweat. The house, which was once the home of so many good times, now seemed to have become a mausoleum. A cold, dank and cheerless tomb devoid of anything that recalled the happy family which once lived there. Seeing Dan watching him, he mentally pulled himself together and entered the hall. His brother-in-law followed at a discreet distance. He waited for Victor to sit down before he picked up the telephone to call his wife.

Victor could not hear what Dan was saying but he could sense that Naomi was not at all pleased at Victor's determination to stay in his own home. Pouring himself a large Jack Daniels from the well-stocked bar, he sat back down.

'Get yourself a drink if you want one Dan. What did Naomi have to say?'

'Well, she still thinks you would be better off coming with us.'

'I am staying in my own home! Don't worry, I am not going to slash my wrists or do anything else stupid. I would far rather be on my own

as I said. If you insist on remaining with me, it's going to be here.'
Dan could see that Victor's mind was made up and that nothing was
going to change it. He decided that 'if you can't beat 'em, join 'em
and, pouring himself a somewhat smaller measure of whisky, sat down
on the couch. Finishing off his drink in a couple of swallows, Victor
said, 'I might just go up and lie down for a few minutes until Naomi
arrives, Dan.'

'Have you taken those tablets?'

'All right, if it is going to make you happy, I will take them. I can tell
you though that they are not going to work. I am far too upset to even
think about sleep at the moment.' He swallowed the pills with another
measure of Jack Daniels. He then made his way slowly up the stairs.
Dan waited for about twenty minutes then followed him. As he
opened the door of Victor's bedroom he found him, as expected,
lying on the bed fast asleep. Covering him with a blanket he then
quietly made his way back to the lounge to await the arrival of his wife.

There was a huge turnout for the funerals. A lot of Victor's col-
leagues from the industry as well as the twins' school friends attended.
Dan and Naomi made sure that only the family and close friends came
back to the house afterwards. Victor had insisted that everyone was to
come back for the traditional gathering and had even gone so far as
to hire a caterer to see to the food side of things.

Everybody had split into small groups and was talking quietly
among themselves, when Victor arrived with Dan and Naomi. He had
given the caterer the key to the house, so that they could get on with
the cooking while the service was taking place at the church, so most
of the crowd had preceded him to the house. As the three of them
entered the lounge, everyone became silent, many at a loss for words.
It is always uncomfortable when anyone has just been buried, but
when it is most of a family, then most people find it hard to come to
terms with such a tragedy.

However, it was Victor himself who broke the tension. 'If someone
would like to open the kitchen door and tell the chef that we are all
starving in here, he might start to roll out some food.' Everybody
laughed and it seemed as though the sun had broken through the
clouds after an extra heavy storm. The atmosphere lifted and people
began to relax. As the food arrived, Naomi grabbed a plate. Piling it
high with goodies, she took Victor's arm and guided him to a vacant

chair. 'Sit down and relax Victor. Everything is under control. It was a good idea, hiring the caterers, although you know that you were more than welcome to use our place.'

'Thank you, Naomi, but I am sure that Amanda would have wanted it to be held here. But I should mix with everybody, they will think me very rude if I don't.'

'Nonsense! People know how hard this has been for you. They also know that when you are ready then you will talk. Just sit there and eat something. I have to go and find Dan. He promised to look out for Granddad and he is not here yet. Knowing him, he is most likely chatting to that blonde woman who was sitting next to him in Church. I really don't know how Gran puts up with him.'

'He is harmless enough and besides it keeps him out of your grand-mother's hair. She is always complaining that he keeps getting under her feet.' Naomi laughed and went off in search of her husband. Victor remained in his chair and had just started to pick at the food on his plate. The doorbell rang. 'I wonder who that can be? I thought that everybody knew to come straight in.'

He started to struggle to his feet when one of his nieces, he could never remember their names, cried out, 'Don't you worry Uncle Victor. I will go for you. You just sit there.' Before he had a chance to make any remark, she had scurried out of the room to the front door. She returned a couple of moments later with a stranger in tow. 'Uncle Victor, this man says that he needs to talk to you. I told him that it wasn't a good time but he said that it was very important and he won't take up too much of your time.'

'Thanks Sugar, I'll talk to him.' The stranger stepped forward and held out his hand. 'Mr Barnes. My name is John Livingstone and I see that you are well into your celebrations. You are a very lucky man.'

'Celebrations! Lucky man! What the hell do you mean? Who are you?' Victor dropped his plate and grabbed the man around the throat.

Just then Dan and Naomi came back into the room and seeing what was going on jumped to the stranger's aid. 'Hey steady on there Victor. Who is this poor guy and what brought all this on? Just let him go, you are choking him,' Dan cried, wrenching at Victor's arm.

'And so I should. How dare he say that I am celebrating,' Victor hissed through clenched teeth. The man swallowed painfully several times and then turned to Victor. 'I am very sorry Mr Barnes but when

Chapter One

I arrived and saw a house full of people all eating and drinking, well, naturally I assumed that you were all celebrating. I am sure that most people would have been of the same opinion, in view of the circumstances.'

'What the hell are you talking about?' Victor snarled. Dan stepped forwards and took Livingstone's arm. 'You are obviously not aware that Victor buried his wife and two boys today. We have all just come back from the cemetery. That is why the house is full.'

'Oh, my lord, Mr Barnes. I had no idea. What a terrible thing that must have been. How did it happen? Just a minute, your wife and two boys?' The man went as white as a sheet, as the impact of the statement hit him. 'That horrible accident on Cup Day, it was your wife and...?' Dan nodded. 'I am so sorry Mr Barnes. What on earth must you think of me?'

'No! It's I that should be apologising to you, Mr Livingstone. I realise now that you weren't to know. What did you want to see me about anyway?'

'I work for Tattersalls, Mr Barnes, and I thought that I was the bearer of some good news. Usually most people are thrilled to see me.'

'Oh yes, I remember. I buy tickets in all the draws.' Victor wearily sat back down. 'I enter them for five weeks at a time. I hardly ever check them, as I am a registered player. I know that if I have a win you people eventually send me the money. Have I won a major prize? Is that why you are here today?'

'Yes and I am very happy to tell you that you have won Division One in Powerball.'

'Is that good? How much did I win?'

'You mean that you have no idea?' Victor shook his head. Taking a deep breath, John Livingstone grasped Victor's hand. 'Mr Barnes, it is my very great pleasure to inform you that you have won ...' He paused with dramatic effect, clearly enjoying his moment of fame. Dan grabbed the man's arm and shook it. 'Come on man don't keep us in suspense. How much has he won?'

'Twelve million dollars, Mr Barnes! You have won a little over twelve million dollars!'*

---

*4.5 million pounds, sterling

19

Chapter Two

Early in the New Year Dan drove up to Victor's house. The drive being empty, he drove right in. Bringing the car to a halt, he cut the engine and then turned to his passenger. 'I am sure that we will find that he is home. Nobody has seen him since Christmas Day but I think that we will find him at home. If not, we can just sit here and wait for him.' He looked around. 'Gee he certainly has let the garden go. Amanda used to be so proud of all her azaleas and rhododendrons but just look at the state of them now. We have had a very hot and dry three months but it looks as though he hasn't even turned the hose on them once. What a shame.' He opened the car door and got out.

'Come on Harley, let's see if the bugger is going to answer his door today. I know losing Amanda and the twins was a great tragedy, but he simply must pull himself together. Maybe you arriving on the scene is just the tonic that he needs to lift him out of his misery.' Waiting a moment for Harley to join him, Dan then marched up to the front door and rang the bell. There was no reply so he rang again. Still no one came to answer it so he put his finger to the bell once more and left it there. It rang continuously. He also hammered on the door as hard as he was able.

'Come on Victor, I know that you are in there. Open the door. There is someone here to see you. He has flown all the way from America so the least that you can do is to offer the poor guy a drink.'

'Hey, I didn't come just to see him,' Harley protested.

'He's not to know that now is he? If he thinks that you did, we might be able to get him to open the door.'

'Maybe he truly is out somewhere. From what you have told me he must had had a pretty rough time of it, the poor sod. It is possible that he has gone into town.'

As he spoke the door opened slightly and an angry voice snarled, 'What are you trying to do? Push the bloody bell through the wall?'

20

'And a good day to you too, old son. Look Victor, open the door properly and let us in. As I said, there is someone here who has come all the way from America to see you. You remember Harley don't you? Why don't you take him through to the lounge and I will put the kettle on.' So saying, Dan pushed open the door and gently propelled Harley through into the hallway.

'Harley? Harley who?' Victor shook his head as he tried vainly to place the face.

'Victor, we met in Canberra. You sold me $10 million worth of gaming machines, You also told me about a horse that I should back that was running on Cup Day. You told me that if I wanted to recoup some of my outlay for those machines, then I should back it. If you remember you told me that it was the bet of the day.'

'Of course, Harley. You will have to forgive me. I have not been myself lately. How did the horse go anyway? Did it win?'

'Win? She cruised in. I won a packet thanks to you. In fact I was so impressed with the way that she raced that I went and bought her. She has already won three races back in the States for me. I have picked up treble what I paid for her in prize money alone. Not to mention how much I won on her with her first start at Belmont Park.'

'How much did you win on her then Harley?'

'I said not to mention it,' Harley laughed. 'I will have the taxman after me and that I can do without.' By now, Dan had disappeared into the kitchen and Victor had led Harley almost automatically into the lounge. 'Sit down Harley. Dan reckons that he is making tea or something. I am sure that you would prefer something a bit stronger wouldn't you?'

'No tea is just fine by me,' Harley said shaking his head.

'Well you won't mind if I do, will you?' So saying, Victor poured himself such a large measure of Jack Daniels that even Harley, who prided himself on being a heavy drinker, flinched. 'Hey Victor, I know that you Aussies are supposed to be heavy drinkers, but you don't have to prove it to me buddy.'

'Actually, I am English and proud of it.'

'I am sorry Victor, I did not mean to slight you. I just assumed that as you lived here, then you must have been Australian.'

'Amanda and the boys were born here but I was not.' Victor muttered.

'Look Victor, about Amanda and the accident, well there isn't

21

anything that I can say really. With such a catastrophe, words aren't nearly enough to say. I mean that at a time like this, I am not certain what I . . .'

'Don't worry, Harley, I know that your heart's in the right place. Now if it is all the same to you I'd rather not talk about it, if you don't mind.'

Just then Dan entered the room carrying three different coloured mugs. 'It must be the maid's day off Victor, I couldn't find any clean cups anywhere, apart from these three. You just can't seem to find good help nowadays. She also seems to have missed the garbage too, the last couple of weeks.'

'Ok Dan, knock it off will you? I know that the place is in a mess but I used to have a reason to keep it clean. I just don't care any more.' Victor gulped down his drink and went to pour himself another. Harley stood up and took his arm. 'Steady Victor, we all know how you must be feeling, but this will not do you any good. I have been down this road myself. My wife was shot in a bank hold up and she died in my arms. She was so full of a zest for life that even as she was dying, she made me promise that I would carry on. She said that I should remember all the good times that we had enjoyed together. I know that you had it a lot worse, losing your two boys as well. You have to know that eventually the pain does subside. What you have to do now is to look ahead. Now I think that I might have the perfect solution for you. That is if you are interested of course. First thing though is that you have to take a grip on yourself, ease off the booze. It is only a short-term cure.'

'I'm ok, just leave me alone.' Victor shook Harley's hand off his arm and going behind the bar poured himself another equally large measure of whiskey.

'Victor, you are far from ok,' Dan interjected. 'Have you looked at yourself in the mirror lately? Besides that, this place is a pigsty. Now why don't you just sit down and at least listen to what Harley has to say? You owe him that much.' Sullenly his brother-in-law retreated to the couch, still clinging to his drink. The other two men were more than a little relieved to see that he made no attempt to drink it though.

Harley moved across to one of the armchairs. Seating himself he then leant forward towards Victor. 'Look Vic, Dan here says that you seem to have a talent for spotting good horses. I must say that on the

performance of the one that you tipped me, I am inclined to agree
with him. I know that you have only given me the one and that could
have been a lucky guess. He insists, however, that you have a gift but
you have never really developed it. Normally it takes years of experience to be able to recognise potential champions. I do know that some
people possess an instinct about a horse though. I have an Indian
working for one of my stables and he certainly seems to have an
uncanny knack for picking the most unlikely looking animals that
have turned up trumps. You could be another like him. Now a friend
of mine in England has just died. He used to own a string of horses
but his wife has decided that she wants to get rid of them. She has no
real interest in racing and also she says that they remind her too much
of her husband.'

'What did he have – four legs and long flowing hair then?' Victor
said with a snigger. Dan and Harley laughed politely at his poor
attempt at humour.

'No not really. Victor, Tattersalls are putting on a special sale for her
at Newmarket. Apparently her husband was in some way connected
to somebody high up in the Jockey Club. These horses are all high-
class thoroughbreds. In fact four of them are entered for the Derby.'

'I don't quite understand, what has all this got to do with me?'
Victor asked. He had put his drink down untouched and the other
two glanced at each other. Was it possible that they indeed had stirred
his interest, Dan wondered. Was this just the right thing to help him?

'I want you to go to England on my behalf and bid for some of those
horses. Racing is a real hobby for me and I can indulge it because of
the money that I make out of the slots. Also, thanks to you and those
new machines that you sold us, business is booming. The gambling
public just loves all those hi-tech games. They are so different to our
standard machines.'

'Hold on a minute Harley. I don't know the first thing about the
English racing scene, particularly the current form. I mean I used to
follow the horses when I lived there. But I have been out here for
twelve years now. The racing world has changed a lot since I was there
last. I don't even know a lot of the jockeys now, let alone the horses.'
Victor protested.

'That is not really an issue. You can buy on instinct. As I said, I trust
your judgement. Dan says that you have more than once picked a
horse that everyone else reckoned was a donkey and the animal has

come out and won. I am prepared to offer you a blank cheque and an all-expenses-paid trip to England. You can buy them and I'll even go as far as to make you my manager over there and you can race them for me. Come on, what do you say?'

Victor stood up and started to pace up and down the room. He stopped, looked at Dan for a moment and then back again to Harley. 'Well I am through selling poker machines and that is for sure. I must say that your offer is very tempting. Let's be realistic for a moment though. Apart from that spot of business that we did in Canberra, you hardly know me. What makes you think that I can do what you want?'

'Victor, I got where I am today by taking chances on people. You may have a talent for picking horses but my forte is with people. Wouldn't you like to visit England again?'

'Amanda and I were actually planning a trip there next year. We were toying with the idea of spending three or four months there to show the twins the more interesting places. They were at an age when they could appreciate what they were seeing. We felt that the trip would broaden their minds somewhat.' A dramatic change had seemed to come over Victor, like a smouldering fire that had suddenly sparked into flame. 'Hang on a minute though, when we were in Canberra, didn't you tell me that you owned a couple of horses that were racing in England?'

'Nags, more like it you mean.' Harley snorted. 'They haven't won a bean between them, at least nothing worth writing home about.'

'But if you have horses in training there, then you must have a manager already working for you?' Victor said, sounding more than a little disappointed and his shoulders seemed to sag a little.

Harley laughed. 'I have a worthless son of a bitch collecting a pay packet from me each month. He doesn't seem to be earning his keep though.'

'All the same, I can hardly manage other horses when you already have someone there doing the job. Unless you sack him, of course, but you would have to have a good reason to do that.'

'I have a very strong suspicion that the bastard is lining his own pockets at my expense. I can't prove it because I am not there, but my gut feeling is that is what is happening.' The American sprawled back in his chair and cast a quizzical eye over Victor. 'Well. What do you say? Are you in the mood for a trip to England to buy me a couple of classic winners? Or do you intend to just sit there and wallow in self-pity the rest of your life?'

'Hey steady on there, Harley, that's a bit strong don't you think?' Dan spoke up, feeling a little uncomfortable for his brother-in-law.

'No he is quite right Dan.' Victor raised his hand in acknowledgement. 'I am acting as though something like this has never happened to anybody else. Amanda and the boys are dead, that's true. However life still goes on. It is about time that I accepted the fact that I am never going to see them again. I am sorry I forget that it must have been really tough on you and Naomi as well. After all, she was your sister. No, maybe this trip will help me to get on with my life again.' He sat back on the couch and for a few minutes appeared to be lost in thought, his thumb and forefinger pinching his lips together. Dan opened his mouth to say something but Harley motioned for him to remain silent. Dan leant back, his unspoken question forgotten for the time being. Suddenly Victor got to his feet and faced the American tycoon. 'I will tell you what I am prepared to do.'

'Go ahead. I am listening,' Harley said with interest. Victor started to pace up and down again as though he was trying to focus on the ideas that had started to race through his mind. The other two men remained silent, as though aware that their friend was, indeed, starting to come back to the real world. 'I accept on the following conditions. Firstly, we both initially go to England to see these horses. I will give you my candid but strictly gut feelings about them. You must realise that I know virtually nothing about the conformation of a horse. Someone once told me about a horse's nostrils I know that a wide-open one allows the horse to breath better and that when he becomes excited or angry, then he dilates his nostrils. I also know that the more supple his knees are, the less likely he is to fall in a race.'

Harley nodded. 'That's right and another important thing to look for is that the haunches should be firm and in the right proportion to the chest and flanks. This will enable the horse to run faster. The main thing that I look for is that the animal looks good and is a decent size.'

'No, that is where I would disagree. You take Rough Habit for instance. He was only a small horse, cost only $1,200 and went on to win almost four million dollars. On your reckoning, nobody would ever have bought it.'

'Rough Habit was different. For a start it was the dam, Certain Habit, that its owner paid that $1,200 for in New Zealand and he bred Rough Habit himself. The horse was a fluke in my opinion. If it had been offered at the yearling sales, the odds are that, from its breeding and size, the horse would never have been sold. You are always going to get horses that are sold for a song that go on to make their connections very rich. Take that horse that won the Japan Cup, the only Australian horse to do it. What was its name? I can't remember.'

'You mean, Better Loosen Up.'

'Yes that is the one that I mean. Now that colt sold for a mere $10,000 and went on to win almost $5 million.' Just then, Dan who had been listening to this exchange with acute interest finally managed to break into the conversation. 'This is all very well fellas, but I have to get back home. I promised Naomi that I would take her out to dinner this evening. It is her birthday. So I am afraid that I shall have to leave you two to your horses.'

'Oh Hell Dan. I completely forgot that today was her birthday. I haven't even bought her a card, let alone a present.'

'Don't you worry about that old son. Under the circumstances she will understand. Anyway, seeing you take an interest in living again would be the best present that you could give her. Now I am going to leave you two horse traders alone and I will catch up with you later. Wait a minute though, I forgot. How will you get back to your hotel Harley?'

'Don't you worry about me, I can get a cab. I think that Victor and I have a lot of details to sort out anyway. He still hasn't told me all his conditions for taking this job.'

'I will get to those in a minute.' Victor replied. 'Wait a moment, I have an idea Dan. I said that I had not bought Naomi a present yet. How about we all go out to dinner, my treat? We can go somewhere nice and while you and Naomi dance, Harley and I can go over this trip thing.'

Dan and Harley looked at each other. Dan grinned widely and Harley gave a small smile.

'See what did I tell you Harley? It looks as though you arrived on the scene at exactly the right time. Right Victor, I accept your offer on the condition that you have a shower and a shave. Looking like you do at the moment, no self-respecting restaurant would even let us past the front door.'

Victor to his credit had the decency to look sheepish. 'I must admit that I have let myself go a bit. I will get on and clean this place up tomorrow also. For the moment though I will just attend to my appearance. Look, let's do things in style tonight Dan. Whilst I go and have a shower, why don't you ring up one of those limo services and hire a car and a driver. I am sure that Naomi would get a kick out of being picked up in one of those things. We shall have to continue this chat later, Harley, but I am definitely very interested.'

'Well, I think that I had better get you to drop me off in town because I feel that I am imposing here. It is a family matter, a birthday. You don't need strangers there.'

'Nonsense,' Dan said. 'You have earned yourself a dinner at the very least. Naomi would be thrilled to have you come along. I insist on her behalf.'

'Well, if you put it that way, I should be delighted to accept. On one condition though. You must let me pay for the limo. That is the least that I can do.'

'No way, my friend,' Victor shook his head vehemently. 'You forget, you are talking to one of the richest men in Melbourne.'

'What on earth are you talking about? Surely the commission that you make is not enough to put you into that category?'

'Hasn't Dan told you?' Victor asked in an amazed voice.

'Told me what, may I ask?'

'That I won the lottery. Twelve million dollars in fact. Or at least about nine and a half in your American dollars. Now you can also believe this or not. I haven't touched a penny of it yet.' Harley gave a loud gasp and rose to his feet. 'Are you kidding me? – $9 million. nine million smackeroos! Buddy! Why didn't you tell me Dan?'

'Well, to tell you the truth, I didn't think that it was my place to do so. In fact, I don't think that Victor had told anybody yet. The last thing that he needed at this time was a heap of begging letters, which is what usually happens when the word gets out.'

The American nodded in agreement. 'Of course. I understand. What a shame though. It would have meant so very much more if Amanda had been there to share it with you, old pal. People dream all their lives of hitting the big one. In your case, however, what a price you had to pay. There are no second prizes for guessing which you would rather have had. I am so very sorry, this should have been such a happy time for you.' For a moment Harley wondered if he had said too much. A look of utter despair and misery swept over Victor's face; the interest that he had in the prospect of a trip was gone and his eyes filled with tears. Picking up his, so far, untouched drink, he raised it to his lips. Harley looked at Dan helplessly, mentally cursing himself for bringing the memories flooding back to the man. Then, to the amazement of both men, Victor suddenly stiffened, his face as white as a sheet; then turning around, he poured his drink down the sink. Replacing the now empty glass on the bar, he stood there shaking.

'Hey, Victor, what is the matter. You look as though you have seen a ghost. What is wrong?' Dan asked him, his voice full of concern.

For a few seconds Victor did not reply, then with his voice quivering with emotion, he said, 'You are not going to believe this guys, I can't believe this myself. Amanda just spoke to me! I actually heard her speak!'

Dan and Harley looked at each other, neither of them knowing what to say. Eventually Dan got enough courage to ask. 'What did she have to say to you Victor?'

'I am not going crazy. I know what you guys must be thinking. I swear to you that I heard her voice. She was asking me to stop punishing myself. She said that the accident was none of my fault and I was to stop blaming myself. She also said that she wants me to go to England and that she will be there with me. I heard her speak, I did, I did.'

Dan took his arm. 'We believe you, old son. I mean, something very profound must have happened to you for you to pour good bourbon down the sink,' he said with a forced smile.

'Look why don't you go and have your shower and while you are doing that I will ring Naomi and also sort out the car. Where do you fancy going to eat? Is there anywhere that you would like to go in particular?'

'I don't really care. Maybe Naomi would like to pick something after all it is her birthday. Wait a minute though, how about that new place in South Yarra, um, what is it called? I heard that it was very good. Gee, what was it called?'

'You must mean Medallions. That opened about six months ago. It is rather exclusive though. I hear that you have to show your wallet before they even let you through the door,' Dan joked. 'Naomi would love it though. She once said that she would like to roll up there wearing jeans and a T-shirt, just to see the look on their faces. Ok, you go and get cleaned up and I'll make the arrangements.'

'Perhaps you also arrange for a decent bunch of flowers to be delivered there for her. That would help make up for not buying her a present.'

'Victor, believe you me, the best present that you could give her is for her to see you out and about again,' Dan said sincerely.

Later on that evening, the four of them enjoyed a wonderful meal of grilled crab sandwich followed by tenderloin Australian. This was all washed down by several bottles of Salinger. The coffee came and Dan and Naomi got up to dance. This left Victor and Harley sitting at the table with their coffee and cognac.

'Right buddy, tell me what you have in mind,' Harley said as he offered Victor a Havana cigar from a silver case.

Victor shook his head. 'No thanks, but you go ahead. This is one of the few places that still allows you to smoke.' He waited until his companion had lit up and was sitting back, enjoying his smoke. 'As I said earlier. I accept on the understanding that we both go to this sale together and that we do it as partners. I have all this money that I won. I haven't really thought about what I want to do with it at the moment. Investing in a couple of racehorses with you seems as good an idea as any. Neither would it do me any harm to spend a while back in England. As I told you, Amanda and I had been planning a trip anyway. As far as being your manager is concerned, it would make things far simpler if we were partners.'

'To be honest Victor, I would rather own my horses outright. I have a silly foible that I prefer my horses to belong to me only. The business is a different matter. I need the other members of the syndicate to help run the company. They are all specialists in different fields and I need their expertise in different facets of the company. Now the horses are mine alone and maybe you might decide to buy a couple of nags for yourself. I should still be only too happy for you to race mine on my behalf. I suppose that I could spend an extra couple of days in England on the way home. Are you able to leave right away, because I have to be back in LA by the 17th for a board meeting?'

'Well my passport is up to date, I just have to get a re-entry visa from the Immigration Dept. That is easily done over the counter. The only thing that I really have to do is to arrange something about the house. I am not too keen on the idea of just leaving it empty. You never know what might happen if people realise that it is not occupied.'

'Maybe Dan could arrange for somebody to look after it for you?' Just then the other two returned, the dance having finished.

'Did I hear someone mention my name?' Dan asked. 'What have you two been plotting while we were out of the way?'

'We were merely trying to work out what I should do about the house if I went to England.'

Naomi sat back down at the table looking very thoughtful. Then she tapped her hand on the table. 'I think that I have the perfect answer for you. My niece got married last week and at the moment they have to stay at his parents' place. They will be there until they have saved enough money for a deposit on a house. You could let them live in your place rent free in return for looking after it until you return. That would solve both problems. They would have their privacy and you wouldn't have to worry about the house. How long do you expect to be away for anyway?'

'At this stage I have no idea. It all depends on what happens with the horses that Harley intends to purchase,' Victor said.

'While you are over there you might also try and find out what my current manager is up to. I need evidence that he is taking me to the cleaners, as I suspect that he is.' Harley waved his cigar at Victor.

Victor drew back from the thick cloud of smoke that the cigar was emitting and said, 'That's settled then. First thing in the morning I will ring my solicitor and get him to draw up an agreement making me your manger. It will save us time in England.'

Harley shook his head. 'No, that won't be necessary unless you feel that you need it. As far as I'm concerned, all that we have to do is shake hands on the deal. I have never been one to worry about written contracts. I am the old-fashioned type that believes that a man's word is his bond. I have sufficient faith in you to count on you doing the right thing. Most times I trust my gut feelings about people. In the case of this guy in England, I never actually met him. The trainer was the one who arranged everything. The only contact that I have with either of them is a report that he faxes to me each month with a breakdown of expenses.'

'Have any of your horses actually won a race?' Dan asked casually.

'Oh yes, although it appears that they were only minor races, no real stake money. That is why I am a bit dubious about what is happening there. I truly thought that these beasts were better than they have appeared to have turned out. On their breeding they should have won better races than the ones that they have raced in. That is why I want Victor to have a nose around and see what he can turn up for me. Everything appears to be Kosher but I have this little niggle that things are not as above board as they appear to be.'

'My, my. Victor Barnes, private eye!' Naomi laughed. 'That sounds really dramatic. What will you do if you catch them in some evil scheme Victor? Arrest them?'

'It seems to me that you all have more faith in my abilities than I do.' Victor blushed slightly. 'I don't really know where to start or indeed what to do.'

'Don't worry about it Victor, if there is anything amiss, I am sure that you will latch on to it very quickly. I have absolute faith in you. Anyway the prime reason for you going is to buy a couple of horses. I'm counting on you to win me a pile of money.' Harley grinned at the embarrassed Victor.

'I am not so sure about that. In Australia only about five per cent of horses win enough to pay their owner's expenses. Bear in mind also that it is far cheaper to train a horse here than in the northern hemisphere,' Victor stated matter of factly.

Harley looked at him closely for several seconds. 'For someone who claims that he knows nothing about being an owner, you seem remarkably well informed.'

'I must admit that I have toyed with the idea of buying a horse. I have never been in a financial position to do so until now. I just wish that Amanda was here to share in all this.' His statement dampened the whole proceedings for a moment and everyone lapsed into silence.

It was Victor himself who broke the mood. 'I am not sure about you lot but I am ready for home. If Harley and I are going to England I have a lot to do. Dan would you give the limo driver a call? Here is his mobile number. He is having a snack next door. Anyone care for a final drink while we wait for him?'

They all declined. As Dan got to his feet to ring the driver, he leaned across the table and whispered to Harley. 'As I told you on the phone, the one thing that Victor can't resist is a challenge. This jaunt to England should be a great tonic. Well done Harley. We owe you big time my friend.'

Chapter Three

Eight days later the Qantas 747 touched down at Heathrow Airport to allow Victor and Harley to alight. It was a fairly typical English, February morning. The air had a crisp but foggy smell to it as a pale, watery sun struggled to push its way through a bank of rain-laden clouds. Victor had passed through customs and immigration with ease. He was amused therefore on meeting Harley at the coffee shop that he had not been so lucky. Being English he had gone through a different gate from the American and had not even had to open his suitcase. Harley, however, had struck a young, career-minded officer. He proceeded in searching everything including Harley's wallet.

'You must have a suspicious looking face, Harley. Never mind, drink your coffee before it gets any colder,' Victor laughed and pushed a cup across the table to his outraged companion.

Harley downed his drink in a couple of swallows. 'I thought that he was going to have me strip-searched as well. He most likely would have done, if the other guy with him hadn't told him to hurry up. Just because I had an American accent, he must have thought that I was a crime boss or drug lord or something equally bizarre.'

'It will give you something to talk about next time you get home. It should be good for at least a couple of drinks.' Victor said with a grin. 'Now let's down to business shall we? How are we going to get to Newmarket, by train or by car?'

'I don't really care. I simply want to get my ass out of this place.'

'Then in that case I will see about hiring a car, it will give us more freedom that way. I will have to pick up some maps also, as I have never been there before. By the way you never mentioned where your other two horses were trained.'

'I am not really sure myself. All that I know is that they are near another town called New something. I would have to get my office in LA to fax me the address. I do remember though that someone told

32

me the place was famous for something.'

'It is most likely to be Newbury then. There are a lot of stables around there.'

'Now I remember.' Harley clicked his fingers. 'The place was the one that book about rabbits was written about. Paul Simon sang a song about it.'

'Rabbits? Oh you must mean Watership Down.'

'Yeah, Watership Down. That was it. The stables are just on the outskirts of that village but I don't recall that name as being the address on his accounts.' Victor scratched his chin as he struggled to place his friend's vague directions. 'I think that in the book the village was called Burghclere or something.'

'Burghclere! Yes that was it. I remember saying at the time that I should never forget the place as it reminded me of McDonald's.' Harley thumped his fist triumphantly. Seeing the blank look on Victor's face he added, 'you know, burgers, hamburgers from McDonald's.

'You must have a great filing system in your office,' Victor said with a quiet chuckle. 'What have you got listed under Kentucky Fried Chicken?'

'You can laugh, but I will have you know that I have a very efficient office staff. They are always able to give me an answer to any query that I might have, no matter what it is.'

'I am sure that you have. However. we shall have to leave your stables at McDonald's for the moment. Newmarket, my friend is in the opposite direction. You hang on here while I go and fix us up with a car. Hey! I've got plenty of money so we may as well get a chauffeur-driven one. If we are going there to buy a champion racehorse, then we might as well arrive in style. We don't want people to think that we are paupers do we?' Before Harley could protest, Victor was away to hire a car.

Sitting back in his chair, Harley smiled to himself. At least Victor had seemed to forget his troubles, for the moment, anyway. How ironic though to win all that money, but to have no family to share his good fortune with. Money will certainly not buy happiness, at least not in his case. Harley looked up to see his friend waving to him. Getting to his feet he walked over to the door.

'Come on Harley, let's grab our bags. There is a car on the way and it will be waiting for us by the time that we collect our luggage.' Some fifteen minutes later saw the two men installed in the rear of a limo and heading towards the M11.

The car seemed to eat up the miles and just over an hour outside London, the driver first spoke to his two passengers. 'No doubt the American gentleman has travelled on the Concorde. Would he be interested in seeing the first prototype? It is but a short detour to Ickleton.'

'What could possibly be at Ickleton that would interest us?' Victor asked.

'Just outside the village, there is an RAF Museum. It boasts a large display of aircraft including the first Concorde prototype. It landed there but before it was ready to take off again the runway was shortened to make way for the motorway. Consequently there was insufficient room for the plane to take off again. A slight misunderstanding, you might say.' The driver's dry humour made Victor smile.

'You are kidding me, aren't you?' Harley said with a gasp. The driver merely shook his head.

'Good Lord! Now I have heard everything. However, much as I would like to see it, I think that we should push right on to Newmarket. I would hate to miss a bargain at the sales because I stopped to see a monumental waste of dough like that. What a balls up.'

'As you wish sir. We should be in Newmarket in about thirty minutes.' The driver then turned off the motorway onto the A11 and lapsed back into silence for the remainder of the journey.

The chauffeur dropped the two men off at Tattersalls' sales yard and Victor paid him off. They had decided that they would spend the night at a hotel in town and catch a train back to London.

'There is so much that I need to discuss with you regarding stables, trainers and nominations for races, etc.,' Victor had told Harley. ' We must have some sort of strategy worked out before you fly back.'

As the two men approached the sales ring, a feeling of panic seized Victor. He clutched at the other man's arm. 'Harley! Are you sure that this is what you want? I mean, in Australia if you want to buy a horse at one of the sales you don't just rush in. First you would try and get a look at what was on offer then make a short list. After that we would then have a vet look at the ones that we were interested in. We would have detailed reports before the sales took place. The sales catalogue

Chapter Three

would be out at least a month beforehand. I mean that here we are
going in completely stone cold.'

'Don't worry so, Victor. For a start this is no ordinary sale. All these
beauties are thoroughbreds. All that hard work has already been done
for us. I told you that four of them have been entered for the Derby.
All that I want you to do is to have a good look at them and let your
instincts make a selection as they are being paraded. I would like to
buy at least two of them. Maybe even three depending on how much
I have to pay. We should be able to up one or two at a decent price.
You might even see something yourself that you fancy. Just as long as
we don't bid against ourselves,' Harley grinned.

'I know that I said that I would like to buy a horse but I think that
these might well and truly out of my class and price range.'

'Out of your price range!' Harley laughed heartily. 'Man you have
$9 million, I don't think that they will fetch quite that much.'

'Yes but I don't intend to spend a fortune on a horse. I would like
to but one just for the thrill of racing it. Naturally I would like it to
win, but it doesn't have to win a classic. That would be nice of course,
but I don't have any real intentions in that direction.'

'Well I do, so let's go and look at some horseflesh my friend.' Harley
grabbed two of the catalogues that an attendant was offering and
marched off to view the horses. Victor shrugged his shoulders
resignedly and followed the American into the ring.

For the next thirty minutes or so, the two men spent their time consulting the sales brochures. They then checked each horse against the
information offered. Victor had not spoken a word the whole time,
content to let his friend do all the talking. It was obvious that he really
was up to date with the current racing scene.

Finally Harley turned to him and barked, 'Well, what do you think?
Am I going to buy a champion here or not?'

'There is just one thing that puzzles me a little,' Victor said in reply.

'What is that, old buddy?'

'It's obvious that this guy was into racing in a big way. There are
forty horses listed here, but not one yearling. I would have expected
to find at least a couple. These are all either two, three, four or five-
year-olds. There is not a single yearling on the list. I must admit that
I find it a little strange.'

Harley looked at him for a moment then, as a thought struck him,
he laughed and slapped his side. 'Victor I think that you have

35

forgotten that you are in England and not Australia. This is February, pal.'

'I know that it is February, you don't have to remind me. The cold does that,' Victor looked at him, a frown creasing his forehead. To emphasise his words he pulled his coat tight.

'All those two-year-olds listed there only had their birthday last month. January in England and August Down Under.'

'Of course!' Victor slapped the side of his head in annoyance. 'How stupid of me to forget. That is why we never have any horses from the northern hemisphere contesting our Derby. They would be classed as a four-year-old. So unless you entered a two-year-old it would not be eligible to race there. Then it would have to be a super horse to even stand a chance of winning.'

'Now that we have got that sorted out, have you picked anything out of these yet?'

'There are a couple of them that took my eye. I wouldn't mind buying them, that is of course if I had the money,' he replied with a grin. 'To be serious for a minute though, I have made a note of five that I like. I'll reserve final judgement until I see how the bidding goes. One horse in particular I fancy but I think that might be for sentimental reasons rather then logic. It was sired by Flying Spur, whose own sire was Danehill, a leading sire back in Australia. Flying Spur won several Group One races as far as I can remember.'

Harley flicked through the pages of his catalogue until he found what he was looking for. He twisted his face into a grimace. 'You must mean Groyne? Now what kind of dumb name is that for a horse? It must have been a woman who named him.'

'If you must know I thought that it was a very clever name. Don't you know what a groyne is?'

'The only groin that I know of is a part of the human anatomy. Any horse named after that has a snowball's chance in hell of ever winning a maiden, let alone a classic race like the Derby.'

Victor almost doubled up with laughter at the pained expression on the face of his friend. 'Harley, you really are a tonic, you know that? A groyne is a kind of jetty that they build out from the shore to protect against erosion. Another name for it is a spur. Hence spur from Flying Spur. As I said a very clever play on words.'

'Well, why didn't they call it Jetty or something civilised then? You Limeys certainly like to screw around with the English language.'

Chapter Three

'You Yanks don't do too bad a job yourselves,' Victor retorted. 'You just call me a Limey. I bet you ten bucks that you don't even know what it means, do you?'

'Hell! You have always been called that as far back as I can remember,' Harley shrugged. 'I don't know but I suppose that you are going to tell me?'

'If you insist. In the very early days of the British Navy, the sailors were made to drink lime juice. It was to help protect them against scurvy on long voyages. So they were known as Lime Juicers which you Americans shortened to Limeys.'

'How come you became a salesman instead of a teacher, Victor?'

'I can't help it if I am a trivia buff,' he replied with a grin.

'I don't know about you, but I came here to buy a horse, not to be given an English lesson. Let's get on with the real business shall we? But you can forget about that Groyne. If you ask me, you would be buying nothing but trouble with an animal with a name like that. Find me something else that you like with a name like Yosemite Sam.'

The two of them went through the list of horses comparing notes. They discovered that each of them had selected two horses the same. A chestnut colt out of Sea Bird and a grey sired by Niniski. Both of them had been entered for the Derby, although, said Harley, greys did not have a great success rate in the race. Both of the horses had been lightly raced as two-year-olds. This fact pleased Victor enormously and his respect for the late owner of the colts grew. Some owners, keen to get back some of their high financial output, tended to race the horses as much as possible, the object being to recoup their outlay as quickly as they could. The end result was that a lot of horses raced this way never trained on as three-year-olds. They of course were prevented from achieving their likely potential.

A bell rang to indicate that the first of the bunch was about to be led into the sale ring. Harley had no intention of bidding for any of the early lots but he wanted to gauge the feeling of the sales. This would be a good guide to the possible price that he may have to go to in order to secure his choice.

Victor, never having attended a sale of this magnitude before, sat engrossed as the first ten horses were brought in. He leaned forward as they were led around the ring. He was more than a little startled at the prices that these animals were fetching. The first ten averaged £40,000 or nearly $90,000. He turned to Harley. 'I had no idea that

37

these horses were so valuable. This guy must have been earning a tidy crust to be able to afford all these.'

'He was in the video games business. Some of the games that he invented made him literally millions of dollars. Judging by what these nags have gone for so far, I may find that I am going to have to spend a lot more than I intended to. Still, that is par for the course. Although if one of them was lucky enough to win the Derby for me, then I could live off the stud fees alone. I am going to grab a cup of coffee before our two are brought in. Do you want one?'

Victor shook his head. He was rapidly becoming caught up in the thrill and drama of the sales. He started to go through the rest of the catalogue, mentally forecasting what he thought that each horse might fetch. He was unfamiliar with most of the sires, having lived in Australia for so long. He discovered that he was indeed, totally out of touch with the current scene. A point that he had pressed on Harley several times.

The next batch of ten had already been sold before the American returned. 'So, Victor, how are things going? Has anything decent caught your eye yet?'

'I cannot believed how far out of touch I am. I have been way out in my estimation of what these would sell for. They are all going way higher than their reserves. That last one for instance was £57,000 above. I am amazed that there is so much money around. I understood that the country was in the middle of a minor depression at the moment.'

'It is usually when there is a depression that the people who have money, are inclined to spend it,' Harley chuckled. 'I know that in the Casino, the tighter the money is, then there seems to be more punters. They all gamble in the hope of winning the big one. Whatever the state of the economy is in this country isn't having much bearing on these buyers. They are mostly from overseas with incomes of at least half a million a year. That little guy over there by the post, for instance. He is nothing to look at but he owns a team of Nascar racers. Then, you see that rather portly fellow, wearing that hideous, orange jacket? Back home in the States, he owns a chain of over two hundred supermarkets.'

Victor shook his head in disbelief. 'Thanks a lot Harley. You are making me feel totally out of my depth here. I think that I had better wait and buy something in a selling race. I don't think that I am quite ready to play with the big boys yet.'

'Nonsense. You have just as much money as a lot of this crowd. Besides, as far as I am concerned, you are one of the big boys. You forget that I have seen you in action in Canberra. It was no mean feat beating off all those other companies to win our business.'

'But that was entirely different. I knew that our product was good and I was up against people in my line of business. This kind of thing is completely new to me. A totally different kind of ball game altogether.'

'The principle is the same thing though, just trust your gut feeling, you will do all right. Look, here is the first one that we are interested in. He is there in the next batch,' Harley pointed to the steward leading in a magnificent chestnut colt. His coat shone like satin, an obvious sign that the animal was well cared for. His deep, broad chest was in perfect proportion to his fleshy haunches. The bones of the shanks appeared to be thick and firm. His knees too showed a pleasing suppleness as he walked around the ring. He held his head high, his wide-open nostrils adding to his already striking demeanor.

'Man, would you take a look at him,' Harley said softly. 'That horse is championship material and doesn't he know it too? I simply have to have this one Victor. Even if I buy nothing else he has got to be mine. What do you think of him, my friend?'

'I think that you are right Harley. You have found your horse. He certainly looks the part. He reminds me of a horse that used to race in Australia named Tobin Bronze. He, too, seemed to know that he was born for greatness. He almost used to bow to the crowd after one of his great wins. Tobin was a born champion. However I think that you are going to have your work cut out for you, trying to buy this one Harley. Have you noticed how the mood of the crowd has altered since they brought him in. There is a definite air of expectancy about. I think that most of them have been waiting for this one.'

'Yes it will be very interesting to see what the auctioneer starts the bidding off at. That should give us a fairly good idea what kind of battle we are in for.'

Even though the two of them had known that the bidding was going to be hard and fast, even they were shaken at the opening price of £100,000. The raises started off at £10,000 then twenties and finally nods of fifties, Some six short minutes later the hammer came down for the third time. Harley was the proud owner of the chestnut colt,

Delmore, at a cost of £339,000.

Taking a handkerchief from his pocket, he wiped the perspiration from his brow. 'Man I don't usually have trouble spending money but this time I think that I have bought something extra special.'

'At £339,000, I should hope that it is special. I am shaking like a leaf and it's not even my money.' Victor gasped and clapped his friend on the shoulder. Just then a sandy-haired giant of a man, dressed in jeans and a faded sheepskin coat, came up to the pair of them.

'Harley you old scoundrel! I might have known that it was you who stole my horse. I came here especially to buy that colt. Though even I wasn't prepared to go to that price for it. I hope that he wins some races for you. I reckon that you will have to win the Derby just to break even.'

'Ambrose! Hell man, I thought that you were dead! The last that I heard of you, you were in intensive care after having a massive heart attack. What were you too stubborn to go or did they throw you back? You really must lose some of that weight, it can't be healthy for you.' He playfully threw a punch at the big man's torso.

'Aw come on Harley you know me better than that. Since when is it going to take a little thing like a heart attack from keeping me of all people from going to the races? As for my weight, it is simply to keep the cold out when I am over here.'

Harley turned to Victor. 'Victor, I would like you to meet Ambrose Mellor. He is one of the original Beverly Hillbillies. He went drilling on his old clapped farm down in Texas. He was looking for water and struck oil instead. So he sold his farm to one of those big oil companies. Now he spends all his time trying to find a horse that can beat mine.'

'From what I hear back home, that shouldn't be too difficult here in England at the moment I can tell you. What is wrong with your horses lately Harley? You usually have much better luck than you appear to be having at the moment.'

'I wish that I knew that Ambrose,' Harley said with a sigh. 'It is a bit of a worry I can tell you. That is where Victor comes in. I am hoping that he can discover exactly what is going on. For one thing I am sure that my trainer is robbing me blind but I need proof before I can do anything about it. If he were just making a few extra dollars for himself then I wouldn't mind. When it comes to big money that is something altogether different. If he is on the fiddle then he is smart

enough to show that the horses are winning. Although in my opinion
they should be winning a far better class of race. Look why don't you
two go and get a drink somewhere? I will go and make some kind of
arrangements for this horse I've just bought.'

'You can send him along to my trainer if you wish to, Harley. The
guy is as honest as the day is long. He won't stiff you. Just mention my
name.'

'Thanks Ambrose, that might be a good idea until we find out what
is happening with my guy. Is your's still Jenkins, here in Newmarket?
Though on second thoughts sending Delmore to my current man,
will give Victor an introduction.'

'Well if you change your mind, just tell the steward when you settle
up. Tell him that you are with me. He will look after everything for
you.' Ambrose then turned to Victor. 'Right then, buddy, let's go and
get that drink. I need one after Harley robbing me like that.'

Victor hesitated for a moment, then said to Harley, 'What are you
going to do about that grey? Are we going to have a look at it?'

'You can if you want to, my friend, but I am all spent out for the
day,' he said with a broad grin. 'Mind you I would have got it much
cheaper if I hadn't been bidding against Shylock here.'

'If you are looking to buy a horse, I happen to have a couple of my
own that I would be only too happy to get shot of. I'll tell you why
don't I take you out to the stables and you can have a look at them?
You can join us out there after you have finalised the details with
Delmore, eh Harley?'

'Sure, why not? I shouldn't be too long anyway.' Ambrose grabbed
Victor by the arm and started to propel him towards the exit. 'Come
on, what was your name again? Ah yes, Victor. Now let me show you
a couple of real nice horses.'

'If they are so good, how come you are selling them?'

'Because,' Ambrose laughed, 'they are not winning any races for me.
The last thing that I need is animals that eat me out of house and
home and are not paying their way. Give them some new surroundings and they could improve.'

'Why do you think that they are not winning?'

'Maybe,' Ambrose laughed again, 'I am not treating them nice
enough. Or it could be, perish the thought, they simply ain't good
enough.' His booming laughter echoed around the ring as the two
men reached the exit and went outside.

It was about an hour later before Harley joined the two men sitting in the trainer's office sipping Jack Daniels. Victor had noticed that it was the new Gentleman Jack, which Jenkins the trainer had produced. He fussed around Ambrose like a broody hen. It was plain to see that he knew where his major meal ticket came from and went out of his way to make sure that Ambrose lacked for nothing.

After Harley also had made himself comfortable with a large glass of liquor, he turned and challenged the other American. 'Now my friend, tell us why you are trying to offload a couple of your horses onto us. Just because you are plying us with this excellent bourbon, you can't fool me. I want the truth now, none of your usual bullshit.'

'To be honest these last two belonged to Hetty. As you know what she knew about racing horses could be written on a postage stamp. She only bought these two because she fell in love with their names.'

'Hetty was Ambrose's wife,' Harley explained to Victor.

'I hope that you don't let your wife run your life for you m'boy.'

'I don't think that there is much danger of that happening,' Victor shifted uncomfortably in his chair as he spoke.

'Women! You have to keep them firmly in their place. I suppose that wife of yours nags you about the gee gees, does she? If she does you have to put your foot down. Women respect a man of action and firmness.'

'Ambrose!' Harley hesitated for a minute. 'Ambrose, Victor has just had to bury his wife and two children. I think that enough has been said.'

Ambrose, however, appeared unfazed. He looked Victor straight in the eye. 'Victor, my boy, I have wed and planted five wives. I am still, however, what the media likes to call a chauvinist. In spite of all that I loved and respected them all. Believe you me, the pain does eventually go away. Now let's go and look at some horseflesh shall we, before Harley has me crying in my whiskey.' So saying he heaved his huge frame to his feet and led the way out to the stables.

Harley shrugged his shoulders helplessly and followed. Victor looked at Jenkins who said simply. 'He is a great guy really. You just have to get to know him a little better. It is all a front to hide his pain. I have known him for many a long year and when his wives were alive, he was truly a devoted husband.' He then followed Harley out. Victor somewhat reluctantly brought up the rear.

By the time that he had caught up with the rest of them, Ambrose had two horses out of their stalls. Jenkins was leading them around for Harley's inspection. There was nothing that truly grabbed Victor about the two nondescript colts and, quickly losing interest in them, he slowly wandered along the rest of the stalls. He had walked three parts along the row, when he came to a stall that was closed. He knew that it wasn't empty because he could hear an animal moving restlessly about. Curious, he stopped. Reaching up he unbolted the top half of the door and swung it open. Immediately a black head with fierce looking eyes thrust itself out. Even to Victor's inexperienced eye, he knew that this was a thoroughbred. His heart began to race. He could taste the adrenaline pulsating through his body. This horse was indeed something special. He could almost feel a bond between them. He reached out his hand towards its head.

The animal snorted and jumped back away from the door. 'Hey steady on old feller, nobody's going to hurt you. I think it would be safer though if Jenkins brought you out. I wonder if you are for sale too?' Noting the number of the stall, he walked back to join the others.

'Hey Victor! What do you think about these two?' Harley called to him.

'I hope that you won't take offence at this. I think that you would make far more money hiring them out for pony rides, than by racing them.'

Ambrose laughed heartily and slapped a huge hand on his back, almost knocking him to the ground. 'You certainly know horses. That is exactly what I told Jenkins that we should do with them. I might even give them to a kids' orphanage or something. I think that Hetty would have liked that. She was very fond of kids.'

'Mind you, I can't say the same thing about the one in bay 17. Is he for sale? I am very interested if that is the case.' Ambrose and Jenkins exchanged glances and the Ambrose looked at Harley. 'I am impressed buddy. At long last it seems as though you have teamed up with someone who could teach you a thing or two about horses. Unfortunately my friend,' he said turning back to Victor, 'he is not for sale. I value my friendship with Harley here too much to sell you that beast.'

'Why not?' said Victor, 'money is no problem. I really feel that horse has a quality about him that makes him something special. How much do you want for him? Harley will vouch for the fact I am good for the money.'

'Victor, I don't doubt for one instance that you have the money. It is just that I wouldn't feel right about selling him to you. You are correct about one thing though, he is something special. That is why I bought him in the first place. I thought that I had a world-beater with him. Sadly, though, things did not turn out as I had hoped. The stable lads call him Satan. He has a killer instinct bred in him. At every race that we have entered him for, he has thrown his jockey before the start of the race. In fact, he has been barred from the track until I can prove to the Jockey Club that he can be ridden. The sensible thing would be to have him put down but I haven't the heart to destroy such a majestic creature.'

'Then sell him to me. I will give you a fair price for him,' Victor pleaded.

Ambrose looked very uncomfortable. 'I don't know. I don't think that he will ever race and it wouldn't be right, taking your money.'

Victor looked across at Harley, who had been watching the proceedings with interest. 'Tell him, Harley. Tell him to sell him to me.'

The two Americans looked at each other. After a moment's pause Harley nodded his head. 'Much against my better judgement, you have yourself a deal,' Ambrose said holding out his hand.

Victor grabbed it with delight. 'Hey Harley! I have just bought myself a horse!'

'I hope that you have got a good trainer, because, believe you me, you are going to need one,' Ambrose said with a huge sigh.

Chapter Four

The next few days were taken up with the formalities of their purchases. It was well into the evening of the third day before the three of them were seated in the lounge bar of the hotel where they were staying. Eventually the subject of a trainer for the newly acquired purchase was brought up again.

Ambrose was adamant that leaving the horse with Jenkins for a short time was no problem. However, neither of them was at all happy about trying to train him. Jenkins had taken Victor to one side.

'I would be taking your money under false pretences sir. I must admit that I can do nothing with him. In fact I have to exercise him by rein from one of the other horses, because none of my lads can stay aboard him. To be honest I don't know of anyone that will be able to handle him. He really is a problem horse.'

Quite undeterred, Victor arranged for Jenkins to look after Satan for two weeks while he found a trainer who would take him.

'You will have no problem finding someone who will accept him, but whether they will be able to train him is another matter. You will have to be very careful that you pick an honest one or you will soon find yourself well out of pocket,' Jenkins had warned him. Victor said that he would check anybody that he found with him first.

'Well my boy, I hope that you know what you are doing,' Ambrose said to him. He signalled for the waiter to bring them another round of drinks. 'I have heard of people buying a pig in a poke, but this is the first time that I have sold a horse in a stable. Because a stable is the closest that I think that you are going to get him to a racetrack.' He laughed so much that Victor thought that the chair that he was sitting in would collapse. His huge girth shook uncontrollably as waves of laughter rolled through the many layers of fat that constituted his stomach.

He waited patiently for the big man's mirth to subside, then asked,

'Speaking of racing, what name does he run under? Also I am not very keen on him being called Satan.'

'His stable name, well you can call him what you like. There is no law to govern that, but he is registered to race as Arcadian Steel.'

'Hey that is a great name! How on earth did you come up with that?'

'Well, to be honest, it is a bit of a misnomer. I once owned a horse that was sired by Diesis. I thought that Arcadian Steel was very subtle as Diesis is an Ancient Greek and is also a double dagger. Arcadia, of course, was a part of Greece and steel for a dagger. However, none of that came to be, because the woman that I was married to at the time had made up some fancy name for the colt. She refused to let it be called anything but Ambrosia, supposedly after me. So I put the name in abeyance until I found something worthy of the name Arcadian Steel. When Satan came along, it seemed to be the ideal colt. Sadly though it seems that the steel is too tough to be tempered.'

'For God's sake Ambrose! Why can't you speak in plain English? You are as bad as Victor here. Abeyance and tempered steel! We are talking about a goddamn horse here not some dictionary you may have swallowed,' Harley broke in, in an exasperated tone.

Both Victor and Ambrose laughed at their friend's outburst.

'Oh come now Harley, where is your sense of drama?' Victor said tossing his hands skyward.

'I lent it to Al Pacino. I thought that he needed it more,' Harley answered with a perfectly straight face that he could not hold for longer than a few seconds, before his features creased into a huge grin and they all convulsed with fits of laughter.

Ambrose caused the waiter to look at him with some apprehension, as he tried to place their drinks on a table that vibrated fiercely with the gyrations of the big man's stomach.

Eventually, some kind of order was restored and Ambrose said that he had to make tracks. He had a horse entered at Lingfield the following day and he wanted to see it run.

'There was a time when at this time of year we could rely on having a bit of a rest from racing. Though now, since the inception of the all-weather track, the flat season does not truly end. It is at times like this that I think that the old days were the best. To me the real season doesn't start for at least another month although the general public seems to prefer it as it is. Since they virtually pay our prize money, I suppose that we have to go along with it.'

'I believe that I read somewhere that Frankie Dettori was very much in favour of these all-weather tracks,' Victor remarked quietly.

'He would!' Harley snorted. 'Anyone who gets as many rides as he does would most likely want more. I have never seen a jockey travel around as much as that guy does.'

Ambrose shook his head. 'No, you are wrong. As it happens Frankie has become far more selective about his rides than when he was starting out. He doesn't need to chase rides. He is too good a jockey for that.'

'He even made the news back home that day he rode seven winners out of seven. When was it? September? October?' Victor broke in.

'Ascot, September 28 1996. That is a day that I shall never forget.' Ambrose spoke with a touch of envy. 'I was there that day and the atmosphere on that last race of his was unbelievable. I also saw Willie Carson ride his six out of seven. That was six years earlier at a Newcastle meeting. I remember thinking at the time that I should never see a feat like that beaten in my lifetime. Then low and behold along comes Dettori and he rides seven. That guy is simply amazing and that is the truth.'

'We even had a jockey in Australia copy his jump off a horse. I personally thought that was a bit over the top. He later gave racing away to become a preacher. There were a lot of punters who could not fathom his reasoning.'

'Well, he should find it a lot easier making a living from the Gospel than the horses,' Harley interjected. 'Although I think that all of us have hoped for divine intervention at one time or another. Especially when our horse is being passed in the final furlong.'

'We shall have to wait and see what happens. A lot of people think that the lure of the track will be too strong for him. I think that he does the occasional interview. He was an excellent jockey and a very popular one.'

'All jockeys are popular if they are riding the winner,' Harley said drily.

At this point, Ambrose struggled to his feet. 'I am going to turn in or I will never get up in time to get to Lingfield tomorrow. Are you guys going to come and see my horse run?'

'Not me, I am afraid,' Harley shook his head. 'As much as I would like to, I have some business to settle in London that can't wait any longer. I also have to get onto my office in LA. I need to get all the dope that I can on the two horses that this rogue trainer has of mine. Plus I simply have to be back home on the 17th for a board meeting. No rest for the wicked, I am afraid.'

'How about you Victor?' Ambrose looked across to where he was sitting, drumming his fingers on the table.

'Yes, why not? I can go to Burghclere next week and check out Harley's horses. That is one advantage of being on your own. You don't have to answer to anybody.'

The other two men looked at Victor as he was speaking. They then turned away, embarrassed as they saw the tears trickling down their friend's cheeks. There was an awkward pause for a few seconds then Ambrose said, 'Right, that's settled then. I shall see you at breakfast I suppose.'

He started to walk away then stopped for a moment. Gently he laid a heavy hand on Victor's shoulder.

'Believe it or not my friend, there are still times that the tears come to my eyes. When I remember my wives, Hetty especially, it all comes back. Never try to hold back the tears, let them out. If you try to keep them inside they can turn bitter on you.' With that, he gently squeezed Victor's shoulder. Releasing his grip he lumbered off to bed.

Harley too got to his feet. 'I am off too. I will see you in the morning. I will fax the office tonight and I should have all the details back before you have to leave in the morning.' With that, he also left the room leaving Victor alone with his memories of Amanda and the two boys.

The trip down to Lingfield next morning was fairly uneventful. Victor was still amazed at the system of motorways that had developed since his departure from England. It was now possible to traverse the country in a couple of hours. This was fine if you were in a hurry to get from point A to B but one saw very little of the countryside, which to him was a shame. The charm of the small picturesque villages was bypassed in favour of speed. Ambrose spent most of the journey talking on his mobile phone, so conversation between them was fairly limited. In fact it was not until they actually reached the track that Victor was able to ask his host about his horse's chances. 'To be honest, not very good. Lingfield is equitrack and not fibresand. The other two are all-weather at Wolverhampton and Lingfield. Also Lingfield is a very sharp track that tends to suit front running horses, which my girl ain't! Then, on top of that, she has drawn the outside barrier, whereas the course tends to favour the inside draw. She runs very well at the other two tracks, but never seems to reproduce that form here. So don't go putting your shirt on her Victor. You will most likely lose it.'

'Then why?' Victor hesitated, and Ambrose laughed.

'Why did I enter her then? Simple! I have never won a race here and I am determined to remedy that. Also it gives me a chance to catch up with all the latest gossip from the other owners. Today is more of a social outing than a working day. But at least it makes Jenkins and the jockey think that they are earning their money. That is one advantage of having plenty of money and no offspring waiting for you to drop dead. You can spend it how you like. I don't believe in shoving all my money in the bank. I like to spend it.'

Victor shook his head, slightly bewildered. 'Well that certainly is a philosophy that, to date, I haven't been in a position to follow. It does make a lot of sense though, I will admit.'

'You can't take it with you my boy. So you might as well enjoy it while you can. You never know what is waiting for you around the next corner.'

By now, they had reached the stables and Victor followed Ambrose to the stall where his chestnut filly was being prepared for her race. Victor was impressed by the animal. She was a light chestnut with a flaxen mane and tail. She was almost a true chestnut apart from a white snip between the nostrils. 'She certainly is a splendid horse. You must have been pleased when you saw her?'

'Yes, isn't she? Actually, I am not all that worried if she never wins a race. I really bought her to breed from. I want a palomino. A pal of mine down in Cornwall has a real show horse and I need to breed one just as good.'

'Don't you need two palominos to breed another? Why a chestnut?' Victor asked in a puzzled tone, his face creased into a slight frown.

'Most people seem to think that.' Ambrose said with a laugh. 'No, if you mate two palominos, you end up with what they call a cremello. It is very, very pale, almost an albino. No, to produce what you want, you need a chestnut or a grey to mate with a palomino. It is preferable also if the sire is the palomino, but it can be the dam. You usually have far more luck with a sire though.'

Victor looked at the other man and then scratched his head.

'All that is a bit beyond me I'm afraid. I think that I will just stick to racing horses, which is hard enough. How long are you going to run this one for, before you start breeding from her?'

'At the moment she is only a three-year-old. Most likely I will race her for two or three seasons before I do anything with her in that regard. I am in no real hurry, as I want the palomino for my favourite granddaughter. She is only eleven at the moment. There is still time for Dolly here to win me a couple of good races.' Ambrose fondled the filly's ears affectionately as he spoke. Then giving her a good pat turned and said, 'Come on, I am starving. Let's go and get some lunch.'

As Ambrose had predicted, Dolly finished a gallant fifth in her race. However, he did not seem at all perturbed by the result. It was only when he invited Victor to share a bottle of Moët with him that he learned that his companion had bet £1000 on the winner at 11–1. Victor, for his part had not backed a winner in the first three races.

The two of them were sat in the bar drinking their champagne when a short very dapper looking man came up to their table. 'Good afternoon Ambrose, drinking Moët eh? You must have backed my filly in the last.' Pulling out a chair he sat down uninvited and signalled to the bar for another bottle.

'Charlie! You know damn well that I never take the slightest notice of anything that you tell me,' Ambrose laughed and turned to Victor. 'A word of advice Victor, when another owner tells you that his horse is a good thing, back anything but. This scoundrel here is the biggest liar in the game. Meet Charlie Frazer, one time jockey and now part-time owner. He also trains half a dozen of the luckiest nags running. His horses don't win races, it is more a case of their opposition losing.'

'Mine was too good for yours today Ambrose,' Charlie grinned and held out a small hand to Victor. As he took it, he was surprised by the strength of the little man's grip.

Noticing the look on his face, Ambrose said, 'He got strong by always pulling his horses when he was a jockey. I didn't expect to see you here today Charlie. I would have thought that you would have been at Ascot.' Without waiting for a reply, Ambrose took Victor's arm and in an exaggerated whisper said, 'Charlie mainly trains jumpers. He didn't have too much success on the flat as a jockey. The same could be said about his horses.'

Charlie grinned and winked at Victor. 'Yes, I only rode 336 winners in my last three seasons. That is one of the reasons that I became a trainer. Ambrose is correct in one respect though. I do seem to have more luck with my National Hunt runners. But then I have more in training at the moment than I have flat runners. That is one of the reasons that I am here today. I am selling Pride of Tintagel and I did promise you first refusal on him.'

'No thanks. I have decided that this year I am going to stick to the flat only. I am getting a little long in the tooth to be going to the races all winter as well. Victor here might be interested in him though. He is in the market for a quality horse.'

'He is a good buy Victor. I am only selling him because I need the room. A couple of other parties have asked me to take their horses on. They are both classic prospects so I would be crazy to turn them down. Pride is entered for Newton Abbott, Cheltenham and Exeter at the moment. I reckon that he is a good thing for all three. I am prepared to let him go for £10,000 for a quick sale. I have him here at the course today. I was hoping to sell him to Ambrose here. Why don't you come and have a look at him? You won't be disappointed I can tell you. In spite of what this guy here says, I do have some good horseflesh. Also I know for a fact that he backed mine because I saw him at the bookies.'

On hearing this, Ambrose threw up his arms in mock disgust. Looking straight at Victor said, 'Is nothing sacred anymore? A man can't even have a wager now without the whole world knowing about it. Seriously though Victor, Pride of Tintagel is a nice horse and you would not do much worse. That is, of course, providing you want a chaser as well as Satan?'

'I had not really given much thought to buying a jumper. In Australia, the jumps are a very minor side of racing. In fact, jump jockeys are regarded as part-timers almost. We did have one rider from Melbourne come over here and work for a trainer called Martin Pipe. Jamie Evans was his name and he managed to ride a few winners for this guy Pipe. Do you two know of him, the trainer I mean?'

'He is only our leading National Hunt trainer,' remarked Charlie drily. 'My horse is not in the same league as most of his but he is still going to win some decent races for whoever buys him. At least come and have a look at him?'

'Well, if you already have him here, I don't suppose that there is any harm in looking. Are you coming Ambrose?'

'No thanks. I already know the horse. I will just sit here and polish off this new bottle of bubbly that Charlie has so kindly bought me.'

So, leaving Ambrose with his bottle of champagne, the other two men left the bar to the accompaniment of cries of 'Nice race Charlie', 'Well done Charlie' and 'Good win Charlie'. They made their way over to where the horseboxes were parked. Charlie led the way down the rows until they came to a twin box.

As they approached, a horse thrust its head out and snorted excitedly. Charlie put his hand in his pocket and pulled out a couple of carrots, which the animal quickly devoured.

'I always thought that feeding horses or donkeys carrots, was a bit of a myth,' said Victor with a slight chuckle.

Charlie shook his head in dissent. 'No, apart from the fact that the horse likes them, they are good for cooling the blood. They also help with poor-winded animals.'

'I can see that I have a lot to learn,' sighed Victor heavily.

Again Charlie shook his head, this time more vehemently. 'As long as you employ a reputable trainer, then you can leave all that sort of thing to him. Now let me lead this one out for you.' Unclipping the ramp, Charlie let it down and then moved into the right-hand stall and untied the horse. As he led it out, Victor could see that it was predominately brown but with three flesh marks and black legs. After parading it up and down in front of Victor a few times, without a word, Charlie led it back up the ramp and into its stall. Securing it once again, he gave it a couple more carrots, patted it on its croup and made his way back down the ramp. He then made sure that everything was secure before turning back to Victor. 'Well what's your opinion? Do you think that you might be interested in buying him?'

'Do you honestly expect me to make a decision just on that showing?' Victor laughed heartily. 'Do you think that I would buy it, without knowing any other details or even having it checked by a vet?'

'Yes,' said Charlie simply.

'Now what would give you that idea? Up until a half an hour ago, you hadn't even met me. You know absolutely nothing about me. Not even if I have the money to pay for it.'

'On the contrary, I know all that I need to know about you, Victor. You see, as we left the bar, Ambrose gave me the thumbs up. He and I have been friends for a long time. So if he vouches for you. Then that is good enough for me.'

'Hell's bells! He himself has only known me for a very short while.' Victor protested, slightly staggered by this revelation.

'Ambrose is as good at judging people as he is horses. Now do we have a sale or not? He truly is a snip at the price. I can arrange to have him shipped wherever you like.'

'I don't even know any trainers apart from you and Ambrose's Jenkins.'

'I could recommend a guy for you if you want.' Victor caught the hint of hesitation in his voice and looked him straight in the eye for a few seconds. 'What is the catch Charlie?'

'Oh, there is no catch. It's just that he is my niece's husband. I don't want you thinking that I am trying to keep the horse in the family. Even though I am selling it. It's simply that he has had a run of bad luck lately and he could do with a lift.'

'How many horses does he have in training at the moment?'

To his credit, this time Charlie did look embarrassed. He kicked at a clump of grass near the float and turned away from Victor. After a moment's pause, he lifted his head and turned back to face his prospective buyer. 'Just at this time he hasn't actually a single horse in his stable. The last three that he had were removed last week. He is a good trainer but things haven't gone his way lately. His parents were recently killed in a car smash, his son died of a drug overdose. Two of his horses broke their legs and had to be put down. Then on top of that . . .'

'Oh stop it Charlie! You are making this sound like a TV soap. I suppose that the bank want to foreclose on his mortgage too?'

'As a matter of fact . . .'

'Shut up! I have heard enough. This is not a run of bad luck! This guy is jinxed. You expect me to throw more money his way. Why, Charlie why?'

'Because I love my niece and I know that this guy is good. He just needs something to go right for a change.'

'Would you still sell me the horse even if I didn't go along with him as the trainer? Suppose I placed it elsewhere? Would I still get the horse?'

'Of course! One is not conditional on the other,' Charlie said in a shocked tone. Victor paced up and down several times, his head bowed. Suddenly he stopped and faced the other man. 'I think that I ought to be committed but, ok, it's a deal.'

'You mean that you are willing to buy the horse?'

'Yes, I will buy the horse and, Heaven help me, your niece and her husband can train it for me.' Victor slapped himself on the head sharply several times. 'I can't really believe that I am doing this. In less than three months, I have lost my wife and two sons. I have tossed in my job, flown across the world. I have bought myself two racchorses and am now proposing to give one to a no-hoper Jonah and all because I won $12 million. It is simply not a logical thing to do, as some TV character once said. On top of all that I have promised an American that I would try and find out if some cowboy is ripping him off. I am sure that I am going to wake up soon and find that this has all been some terrible dream. A fool and his money are soon parted, so they say. Well, at the rate that I am going, I am not going to have much of mine left before long.'

Chapter Five

Victor had declined a ride back with Ambrose. He felt that he should travel to Burghclere and make his presence known to Harley's trainer. He had arranged with Harley that all the information that his office had concerning the stable and his two horses would be sent to the local post office for him to pick up. So, giving Charlie a cheque for Pride of Tintagel he received instructions on how to find his niece's place. He then made his farewells and set off to hire a car.

'Aren't you going to stay for the last two races at least?' Ambrose had asked him. However he had refused, saying that he couldn't afford to meet any more of his friends. 'They might all try to sell me a horse,' he had retorted. This had highly amused the American but he could see that Victor could not be swayed. Having extracted a promise to call on him again he had almost shaken Victor's arm out of its socket in his farewell. Then giving him a cheery wave he had marched off to find another unsuspecting bookie.

Having found a car hire firm, Victor settled on a small Rover. He did not want to give the stables the idea that he had plenty of money. Before he had left Australia, he had applied for three master cards. He had then paid $50,000 into each of them. He had also opened a bank account with a further $500,000. Of course he still had access to his savings account through his key card. This of course was not very useful to him with the amounts that he needed to draw on to buy such things as racehorses. The exchange rate, too, on the Aussie dollar, had fallen quite some way since his arrival. This was another reason not to spend more than he needed to on a car. The details complete, he consulted the map that he found in the glove compartment. He then headed north towards the M25 and thence to Newbury.

By the time that he reached the town it was quite dark. So, rather than try to find the stables in poor light, he decided to stay the night there. Seeing an old inn displaying a bed and breakfast sign, he pulled into the car park. Half an hour later, having freshened up in his room, he made his way down to the restaurant. Being a Saturday night the place was extremely busy. He could not find a free table anywhere. Just as he was about to leave, he felt someone tug at his arm. He looked around and was confronted by an attractive, dark-haired girl about twenty years of age.

'Dad says that you should share a table with my boy friend as there is no room at the moment. That is, of course, unless you would rather eat on your own?' she added hastily. Victor shook his head and allowed the girl to lead him to a small, corner table. A fair-haired, crew-cut lad was sitting there, busy tucking into what appeared to be a huge meat pie.

Telling Victor to take a seat, the girl disappeared into the throng and returned a few minutes later with a menu. Victor declined it. 'I will have whatever it is that he is eating,' he said pointing to the boy's plate.

'Steak and kidney pudding, the house speciality,' the girl smiled. 'Mum will be pleased. She says that no one knows what a home-cooked meal means in here anymore. They all want lobster thermidor or braised pheasant. Things like steak and kidney are considered too parochial for the racing set.'

'I suppose that you must get most of the racing fraternity in here?'

'We get our fair share. Most of the stable lads tend to treat this as their local. We don't get too many of the owners though. Most of them go to the new hotel, about half a mile further on. Anyway, I will go and order your meal. Mashed potatoes ok or would you rather have a jacket potato?'

'No mashed will do just fine.' The girl flashed him another smile and disappeared again. Victor watched as the boy quickly polished off his meal. 'You appear to have enjoyed that,' he remarked with a smile.

'Yeah, the grub's first rate here.' The boy grinned. 'That's one of the reasons why I go out with Becky. Her old man is ok too. He lets me work behind the bar on race days. Cash in hand too. My name's Billy. Me and Becky have been going together for ten months now. We plan to get married next year but I want to finish my course first. I have almost got it done.'

'What is it that you are studying?'

'Computer programming,' Billy replied. 'What I really want to do though is to design my own computer games. You only need one good one and your fortune is made. Then it's off to America and the high life for me and Becky. I have almost finished writing a program for a great game that's going to be my meal ticket.'

Victor was quite captivated by the boy's enthusiasm. He held out his hand. 'My name is Victor. I actually used to sell video machines for a living in Australia.'

'What, you mean arcade games and such?'

'No, no. The machines that I sold were poker machines that you find in casinos and such. I even sold some to a casino in Las Vegas.'

'Money for old rope, those kind of machines. Naw, I want to sell mine to Sony or someone like that. You get one game accepted for their Play Station and you can sit back and watch the money roll in. I have already written to them and sent them some of my ideas. I am just waiting for them to offer me a job.'

Just then Becky arrived back with Victor's meal and set it down before him. His eyes popped at the size of the serving. Seeing the expression on his face, she laughed. 'You got extra because you had to share a table with Billy. I hope that he hasn't been bothering you too much?'

'On the contrary, what he had to say was very interesting.'

'I can't believe that. He only knows about one thing. Computers. Computer mad he is. I sometimes wonder if I am going out with a man or a machine.'

'Just you wait until I sell my first game, Becky, then you will see. The things of the future computers are. They will be able to do anything. Vic and I, were just talking. He sells poker machines. You know that you can sell them with the help of a computer, Vic. All you have to do is to set a page on the Internet. You wouldn't even have to leave your room.'

'I used to sell them,' Victor corrected him. 'The ones that I sold though are nothing like the machines that you have in your clubs here.'

'They all work on the same principle though and besides . . .'

'Billy! Let the poor man eat his dinner.' She turned to Victor, 'I am sorry, but once he gets started on his precious computers, there is no stopping him,' Becky apologised. 'I will say one thing for him though, he is good. He can do almost anything with his computer. I just wished that he paid as much attention to me as he does to his electronic circuits and things. I still love him though in spite of his faults,' she said as she scratched him affectionately on his head.

Victor laughed and started to tuck into his meal, then suddenly paused as a thought struck him. 'Billy, if I were to give you a heap of data. Could you work out if there was any sort of pattern to it?'

'Should be a piece of cake,' Billy frowned. 'That is as long as I have enough information to feed the computer.'

'Oh you will have enough data, I can assure you. Yes, I think that I might have a small job for you. Cash in hand, of course,' Victor said with a smile.

The boy stood up. 'Just let me know when you are ready Vic. But, I must be off now, as I have a class to go to and I don't like to be late. It is a private tutor who gives extra lessons if you want.'

'Sure thing, well I won't keep you. Oh, and Billy,' the boy turned to look at him. 'Please would you call me Victor? I hate Vic.'

'Anything that you say Vic,' Billy laughed. Planting a kiss on Becky's cheek, he raised his hand in farewell and left the table.

Becky, smiling shook her head. 'I am sorry Victor, he is hopeless. Now I will leave you to finish your meal in peace. I will be back soon for your sweet order. The rhubarb and apple pie is nice.'

'I still have to get through all this first,' he protested. 'Though don't you go worrying about Billy. At least he has ambition and I am sure that he will make a go of anything that he tries. He obviously thinks the world of you.' Becky blushed and laughing, walked off leaving Victor to enjoy his meal.

That night Victor could not sleep. He tossed and turned and eventually decided to get up. He glanced at the clock: it showed 2.25. He felt like a cup of coffee. Switching on the jug beside his bed, he waited for it to boil. Having made his drink he sat on the edge of the bed. In his mind he tried to sort out what he was going to do when he reached the stables later that morning. It was all very well, Harley saying 'Find out what he is doing with my horses Victor.' Where on earth was he supposed to start? Also he should think about renting somewhere to live for a few months. It was interesting travelling around the countryside, staying at hotels and pubs, but he needed a home base if he was going to remain in England for any length of time. Although he was not strapped for cash, his budget-conscious mind bulked slightly at all the unnecessary expenditure. Then there was his own home to consider. He had no doubt that Naomi's niece and her new husband were taking good care of it. There was always the chance that they had found their own home by now.

Victor looked at his watch. 'H'm, it should be about four in the afternoon in Melbourne,' he mused. 'I might give Dan a ring and find out what is happening down there.' As he picked up the phone and dialled, he felt a slight tinge of guilt. He had not been in contact with anyone since he arrived in England. They must all be wondering what was happening to him.

Some fifty minutes later he replaced the phone. Having sorted out his home in Melbourne with Dan, he promised that he would let them know from time to time what was happening with him. He then began to feel a little drowsy. Getting back into bed again, within ten minutes he was fast asleep.

His was not a restful repose, however. He dreamt of being chased by men riding black horses. They were all waving house keys at him and crying out that theirs was too good an offer to miss. Visions, too, of Amanda and the twins, driving around town being pursued by runaway trucks, passed before his eyes. He became very agitated. Then he saw Amanda dressed all in white, walking towards him. She stretched out her arms to him. He screamed and woke to find himself soaked in sweat. He sat there in his bed until the shakes in his body had subsided. He then hauled himself out of bed and into the shower.

For the next ten minutes he let the water run over his body, washing away the sweat and tiredness. By the time that he had finished his toilet it was a little over 7.30. He then dressed and made his way down the narrow staircase and into the restaurant.

Discovering that he was the first down to breakfast, he wandered into the bar, in search of a newspaper. He could not remember the last time that he had bought one.

'Good morning. Did you sleep well?' Becky's cheerful voice surprised him.

'Good morning. Do you work here too?'

'No. I just help Mum out when we are busy. I work in the estate agents but I don't start there until ten o'clock on Sundays.'

'Estate agents eh? I might come and see you later. I am looking for somewhere to rent, I might as well try you first.'

'Right then. Now if you want to go and sit down, I will tell Mum that you are up and ready for your breakfast. Being Sunday, it is fairly relaxed.'

'I am in no hurry, in fact I have all day,' Victor protested, but before he could say anything else, Becky had gone into the kitchen. He strolled back to the table where he had eaten the night before. Sitting down, he awaited his meal.

Once he had finished his breakfast, Victor inquired whether or not his room was available for another night. He had decided to take Billy up on his offer to see if there was any sort of pattern to the way that Harley's horses were being raced. Being Sunday, he would be unable to pick up the notes that Harley had sent him till the following day. Having secured his bed for another night, he then drove through the town and took the A339 to Burghclere.

Ten minutes fast driving took him to the twisting village of Kingsclere. As he drove through, his eyes roved the signposts, looking for the one that he had been told about, pointing the way to the stables. He was almost into Basingstoke before he came to the conclusion that, somehow, he had missed his way. Seeing that he was not in any hurry, he decided to carry on to Whitchurch and approach it from that direction.

Eventually, though more by luck than judgement, he found the turn-off to the stables. Pulling off the main road, he followed the narrow lane until he reached his destination.

'How on earth do they manage to drive those big horse floats down here?' he wondered to himself. Unhooking the gate he drove through. Making certain that he had closed it behind him, he drove up to the house. A large sign hung over the door: 'Palladian Lodge. For Winners Only'.

Stepping out of the car, Victor looked around him. The house was built of a dark red brick with a gable roof. The dormer windows all had bars affixed to them. The brass knocker on the front door was of a rearing horse, evidently custom-made. The bell pull too was unique, a tightly twined horse's tail. He gave it a sharp tug but was unable to hear what kind of sound it made. After about twenty seconds, the door opened and a short stocky man, dressed in a tweed jacket and riding breeches, peered out at him.

'Yes, what do you want?' he barked.

Victor was slightly taken aback. 'Mr Oxford?'

'Yes. I'm Oxford. What do you want?' He repeated the question.

'My name is Victor Barnes,' Victor said offering Oxford his hand. 'I am a friend of Harley Klugman. He was thinking of sending you a colt that he has just bought. I understand that you already have two of his horses here, don't you?'

'Um, er, yes I do but I haven't received a third. Not as yet anyway. Is, er, Mr Klugman coming here too?'

Victor could sense an air of panic in the man's voice. So Harley was right, something was going on here. 'No. He had to fly back to the States, some meeting or other he told me. You know what these Yanks are like. Always on the move, never still for a moment.'

Oxford visibly relaxed and his manner changed completely as he received this bit of news. 'Now that is a shame. I am always only too pleased to see him whenever he is in town. Which is not often I must admit.' He stepped forward and grasped Victor's hand with both of his and shook it heartily. 'Why don't you follow me around to the office Mr Barnes? You would like a cup of coffee, I am sure. Tell me is that an Australian accent that I detect? A great horse race that you have over there, the Melbourne Cup, isn't it? Then that guy, Kerry Packer, one of the world's biggest gamblers I believe. Do you happen to know him at all?'

'I am afraid that I don't move in his type of circle. Nor do I have a strong enough heart to bet the way that he does. Also, I am English, not Australian Mr Oxford, but admittedly I do live in Melbourne.'

'Please call me Colin,' Oxford gushed. 'Are you over here on business or holiday, er, may I call you Victor? Mr Barnes sounds so formal doesn't it? The office is just around the corner here. I had it built so that I could keep an eye on the yard. My staff on the whole is pretty good, but you still have to watch them. What line of business did you say that you were in? Here we are at the office.'

Oxford opened the door of a small cottage that had been constructed at the rear of the main house. The wall that faced the yard consisted almost entirely of glass. He was obviously true to his word, when he said that he could keep an eye on everything, Victor thought to himself. There was no way that anything could come or go without being seen. The yard itself consisted of two blocks of stalls in a reverse L shape. There were five boxes in the straight, with another three in each bend. At least half of the stalls had their doors hooked open.

Ushering Victor into the office, he told him to take a seat. The big, oak desk that took up most of the room was piled high with books and papers. Oxford pushed these to one side and, opening a drawer in the desk, pulled out two glasses, which he placed on the cleared space on the desk. 'A nice single malt Victor?' He asked without making any attempt to produce a bottle.

'I would prefer coffee, if the offer is still good?' Victor replied smiling to himself. It was fairly obvious that the man was not too keen on sharing his scotch.

'Of course. Coffee it shall be.' Oxford leaned forward and spoke into the intercom on his desk. 'Lilly dear, could we please have a pot of coffee and two cups in here when you have a moment?' He then sat back in his huge, leather chair, folded his hands across his stomach and stared at Victor. 'Now, how can I help you?' Victor was silent for a moment, not quite sure what approach he should adopt with this man.

'Well, as I said, Harley had to fly back to the US so he asked me if I would drop in and have a look at his two horses. I am also to discuss the possibility of his new acquisition coming here. He is a trifle disappointed that his others haven't lived up to expectations.'

'The curse of all trainers, Victor,' Oxford threw up his hands in an exaggerated gesture. 'Almost every owner thinks that his or her horse should be doing better than it is. At least Harley's have won a few races between them, which is more than a lot of them do. This new one that he has bought, do you happen to know its name? No paperwork has arrived for it as yet. Although Harley usually manages to buy something that looks as though it might be a handy type.'

'A handy type! I shouldn't let him hear you call it that! He is convinced that it is going to win the Derby for him. It certainly needs to in order to get back what he paid for it,' Victor laughed heartily.

Oxford's interest quickened visibly. 'How much did he lay out for it exactly?' The beads of sweat were clearly visible on his brow. Victor was also certain that, were they to shake hands, he would find the other man's palms the same. Still, it could be genuine concern over an expensive thoroughbred, but somehow he doubted it. He could almost see the dollar signs in the other man's eyes. He decided that it was time to go on the attack and see what happened.

'Let's just say that if it wins the Derby, he will show a small profit. Now can I see his horses Colin? I presume that they are here?'

'Actually they're not. They are with the second string and not back from exercise yet. I am expecting them very shortly though. Ah, here is our coffee.' He broke off as a girl appeared with a tray of coffee and sullenly dumped it on the desk. 'Thank you Lilly.' The girl glared at him and left, slamming the door behind her. Oxford squirmed in his chair. 'Sorry about that, she is not herself today. Wrong time of the month I expect. It is hard for her I suppose since her mother left. A girl needs a mother to talk over these women's problems that occur.'

'Is she your daughter then?' Victor was quite taken aback. He was more than convinced that it had been malevolent hatred that he had seen in the girl's eyes. He wondered what Oxford could have done to warrant such passion from a young girl.

'Yes, that she is. I don't think that she has ever forgiven my wife for walking out on us as she did. But that is my problem and certainly not yours.'

Victor took a sip of his coffee and shuddered. It was terrible. Evidently Lilly was not backward in taking out her emotions on her father's guests. He wished now that he had accepted the invitation of the malt whisky. He tried to drink his coffee without tasting its bitterness. 'Perhaps I could see what type of programme you have mapped out for the pair then? You must have them entered for some future events. I mean that the season proper gets underway in about five weeks.'

'To be honest, I was thinking that they both might need spelling for a while,' Colin paused for a moment. 'I must admit that I am having a few problems with them lately. They seem to have lost that edge that they need to race. I thought that a spell might freshen them up and do them some good.'

'I understood that they haven't raced since November. Surely that is a long enough spell for any horse?'

Colin regarded him silently for a while and then said quietly, 'Tell me, have you had any experience in training horses?'

Victor shook his head.

'No? Then may I suggest, quite respectfully of course, that decisions like that are best left to people whose business it is?'

Victor was not sure, but he thought that he detected an undertone of a threat in Oxford's voice. For the time being he decided to let it pass, but he made a mental note of it. 'I meant no disrespect, I can assure you. It's just that as an owner you like to see your horse at least racing. Even if it is not winning as it ought.'

'Oh, so you have some horses yourself do you? May I ask who your trainer is? Perhaps I know your animals. I presume that they have raced have they?'

'Horse,' Victor corrected him. He thought it prudent that he didn't mention Pride of Tintagel at this juncture. 'Actually, I have only just bought it, so at the moment I am looking for a trainer. That was my second reason for coming to see you. I wanted to know if you were interested and if you had the room, should I decide to place it here. The sale is not yet finalised but it is almost a done deal.'

Colin's face almost lit up with greed. He leaned forward across the desk. 'I most certainly do have room here at present. I would be honoured to take your horse, Victor. I am sure that Harley has vouched for my methods. Would I know of this horse or is it yet to race?'

'I think that the answer might be yes on both counts.'

'I am not sure that I quite understand you. If it hasn't raced yet, then how would I have heard of it?' Oxford looked genuinely puzzled.

'It is called Arcadian Steel. I am sure that you must have at least read about it,' Victor said softly.

Oxford's eyes narrowed thoughtfully and he looked at Victor. 'What made you buy that brute? Surely you must have been told of its reputation? I sincerely hope that someone hasn't taken advantage of you being new to the game.'

'No, I bought it with my eyes wide open. For a start it is entered for the Derby and I have always wanted a runner in the race. Because of its reputation I got it at a good price. Far cheaper than you would normally expect to pay for a Derby hopeful. Secondly, and far more importantly as far as I am concerned, I like the horse and think that it has real potential.'

'All that I can says is that I hope that you got it dirt cheap. Forgive me for saying it but as for winning the Derby, you are day dreaming. It hasn't even had a run yet.'

'Lammtarra ran only once as a two-year-old and then had the Derby as its first run of the season, after that disastrous time in Dubai.'

'I have to give you that but it will never happen again, I can assure you. That Lammtarra was something extra special. Still, if you are serious about racing your colt then I can tell you that if anybody can get him to run, I could. I should be more than happy to train him for you. You never know, he could make us both famous.'

'At least we have that settled then. If I decide on you as his trainer I'll let you know when everything is finalised with the sale. Now to get back to Harley's two, if you have any details on them I would like to take them with me. His office is sending me everything that they have but you of course are a lot closer to the problem. Harley has asked me to go over their form and results. I will have a vet look at them too. I have then to report back to Harley. Depending on what I come up with, he will make his decision.' Victor then leant back in his chair and looked at the other man steadily.

'What decision are we talking about here?'

'Oh, whether or not we sell them,' Victor replied sweetly, turning the screw. He inwardly laughed as he saw Oxford wince.

The sound of horses' hooves clattering across the cobblestones of the yard,stopped the conversation from going any further. Six horses, ridden mainly by apprentices from what Victor was able to see, pulled up alongside the taps. Their coats steaming in the cool morning air, they waited patiently. After dismounting, their riders started on the task of unsaddling them and cooling them off.

'Are Harley's two in that bunch there?'

Oxford nodded. 'Come and have a look at them if you like.' The two men got to their feet and went out into the yard. As they approached the group, one of the riders, who appeared to be the eldest, handed the reins of his mount to one of the young lads. After a muffled protest the boy led the horse away. The elder lad walked towards them. He was about to speak when Oxford held up his hand. 'Was he warning him to be quiet?' Victor thought to himself. 'Maybe I am becoming paranoid about the whole thing.'

Oxford turned to him. 'Victor, I would like you to meet Jimmy. He is my number one jockey.' Victor offered him his hand, but Jimmy ignored it and merely nodded at him slightly. 'Any problems Jimmy? They all look fit,' Oxford asked.

'None apart from that bay colt again. You need to put a stronger rider on him. Harrison just can't hold him. The horse is stargazing far too much.'

'Stargazing? What do you mean by that?' said Victor with a chuckle. 'I have never heard that expression applied to a horse before.'

Oxford gave a little sigh of frustration. With a slightly disparaging tone, like a teacher to a very young and ignorant pupil, he explained. 'Stargazing means that the horse is riding above the bit. You see, you cannot pull a horse's head down. The more that you pull, then the higher he will put his head. To correct this, the rider has to raise his hands five to six inches above the normal position. Now Jimmy here says that the boy has not yet learnt how to do this properly. Personally, I don't think that he will ever be strong enough to be a jockey. We try to do our best with him. We have to at least give him a proper chance. Some lads just don't have it in their make up to become jockeys.'

'Thank you Colin. This is my first venture into racing. I can see that there is a lot more to learn than I ever imagined,' Victor said, looking suitably humbled. Inwardly, again, he was laughing. Still he did want to give the impression that, as far as horses went, he was a complete novice. If he was to find out what was going on then he didn't want Oxford thinking that he represented any danger to him.

'Ok Jimmy. I will get a full report from you a little later on. Carry on for now.'

'Colin, which two belong to Harley? I should like to see them if I may.'

'Yes, of course. They are the two at the rear there.' He pointed out two horses that were just being led into their stalls. The two men strolled across to the opposite side of the yard. Stopping at the first stall, Victor waited until the boy had tied the colt to its tethering ring. He then entered the stall. He studied the animal with interest. It was bay brown on colour, with black legs, mane and tail. Its head was bony with a fairly small cheek and prominent eye. Its haunches were broad and fleshy. Victor ran his hands lightly over them. They appeared to be firm all over, which indicated to him that the colt should be speedy. He reached up and felt the jaws. They both felt of equal firmness. Continuing to run his hands down the animal's neck, he found a muscular depression in the shoulder. He whistled lightly.

Oxford looked at him hard. 'Nothing is wrong is there?'

'Oh no. It's the Prophet's thumb mark. I thought that was normally found in the neck of thoroughbreds. It is the first time that I have ever seen one in the shoulder.'

'You know what it is then?' Oxford said quizzically. 'So you do know something about horses! Have you been trying to make me look like an idiot? I do not like being taken for a fool, Victor!'

'Oh no! There was never any intention of that,' Victor protested quickly. His brain raced quickly to find a suitable answer that would placate the man. He also cursed himself for slipping up in this way. 'Uh, I have a friend in Australia who breeds Arab horses. He showed me the mark once. He told me that some people believe Arabian horses were touched by Allah to give them speed. Hence the name.'

Oxford considered this for a moment. Then, evidently thinking it plausible, nodded. 'Did you know that you can find it sometimes in the hind quarters too. Although I must admit, that is not very often.'

'Well, I have certainly learnt something new today' Victor stood away from the horse. Time for some damage control, he thought to himself. 'To be honest, I was trying to impress you. I was merely copying what I saw them doing at the sales. I didn't want you to think that I was a complete dunderhead when it came to horses. If I could just have a quick look at Harley's other horse. That way I don't have to lie if he asks if I saw them. Then I will get out of your hair. You must have a lot of work to do.'

The trainer considered this explanation for a minute. Then nodding, led the way into the next stall. A brown colt was quietly munching on some oats.

'If this horse raced half as well as he eats, we would all be happy,' Oxford said in a jovial voice. 'Tell me, what do you think of this one's list?' Alarm bells sounded in Victor's brain. Was this a genuine question or an attempt to trick him? He walked around the animal, peering at it intently. 'It doesn't appear as though he is listing at all. I thought that term only applied to ships,' he replied innocently. The other man gave him a long, hard look. He then laughed and slapped him on the back.

'You will do, Victor. A list, my friend, is a band of black hairs. It has nothing to do with the way that he stands. In fact this horse doesn't even have any. Now when can I expect Arcadian Steel to arrive?'

About half an hour later Victor drove out of the yard and headed towards Andover. He had arranged with Oxford to call back the next day for some details on the horses' future plans. He had also promised to consider placing Arcadian Steel with him. He had no intention of doing so but he wanted to keep the man sweet. He was still mystified as to what was going on exactly. He was more convinced than ever that the stable was running some kind of fiddle. It was a gut feeling as everything appeared above board. He knew that he could do nothing until the next day. He would be able to pick up Harley's data when the post office opened. In the meantime, he thought that he might as well do some sightseeing.

At breakfast that morning, he had remarked to Becky that the one thing that he missed about England was the old pubs. Being only two hundred years old, the Australian pubs were not in any position to have a comparable history. The whole atmosphere of the 'English local' was missing from their Aussie counterparts. In Melbourne, the hotels on the whole were merely for drinking in. Victor missed the old inns that had stood the test of time over, literally hundreds of years. The thatched roofs, the little snugs, the old smuggler haunts and such like.

Becky had told him about a place called Wooton Rivers, a village full of thatched cottages. The main attraction was a sixteenth-century free house, complete with oak-beamed bars, called the Royal Oak. She had also told him that the food was really good there. 'While you are there, you should go and have a look at the canal. It passes through a lock at the end of the village. The canal itself was featured in the TV series, *The River.* David Essex starred in it.'

Victor told her that he didn't think that it had been shown in Australia. If it had he had missed it.

'There is also a thirteenth-century church there that has a very unusual clock. It was built by one of the villagers for the coronation of George V. Instead of numbers it has the words "Glory Be To God" attached to its face. It is a nice trip.' He had laughed and told her that she should have been a travel agent instead of an estate agent.

So here he was, driving through the Wiltshire countryside, wishing again that Amanda were with him. When they had first talked about a trip to England, she had written away to every source that she could find. She wanted details of tours, bed and breakfast places and maps of the southern counties. She had been so excited at the prospect of coming over. Now here he was, touring on his own. Never again to see the smile on her face or hear her laugh. Life can be so cruel at times. Victor brushed the salty tears from his eyes and concentrated on his driving.

Upon reaching Andover, he took the A342, then turned right on the A345 at Upavon, to Pewsey. Becky had told him to watch out for the turn off to Wootton Rivers about four miles outside Pewsey. As he drove through the Saverake Forest he wished that it had been a little later in the year. The leaf-bare trees that faced him seemed somehow inhospitable. Turning off the main road, he slowly made his way down the narrow, twisting lane until he reached the village. Deciding that it was too early for lunch he parked the car in the car park at the rear of the pub. He then set out to explore the village on foot.

Chapter Five

Becky had been right. Almost the entire village consisted of cottages with thatched roofs. Most of them, too, were whitewashed with blackened, oak beams, in the Tudor style. Dotted amongst them was the odd one constructed of the more modern red brick. He walked as far as the canal in order to view the lock. The lock-keeper's house was evidently a far newer residence than most of the village houses. It was built of brick, painted white but with a tiled roof. He remained gazing down at the canal for some fifteen minutes before slowly making his way back up the village.

Coming to the old church, he decided that he should have a look at the clock that Becky had spoken of. Pushing open the gate he made his way up the narrow path to the ancient building. The going was wet and slippery underfoot and he had to tread warily. He found that the front door was locked against vandals. A sign of the times Victor sighed. There were instructions, however, on how to obtain a key if required. Victor contented himself in merely picking his way through the stone tombstones. Most of them were too old to read any description. He then gazed up at the object of his visit, the famous clock. The hands on its face were pointed at an 'O' and a 'D'. He decided that this indicated time for lunch. With a last look around at the well- kept grave yard he retraced his steps back down the greasy path. Securing the gate once more behind him, he continued on his way back to the Royal Oak and lunch.

The inside of the inn was as Becky had described it, low ceilings with light oak beams, the walls decorated with lamps and china plates, the wooden tables and chairs blending ideally with the brick of the bar. Having studied the menu with great interest he settled on roast venison with madeira sauce. To wash it down, he chose something that he had not seen since leaving England: a glass of hot, mulled red wine. A house speciality, he was informed.

Just over ninety minutes later, feeling fully nourished and at peace with the world in general, he was once more back on the road. He decided to return to Newbury, via Marlborough, a town that he had not visited since his schooldays. It was just starting to get dark by the time that he arrived back at the inn. Seeing that the place was busy, he decided against trying to talk to Becky. Instead he made his way up to his room, fully planning to come down later for a drink. He lay on the bed and within minutes was fast asleep.

The next morning, Victor partook of a late breakfast. He then headed to the post office to pick up his mail. Harley's office had certainly done him proud. Every scrap of information that they possessed on Colin Oxford and the horses was there. Taking it back to his room he sifted though all the paperwork that he had received. He made three separate piles. One for each of the horses and the final one for Oxford and his stables. Having completed this he then went in search of Billy. He had been told that he would find him in the public bar from eleven o'clock. Sure enough, Victor found him there playing darts. He nodded at Victor as he approached. He threw his final darts and told his opponent that he had to leave. Picking up his coat he told Victor to follow him. Leaving the bar he walked down the street some twenty yards and stopped. Taking a key from the pocket of his coat, he unlocked a door. 'Come on up. I have a bedsit on the first floor.' Victor followed him upstairs and into his room.

Once inside, Victor glanced around and was pleasantly surprised. Instead of the disorder that he had expected to find, the whole room was neat and tidy. The bed was made and nothing seemed to be out of place. Billy saw him looking around and grinned. 'Becky says that she won't come into an untidy room. If there is any mess when she arrives, she leaves. As I never know when she is likely to come, I have to keep it neat and clean all of the time.'

Victor was impressed. She evidently had her head screwed on right. Train him well before they got married and it would continue when they decided to tie the knot. The only other piece of furniture in the room apart from a small dressing table and chair was a large walnut desk. Billy used this to house his computer and keyboard. 'I need plenty of room when I work,' he said.

Victor nodded in agreement and silently handed him the two piles of notes on the horses.

Billy took them and quickly glanced through them. 'What is it exactly that I am supposed to be looking for?' he asked curiously.

'I am not really sure to be perfectly truthful. Anything that represents a pattern or any abnormalities that the computer can throw up, I guess. Keep anything that you find to yourself of course.'

'Well, leave it with me for a couple of hours. It will take me that long to feed all this data in. I should be able to give you some kind of answer by then.'

'That's fine by me. While you are doing that I will go and pay a call on Becky. I am anxious to see what she has to offer me in the way of places to rent. Any message for her?'

'Naw. I will have something for you later.' Billy was already busy typing into his computer. He almost seemed unaware of the other man's presence. 'I will see you anon, Billy.' Victor laughed and left the room, quietly closing the door behind him. Once outside he cursed softly. He had meant to ask Billy how to get to Becky's office. Still, it shouldn't be too hard to find an estate agent in a town of this size.

Luck was with him for once because the first one that he tried turned out to be the correct one. Becky was with a couple as he entered. Looking up, she smiled at him and motioned for him to take a seat. She was with the young couple for about five minutes. They then left, clutching several sheets of paper. She invited him to take a seat at her desk. She finished writing up some notes. Placing them in a file she then pushed it to one side. 'Now, Victor, what exactly are you looking for?'

He hesitated for a short time and then stroked his chin. 'Do you only deal with property in the Newbury area or do you go further afield?' He then sat back in his chair, feeling strangely apprehensive.

'How far further afield? We don't go as far as the Continent, if that is what you want. We cover Berkshire and Hampshire. Is that what you mean?'

Again he hesitated, then asked quietly, 'How about Cornwall? Do you have anything down there at all?'

'Cornwall. How nice. Well, I am not sure. Just give me a minute and I will have a look. Nothing immediately springs to mind. But then I don't normally get asked that.'

'I realise that it is not a local spot, but I just have a fancy for Cornwall. Or even Devon would do. I am not really fussy about the exact location,' Victor could almost feel his blood pressure rising.

Becky typed some details into her computer and waited patiently for an answer. 'Why, yes, as a matter of fact, we do have a couple of listings for Cornwall. Though I don't think that this first one would be much good to you,' she laughed. 'It's a betting shop in Redruth. There is also a hairdressing salon in Newquay. Wait a minute, this looks more interesting. I think that it could be a bit on the large size for you though. It is Seven Oaks, a four-bedroom house, short-term lease, unfurnished though. Now that might be a problem for you.' She looked up at him expectantly.

'It certainly sounds a distinct possibility. Where in Cornwall is it?'

'Um, six miles north of a place called Perranporth. Let's see now, your biggest town would have to be Newquay I suppose. Or maybe Truro, they are about the same distance away. Hold on a second and I will get a print out for you.' So saying, she clicked the mouse and moments later the information issued forth from the printer.

Victor took the sheet and studied it closely. 'This one looks quite promising. The size doesn't really worry me, I like plenty of room. There is a contact number written here. Do I just ring it or what?'

'I can do that for you. When would you like to go down and see it?'

'Well, I have to wait for Billy to get me some results from his computer. How about Wednesday or maybe Thursday?'

'Just give me a moment and I will see what can be arranged.' Checking the telephone number, she picked up her phone and dialled. Victor couldn't quite catch all of the conversation as a convoy of heavy trucks took that moment to drive by. A few minutes later she replaced her receiver and smiled at him. 'All arranged for you. Any time after noon. The agent has another appointment in Truro. However, he will arrange to have the house opened for you if there is any likelihood of him being late.'

'Becky, I am impressed, but what do you make out of this? Something I hope.'

'Oh, on these multi-listings, we get a percentage of the commission.'

'Perhaps I can take you and Billy out to dinner tonight? My way of thanking you both for your help.'

'No. There is no necessity for anything like that. This is what I am paid for. Billy loves to show off what he can do so thank you, but no.'

'I insist. You can let me know where you would like to go later. In the meantime, I might go back and see how he is getting on.'

'No,' Becky shook her head. 'If he told you a couple of hours then it's better if you let him have the time. When he gets involved with that gadget of his, he is not aware of anyone else. Not even me,' she added rather ruefully.

'Well, you should know.' He laughed. 'You must be the first computer widow that I have met. Can I buy you a cup of coffee while I wait then?'

'No, I am sorry. I can't leave the office until the boss gets back. Why don't you take a walk around the town and I will see you tonight.'

Later on that evening, after a very pleasant meal at the local Chinese restaurant, washed down by a couple of bottles of Riesling, the three of them adjourned to Billy's place. He had placed all the print-outs on the table for Victor to see. He had gone over them several times but could not really find any kind of pattern. He asked Billy what he thought about them.

'The only thing that seems to stand out is that they both have only won minor class races. Neither of them has won above a class G race. There is one strange thing though that the computer shows. If either of them ran in a class D or above, then their time is at least three seconds slower. Even if the lower class race is over the same distance.'

'Now that is interesting,' said Victor slowly. 'Are you sure about that? There couldn't be any error at all?'

'The computer cannot lie.' Billy's expression was so pained that they both had to laugh at him. His features changed into a pout.

'I am sorry Billy, I shouldn't laugh. Tell me, though, if both horses are at least three seconds slower in a higher-grade race, regardless of whether they won or not, what does it suggest to you? Their actual times shouldn't be affected by the quality of a race.'

'This is only a guess on my part of course, but . . .' He hesitated for a minute. 'I know that it seems highly unlikely of course . . .'

'Go on.'

'It does suggest that they have been got at. It is the only logical explanation, but why? It doesn't make any sense. If we hadn't have been looking for an anomaly, most likely nobody would have picked it up.'

'Now why would anyone want to stop a horse from winning a decent prize.'

Becky meanwhile, had also been reading the sheets that Billy had printed out. She looked up with a puzzled air about her. 'Victor, I thought that you said that you had all the data on these two horses. Not everything is here, not for Alaskan Jack anyhow.' She named the bay brown that Victor had examined yesterday.

'What do you mean, not all there?' He asked, frowning. 'Every race that he has been entered in is supposed to be listed. I can't see Harley's office messing up.'

'What about the two-year-old races in France? I know that he ran because his stable lad came into the bar all excited. It was the end of last year and the first time that he had driven through the Channel Tunnel.'

'France!' Victor said astounded. 'Harley never mentioned about racing in France. I think that I had better give him a call right now and find out. That is too big of a mistake for his office to have made.'

'You can use my phone if you like,' said Billy.

Victor thanked him and, after checking his notebook for the number, rang Los Angeles. He got through almost immediately and quickly explained what they had discovered. After a few minutes he put the phone down with a thoughtful look on his face. 'I shall have to ring the *Racing Post* in the morning to check. As far as Harley is concerned, none of his horses have ever raced in France. So what does Mr Colin Oxford think that he is playing at?'

'I will lay you 10–1, the horse won in France,' Billy cried excitedly.

The next morning proved Billy's forecast correct. After several phone calls and checks with various bodies Victor had the faxed proof that he needed. It turned out that both horses had won at Deauville, not once but twice. In doing so they had amassed prize money amounting to £101,300. The horses had raced in the name of Klugman Nominees, so at least Harley's name was registered. So where was the money? Victor knew that it was no good phoning Harley for several hours. The time difference between the two countries made it impractical. What should his next step be, he wondered? Also he needed to find out how many people were involved in the scam.

Victor suddenly realised that as yet he had not spoken to the guy who was supposed to be Harley's manager. Rummaging through the papers again he found that the manager lived in Salisbury. He toyed with the idea of just turning up at his house but quickly dismissed this. He didn't want to drive all the way down there, only to find that the man was not at home. He dialled the phone number and waited.

'Hello. John Cassidy,' the voice at the other end boomed out.

'Oh good morning. My name is Victor Barnes and I am . . .'

'Ah, yes, Mr Barnes. I have been expecting your call. Where are you exactly?'

'Expecting my call? How did you know about me?' Victor was a little amazed.

'Mr Barnes, there is not much in the racing world that I am not aware of. Also I had a call from Colin Oxford. He told me that you were preparing some kind of report for Harley Klugman. Anything that you wanted to know about his horses, you should have come and seen me about, After all I am supposed to be his manager.'

'I see, I do apologise. Well, I am in Newbury at present. I was thinking of driving down to see you. There are some things that we need to discuss.'

'No problem. I am only too happy to oblige. How about if we meet for lunch?'

'That is fine by me.'

'Ok. How about meeting me at one o'clock at The Haunch of Venison. You will find it opposite the Poultry Cross. You can park in the Market Square, which is right in the centre of town. You will find the Poultry Cross is at the rear of the square. You can't miss it. I will look forward to meeting you.' Before Victor had a chance to reply, Cassidy hung up.

Victor slowly replaced his receiver. 'Well now, so Colin has already been on to Mr Cassidy. It certainly looks as though they are in this together. I shall have to be careful,' he said to himself.

Forty-five minutes later saw Victor motoring through the Wiltshire countryside towards Salisbury. He drove at a steady pace trying to work out in his mind the best tack to adopt. He didn't really want to bring up the subject of Deauville until he had spoken to Harley again. He concluded that his best bet was to continue along the line that he had adopted with Oxford. He would say that Harley was not happy with the returns from his charges and was considering selling them.

The pale, watery sun was struggling to make its presence felt as Victor drove into the old market town of Salisbury. He had not been there since he was a child, when he had occasion to sing with his school in the magnificent old cathedral. There was a decided bite in the air as he parked the car in the market place. He quickly made his way towards Minster Street. The cold weather was one thing that he did not miss about England, although Melbourne too could experience some very cold days. In fact he had even seen it snow there on more than one occasion. When he and Amanda had been discussing their proposed trip, they had agreed the best time to visit England was June or July.

Pulling his newly acquired sheepskin coat closer around him, Victor walked on until he found the restaurant. The original building dated from 1320 and he was fascinated by its wealth of beams and panelling. The odd floor levels also caught his eye. He enquired of a waitress if a Mr Cassidy was there yet. Nodding, she pointed to a table by the window where a man that Victor judged to be in his late twenties, with wild, sandy-coloured hair, sat drumming his fingers on the table. As Victor approached, he looked up but made no attempt to get to his feet. This rudeness of manner caused Victor to take an immediate dislike to the man. His defences went up sharply.

'Mr Cassidy?' he asked holding out his hand. The other man raised his own hand in greeting. He made no attempt to shake hands. 'Mr Barnes,' he drawled. 'I see that you found the place ok. I picked it because it is fairly central and the food is good.'

'It certainly is an interesting old place. We have nothing like this at home. Then the country is not old enough.'

'Yeah, there is actually an identical replica of this built in the US somewhere. Some rich Yank liked it so much I suppose. Maybe you should think of doing something similar in Australia. A far sounder proposition than horse racing eh? Ah, here is the waitress now. How about we eat first, then talk business? If I am going to fight you, I would rather do it on a full stomach.'

'Who said anything about fighting me?' Victor protested. 'Harley has merely ask me to do an assessment of his horses and their possible future. Even if we decide, or rather Harley decides, to move them, it doesn't necessarily follow that you won't still manage them,' Victor tried to placate the man. He needed him until he discovered whether or not he was working with Oxford. At this stage there was every indication that he was. In fact, reason demanded that he must be or else he was a fool.

'I don't see what all the fuss is about. The horses have won a couple of races each and at least that is something. Some owners have horses with Colin that have never won, nor do they look likely too. They don't talk about pulling out, they just keep hoping for that lucky break,' Cassidy said sullenly, his eyes glaring at Victor as he spoke.

'Look as you said, let's eat first and talk afterwards. Now can you recommend anything on this menu? It all sounds very good.'

'You can't really go wrong with the venison. This place is famous for it, or the chicken's not bad. That is if you want something a little lighter.' So, in spite of having enjoyed a similar dish only a couple of days earlier, Victor ordered the man's recommended choice. The meat was indeed very tender when it arrived but he was disappointed to find it was on the tepid side, as were the vegetables.

Chapter Five

Hardly a word was spoken as both men ate their meal. Victor waited until the waitress had brought their coffee, then leant back in his chair.

'How is the security at Colin's stables John?' He asked the other man looking him straight in the face. Clearly the question had caught the other by surprise and his drumming fingers slipped off the table. 'Security! Why, what do you mean?'

'I have had a computer analysis done of the races that the horses have run in. It has come up with some very interesting facts.'

'Computers! You can make them say anything that you want to.'

'Maybe you can. But there is no denying the facts. Every time that one of them runs in a D class race, their time is at least three times slower than when they run in lower grades. This would suggest to me that when they race in better-class events, that someone doesn't want them to win.'

'That's ridiculous! What would anyone achieve by that?'

'Of that I am not quite sure,' Victor said shaking his head. 'As you say, how would anyone benefit by stopping the animals? However, the fact still remains. In better class company the horses run slower.'

'Well I can assure you that Colin's security is as good as anybody's in the country. There simply is no way that anyone can get at his horses. All you have to go on are a few figures from a computer. Well, quite frankly, I think that you are wasting your time.' He paused. 'I also resent the fact that you could even suggest that Colin does not look after his charges. Why can't you and Harley accept the fact that his horses are not good enough to win any major races? It does happen, you know.'

'If that is the case, you would not have any objections if we pull them out. He would be better off selling them,' Victor dropped his voice a tone. 'After all, if they are the hacks that you are implying, he might as well cut his losses. There is no point of throwing good money after bad.' Victor looked Cassidy straight in the eye as he spoke. His interest mounted as he saw all the colour drain from the other man's face. 'I'll tell you what I'll do. I'll leave things as they are until their next race. I can see them run for myself and then I'll make up my mind. Now, just to show you that there are no hard feelings, let me pay for this lunch. Is there anything that you need to know from me?'

'No, nothing. I will find out from Colin when they are due to race next and get in touch with you.' Angrily, the other man got to his feet.

'Where are you staying, so I can find you?'

'There is no need to do that. I will just watch the papers until I see them entered. Then I will be in touch with you. On that you can rest assured.'

Chapter Six

The approach to the house was nothing short of spectacular; the narrow lane flanked on both sides by hedgerows of blackthorn standing atop moss-green embankments. These in turn were ablaze with hundreds of daffodils, their brave trumpets proclaiming spring. They were interspersed with clumps of azure bluebells, almost seeming like interlopers in this blanket of yellow.

The weather worn wooden gate wedged between four-foot-high dry-stone walls opened onto a crazy paving pathway. This wound gently between rows of azaleas and rhododendron bushes, whose bases were lifted by clumps of late-flowering double primroses and white bluebells. Away to the left, a dilapidated scarecrow stood sentinel over an overgrown and neglected vegetable garden. To the right was the servant's cottage – a circular, white-painted thatched dwelling surmounted with a cross. Legend had it that it was devil-proof as it had no corners. Therefore Satan could not lie in wait for its occupants. Ancient Cornwall was a land full of superstitions; many were still believed in today by a very large percentage of its inhabitants.

The house itself was the result of the remodelling of three miners' cottages. They had been built of local granite with slate roofs. From the walls of the house grew climbing roses instead of the more common green ivy. The windows, fanciful nineteenth-century Gothic style and the solid oak front door, were all blossom-capped with honeysuckle and columbine. These had been planted originally to ward off the plague. To the left and right of the front entrance, elder bushes (placed to prevent the passage of witches into the house) thrived in oaken tubs.

Almost dwarfing the house grew the seven giant oaks that gave the house its name. The original owner had planted them to protect the house from the Atlantic gales that constantly swept in from the west coast and buffeted it during the winter. Time had taken its toll and they had been beaten into somewhat grotesque shapes by the ever-ravaging wind. The front door opened into a small entrance hall, the floor of which was Cornish slate, very smooth and cool, with a texture of smoky, dark blues and greys. Each flagstone was like damascene where the passing of many feet and provisions had worn small grooves and patterns.

Across the narrow passage from the entrance hall was the doorway to the kitchen. This, too, was paved with banded slate. Two distinctive features dominated the airy kitchen. The first to strike the eye was a huge fireplace with a wood-fired oven and range. The surround of which was white-painted plaster, sharply contrasting with the blackened oak mantle and surround. The second was a far more spectacular item: the gnarled and smoke-bombarded trunk of one of the seven oak trees that actually grew out of the kitchen floor. It climbed nobly past and through the black poplar beams that supported the upper level. To the left, a wooden settle with a faded patchwork seat had been set back into the actual wall of the room. A table carved from solid red stone, imported from Devon and polished as smooth as glass, took up most of the centre of the room.

A massive fireplace, too, dominated the lounge, where over the years many people had sat to warm themselves in winter. Whilst enjoying the warmth they listened to the hiss and crackle as the huge logs burnt through the dark nights, their glow emanating throughout the room, occasionally cracking and spitting, sending a myriad of brightly hued sparks into the dark, sooty depths of the stone chimney.

The remainder of the downstairs area consisted of a den, cobble-stone laundry and a small scullery. To reach the upper level it was necessary to climb a set of wooden stairs at the end of the passage. These too, were somewhat different from the norm with the rises being a foot in depth instead of the customary nine inches. They had been worn smooth by the constant traffic over many years.

Upstairs, the master bedroom occupied virtually the whole of one side. The entrance to it was gained off a narrow landing. A rather dilapidated four-poster bed, badly in need of restoration, had been left by the previous owner, most likely deciding that it was too much trouble to try and remove it. However, the crowning glory of this room was the view from its almost palatial-sized bay window. This was in complete contrast with the windows in the rest of the home.

Chapter Six

Looking out through the multi-paned glass, the view was spectacular in all directions. To the north, the land climbed to the sky. The landscape was dotted with the decaying engine houses of derelict tin and copper mines, their tall chimneys standing reminders of past riches, lost dreams and noble causes. To the south, the hills sloped away to the sparkling blueness of the bay. Here the Atlantic rollers came crashing in to beat resoundingly upon the rocks at the foot of the wind-carved, granite cliffs, great columns of water being hurled high into the sunlit sky.

The other three bedrooms were situated on the opposite side of the house and their uneven floors all sloped towards the front. This gave the occupants a great view of the straw-thatched cottages of the nearby village.

Having fully explored the upper floor, Victor stood for a while gazing at the varied arrays of chimney stacks that, almost lazily, discharged smoke from many fires towards the heavens. So much for the smokeless fuels, he thought, but then there was nothing more comforting than a blazing log fire. For a moment, a feeling of deep remorse gripped him. He felt almost guilty standing there. This was meant to be the year that he was finally going to bring his family over here. Amanda in particular, had been so looking forward to doing a tour of the many famous old inns and places that he had told her about. She had especially wanted to see the south west and visit places like Mousehole. She had insisted on calling it as it was spelt instead of pronouncing it Mouzel as it should be. She had fallen in love with Cornwall through watching such TV programmes as *Poldark* and *Wycliffe*. She had also been intrigued by the number of towns and villages that were called St something. She had discovered at least twenty such places on an old map that she had bought in a second-hand bookshop. She declared that one to be a fine place to have such a God-like air about it, yet be so famous as a smugglers' haven. 'She would have absolutely adored this place,' Victor thought to himself.

'I am not sure whether I will be able to stand renting it without her. Still, it is not as though I am going to buy it. Just rent it for a couple of months while I race Pride of Tintagel,' he thought, 'Oh Amanda! How I miss you and the boys. Whoever said that money couldn't buy happiness certainly knew what they were talking about. Here I am, rich beyond my wildest dreams, yet so very alone.' Yet there was an air of calmness about the house that seemed to pervade his very bones, leaving a sense of belonging. 'I suppose that if I am to settle anywhere, it might as well be in a place like this, that I know she would have loved,' he reflected.

Just then, a car up and stopped in the lane, distracting his thoughts. 'It must be the agent,' Victor said to himself.' I suppose that I ought to go down and see what he has to say.' He made his way back down the stairs and was just reaching the end of the passage when the front door opened. A stockily built man about forty years of age and carrying a shabby old briefcase came in.

'Good afternoon. You are Mr Barnes I take it?' he asked in a breezy tone.

Victor nodded and shook the outstretched hand.

'I hope that I haven't kept you waiting too long. I am afraid that I got held up in Truro longer than I anticipated. Have you looked the place over yet? I know that it smells a trifle damp but it has been closed up for six months. It just needs a little airing out.'

'You haven't been able to let it then?' Victor asked.

'No. There is not a lot of call for these types of places in the winter. Too bleak and far away from town for most people.' He saw Victor smile and added hastily, 'We won't have any trouble when the holiday season and warmer weather arrives. I could even rent out a garden shed in the summer months. People are prepared to accept anything that they can get then. Plus of course they have to pay a lot more money for the privilege.'

'Why don't you let the servant's cottage then? That looks as though it could hold at least a couple.'

The agent shook his head and sighed. 'It needs too much money spent on it. The council will not grant a permit to occupy until all the plumbing and wiring have been completely renewed. Nothing has been done to the place for at least fifty years. A great shame too, as I could let it as easy as winking an eye. It would fetch a handsome rent, too, in the summer months.'

'Who exactly owns the house at the moment?' Victor asked curiously. The agent laughed and said with a grin, 'The building society! The couple who used to own it, well it is a tragic story really. Mr and Mrs Humber, a couple in their late fifties, he used to be a merchant seaman but he retired. They bought this house and he had this dream of opening a theme park, similar to the Poldark Mine down at Wendron. Everybody told him that he was crazy but he wouldn't listen to any one. He sank all his savings into this scheme. He even mortgaged this house.'

'What happened? There doesn't appear to be any sign of development around here, not that I passed driving up. In fact apart from the village, I haven't seen anything that even suggests any occupation of any kind.'

'No, he started building over St Agnes way. People warned him that the ground was not safe because of all the old mine workings there. Like a fool he went ahead, heeding no one. One afternoon he was driving a lorry loaded with steel beams. He turned off the road and started driving towards the cliff. As far as we know, a sudden wind must have sprung up and hit the lorry. We get some real violent gusts up here, you have to be careful. Anyway, the lorry overturned and the weight of all the steel must have made it impossible to control. Evidently he had been driving across an old mine working. The ground gave way beneath him and the whole lot fell well over two hundred feet. They never ever found his body or half the steel.'

'How awful. I suppose that Mrs Humber couldn't afford to pay the mortgage? So along comes the building society and repossesses the house?'

'That's right,' the agent nodded. 'It really hit her hard. Folk say that she misses the house more than she misses him. She adored this place and I know that she tried to talk him out of the crazy venture. She felt that they were too old to try to start a scheme like that. Most folks around here agreed with her. She would have been quite content to live out the rest of her days just pottering around the garden.'

'Whatever happened to her?'

'The couple who own the inn in the village took pity on her. She has a room there and in return she helps out in the kitchen. I am told that she is a wonderful cook. Every once in a while, she comes back here and does a bit of gardening. You don't have to worry,' he said quickly, 'she is no bother and she won't come inside the house at all.'

'Oh I'm not worried,' Victor laughed. 'In fact she sounds just the person that I am looking for. I have to be away quite a lot on business and I need someone to look after the place when I am not here. I might have a chat with her and see what arrangement we can work out, that would suit us both.'

'So you have made up your mind to rent it then?'

'Yes, I will take it for three months with a three-month option. I am not absolutely sure how long I shall be in England.'

'I thought that you were an Aussie,' the agent said looking at him. Victor gave him such a look that it made the man squirm. 'I was born in Bristol,' he said icily. 'It really is amazing, out in Australia, people know instantly that I am English. Yet come back to this country and everyone mistakes me for an Australian.'

'I do apologise. I meant no offence, please believe me but you do have a very strong Australian accent. The man put his hand into his jacket pocket and brought out a document. 'Once again, I am very sorry but, er, would you like to sign the lease and get it over with or would you prefer to wait?'

'Afraid that I am going to change my mind are you?' Victor laughed. 'Don't worry, it will take more than you to make me change. Come on through to the kitchen and I will give you a cheque for the three months' rent.' So saying, he turned and led the way into the kitchen and, on the red stone table, he signed the lease and wrote out a cheque for the rent.

The other man took it and after carefully folding it in half placed it just as carefully in his battered briefcase. 'Well, if that is all, I had better be on my way and leave you in peace. When were you thinking of moving in?'

'As soon as I can, actually, which brings me to another point. I shall be in need of some furniture. Can I get all that in the village or will I have to go somewhere like Truro or Newquay?'

'Well, there is a woman in the village who could run you up some kind of curtain. I'll write her address down for you. As far as furniture is concerned, yes, I think that you will have to go to Truro. I presume that you only want some second-hand stuff as you won't be here all that long, will you?'

'Yes, I suppose that I could make do. As you say, I most likely won't be here very long and it does seem a bit pointless, buying a lot of new stuff.'

Five minutes later both men were on their way to Truro. Victor had decided to follow the agent as it was quicker with a guide than him going later and having to find his own way. Arriving in the town, he parked his car in the car park and for the next couple of hours wandered around the shops until he had bought all that he needed. Having arranged for a carrier to deliver his purchases the next day, he realised that he was quite hungry. Seeing a pub on the corner, he made his way inside in search of sustenance. He was pleasantly surprised at the quality of the meal that he was served.

Some sixty minutes later, feeling comfortably full, Victor made his way back to his car. He was about to open the car door, when he remembered that, as yet, he had not been able to get in touch with Harley. He had phoned several times without success, so he decided that the best thing to do was to fax all the information that he had uncovered. He asked a local constable, 'Who says that you can't find a policeman when you need one?' the way to the post office, and having followed his rather colourful directions found his way there.

About twenty minutes later, feeling fairly satisfied with his day's work, he was again making his way back to his car, when another thought struck him. With all the excitement regarding Harley's horses in France, plus renting the house, he had still not found his way to the stables to see Pride of Tintagel. The horse was supposed to have been delivered there that day. He had meant to call and introduce himself to Charlie's niece and her husband that morning. He had been so taken up with the house he had forgotten all about his horse. The stables were situated about ten miles from the house at a village called St Mawley. He decided that there was still time and enough light left in the day to drive over and visit them straight away. He reached the car and, after checking the map, drove off with some trepidation.

Charlie had told him that the stables were situated on the edge of the village. 'You can't miss them. Turn right at the duck pond.' Those words from Charlie were still ringing in his ears as he drove into the village. The duck pond was similar to the many dams that one could find in Australia, except that this one was choked with weeds and the water was stagnant.

There was a small track at the side of the pond, so, with some reservation, Victor took it. He drove for about a further half mile and was pleased to see that the track widened almost enough for two vehicles to pass each other. He continued for another hundred metres or so until he came upon a gate. Stopping the car, he got out and peered over the gate. There was a path of sorts that ran away from the road until it dipped out of sight. In the distance he could see the roofs of some buildings. 'This must be the place I suppose,' he thought to himself, though far from confidently. He opened the gate and drove through, stopping the vehicle to fasten the gate behind him. He then proceeded down the path towards the buildings. The track, overgrown with weeds and thistles, curved slightly and took him past what appeared to be a derelict barn and a couple of outhouses. All the buildings were obviously in need of urgent repairs. Eventually the track petered out in front of a small cottage. Stopping the car, he got out and slowly looked around him. If this place was a racing stable, it did not inspire confidence. Thinking that he must have made a mistake, he was about to return to his car when the door of the cottage opened to reveal a young woman dressed in overalls.

'Hello,' she said with a smile. 'Are good news or bad news? If the answer is good, then come on in. But if it is bad, well, we have had enough of that lately. If that is the case then you can call back another time if you don't mind.'

'Well I must say that is the strangest greeting that I have ever had,' Victor replied with a grin. 'I sincerely hope that you don't regard me as bad news. I am Victor Barnes and, quite possibly, you received my horse here today.'

The woman flushed and raised her hand to her mouth, biting her finger. 'I am so sorry. I was not expecting you to call for several days. You must think me awful. Please forgive me and do come in.' She stood back to allow Victor to enter. As he approached, he noted that she was a lot younger that he had first thought. Put her in a dress and remove the scarf from her head, then she really was quite attractive. As he entered, he was surprised to find that the inside of the cottage very much belied its outward appearance. The small entrance hall that led into the lounge was warm and welcoming. The polished floor-boards shone with a gloss that would have done a dance floor proud. The lounge itself, although sparsely furnished, was spotlessly clean. Three small, brightly coloured scatter rugs lay in front of two armchairs. There was a Welsh dresser in one corner of the room, upon whose shelves was a collection of cups and trophies. These too were all highly polished and sparkling. The wall above the slate fireplace was adorned with three photographs of horses. They were evidently taken with the animals engaged in a steeplechase, as they were shown sailing over brush obstacles. The woman saw Victor admiring them and she nodded.

'Yes, they are Uncle Charlie's horses,' she exclaimed proudly. 'The one in the middle is Pride of Tintagel winning at Exeter. I am so pleased that he has come back here to be trained. He is almost like one of the family.' Victor moved to have a close look and then said with surprise. 'That looks like a girl riding him, or am I seeing things?'

'No, you are not. That is my cousin Mary. She mainly rides at point to points, but sometimes she is persuaded to ride at recognised courses. She is an excellent rider but she prefers the fun of point to points, rather than the more cut-throat pace of the National Hunt.'

'We have female riders in Australia but as far as I know they only ride on the flat. I don't know of any female jump jockeys.'

'You have to be so much stronger to ride over the jumps. You only have to look at the results. Take the National for instance. No female rider has ever been placed and I think that only two have ever completed the course. The last one to do so was Rosemary Henderson on Fiddler's Pike.'

'Yes, but be fair, you are citing probably the toughest horse race in the world there. On a racetrack at least,' Victor protested. 'Even in Australia we respect that.'

'Well, please take a seat Mr Barnes. My husband Mick is in the stables at the moment. I will go and tell him that you are here.' She hesitated a moment and then continued. 'Mick has had a very hard time of it lately and he is under a lot of pressure. He is not in the best of moods at the moment and you may find that he is . . .'

'Don't worry,' said Victor putting up his hand. 'Charlie has warned me about him. But please call me Victor; only my bank manager calls me Mr Barnes.'

'Fair enough,' she laughed. 'My name is Sally and now, Victor, why don't you come down to the stables and meet Mick? I expect that you would like to see your horse anyway.'

Victor agreed and followed her through the kitchen and out of the back door. She led the way to a Dutch barn that had been built about one hundred metres from the cottage. Pushing open the big, wooden door they went inside. Victor was surprised to find that the interior had been arranged to accommodate at least a dozen horses. The first one housed a bay mare that regarded them with disinterested eyes until Sally stroked its ears. Then, it whinnied softly and made a playful nip at the girl's neck. Laughing, Sally backed away and turned to Victor. 'Meet Emma. She is going to be our brood mare, unless we decide to race her instead. Now, where is Mick I wonder? Mick where are you Honey?'

'What do you want now?' a voice growled from the other occupied stall. A man stood up from behind a horse, which Victor guessed was Pride of Tintagel. Seeing him standing there, the man scowled at him. 'I suppose that you are the one that bought Pride? Charlie should never have sold him. If he didn't want to race him, he could have let me have him. I told him that I would pay him eventually. Now I am expected to train him for some stranger.'

'There is no expected to about it. If you don't want to look after him then I can easily take him elsewhere,' Victor said mildly. 'Finding another trainer for this horse is easily done. I am told that he is a very promising prospect.'

'No! No! Please don't do that Victor. Mick didn't mean it like that. He is just upset that we couldn't afford to buy him ourselves,' Sally pleaded. 'Come on Mick, come out and meet Victor Barnes and for goodness sake behave yourself. That kind of attitude will get us nowhere. Now this is Victor and he is offering you a chance to train his horse.'

Her husband came out of the stall and somewhat reluctantly held out his hand to Victor.

Victor looked Mick squarely in the eyes for a moment and then shook his hand. 'I can see why you would be upset, he is a magnificent animal. You can still have the satisfaction of seeing your name in the race books as his trainer. However, if there is going to be any animosity or ill feeling between us, then I think that it is best if we part company now. If we are not going to get along I would always be afraid that you would not be doing your best for my horse. It is entirely up to you Mick,' Victor made his point, clearly and firmly.

'No, I should love to train him for you. Sally is right, of course. I am upset because I did not have enough money to buy him myself.' With that he put his arm around his wife and gave her a big squeeze. 'I don't know what I would do if she wasn't here to look after me. It's her job to make sure that I don't make too big a fool of myself.'

'Well, I am glad that we have got that settled and out of the way. I don't imagine that you have had enough time to map out any sort of schedule for him yet? I can't wait to see my first horse running in a race for me.'

'Charlie had got him entered for Newton Abbott on Monday week. I don't see why we can't still run him then. He is fit and the work out should do him a world of good. I can't promise that he will win first

up for you, but he should give you a good sight for your money. I will
have to find a rider for him, though. I don't have any working for me
right at the moment. Most of the lads will have already been booked.'

'What about that girl, Mary, I think her name was? The one that I
saw in the photo in your lounge. Perhaps she might be free to ride
him?'

'No she wouldn't,' Mick snapped sourly. 'Don't you worry, I shall
find someone.' He then marched out of the barn and back towards
the cottage.

Victor looked at Sally. 'Did I say something wrong? I certainly seem
to have upset him for some reason.'

'No, you didn't do anything wrong. It's just that the two of them
have had a fight and Mick won't apologise,' Sally replied sadly. 'Oh it's
so stupid.' Victor could see that she was close to tears so he refrained
from making any other comment. He was about to follow Mick up to
the house when Sally spoke again. 'Wait a minute, though, I have had
an idea. She may ride him if you were to ask her. Yes, that is it, you
can ask her, Victor. You are the owner after all.' She clutched at his
arm. 'She will be riding in a point to point on Saturday. You could go
and see her ride and ask her then.'

'I am not too sure about this at all, Sally,' Victor shook his head
slowly. 'I mean, that Mick is not too happy anyway right now.
Somehow I don't think that this would go down too well with him.'

'Forget about Mick. You want the best for your horse, don't you?
Pride always goes really well for Mary. I am sure that she would be
thrilled to be able to partner him again.'

Victor could hear the excitement in her voice and looked at her
quizzically until she blushed.

'What would you say to Mick about Mary riding?'

'I wouldn't say a thing to him. I will leave that part to you,' she
replied with a mischievous grin. 'Don't you think that we should leave
that part until we have asked Mary? Where is she riding anyhow? I
may not be able to get there.'

'At Buckfastleigh, not far from Plymouth. Say that you will at least
go and see her race. She really is a splendid jockey and you will enjoy
the atmosphere.'

'Would you and Mick come with me?'

'We can't I am afraid.' Sally gave a rueful grin. 'We are going to see
his father to see if we can borrow some more money from him. I have

to go as moral support. Mick's family was dead against us going into this place from the start. Now that we are in real trouble, they like to remind us that they said that it wouldn't work from the outset.'

'Why a stable right down here anyway? Wouldn't you have been better off nearer to one of the major tracks? I mean your travelling costs would be very high to start with.'

'So would the cost of premises nearer to the tracks. We were lucky to be able to buy this place at the right price. Even so, we will be in hock for the rest of our lives unless Mick can train a few winners. To do that, of course, he needs horses here that he can work with. If Pride wins some good races, then maybe some of the bigger owners will bring their stock back here. Mick really needs Pride to win which is why he needs Mary.'

'Well, first things first. I suggest that we rejoin Mick at the house. We have not even discussed fees etc and I might just be in a position to help you with your immediate cash problem.' Taking her arm, Victor gently but firmly propelled Sally through the door and towards the house.

Some twenty minutes later, the three of them were sitting around the kitchen table. Sally had made coffee and brought out her home-made muffins. Victor finished munching on his and, after licking his teeth to clear the last of the crumbs, sat back in his chair. He looked across the table at Mick. The man was obviously unsure as to Victor's intentions.

'Let's talk money shall we? Now I am not sure what the going rate for trainers is in England, but in Oz, it is about $50 a day. Then of course we have the nomination fees, vet, track fees, floats and things. I think that we can disregard the spelling costs for the time being. So we are looking at, what, about five to six thousand pounds for the next six months? Is that a fair figure would you think Mick?'

'It sounds about right,' Mick shrugged, 'but where does that get us?'

Victor did not reply but stroked his chin a couple of times. Then putting his hand in his jacket, pulled out his cheque book. Next, taking a pen from his inside pocket, he looked Mick straight in the eye. 'Six thousand pounds for the next six months, are we agreed then?' Without waiting for an answer he wrote in his cheque book. Tearing the cheque out, he pushed it across the table towards the other man. Mick looked at the sum written there, then regarded Victor thoughtfully for a moment.

'This is for seven thousand, not six.'

'You have to pay the strapper and farrier on race days don't you?'

'I can do without your charity thank you! 'Mick replied, flicking the cheque at him. Sally gave a small gasp of dismay at her husband's attitude.

Victor calmly pushed the cheque back again across the table. 'It is not charity. I am simply protecting my investment. I will never get my money back if you go broke now, will I? Where is your business sense Mick?'

Mick was silent for a while, then picking up the offending piece of paper, he folded it in half and placed it in his shirt pocket.

Sally jumped to her feet and moving, round the table, flung her arms around Victor's neck. Pulling him towards her she kissed him passionately on the lips. Embarrassed, he flushed bright red and tried to push her away, without much success.

'Don't worry, I am not going to punch you out. As a matter of fact, I could almost kiss you myself. You cannot believe what a life-saver this cheque is. I am sorry for being such an ass too, I should indeed be grateful to you, not antagonise you.' Mick got to his feet and then held out his hand. Finally, after managing to prise Sally's arms from around his neck Victor too got to his feet. Grabbing Mick's hand he shook it heartily.

'This calls for a drink, Victor. We should toast our new partnership. Sally, where is that bottle of Mumm that we were saving for a special occasion? I think that this comes under that heading don't you?'

Before she was able to answer her husband, Victor chipped in: 'I am afraid that I must be making tracks. Perhaps we can save it and open it when Pride wins that race at Newton Abbott?'

'No, I have an even better idea,' Sally said with a laugh. 'We will keep it until he wins the Grand National.'

Chapter Seven

That Saturday found Victor attending his first ever point to point meeting. He was surprised at the informality and carefree atmosphere that he prevailed. In fact it reminded him of the picnic races that they held in Australia. He had often been to the New Year's Day meeting at Hanging Rock, a short drive out of Melbourne.

Mary Collins had two rides that afternoon. He watched her win her first and be thrown in the second, as her mount stumbled at the seventh fence. Victor waited for her to change and caught up with her as she was leading her own horse back to its float. He watched her secure the animal and then as it appeared that she was about to drive away, called out to her.

'Mary Collins. Could I speak to you for a minute?' She turned around as she heard her name called and gave him a long, hard look. He moved in closer. 'I promise that I won't take up too much of your time, Miss Collins. My name is Barnes, Victor Barnes.' She still did not speak but gazed at him intently. 'I saw you ride. A nice profitable afternoon in spite of that second race, I take it?'

'Your first time at a point to point, I take it?' she said icily.

'Why yes, but how did you know?' Victor did not have to fake his surprise.

'Point to point riders are all amateurs. We do it for the love of the sport, not for any monetary gain. Now what do you want with me? I am rather busy at the moment.'

'I am sorry. I meant you no disrespect. Sally Richards sent me. I say, I hope that you weren't hurt in that fall were you?'

'Only my dignity,' she said with a chuckle. 'So Sally sent you did she? How is she and that ratbag of a husband of hers, anyway?' Her demeanour seemed to soften with the mention of her cousin's name. 'This wind is more than a little chilly. Do you mind if we sit in the Land Rover and talk?' Without waiting for his reply she unlocked the passenger door. Motioning him inside, she then went around the front of the vehicle and clambered in the driver's side. 'That's better. Would you like some coffee? I have a thermos here somewhere.' She rummaged around in a canvas bag until she found the thermos and two cups, which she then placed on the dashboard.

'Do you always carry two cups with you?' asked Victor, raising an eyebrow.

'Yes. I am always hoping that I shall meet my knight in shining armour. You always need to be ready to offer him a cup of coffee at the very least.'

Victor could feel the colour rising in his cheeks and felt slightly ashamed. He had no right to be flirting with a girl with Amanda being buried less than four months ago. Mary seemed to sense his discomfort, although she was not certain why he was becoming so upset. She was used to having guys making a pass at her but somehow this did not feel like a pick up. She poured him a cup of coffee and handed it to him silently. He took the steaming liquid gratefully.

'I am sorry. I did not mean to embarrass you,' she said softly.

'Oh you didn't embarrass me, it was that I felt just a trifle guilty.'

'Ah, just my luck! Another married man! I seem to be able to pick them,' Mary said with a deep sigh and a wry smile.

Before he could stop himself, Victor found himself pouring out his heart to this girl that he had just met. She listened without a word, then when he had finished speaking, gently took his hand and touched it to her lips. Victor felt a tremor run through his body and he felt his face colour again. 'I think that we had better talk about why I came to see you,' he said huskily.

She looked at him for a moment and then smiled. A huge, warm smile that seemed to engulf him in its ardour and intensity. Once again, he felt a warm wave of emotion sweep over him and he gasped slightly. Angrily, he tried to shut her closeness out of his mind and concentrate on what he was here for. 'I have bought Pride of Tintagel and I want you to ride him for me at Newton Abbott next week. Sally says that he always goes well for you.' He blurted out the words in a hurry.

She looked at him in surprise for an instant, then said quietly, 'Does Mick know that you were coming to see me here today?'

'No,' he admitted, 'it was Sally's idea. What is it between you and Mick anyway? Sally just told me that the pair of you had a fight, but is that all?'

'He wanted me to ride a horse for him. He had had some trouble with this horse and its owner told Mick that if it didn't at least run a place, then he would take it and two others that he owned to another trainer. Well, I couldn't ride for him that day. I had already promised someone else that I would ride for them at Taunton that same day. Mick's horse did not even get a run. It threw its rider at the start and bolted. Mick, of course, blamed me. For some reason I have never had any trouble riding that one, but others do. The owner was as good as his word. He took his three horses away from Mick the very next day. This was a month after his son died. You knew about that, I take it?'

'Yes. Charlie told me. I must admit though, when I met Sally, I was more than a little surprised. I didn't think that she looked old enough to have a son who was into drugs. Still, I have never been very good at judging people's ages.'

'Sally wasn't the boy's mother. Mick was married before and what do you mean, he was into drugs? I don't understand. Steven died because they made a mistake with his medication while he was in the hospital. There was nothing that anybody could do.'

'Charlie told me that the boy died of a drug overdose. Naturally I presumed . . .'

'He loves to dramatise everything, Charlie does. I suppose that, technically, he is correct, but it puts a completely different slant on things. I suppose that you thought that he was into coke or heroin?'

'I have to admit that I did,' Victor replied ruefully. 'Speaking of horses that run for some people but not for others, just to change the subject for a moment. I have another horse that nobody and I mean nobody, appears to be able to ride, or so I have been told.'

'There is no such animal. You just have to know how to treat them, that's all. Horses are very much like people, you have to pander to their egos. Also a little TLC goes a long way. Maybe someone has mistreated this horse of yours and that is why he is so unco-operative. Are you going to bring him to Mick as well?'

'No, he is not a chaser, this one. In fact I am not sure that Mick could even handle him. He has a somewhat dubious nature for a start.'

'If he isn't a chaser, you will need a trainer who is licensed for the flat. My father might handle him for you. I'll ask him if you like.'

'Your father is a trainer? I didn't realise that. Sally certainly didn't mention it.'

'He is semi-retired now. He still likes to keep his hand in with a couple of horses though. Actually, I am apprenticed to him, though I prefer riding over the jumps to the flat. There is nothing that gets the blood flowing more than to be astride a magnificent stallion as he leaps over a four foot plus obstacle.' She looked straight at Victor and grinned, 'at least nothing that I have tried so far.'

To his obvious chagrin, he felt himself blush fiercely again. He had never met a girl quite like Mary before.

She roared with laughter, obviously getting a huge charge out of his undoubted embarrassment. 'Do you still want me to ride this horse of yours?'

'Yes. I would appreciate it very much.' He looked straight at her twinkling blue eyes.

For a brief moment she held his gaze then looked away. 'Right then, I will see you at Newton Abbott on Monday week. You can tell Sally that I'll give her a ring during the week to work out what to do about Mick. I am not sure that he is going to welcome me with open arms. In fact you can take it from me, he will not be pleased to see me at all.'

'Leave that to me. After all I am the owner of the horse and I pay his wages.' He opened the door to get out. 'And Mary, thank you.'

'A pleasure Victor,' she smiled at him. 'And Victor,' she paused and waited for him to look back at her. 'I am very, very glad to have met you. Bye for now.'

Victor had left Buckfastleigh and was driving across the Tamar River, via the spectacular bridge, when he happened to glance out of the window. His eyes met the iron railway bridge built by Brunel. Below it he could see the huge expanse of water that formed a natural boundary between Devon and Cornwall. Suddenly he felt very much alone. He increased his speed and drove until he came to a layby and pulled in. By now, there was a decided nip in the air. He somehow seemed oblivious to it as he stood and thought about his ravaged family. Flirting with Mary had brought home to him how much he felt their loss. The tears ran slowly down his cheeks and all that he was conscious of was a tightness across his chest and a bitter taste in his mouth. In his mind all that he could see was Amanda sitting on the couch with James and Ricky sitting on the floor playing one of their video games on the TV. How he wished that he was able to yell at them to tidy up their mess. His pain was released in a sea of salty tears that cascaded down his face and fell to form puddles on the bitumen sealed ground. It was almost a quarter of an hour before he was able to stop crying enough and was sufficiently back in control of himself, to consider driving again.

Wiping the last remaining tears from his face, he got back into the car and started the engine. As he drove out of the layby, he decided that he could not face being all alone in the house tonight. He made up his mind that he would find somewhere to stay in Liskeard that night. He put his foot to the accelerator once more and continued on his way down the A38. Reaching the Liskeard turn-off, he slowed and followed the road into the centre of town. After booking into a hotel, he decided that he did not feel like a full meal but wandered around until he found the local fish and chip shop. His cod and chips, so different from any fish in Australia, brought back childhood memories of his life in England. He could feel the tears welling in his eyes again. Angrily, he remonstrated with himself. 'Pull yourself together Victor! You are becoming quite maudlin.' Finishing his supper, he screwed the paper up, tossed it in the litterbin and walked into the hotel lounge bar.

He seated himself at a corner table with a coffee and a large brandy and contemplated what he should do next. Part of him wanted to throw the whole lot in and return to Melbourne. The rest of him argued that he had never been a quitter. He should try at least to do something with his horses. Still undecided, he finished his drink and made his way up to his room. He sat on the bed and glanced at the wall. There was a picture of a horse race hanging there. Idly, he got up to have a closer look. It came as a bit of a shock to him to see that it was actually a copy of a photograph that was framed there. A photo of perhaps one of the most famous race finishes in chasing history. The mighty Arkle, giving Stalbridge Colonist 35 lbs and being beaten by just half a length in the 1966 Hennessey Gold Cup. Victor himself had only just been born when the race took place. Arkle to the English public was like Phar Lap to the Australians, one of a kind. He knew that the modern day racegoers tended to regard Red Rum as the greatest ever chaser, but to many there would never be another horse like Arkle. Having already won the Cup in 1964 and 1965, he had been simply majestic in defeat in 1966. If he had ever needed a sign to point him in the right direction, Victor knew that this was it. He felt a shudder run through the whole his body and his mind was made up for him. He knew that he would never be a Sheikh Mohammed with around 450 horses in training. He did have two, however, that he was going to do his utmost to see win at least one race for him.

The next morning saw him making an early start back to the house. As he entered, he remembered with annoyance that he had meant to stock the pantry. Opening the fridge door, he found that the milk had gone off. The piece of steak that he had left there a few days ago also smelt decidedly strange. 'Damn! I haven't even got any coffee. I will have to go and do some shopping,' he spoke savagely to himself and looked around for his car keys.

There was a knock at the door and he opened it to be confronted by a wizened old man, dressed in shabby blue overalls that had obviously seen better days. Dark stains of what looked like grease, were sandwiched between streaks of paint and multi-coloured patches. These had evidently been sewn together over the years to piece together the many holes and tears that they now mostly consisted of. His shoes, once good suede, were almost threadbare and completely down at the heels. On his head he proudly sported a tartan beret that was pulled to one side of his weather-beaten, craggy face. Tugging off the beret with one hand he grinned at Victor, somewhat grotesquely, as his mouth was almost bereft of teeth. Those that did remain were stained a dirty yellow from years of chewing tobacco.

'Yes, what is it that you want?' Victor snapped rather testily.

'Is aught amiss sur?' The old man answered with a question of his own. He transferred the beret to his other hand and grinned at Victor once again.

'Who are you and I said what do you want?'

"Tis Josh Penhalon, sur.'

'So for the last time, what do you want with me?' Victor shook his head angrily. 'If you are here looking for a free handout, then you are out of luck. I have no food in the house until I manage to get down to the village.'

'No sur, tedn't that at all. Have ee forgotten? That old bed of yourn, I be come to do un up for ee.' The man tried to peer around Victor and into the house.

'Oh yes, the woman who delivered my curtains told me that there was a French polisher living in the village. To be perfectly honest, I wasn't expecting someone as quite as old as you appear to be. She told you about my bed, did she?'

'I do know she. She'm Tom Carnes' dattur, they d'live over to Trengavon.'

'Well, you had better come in and have a look at it, I suppose. I am sorry but I don't even have any cider that I can offer you at the moment.'

'I wudn't drink thee zider this year sur, twuz a poor zummer for frewt, but thank ee kindly all t'same.'

Just managing to understand his broad dialect, Victor stepped back to allow the old man in. He was more than pleasantly surprised to see him take off his shoes. He placed them next to one of the tubs on the front porch, before entering. However, he was not quite as taken aback to see both of Josh's big toes poking out from the front of his rather poorly darned woollen socks.

Leading the way up the wooden stairs, Victor showed him into his bedroom and the four-poster bed. He watched in silence as the old man slowly circled the bed. He prodded at the mattress and gently pulled at the torn and grimy curtains, which hung from the canopy. He paused at the ornate, carved headboard and peered at it intently. Victor felt slightly ashamed that he had made no attempt to even clear the cobwebs from it before Josh arrived. Having completed his circuit and inspection of the bed, the old man stopped at the window and looked out.

''Tis a fine sightin' that ee 'ave 'ere sur.'

'Never mind about the view, what about the bed man? Can you do anything with it?'

'Mebbe. Mebbe not. Tedn't right that folks cudn't fix it afor now. Me dattur in Trurraw, mebbe she can fix the bed cloth and ribands putty quick. Fust, I'll go and see hur fur meself.'

'What about the bed, man? Is it worth doing up and are you able to put it right?' Victor asked him again in an exasperated tone. He was having great difficulty in understanding all that Josh was saying.

'Tedn't a 'ard thing to learn, once you gotten the knack . . .'

'I give up. Here.' He took out his wallet and pulling out a fifty pound note, thrust it into the old man's eager fist. 'Take this, get whatever you want and I will give you the rest when you have finished working on it, ok?'

'I thank ee, sur.' The Cornishman gave him another big grin. Pulling the beret back on his head, he made his way back down the stairs. Victor went to the window and stared out towards the bay. He was so engrossed in watching the white caps out on the ocean that he did not hear Josh return. His heart leapt as he felt a gentle tug on his sleeve. He whirled around angrily. 'I thought that you had left. What do you want now?'

'If ee plaise, sur, thur be a leddy to see ee.'

'A lady? Who is she and what does she want?'

'Tes naught to do wi' me, sur,' Josh said shrugging his shoulders.

'Ok. I will come down.' Victor took one last look out of the window and then followed the old man down the stairs. He made his way along the passage to the front door. There he found a large portly woman that he took to be in her late fifties standing clutching a large willow basket. She looked up as he approached. 'Mr Barnes? They told me down at the inn that you might be in need of a housekeeper. I hope that I haven't come at an inopportune time? My name is Mrs Humber.'

'Ah yes, the lady who used to live here. Please come in. Mr Penhalon was just leaving, weren't you?' he said to Josh who had followed him down. He merely grinned again, touched his forehead to Mrs Humber and shuffled out the door to put his shoes on. Mrs Humber marched straight through to the kitchen and placed the basket on the table.

'I have bought some milk and eggs and things with me. In case you didn't have much in the house yet. They told me that you have only just moved in. Would you like me to light the fires and the stove? A nice fire and things look a whole lot brighter don't you think?'

Victor stood back in amazement. Evidently she had arrived with the intention of working, whether he needed her or not. He was almost afraid to ask her if she knew that the position might only be for a short time. He decided to let things go for the time being.

'Please carry on Mrs Humber. You must know this house better than I do. I will leave everything to you. Tell me though, there is one thing that puzzles me. That four-poster upstairs, it doesn't look as though it has been used for years.'

'That old thing was here when we bought the house. We never used that room. We slept in separate rooms because Mr Humber, God rest his soul, was a poor sleeper. He used to walk about a lot during the night so we had different rooms so as he didn't disturb me.'

'I see. So goodness knows how long that it has been there then. Now I have to go out for a while on business but I shouldn't be gone long.'

'Lunch will be ready at one o'clock. Don't you worry about getting me a key. I can get one from the agent. I will just have a clean around and see you on Tuesday if that's all right with you. I was told Sundays, Tuesdays and Thursdays.'

'Mrs Humber, you amaze me. Yes, those days are fine by me, although there is not very much here to keep clean. I only bought enough to see me through. Just the bare necessities you might say. Oh yes, that Josh Penhalon and his daughter may call in. They are going to fix up that old bed for me. I might as well make use of it while I am here.'

'I will see to it that they don't make a mess. It will be nice to see that brought back to its former glory,' she said wistfully. 'I always think that four-posters are so romantic. Will your wife be joining you in a little while then?'

'No Mrs Humber. Unfortunately, my wife can't be with us.'

'Oh that is a real shame. I am sure that she would have loved this house.'

'Yes, you are so very right. She would have loved this place,' Victor said sadly.

Victor thought that he might drive into Newquay instead of Truro for a change. He needed to buy a mobile phone, as he hated not being able to get in touch with people whenever he needed to. His notebook was filling fairly rapidly with new numbers. BT had told him that it would be at least another two weeks before they could connect a phone to the house.

When Victor arrived at Newquay he found that the post office was not open. Then he remembered that it was Sunday. He still needed to talk to Harley, as he was not sure what to do next. He tried to find a shop that sold mobile phones, but he was hard pressed to find anything that was open. He had forgotten that, unlike Melbourne, where they had seven-days-a-week, twenty-four-hour shopping, he was in Cornwall. At one time, England was a forerunner in new ideas, but lately it was lagging behind the rest of the world. He drove around the town for a time but was unable to even find a pub open. Annoyed with himself, he decided to head back to the house. He would try his luck again tomorrow.

As he opened the front door, a delicious aroma met him. He made his way to the kitchen, where he found Mrs Humber was in the process of taking some kind of pie out of the oven. On the stove a pot was steaming gently. She turned to greet him as he entered.

'Why Mr Barnes, what good timing. There is a beef stew in the pot and I have baked you an apple and rhubarb pie for afters. I hope that you like it.'

Victor lifted the saucepan lid to expose a thick, meaty stew. 'You must join me Mrs Humber, I shall never eat all this. There is enough here to feed a family of four.'

'Oh sir, I couldn't. It wouldn't be proper,' she replied in a shocked tone of voice. 'I am only the housekeeper, sir. I know my place.'

'Nonsense. I insist that you join me. Now sit down and I will find some plates. Besides we need to talk. We have not even discussed your wages yet.'

'Oh I am sure that you will pay me what you think is fair, sir. I am only too happy to be back in this house again. I loved this place when we were here,' she sighed wistfully. 'It has such a friendly atmosphere. Don't you find it so? You could sit on the settle and you feel as though you are safe and protected by the oak tree there. After Mr Humber, God rest his soul, passed away, I used to sit for hours doing my knitting and just listening to the fire. If you look real close at the trunk of the tree, you can see all manner of things and faces, hiding there in those cracks.' She stood up suddenly. 'This is no good, you can't live in the past. I will be crying in my cups next.'

Victor laughed and started ladling out two plates of stew. He pushed one of them towards her. 'Tuck in Mrs Humber, you have earned it and no mistake.'

She started to protest again, then changed her mind and sat down.

Victor took a mouthful of his and a surprised look came over his face. 'I have never tasted a stew quite like this before. What is it that gives it that wonderful flavour? I can't quite place it.'

'I cook the beef with blackberries. Of course, this time of year you have to make do with frozen ones. When you are able to use the fresh ones then the flavour really comes out. Very popular down at the inn, especially in this colder weather.'

'I am not surprised, it's marvellous. Speaking of the inn, I believe that you have a room down there? At least that is what the agent told me.'

'Yes. They have been very good to me since I lost this house.' Victor took another couple of mouthfuls of the stew and a thoughtful look came over his face.

'I have an idea. I have this place for at least six months and I have to go away a good deal. How would you like to be a live-in house-keeper? Naturally, I would have to get you some furniture.'

'Mr Barnes! I couldn't! Just think of the gossip that would arouse in the village. Oh no, sir, that would be quite out of the question I am afraid.'

'I don't think that the gossip, as you put it, would faze you one little bit' Victor said with a laugh. 'Have a think about it anyway. You would be doing me a big favour. I could go away, knowing that the place was in good hands. Apart from that, be honest now, wouldn't you rather live here? Stay in a home that you love rather than stay in a room at the inn? Anyway, you don't have to make up your mind right away, just have a think about it. You can let me know your answer the next time that you come.'

She slowly looked around at what once used to be her kitchen. 'It would be nice, I suppose.'

Later on that afternoon, Victor strolled down to the village and phoned Harley from the pub. The outcome of the conversation was that he was to do nothing at this stage. 'Just keep an eye on things. I shall be flying over in two weeks. We can decide on tactics then,' Harley had told him. Victor then rang Mick and informed him that Mary had agreed to ride at Newton Abbott. Sally came on the line afterwards and said that she was sure that Mick was pleased. However, he had made no comment and showed no emotion. He next rang Mary to confirm that her father would take Arcadian Steel. When she told him that he would, he said that he would arrange delivery of the colt on Wednesday.

'You had better come and meet Dad then. As long as you are going to be here, you might as well stay for dinner.' She refused to take no for an answer. He arranged to meet her at Milverton at noon, when she would take him to the stables.

Lastly, Victor made contact with Jenkins at the Newmarket stables and instructed him to have the horse shipped to Milverton. Feeling that he had at last achieved something, he wandered into the off-licence, bought himself a bottle of Jack Daniels and one of Bisquit, then slowly made his way back to the house.

Chapter Eight

Wednesday morning saw Victor driving along the A30 to Exeter. He stopped there only long enough to pick up a couple of bottles of wine. He was amazed at the variety of Australian wines that the shop stocked. Having made his purchase he then turned onto the motorway. Mary had told him to exit at Junction 26. As he turned off and headed for Milverton, the sun managed to break through. By the time that he reached the village, the sky was blue and cloudless. He found Mary waiting, sitting on the ramp of a float. He pulled beside her and stopped.

'I thought that we may as well take him from here. That way the guys can start right back. Also the stables are a little hard to find if you haven't been there before. That's ok with you is it?'

'Whatever you say. You are the one in charge of this little jaunt it appears. By the way, hello Mary. How are you? You're looking well,' Victor said with a chuckle.

'I am sorry. Hello Victor, how nice to see you again. Are you going my way by any chance?' Mary giggled and got to her feet, brushing a few strands of straw from her jeans as she did so. He got out of the car and walked over to her. She lightly brushed his cheek with her lips. 'Dad can't wait to see this horse of yours. I told him that it was a real brute, so he said that it must be a kitten then. I think that he is going to get a bit of a shock if it is as wild as you say.'

'I told you that the stable lads used to call him Satan,' he reminded her quietly.

Before she could think of a reply, another float drew up besides them. The driver wound down his window and called out, 'Are you by any chance Victor Barnes?' Victor nodded. 'Well I can't say that I'm not sorry to get rid of this bastard. He has nearly kicked the side out of the float on the way down here.'

'I hope that he's not hurt,' cried Victor in a panic.

'Not him mate! This one is tougher than a bloody rhino.'

'Shall I fetch him out for you?' Mary asked.

'Begging your pardon Miss but I should stand well clear of this one if I were you,' the driver said as he got out of his cab. 'We will load him for you.' Another man got out of the other side and both of them went around to the back. As they unhooked the ramp, the horse lashed out and his hoof caught the top edge causing it to fall. The two men were sent sprawling in the roadway.

'Jeez, he's got a temper this one!' the second man said. The driver's words were a lot more colourful than his partner's, the man forgetting Mary's presence for the moment. They started to pick themselves up when they noticed her standing on the ramp.

'Hey Miss, you be careful there. I said that we will get him for you.'

She took no notice, however, but started talking softly to the horse. It tried to rear up but was tied too tight. Slowly, she reached out and took a hold on the rope, still talking softly to him. Her hand crept up the hemp cord until it reached the animal's neck. She then gently stroked it while the other hand came up just as slowly until she held the bridle. 'Would one of you be able to untie the rope for me please, but slowly. Don't make any sudden moves that might startle him.'

Both men looked at each other apprehensively, with neither of them wanting to make the first move.

'I will have a try, after all it is my horse,' Victor said at last. Mary flashed him a grateful look.

He moved in cautiously, with his heart in his mouth and slowly started to untie the horse. On seeing him enter his box, Satan snorted and tried to lift his head. He was unable to do so as Mary had too firm a hold on his bridle. 'Steady boy, steady there,' she whispered.

'Are you talking to me or the horse?' Victor queried as his fingers fumbled with the knots. She laughed inadvertently and the sound had an almost a magical effect on the horse. He stopped straining and tried to nuzzle her hair. At the same time Victor managed to free the rope. Mary slowly led the horse down the ramp and across to the other float. He went in as quietly as a lamb and even stood there as she secured him to the tethering ring.

'Blimey! If I 'adn't seen it wiv me own two eyes, I'd said that you was lying,' the driver gasped. 'Ow d'you do it Miss?'

'Just a woman's touch I suppose,' she replied, smiling. 'Victor how right you were, he is absolutely magnificent. No wonder you wanted to buy him. You can just sense the awesome power in him. Dad will be over the moon with a horse like this to train.'

'We still have to find a jockey that can stay on him long enough to run a race,' Victor remarked drily. 'It's no good having a champion horse if nobody can ride him. He could be the fastest thing on four legs but he can't race without a rider.'

While Mary secured the ramp of the float, Victor took out his wallet and pulled out two fifty pound notes, handing them to the two men, one each. 'I am sorry that you had such a hard time with him, but this should ease your troubles.'

'Why, thank you very much, sir. The young lady is right though, he is a great-looking horse. He looks as thought he ought to win more than a couple of races for you.' Carefully pocketing their bonus, the two men shook hands with Victor, then returned to their now empty float and drove away. Mary, meanwhile was jumping up and down with excitement. She grabbed at his arm. 'Come on Victor! I can't wait to ride him. Let's get him home so that I can give him a gallop.'

'Now hold on just a minute, Mary. I honestly think that this one might just be a bit too strong for you to handle. I couldn't bear to see you get hurt on my account. I suggest that we wait and see what your father has to say before you make up your mind to ride him.'

'Victor Barnes!' Mary stood there, legs astride, hands on hips and glared at him. 'If you don't let me ride him, then I swear that I'll never speak to you again.'

'Is that a promise?' he replied with a grin and then ducked as she took a wild swing at him. 'Ok, but first let's get him home. I will follow you, as I haven't a clue as to where we are going. I saw a sign on the way here, for some stables, but I can't remember what they were called. Would they have been yours?'

'That was most likely for Martin Pipe's place at Wellington. Ours are far more off the beaten track.' After checking that every thing was secure, she got back in her Land Rover and started off. Quickly Victor jumped in his car and followed her. They drove for about ten minutes before she turned off the main road and then drove down a lane. Another five minutes driving brought them to a farm. A painted sign informed Victor that they had reached Hill Top Stud. The main building was a large, colonial-style house painted white, with pale, yellow shutters. Thin wisps of grey smoke could be seen coming from most of the chimneys, indicating to Victor that the house had several occupants.

Mary parked the Land Rover in front of two huge, solid, wooden doors and ran inside the house. Victor pulled his car alongside and got out. He then calmly waited for her return. She did so in a few minutes, dragging a man by the arm. He was well over six foot tall with a shock of snowy white hair. His weather-beaten face was creased in an amused smile at his daughter's excitement. Mary pulled him towards the float.

'Come on, Dad, you just have got to see him. He is the most beautiful animal that you have ever clapped your eyes on. Oh yes, this is Victor by the way,' she said waving a hand in his direction as they passed. Victor was highly amused. He had never seen someone so pumped up about something that wasn't even hers. By the way that she was carrying on, you would have thought that the horse did belong to her.

'Wait up, just a minute Mary, where are your manners?' The man managed to stop in front of Victor and hold out a hand. 'I am sorry son. I am John Collins.' Victor took the man's outstretched hand and was not at all surprised by the strong grip. He had summed up John Collins as a man of substance and integrity. 'This must be some kind of racehorse that you have brought me. I have never seen Mary so ecstatic over a horse before. I suppose that I should take a look at him before she bursts a blood vessel.' He walked over to the float and unhooked the gate.

Satan immediately tried to rear but Mary had tied the rope fairly short, so he could not move far. As the tailgate hit the ground, she was already making her way up the ramp. Again, as she took hold of the bridle, she started talking softly to him. The animal eventually calmed down until she thought him quiet enough to untie the restraint from the tethering ring. She then led him gently out of the float and onto the driveway. By now, many of the stable hands had gathered to have a look at this new arrival. There were whistles of approval from the onlookers as Mary led the horse around.

John Collins moved up and ran his hands expertly over the horse's feet, pastern, knees, chest, neck and jaws. Stepping back he asked his daughter to parade him around some more. He then checked the beast's nostrils and found that they were still wide and open. 'Jimmy, run and fetch a saddle will you? Let's see how he reacts to that.' The lad in question disappeared around the back of the house.

Victor stepped forward and laid a hand on the man's arm. 'Please don't think that I am trying to teach you your job, but I am not sure whether or not Mary has told you, he throws everybody. You might need to tie him up before you try to saddle him.'

'Yes. I had forgotten that. He seems so calm with Mary there. We had better put an extra line on him just in case though. Tom, there should be another rope in the float. Just make sure that he is secured properly will you? By rights we should just let him settle into his new surroundings for a couple of days before we even try to put a saddle on him. I must admit though, just looking at him, that Mary's obvious enthusiasm has got to me somewhat. Apart from that, she is not going to give me a moment's peace until we have given him a run. He certainly looks the goods all right. Real championship material.'

By now, Jimmy had arrived back with a saddle and John cautiously slipped it on the horse's back. Mary was still stroking his muzzle and whispering gently to him. Her father moved in to tighten the girth and still Satan stood there, quietly moving his head up and down.

'Can I ride him please Dad?' Mary pleaded.

'I am not sure. If what Victor says is true, then he . . .'

'Victor fusses too much. Come on, Dad, you know that I can ride anything.'

'I'll tell you what, if nobody else wants to volunteer then you can give him a try.' He turned to the others. 'Is there anybody here willing to give him a try?'

Jimmy started to raise his hand but a glare from Mary halted him.

Her father laughed heartily. 'Ok, you win Mary. Though hold on a moment, if you are going to give him a try out, we might as well do this properly. Jimmy, you and Tom go saddle up Blue Bayou and Pepper Pot.'

John had named the two best horses that he had in training. The two lads hurried off to do his bidding. They returned some ten minutes later riding their allotted horses. Victor was thankful to see that they had brought a helmet for Mary also. Setting it firmly on her head, she walked around to the side of her mount. She placed a foot in the stirrup and waited. Nothing happened so, taking a deep breath, she got her father to hoist her into the saddle. As she settled herself, the horse began to lower his head. As quick as a flash, Mary moved her hands towards his mouth, allowing the reins to slacken slightly. She then snatched at them abruptly, pulling his head up, while at the same time she pushed her heels down and well forward. She then leant back in the saddle.

'Well done, girlie! Well done!'Her father's praise came almost automatically.

Victor looked at him, questioningly.

'He was getting ready to buck, but she stopped him. A horse can only buck if he can lower his head,' John explained.

Mary leant forward and patted Satan's neck whilst she whispered in his ear. The horse gave a couple of snorts and then seemed to settle. Mary looked down at Victor.

'Well as you can see, I am still on him,' she smirked. 'Maybe he just needed a woman's tender touch.'

'Mary I am impressed and I don't deny it,' he said sincerely.

'All right everybody, let's move 'em out. Mary give him a good warm up over four furlongs, then you can let him have his head for about another six. It won't do him any harm to have a good stretch out after being tied up in a float for most of the day. Now Jimmy, you and Tom can keep her company. This is not a race mind you. I just want to see how he behaves with some competition.'

The two boys started off first and then Mary gave her mount a light kick and followed them. They had only cantered for about twenty yards when Satan suddenly propped, his legs as stiff as boards. She leant forward and spoke in his ear again. The animal snorted a couple of times again, then continued on.

'Well, I'm blessed. He is certainly trying her out. That horse of yours evidently has a better than average brain. Let's hope that he runs as well as he thinks,' John said.

'I don't understand, what happened exactly?' Victor was more than a little confused. He looked at the other man with a frown on his face. John saw his expression and smiled at him.

'When a horse props like that, it is usually the first step in refusing to go forward. Now I am only guessing but I would say that if Mary had kicked him or hit him, as most people would have done, then he would have definitely refused. Instead she spoke to him as you saw. You see, both horse and rider have to have respect for each other. They need that to function as a team. That is why Mary is so good with horses, she is very patient with them. Now come on, we had better get down to the track. Mind if we take your car, mine is in the garage?'

Chapter Eight

Victor silently handed him the keys and then got in the passenger side. John started the engine and slowly followed the three riders.

Victor was amazed to find that Hill Top Stud boasted a training track that would not have been out of place at any racetrack. Although devoid of any grandstand, there was a fairly large timber shed with steps leading up to its roof. This provided an excellent vantage point from which one could view the whole course. John parked the car and the led the way up onto the roof. Victor followed and looked around him slowly. He then turned to the other man. 'Am I imagining things?'

'No, you are not.' John gave a hearty laugh. 'I wondered if you would spot it. Yes, it is modelled on your Flemington Racecourse. The guy that I bought this from also came from Melbourne. He had this developed some ten years ago. We should be able to get a good idea of the speed of your horse. Once Mary has him warmed up, she will take him down the straight six.' He took a stopwatch from his pocket as he spoke.

The two men watched as the three horses and their riders wheeled about and made for the six-furlong marker. Jimmy was leading the way, closely followed by Pepper Pot, with Arcadian Steel some two lengths further behind. As they passed the six-furlong post, John started his stopwatch. Coming to the five-furlong marker, the three horses were neck and neck. Then Arcadian Steel seemed to lengthen his stride and began to pull away from the other two horses. By the time that he passed the finishing post, he was a good five lengths clear of Blue Bayou. Pepper Pot finished a further length away. John looked down at the watch in his hand and then shook his head in disbelief. 'Come on Victor, let's get down there,' he cried excitedly.

'What was his time?' Victor asked, but the other man was already out of earshot. He raced down the steps, taking them two at a time. By the time that Victor had caught up with him, all three riders had dismounted. Mary, her eyes shining, was hugging her mount around the neck.

'Did you see him go, Dad? What a horse! This is without a doubt the best animal that I have ever ridden. You can just feel the enormous power in his legs and he is hardly blowing. Oh Dad, I think that you finally have a chance of winning the Derby.' She kissed the horse on the nose once more. Leading Blue Bayou by the reins, Jimmy approached his employer.

109

'I am very sorry boss, we just weren't able to catch him. He was way too good for us.'

'I told you that it was not meant to be a race Jimmy,' John said angrily. Then seeing the lad's crestfallen face, relented. 'I am sorry lad. I would most likely have done the same if I had been in your place. After all, Blue Bayou was expected to be our best hope. Now, out of the blue, this fella has come along and blown him right out of the water.' He turned to his daughter. 'Have a stab at his time Mary.'

'Oh Dad, I couldn't. I just know that he is very fast.'

'One minute eight! Now whether he can maintain that type of speed over a mile and a half is another thing. Mind you, he has finished so full of running. Remember too, that was over soft going and on his first run. How much will he improve when the weather gets better, I can't imagine. But right now though, we had better get these animals washed down and stabled. Well done, all of you.'

Just as she was about to remount and ride off, Victor went up to Mary. 'I take my hat off to you Mary Collins. I honestly didn't think that you would be strong enough to hold him. There is one thing that is puzzling me though. What did you say to him to make him go all docile like that? After he propped as you were going out, I mean?'

'I merely told him that if he did that to me again, then I would send him to the knacker's yard, that's all. The main thing is that it worked,' she said with a wicked grin.

Later that evening they were all seated around a massive walnut dining table. They had just finished dinner and were drinking the last of the wine that Victor had brought with him. John Collins sat at the head, with Mary and Victor on one side. Jimmy was at the bottom and Ginger, a lad that Victor had only just met, sat on the other side with Tom. Apparently the three boys were all apprentices but were treated as though they were part of the family. Mary told Victor that Susan, her mother, was away at the moment. She was up in York looking after her own mother. Unfortunately, she had slipped on some black ice and broken her hip. Susan was staying with her until she was able to move around by herself again.

Of course, the main topic of conversation at the table was the new addition to the stable, Arcadian Steel.

'There is only one thing that I don't like about this horse,' said Victor slowly. 'That is the name of Satan that they gave him at the Jenkins's stable. To me it has an ominous air about it and I think that is wrong.'

'I agree. Satan makes him sound as though he is nothing but trouble,' Mary joined in. 'We shall have to come up with a name that has both power and dignity.'

'Gee, Girlie,' exclaimed her father, 'you are making him sound like a Jane Austen novel.' Everybody laughed. 'Besides we still don't know how he is going to go for anybody else. No one but you has had a chance to ride him yet. You are not going to be here to ride him in work all the time, either. Another rider may not get along with him as well as you. He would not have acquired this reputation he has without some reason. Also, if he does race, then I think that we had better look for a male jockey. You are fine on chasers but, be honest, you are getting just a tad too big for the flat. Now don't go and get upset about this.'

'I won't Dad, because I know what you say is true.' She gave a big sigh. 'I really am too tall, I know. I can still ride him though most mornings, at training.'

'What about Samson?' Ginger's voice broke in hesitantly.

'Who is Samson, Ginger?' Mary asked curiously.

'No. I mean Satan. How about Samson for a name? He was pretty strong,' Ginger said shyly. Everyone looked at him and he blushed furiously. It took a moment for them to take this in. 'Hey! I reckon that is a great name for him Ginger. Well done.' Victor applauded.

'Out of the mouths of babes,' said Mary with a smile. 'Yes well done Ginger. If Victor is agreeable, then that is his new name from now on.'

'It is fine by me. I just didn't like Satan, that's all.'

'Well, that problem appears to be settled then,' John said, with a sigh of relief. 'Now we can get down to the serious stuff. Firstly, we have to map out a plan of campaign for the horse. Next we have to find somebody who is able to ride him. That won't be an easy task I can assure you, otherwise the owner wouldn't have sold him. Then, lastly, the biggest hurdle of them all. We have to get Jockey Club approval for him to race at all. If we can accomplish all that, then winning the Derby should prove a breeze.'

'Oh Dad, don't be such a pessimist!' Mary snapped. 'You will have Victor thinking that he has made a grave mistake by bringing the horse here in the first place.'

'No, your father is quite correct Mary, we have got problems. But then I knew all this when I bought Satan, er, I mean Samson, in the beginning,' Victor, said placing special emphasis on the colt's new pet name. 'We can only try our best. If the horse never races, well that is my problem. However, after seeing you ride him today, at least in my own mind, I shall know that I own a champion. I bought him at a fair price and I knew what I was getting. As for your father having doubts, God, I have them myself but we have to try. As one of our prime ministers once said, "Life wasn't meant to be easy." You have to be in it to win it. This is a challenge that I relish and welcome. It helps to take my mind off other things and also helps me . . .' His voice faltered and he started to shake. He clenched his fists, angrily.

'I think that it is about time for some coffee and Brandy, don't you Dad. We can't do anymore tonight.' Mary came to his rescue. Her father nodded, so she got up and went out to make the coffee.

A short while later, they were all sitting in front of a huge log fire that was burning merrily in the lounge, the leaping flames casting their warm glow throughout the room. John and Victor were sipping brandy while Mary had a crème de cacao. The three boys, having enough sense to refuse the alcoholic beverage in front of their employer, were enjoying their coffees. 'You know we are not going to get somebody like Pat Eddery or Frankie Dettori to ride him. David Campbell would not have a hope with him,' John said, naming his own stable's jockey. 'I wonder why he doesn't seem to mind you Mary?'

'Possibly, because I talk to him. I also treat him with respect and he is not afraid of me. I warrant you that he has had someone give him a couple of good belts when they haven't been able to control him. You know that you have to build a horse's confidence by being gentle and soothing with him. You won't get anywhere with a heavy-handed approach. You know, I have just thought of someone who might just be able to handle him.'

'I am all ears,' said her father, 'just who is this superman?'

Mary hesitated for a minute before replying, knowing what her father's reaction was going to be. Taking a deep breath, she said boldly, 'Jason Carter.'

'What! That arrogant prick!' John sat bolt upright in his chair and turned to face Victor. 'This guy reckons that he is twice the jockey that Piggott was in his heyday. He also considers himself God's gift to women.'

'I know that you don't like him Dad. But even you have got to admit that he is an excellent jockey. Plus I have seen how he behaves to the horses that he gets to ride. It wouldn't do any harm just to give him a try.'

'Oh, he is certainly a good jockey, I'll grant you that much. However I can't stand the man himself. He is so arrogant and well, smarmy.'

'Well I am going to leave you two to fight it out.' Victor finished his drink and stood up. 'I had better make tracks as I have a fair drive home.'

'You can stay the night if you want. We have plenty of spare rooms. You wouldn't mind now would you Dad?'

Before her father had a chance to answer, Victor spoke again. 'I appreciate the offer Mary, but I should get back. I have a few things that I must attend to in the morning.'

'As you wish. I will see you at Newton Abbott then.' She turned to her father. 'I think that I might go to bed as our guest is leaving. Good night all.' She then turned around and without as much as a glance back, left the room. Her father tried, without much success, to prevent a broad smile from creeping across his face.

'Well Victor, it was a pleasure meeting you. We might try Samson at Doncaster at the end of the month. I will see how he shapes up in the morning. Come on, I will walk you out to your car.' After saying his goodbyes to the three boys, Victor followed his host outside. The night air made him shiver slightly after the glowing warmth of the lounge fire.

'Son, Mary has obviously taken a shine to you. I am glad. You are her first real interest in almost eighteen months.' He paused and put an arm around Victor's shoulder. 'Her last guy went and left her at the altar. I don't think for one minute that you would do anything like that. She has told me about your wife and family. About that I am very sorry and I feel for you. However, I love my daughter and I don't want to see her hurt again. I don't care how good your horse is, you cause her any pain, and we are history. Do I make myself clear?' The older man's grip tightened on Victor's shoulder.

Victor stood still for a moment then he broke from the other's grasp. He turned to face him. 'Mr Collins. I think that Mary is a terrific girl but just at the moment the last thing I want or need is to become involved like that. At present I don't think that I am capable of handling a relationship with anybody. I appreciate your concern but, quite frankly, I think that you would be better off talking to your daughter. Not for a minute do I think that she would take any notice. She is a very strong-minded young lady. One who I suspect is not easily swayed. Thank you for an excellent dinner. I hope that we meet again soon. I wish you a very good night, Mr Collins.'

'Victor,' John slapped him heartily on the shoulder. 'Victor, you would have made a great son-in-law. I bid you goodnight.'

Chapter Nine

Victor awoke early. He yawned and stretched lazily, then swung his feet onto the floor. He was sleeping on the couch in the lounge as Josh was still at work on his bed. He had tried to get into the bedroom yesterday to see what progress had been made. Josh shouted him away. He apparently was a craftsman and wouldn't allow anyone to see his work until it was completed. Victor had heard him nattering away to a woman, whom he presumed was his daughter. Their dialect was so thick and broad that he had trouble deciphering what they were saying. In the end he just gave up trying and left them to carry on.

Mrs Humber had refused Victor's offer of accommodation at the house. She told him that the folk at the inn had been very good to her and that she did not like to leave them. He later learnt that they had increased the small wage that they paid to her for her cooking. When they discovered that they could possibly lose their biggest drawcard they had acted quickly. Mrs Humber's culinary art was appreciated throughout the county and was the principal reason for the inn's popularity. The only positive thing that Victor had accomplished since arriving back from Hill Top was that he now had a mobile phone. He had also bought himself a car. He decided that for what he was continually paying out for hire cars, he might as well have his own. He knew that he could always sell it before returning to Oz. Though at this particular point in time, a return to Melbourne was the furthest thing from his mind.

Today, he was going to see a horse that he owned run its first race for him. Victor ambled into the kitchen and put the jug on for his coffee. Drawing back the curtains, he looked out onto a grey sky. Heavy rain clouds were scudding across the heavens in a frenzied race to the horizon. A typical English spring morning, he thought to himself with a wry smile. He didn't think that too many people would venture out onto the course today. Most would prefer to stay at home and watch the major races on Channel Four. He sighed. Pride of Tintagel would not have a great live audience, that was for sure. The shrill shriek of the jug boiling brought him back to basics. He made himself a cup of strong coffee but decided against eating anything. He was not sure that his churning stomach would keep anything down anyway. This was ridiculous. He felt like a small child about to face its first day at school. He was not certain of the real cause of his apprehension, either. Was it due to the fact that this was his first race as an owner? More to the point, he thought that it was the prospect of seeing Mary Collins again. For whatever reason he was as nervous as a kitten.

The night that he had returned from dinner with the Collins', Victor had dreamt about Mary. She had been chasing him on Arcadian Steel and every time that he thought that he had given her the slip, she had turned up again. She was always sitting there on the horse with her arms outstretched towards him. At one stage her father had appeared carrying a shotgun. When Victor had tried to run away from him, he found himself falling over a cliff. To his amazement he landed on a feather bed at the bottom. He had woken up sweating. God, he had thought, Freud would have had a field day with this one. He had been unable to get back to sleep and had gone for a walk along the cliff tops. He had stood and listened to the waves, pounding on the rocks below, until the sun had risen. The remainder of that day he had spent catching up on his correspondence. He wanted to chase Mary from his mind. He knew that Dan and Naomi would immediately assume that, because he now owned two racehorses, the likelihood of an early return to Melbourne was fast diminishing. 'You don't buy horses if you don't intend to race them,' he could hear Dan saying.

Finishing his coffee, Victor, cleared the blankets from the couch and finished dressing. He then rang Mick and arranged to meet him in the Red Rum bar at midday and they would have lunch together in the Terrace Restaurant. Finally, he rang Charlie to let him know that the horse was still going to run as he had planned for it. The ex-owner wished him luck and said that he would have a tenner on the horse, 'for old time's sake'.

Realising that he had plenty of time to get to the racecourse, Victor decided that he would take the longer, more scenic, coastal route. Just for luck, he would stop at Tintagel before turning off for Launceston. After all, Pride of Tintagel was named after the place. When he arrived, he stopped in the centre of the village and got out of the car. He found the old fourteenth-century house that had been used as a post office for fifty years and gazed in awe at the tumbled roof and walls. These had been weathered by the elements over five hundred years, but had stood the test of time well. The National Trust now owned the building. He went in and bought a couple of post-cards to send to Dan and Naomi. As he was making his purchase, the realisation that he did not own a camera came to him. He had never been one for taking photographs, having left that kind of thing to Amanda, so he had never bothered about buying himself one. He made up his mind, there and then, that the very next time that he was in Plymouth or Exeter, he would make the purchase of one a priority.

Having plenty of time up his sleeve, he walked through the village towards the cliff tops and the remains of Tintagel Castle. He knew that the Cornish were very proud of their legendary King Arthur, the famed leader who had led the Celts against the Saxons so successfully in the sixth century. He also remembered that Merlin the Magician was held in such high esteem throughout Cornwall and Wales that countless places claimed the honour of Merlin being born there. He certainly was a magician if he lived in only half of the places that he was suppose to.

Victor paused at the edge of the cliffs and watched idly as the tourists clambered down the steps. These were cut into the cliff and he could see the people making their way across the bridge that linked the two jutting outcrops of rock. Through the expanse of time the pounding seas had cut the channel below. This was now formed into quite a large passageway. He made up his mind that he would have to return here when he had more time as he needed to fully explore the ancient remains. For now, however, he hoped that he was going to see his horse live up to its name.

The remainder of the journey was uneventful. He turned onto the A30 at Launceston and followed that until the map told him to take the A382. This last move took him direct to Newton Abbott. On reaching the town he found the racecourse without too much difficulty. He parked in the owners' car park, behind the public stand. He saw that he was still a little early. Knowing that Mick and Sally wouldn't be there yet he took a stroll around. He admired all the

excellent facilities that the course had to offer. Several marquees had
been erected near the parade ring and he glanced inside one of them.
He was impressed to see that it was even equipped with close circuit
television. Nor had the means for Tote betting been forgotten. He
eventually found the Red Rum bar and went in. Even he knew of the
fabulous horse that the bar was named after. Mainly because of the
year that Australia's champion chaser, Crisp, had done battle with him
in the National. Crisp on that occasion was beaten by an even greater
horse.

As he entered Victor was greeted by Mary's cheery voice calling out.
He looked over and saw that she was standing at a corner table and
waving at him. He was also a little surprised to see that her father was
with her. He walked over to join them.

'Hi Victor, all set for your first winner?' Mary greeted him enthusi-
astically and kissed him on the cheek. John Collins rose to his feet and
offered him his hand. With some difficulty Victor managed to grasp
it, as Mary was pulling at his arm the same time. Her father quickly
came to his rescue. 'Steady on Mary, at least let the poor guy catch his
breath. How are you today Victor? Butterflies in the stomach I betcha.
I know that I still feel that way each time I have a runner.'

'No, actually I am fine at the moment. No doubt that will soon
change as the time for the race gets closer. I didn't expect to see you
here today though.'

'I couldn't have stayed away even if I had wanted to,' he said with a
broad grin. 'Mary here threatened me with all sorts of dire punish-
ments if I didn't come to see your horse run. Your horse, mind you,
not to come and see her ride it.'

'Oh shut up, Dad. You know full well that you love coming here. It
didn't need much persuasion on my part for you to make up your
mind.' She slapped him playfully on the arm, then turned back to
Victor. 'Are Mick and Sally with you?'

'No, they don't appear to have arrived as yet, but still, it isn't quite
twelve o'clock. Can I get you a drink John? I don't suppose that you
are allowed one Mary? I must say though that if it was me out there
riding over those jumps I should need more than one drink inside of
me first, before I could tackle them.'

'Mary doesn't need Dutch courage, she rides on adrenaline. I will
just have a beer, thanks, and she can have an orange juice.'

Victor went across to the bar. He was on his way back with their drinks when the door opened to allow Mick and Sally to come in. Giving Mick the tray to take to the table, he went back to the bar and returned a couple of minutes later with two more beers. As he put the glasses down on the table, he could sense the unmistaken hostility between Mary and Mick. He looked across at John who merely shrugged a little resignedly.

Taking a deep breath Victor plunged in. 'Okay you two, you might have a war going on between you both, but you can call a truce while you are dealing with my horse,' he said forcefully. 'Mick what has happened is past, so forget it. You cannot give Mary proper instructions if you are not talking to each other. Mary, I am not saying that you have to be told how to ride but Mick is the trainer so you will follow his instructions. Do I make myself clear? Or do I have to spell it out to the pair of you in plainer words?'

'Gee, Victor, you look so sexy when your eyes blaze like that,' Mary replied giving him a wicked look. Everyone laughed and it seemed that this was just the tonic needed, because Mick held out his hand to Mary.

'He is absolutely right, Mary. What occurred is in the past. I had no right blaming you anyway. Let's shake on it and forget that it ever happened. We have to concentrate our energy on today's race.'

'Give me a kiss and I will. Shaking hands is way too formal for family affairs.' She walked over to Mick and gave him a kiss right on the mouth. He in return hugged her. 'Don't mind us, you two,' drawled Sally. 'We can always come back later.'

At least the ice was broken. Victor was pleased to see that the pair of them appeared to be far more at ease with each other.

John looked across at him and nodded approvingly. 'Well done,' he mouthed. Sally too squeezed his hand. She had been upset with the strained atmosphere between her husband and her cousin. With all the bad feeling out of the way the conversation naturally turned to the race and the various chances in it.

'As much as I would like to see Pride and Mary win, you are going to have your work cut out trying to beat the favourite,' John stated quietly.

'I am afraid that I have to agree. Spellbound is a champion Irish chaser and he is using this race as a final hit out before the Gold Cup at Cheltenham next week,' Mick said. 'I think that he is our only real danger.'

'Well, he did win the National Trial at Uttoxeter by fifteen lengths and his last run at Leopardstown by twenty. Why the connections are even running him here today is quite beyond me. He is several classes above the rest of this field.' John commented slowly and shook his head

'There is no doubt that he will certainly be a drawcard here today. The course needs something to compensate for the weather. Although, as we came in, it looked as though the sun was finally going to break through. That might encourage a few more to come along. As I said before, I think that the whole point of the exercise today is just to keep him at his peak. Whatever the reason, he is going to take some beating,' Mick sighed gently and finished off his beer. 'I suggest that we go and have lunch and let Mary worry about Spellbound. I think that it will be entirely up to her to find a way.'

'Thanks a lot Mick and thank you for your vote of confidence too.' She got to her feet angrily and was about to storm out when her father grabbed her arm.

'Steady on Girlie. He wasn't slighting you. Don't forget that Pride hasn't even had a run for a while, whereas this other horse is right at his peak. Nobody is saying that you can't win but you have to be objective. That horse is our main danger. Now let's go and have some lunch. All this fresh air is making me hungry.'

'Hungry enough to eat a horse?' Sally asked with a grin. They all laughed and finishing their drinks, got up and made their way to the Terrace Restaurant.

The restaurant was situated on the first floor of the main grandstand, overlooking the paddock. They all ordered lunch, with Mary settling for a small salad. Pride of Tintagel was not running until the fifth race so they had plenty of time to sit and enjoy their meal. The waitress had just brought another pot of coffee when Mary said that she had to go and get changed.

Victor walked her to the door where he took her hand in his. 'Now don't go doing anything silly out there today. I would like to win of course, but you are not to take any unnecessary risks, ok? If we don't win today there is always tomorrow. So you just go out there, take care and enjoy the ride.'

'This is really silly, but I feel as nervous as a schoolgirl on her first date,' she said with half a smile. 'I just don't want to let you down. I can imagine what all this must mean to you.' She then grinned at him,

'This being your first time with a girl riding and all.'

'Mary Collins! You are incorrigible!' Victor was slightly shocked. He was not used to a girl flirting with him like this. She smiled at him and he relaxed.

'You won't let me down. Now go out there and break a leg,' he said repeating the old theatre good luck maxim. As he said it he realised the implication of his words. He became flustered and tongue-tied. 'Um, er you know what I'm trying to say.'

Laughing she reached up and gave him a peck on the cheek. 'I prefer black grapes to green ones thank you.' He looked at her in bewilderment for a moment. Then, as the remark sank in, he too laughed.

Rejoining the party, Victor discovered that they were not talking about the race. In fact they were discussing Arcadian Steel. 'Mary is the only one who has ridden him in work so far. I have been in touch with Carter. He wasn't very interested until I told him some of the times that the horse has been doing. He then changed his mind quite quickly. He is coming down early next week to have a look at him. Whether he will be able to stay on the horse is another matter. I am not sure what our next step will be if he has trouble with it,' John said with just a slight touch of gloom in his voice.

'How about the Jockey Club, have they passed him yet? I mean Mary has proved that it can be ridden,' Mick queried.

'I shall not bother with them until I know that I am going to have a jockey for him. It is a bit pointless getting them involved at this stage.'

'Have you tried him over a mile and a half yet?' Victor cut in.

'No, we are still working him up to it,' John said shaking his head. 'All his times have been first rate so far. I can't see that he will have any bother getting the distance. No, I am more than happy with his progress up to now.'

'Well, I am keeping my fingers crossed. Right now, though, I think that I will go and see today's centre of attraction before he runs,' Victor said picking up the bill that the waitress had just deposited on the table. He stood up to leave but Mick grabbed his arm.

'Not without me, you won't,' he piped up. 'You won't even get past the security guys let alone make it as far as the stalls. Since there have been all those doping scares, even the stable lads have to wear photo IDs.'

Victor looked at him sharply and with a great deal of interest. 'What doping are you talking about?'

'There is supposed to be a gang of dopers operating again this year, like before. They found traces of ACP in both Avanti Express and Lively Knight after they were checked. The same back in 1993 there was the occasion of two horses on the flat. Even one of Martin Pipe's was found to be the victim of ACP doping. The trouble is that, in tablet form, ACP fits into a polo mint, and therefore, can easily be given to a horse.'

'What exactly does this ACP do?' Victor asked curiously.

'It was originally intended as a tranquilliser for use on nervous horses when it was time for clipping. If it is injected directly into a vein, then the effect is almost immediate. It can last for up to four hours or so. It would take a fairly heavy dose if it were to last the journey from home until the time of the race. Why all the interest in ACP though? You are not thinking of using it on Arcadian Steel are you?' John asked.

Victor then told them about Harley's horses. 'What I can't fathom out is why Oxford would let the horses win minor races but then prevent them winning better ones. That is, if that is what he is doing. It certainly looks that way at the moment.'

Both Mick and John remained silent for a while then Mick gave a grunt and said to Victor. 'Would you know if he has them entered for any of the big races in the near future? Say the 2000 Guineas for instance?'

'Not that I know of. I am still trying to get some details out of him. What we do know is that they are capable of winning better class affairs. They both proved that in France. He never mentioned to Harley that they even ran there let alone won four races between them.'

'What happened to the prize money from France then?' John queried. 'Somebody must have collected it, so where is it?'

'I asked Harley the same question,' Victor shook his head, somewhat sadly. 'He told me that he had given his manager, John Cassidy, power of attorney. This was so he was able to sign cheques for the general running expenses of the horses. He did not want him to have to go running to him each time a bill needed to be paid.'

'A trusting man, this friend of yours. To my way of thinking though, he was asking for trouble. Particularly as he seems to spend most of his time in the States.' John stated forcefully.

Victor coloured up slightly and, in almost apologetic tones, said quietly, 'He has done exactly the same for me, you know, John. I said not but he insisted on it.'

'I agree with Harley there,' Mick broke in. 'If you are in business then you have to put your trust in the staff that you employ. More so if you are not there to oversee them all the time. Mostly you are okay and there is no trouble. Sometimes you can strike a bad apple but that is a chance that you have to take. All in all, most people are basically honest. The odds of you employing someone who purposely sets out to rob you blind are fairly minimal I would say. In this case though it does appear that he may have been unlucky.'

'Well, if I were you, I would try and find out just what his plans are,' John told him and Victor gave a slight chuckle.

'At the moment he thinks that Harley is waiting for my recommendation as to whether he should sell them or not. Oxford got quite panicky when I suggested that as a possible course of action.'

'These horses, are they any good, do you think?' John asked softly. 'Maybe they are just average and won't win big races. The most expensive animal can sometimes turn out a dud.'

'Harley is convinced that they should be showing better results than they are. All the breeding suggests that they are capable of much better. The way that they won in France tends to back up that assumption.'

'It sounds to me as though he has let them win a couple of minor races to keep your friend at bay. Most owners would be happy with that. Then if he is stopping them in the better class he must have something in mind. If he is running true to form, he will have them entered in something like the Chester Vase or 2000 Guineas, as Mick suggested. Then, if they do happen to win they would have cleaned up on the ante-post betting. I would imagine that they would have to be at the very least, 25–1. To me that is the only logical explanation that comes to mind. How did they manage to run them in France without Harley's knowledge?'

'Well, he travels around quite a bit and of course relies on his manager to keep him up to date. That ante-post betting though does make a lot of sense. The thing is, what can we do about it? Can we go, to the Jockey Club and tell them what we suspect? I mean, if they do happen to run true to their proper form and win?'

'You will be too late. They cannot prosecute a trainer for letting a horse run on its merits,' Mick said with a laugh. 'It is far too late now to try to do anything about the races that they have already run in. Another thing, even if you do take the animals away from the man he can still achieve his purpose. Another trainer would most likely get the best out of them. If they win Oxford would still collect on his bet.'

'But why would he be so upset at the prospect of me taking them from the stable?'

'Because it is quite likely that he is working the same scam with other peoples nags. He would be afraid that they might start asking some awkward questions. It doesn't take much for other owners to withdraw their horses from you if one owner suddenly does it. I should know about that,' Mick said rather bitterly. He looked across at John who reluctantly nodded in agreement.

'I can see that Harley and I have a fair bit of work to do when he gets here,' Victor sighed. 'At least I can now go to him with some possible theories.'

'You should be able to do something about those French wins, although the trainer could always say that he had no idea what the manager was doing. The money must be shown somewhere in Harley's accounts. The prize money would not have been paid to a third party. To be honest though I don't know quite how you could handle the rest of it.' Mick looked across at John again. 'Have you got any bright ideas John?'

The other man shook his head. Victor gave a big sigh and admitted, 'I am really at a loss for the moment. Let's drop the whole thing for the time being and go and see my horse. By the way, neither of you as yet has told me what ACP stands for. I need to know in order to tell Harley when he arrives.'

Both the other two men looked at each other, then roared with laughter. Finally John calmed down and said, 'Acetylptomazine. Do you think that you will be able to remember that when the pair of you have had a few bevvies?'

Some fifty minutes later they were all down at the saddling boxes, which were situated at the rear of the parade ring. Mick was in earnest conversation with Mary while the others were admiring the other entrants in the race as they were being led around by their handlers.

Sally, who wisely had kept out of the conversation regarding the doping controversy, was now able to join in. 'Just take a look at that fella. Now that is one giant of a horse,' she said pointing to a magnificent looking chestnut that was being led out. John checked his race card and then turned to her. 'Well done Sally. Trust you to pick on that one. That is Spellbound and the one that Mary has to beat.'

'I don't care what you say, that is one great looking horse.'

'I agree,' said Victor. 'To be beaten by something like that is no disgrace. He really looks like a champion even in the way that he walks.'

'Go and tell that to my daughter. I am sure that it will boost her confidence no end,' John gave a good-natured laugh. 'You are right though. You wouldn't feel quite so bad if you were to be beaten by something like that. Mary would not agree with us of course.'

Victor was about to make some comment when he spotted a grey horse being led out. It was a nondescript type of an animal that you would not look twice at in the parade ring. He sensed, however, that there was something special about it. He experienced that gut feeling that Dan had spoken about, his gift. He pulled John's arm. 'What horse is that John? He came out of number seven?'

John consulted his race book again and replied, 'Miner's Curse. He is having his first run today as a matter of fact. A bit of a dark horse if you ask me, no form and no pedigree.' He laughed heartily at his own joke. Just then the clerk of the course rode up to lead the first of the field into the parade ring and for the moment the grey was forgotten. Telling the others that he would see them in the grandstand, Victor waved to Mary and strode off in the direction of the betting ring.

The other horses had started to follow the leader around the parade ring. Mick gave Mary a boost into the saddle and looked at her. 'I'll leave it up to you now Mary. Just try not to finish too far back for Victor's sake. I honestly think that he is in need of a run and is not yet anywhere near his peak, but you are in charge. And Mary,' he paused for a moment and looked her straight in the eye, 'best of luck.' She held his gaze for a moment then lightly kicked her heels and rode off to join the others.

The horses were all milling around the starting tape as the starter tried to get them into some kind of order. Mary watched the man's hand as it hovered near the lever. She knew that in this race she had to be ready at the jump in order to miss the usual mêlée at the start. Either that or wait until the cowboys had got away. Lying close along Pride's neck she watched the starter's hand and as it came down to the lever, she kicked her horse's flanks. The tape flew up and the horses bounded forth like a cavalry charge. The first hurdle approached and Mary's mount sailed over it. Coming up to the second, she had Pride properly balanced before they met it; the powerful hindquarters tensed and leapt.

At the end of the first circuit, the favourite, Spellbound, held a close lead with Mary half a length behind. As she approached the next jump she was conscious of a riderless horse coming up fast on her outside. She pulled back on the reins slightly, aware of the fact that if she was within half a length of the riderless animal when it jumped, then her mount too would most likely leap. That is exactly what happened to Spellbound. The riderless horse cleared the fence easily but the favourite took off too soon and met the obstacle with his massive chest. His rider went sailing over the horse's head and landed in a sorry heap on the other side of the fence. Mary urged her mount forward and he cleared the obstruction with ease.

Coming into the final jump, she was a little startled to see the grey looming up on the inside of her. They met the fence together with Pride of Tintagel landing a full half-length ahead of Miner's Curse. Mary settled her horse and gave him a slight kick to keep his mind on his job. He responded but the grey horse was not yet finished. Mary urged Pride forward with everything that she had. In the last stride, the little grey stuck its nose in front and passed the winning post just inches in front of her.

Cantering back to the weighing room, Mary saw Victor waiting to greet her. Reining in beside him, she dismounted, her silk breeches soaked in sweat and spattered with mud. Taking off her helmet she turned to him with tears in her eyes. 'I am so sorry Victor. As Mick said, I think that he needed that run. He just ran out of steam at the last minute. I really tried for you.'

Victor went up and patted Pride on the muzzle and then looked at her, admiration in his eyes. 'You did just fine Mary, I am really proud of you. You rode a great race. I couldn't have asked for more.'

'But I didn't win. I truly am so sorry. You must be disappointed.'

'I said not to worry. The forecast paid almost £28 and I had £10 on it. That, plus the prize money for coming in second. I reckon that I have had a good day. I really liked the look of that grey.' The crowd looked on in amazement as she clobbered him with her mud-streaked helmet, before striding off angrily to weigh in.

It was about thirty minutes later that they were all sitting in the

Cromwell Bar holding a post-mortem on the race. Mary was still annoyed at Victor and so she was not an over-eager participant in the conversation. At length her father could stand it no longer and grabbed his daughter's arm. 'Mary for goodness sake stop sulking! We all said before the race that we thought the horse would need the run. We also thought that Spellbound would be the one to beat you. In fact I took it and Pride as a forecast myself. Now it just happens that Victor had better luck than I did and actually picked the winner. I say good luck to him and his better judgement. After all Pride, is his horse so he is the one who misses out on the winner's purse.'

'In Australia, Mary, it is common practice to pick a second horse with the one that you fancy. Over there though we call it a quinella and it doesn't matter in which order the horses finish. Here I had to have two bets to cover them both. You are not going to tell me that you have never backed another horse as a saver, when you are betting on your main selection?'

'I hardly ever bet and, if I did, I certainly would not bet against myself,' she replied.

'Ok, I am very sorry. I promise that I will never bet against you again. Now don't let's spoil the day by arguing. I have had a great time and I was very happy with the way that Pride finished today. I can't wait for the next time he runs because we shall be celebrating as winners. Now, if the rest of you have no objections or any other plans that involve her, I should like to take Miss Collins to dinner. Is that ok?'

'That's fine by me,' John replied, 'but first I should be far more interested in knowing what your future plans are for the horse.'

'Naturally now, he won't be running at Exeter tomorrow. I feel that he has a real chance at Cheltenham next Wednesday. The race is ideal for him and he will be fitter of course after today's workout. What we do with him after that will depend on how well he goes at Cheltenham. We could always try running him in the National. It would be entirely up to Victor to decide. If you would like to have a runner in the race then we could have a go at it. I don't think that he will disgrace us. In the National anything can happen and usually does. Though I sincerely hope that we never have a repeat of the 150th running of the race when we had that bomb scare and the course had to be cleared. Unfortunately that year will always be remembered for the chaos that it caused rather than Lord Gyllene's great victory when they finally got round to holding the meeting.' Mick shook his head sorrowfully as he recalled the drama of that fateful day.

'The worst thing about it though was the fact that everybody was forced to leave their horses behind. If there had have been a bomb go off, then the best part of Britain's prize chasers could have been lost. I remember that Jenny Pittman was in tears when she was interviewed.' Mary was almost in tears herself as she too thought about that dreadful day.

'Jenny Pittman? Isn't that the lady that they call the Queen of Aintree?' Victor asked.

'We used to be able to see the race televised every year but now you only see it if you are lucky enough to have cable. I am sure that I have heard her name mentioned.'

'Having trained the winner twice I think and had several placed horses, I expect that you would have heard of her. Even over there in Australia, my boy.' John laughed, hitting the table with his fist.

'Seriously though Mick, do you honestly think that Pride would have a chance in the National? I would love for him to run in it. I reckon that is possibly the best horse race in the world. I know that we have our Melbourne Cup and the Yanks, the Kentucky Derby, but for sheer spectacular racing it takes a lot of beating. I have always loved watching it. To think that I could possibly have a runner in it and then Samson in the Derby. I simply can't believe that I am sitting here discussing the prospect.'

'As I said before, anything is possible as far as that race is concerned. Look at the year that Foinavon won at 100–1, I think. He only won because all the other horses that were in front of him fell. If you are prepared to have a go at it, then run him we will. I am sure that Mary would love to have a ride in the Grand National, wouldn't you?' Mick said in a teasing tone.

She playfully shook her fist at him. 'Just you try and stop me. In view of that I think that I should cry off him for his next run. Even if it is at Cheltenham where I would love to race. I must be getting pretty close to my limit and I would hate to miss a chance at Aintree.'

Victor looked at her, a puzzled frown on his face. 'What limit are you talking about? Can't you ride as many times as you like or do they have a limit on women here?'

Mary gave an exaggerated sigh and wrung her hands together in a symbol of despair. 'How soon we forget. I told you at Buckfastleigh, I am regarded as an amateur. This means that I am only allowed to ride so many races a year or else I have to turn professional. It is something to do with not taking rides away from jockeys who race for a living. So I am afraid that you will have to find another jockey for Pride at Cheltenham, Mick. I am sorry but if I have to make a choice then naturally it's going to be Aintree.'

'Just a minute there Mary. You are getting me totally confused now. Didn't you tell me that you are apprenticed to your father? How can you be classed as an amateur and still ride as an apprentice?' Victor looked totally confused and they all laughed at him.

'Shhh. That is something that Dad worked out for me with the Jockey Club. Technically a jockey riding on the flat is a different occupation to a jumps jockey. I am never going to be able to pursue a career on the flat anyway as I am getting too big. Officially I am an amateur National Hunt jockey.'

'This is getting too involved for me. Sally, you are very quiet over there. Haven't you got anything to say at all?'

'I might if I were able to get a word in edgeways,' she laughed heartily. 'You lot seem to have taken over the stage. I should be very happy to see Pride of Tintagel run in the National though. It would be great for all of us.' She took her husband's hand and squeezed it gently. He looked at her. 'We still have to find a rider for Cheltenham. Most of the top ones will already be booked for the meeting.'

'Don't fret so, love. We will find somebody even if we have to get one of Mary's point to point friends to ride.' Hearing this Mary sat bolt upright in her chair so suddenly it made Sally jump. 'That's a great idea. I know several who would give their back teeth to have a ride at Cheltenham. Just you leave the jockey to me. I will find you one, I promise.'

'Good. Well, if that is settled how about us going to dinner Miss Collins?' Victor asked her. 'All this excitement is making me feel extremely hungry.'

'The same goes for me. All right then, where would you like to go?'

'I don't really mind but I seem to remember a restaurant in Exeter that used to be very good. Of course it is twelve years at least since I have been there it could have changed. I cannot even remember its name but it used to be in a small laneway near the cathedral. It might not even be there anymore.' The others all looked at each other for a moment, all thinking furiously trying to name the place that he was referring to. 'I know! You must mean The Ship,' Mary said at last.

'Yes that's the one. Okay then, Ship ahoy,' Victor said with a chuckle. 'Come on, then, let's get going, if that place will suit you.'

'After only being allowed a salad for lunch, I really do think that I could eat a horse this time,' she exploded with laughter at their shocked looks. 'See you later Dad. I shouldn't bother waiting up for me.'

When they reached Exeter they both decided that it was still a little early to eat so they would go to the cinema first. After seeing Pierce Brosnan as James Bond doing battle in the latest 007 movie, they finally found their way to The Ship. Victor could remember the galleon on the vivid blue sea from years ago when he had last visited the town. The timbered windows built over white stucco panels with the words 'Famous Fish, Steak & Ale House' emblazoned in gold, made him think that a place such as this would go down really well in Melbourne. Maybe he could do as that Yank had done with The Haunch of Venison in Salisbury. He could build a replica of it there somewhere on the banks of the Yarra. Pigeon holing this idea for another time, he opened the door and said, 'Come on Mary, let's eat.'

They took their time over the excellent meal. Victor told her about his previous job selling gaming machines and Mary constantly asked him about his lifestyle in Melbourne. 'It must be great living in that sunshine all the time. You seem to have so much freedom out there too,' Mary said with a slight touch of envy.

He was thoughtful for a moment and then shook his head. 'No, I think that it just sounds good to you because you haven't experienced it. As for the weather, people joke that Melbourne can have all four seasons in the one day. I have also seen it snow right in the city itself. But then I think that you are lucky also. I miss the pubs and places like this restaurant. I also miss the history; Australia is so young in comparison. When you fully analyse it though, life is what you make it. No matter where you live. Every place has its positives and its negatives.'

'Have you become a citizen there?'

'No. I suppose that I should but I only moved to Melbourne because Amada was born there. I also thought that our children would have a better chance growing up there. As far as I am concerned, though, I was born in England and will always hold an attachment for the place. It's in my blood I guess.'

'Would you come back here to live now, now that, now you? You know what I mean?' Mary was becoming quite flustered and uncertain of herself.

'Now that my family is dead you mean.' Victor said bluntly. 'I honestly don't know Mary, not at the moment anyway.' He glanced at his watch. 'Good God! Do you know what time it is? It is after ten o'clock. We had better make tracks because by the time that I take you home and then get home myself, it will be the early hours of the morning. I didn't realise that the time had gone so quickly.'

'That's what good food, fine wine and exhilarating company does for you.' She grinned then her voice took on a more serious tone. 'Are you sure that you are ok to drive though? I don't know whether you realise or not but we have had two bottles of wine plus those drinks that you had at the racecourse. I think that we would be far better off and a lot safer if we spent the night here in Exeter. We can leave early in the morning and drive home then safely.'

'I suppose that you are right, but what would your father say?'

'I'll phone Dad. I am sure though that he would far rather that I stayed here the night with you, than have a fatal accident driving home tonight,' she replied brightly. 'Now, if we are going to stay the night, I could do with a nice brandy with some more coffee please Victor.'

'I think that we should try and find somewhere to stay first, don't you?'

'The Royal Clarence Hotel is right opposite, I noticed it on the way in. Now you order the coffee and brandy and I will see about getting us some place to sleep. There is just one thing Victor,' she looked him straight in the eye and said softly, 'one room or two? You decide.'

His mouth went dry and he took her hand in his. Then in a voice little more than a whisper he replied, 'Mary, I am so sorry. You are such a wonderful girl.'

'A wonderful girl but. Victor it is not as though you would be cheating on your wife. That I could understand but Amanda isn't there for you any more.'

'I know but it still feels that way. I am truly sorry Mary, but it is just too soon for me. I know that most men would think me crazy to knock back such an offer. I would still have her on my mind. That wouldn't be fair to you.'

She stood up and, brushing a tear from her cheek, in a faltering voice said, 'Just my luck. I meet a man that I could really go for in a big way and he wants to remain faithful to his wife. Even though she is dead and buried.' She grabbed at his arm. 'Oh, I am so sorry Victor! That really was uncalled for. I simply wish that I had met you twelve years earlier, things might have been so different.'

He stood up and gently wiped the tears from her cheeks. 'Just give me a little time Mary. Try to be patient with me, that's all that I ask.'

'Victor, you can have anything that you want,' she said softly, 'and I mean anything. Get the drinks in and I will go and book two rooms for the night.'

Chapter Ten

The following Tuesday morning Victor was once again at Heathrow Airport in order to meet Harley's plane. This time, however, the American had no trouble with the Customs or Immigration. Within twenty-five minutes of the flight landing the two men were speeding down the motorway. After some discussion, they had decided that they would go and see Colin Oxford and confront him. They needed to know whether or not he had entered either of the horses in any race in the not too distant future.

Pulling off the motorway at Newbury, they agreed that they would have an early lunch before going on to the stables. Victor led the way into the bar of the inn where he had stayed on his last visit to the town. Moving through into the lounge bar, Victor was a little surprised to find Billy behind the counter. 'Hi there Billy. I thought that you only worked in here on race days?'

'Yeah, but Becky's old man had to go to London for some meeting or something so he asked me if I could fill in for a while. You know me; I'll do anything for a few readies. Have you come for lunch or do you just want a drink? It's toad in the hole today, good stuff. I can't wait for mine.'

Harley could scarcely contain his amusement at this news. 'Hey don't tell me that you Limey's eat toads? I know that the French eat frogs' legs, but eating toads! Really Victor tell me that he is kidding.'

'Very funny Harley, just for that we will both have it, thanks Billy. By the way this is Harley. You know the Yank who owns those horses that you ran through your computer for me. Harley, this is Billy the computer whiz that I told you about.'

'Pleased to meet you Billy. Victor here told me what a great job you did for him on my horses. I am impressed. I might be able to put some more work your way, if you are interested. I want to build up a database on all my business holdings. Horses, properties, shares and

133

such like. Do you reckon that you can handle something like that?'

'No worries. I can do it whenever you want it. I will need your files or at least access to them. Right now though I had better go and order your lunches. Are you serious about the toad in the hole? There is also gammon steak if you prefer that?'

'No, you have got me intrigued with this toad stuff. If Victor says that it is good, then it's fine by me,' Harley said with a laugh. 'Before you go though Billy, you had better pour us a couple of beers.' Billy poured out their drinks and then went off to order their meals.

A short while later a young girl brought out two plates from the kitchen and set them down in front of the two men. Harley's mouth gaped open at the sight of four, thick juicy sausages, nestling in a bed of golden brown batter. A rich, onion gravy had been poured over the sausages and had overflowed into the accompanying peas and carrots. The girl then returned with a bowl of apple sauce.

'Are we supposed to eat all this?' Harley gasped in amazement. Victor, however, was too busy tucking into his to answer him with more than a muffled grunt.

Their lunch over, the two men continued on their way to the stables. Harley arranged with Billy to meet the next day to discuss job prospects. By the time that they reached Palladian Lodge it was almost three o'clock. Victor parked the car and they walked up to the house. Harley grasped the brass horse and rapped sharply on the door. No one answered so next he tried the bell. Still not receiving a reply, Victor led the way round to the office at the rear. Peering in through the glass wall, the two men observed a young dark-haired girl typing at the desk.

'That looks like his daughter,' said Victor as he lightly tapped on the glass. The girl took no notice of them but continued with her typing. He tapped again, harder this time, and slowly she looked up. After a moment's hesitation she got up and opened the door slightly.

'Hi. It's Lilly isn't it?' he queried, flashing her a smile. She nodded. 'I don't know whether you remember me or not? I was here a couple of weeks ago to see your father.' He pointed to his companion, 'This is Harley Klugman. Your father has two of his horses here. Is he around at all? There was no answer at the house when we knocked.'

Lilly looked at Harley. 'Aren't you the lucky one? Two horses with Dad. He isn't home, he has gone to Southwell. We had a couple of runners there. He won't be back for hours yet.'

'Is there somewhere that we can go and have a chat, Lilly? Harley here is a little concerned about his horses. He would like to know exactly what plans your father has for them. Perhaps there is somewhere nearby that we can go for coffee. I am afraid that I am not too keen on your father's blend.'

The girl giggled and a complete transformation came over her. The sullen vanished and she actually smiled. 'Yes, I do remember you. I am sorry about the coffee but if you would like to come up to the house, I will make you a proper cup. You caught me on a bad day I'm afraid. Dad had been particularly spiteful that day and I am afraid that I took it out on you. I am very sorry, it was not aimed at you.'

'I did rather get the impression that all was not well between you. Do you want to talk about it? It sometimes helps and Harley here has shoulders broad enough for anyone to cry on' Victor said, grinning at his friend.

'You seem like nice people. Come on up to the house and I will tell you what has been going on here. I do really think that it is time that I told someone. I can't keep all this to myself much longer.'

Victor looked at Harley who merely shrugged his shoulders and raised his eyebrows. They followed Lilly up to the house.

A short while later they were all sitting comfortably in the lounge drinking coffee. Victor could not believe what a vast improvement that this coffee was on the one that he had been given on his previous visit. Lilly seemed to be so nervous and ill at ease that the two men waited patiently. Eventually it seemed that she was ready to talk without them prompting her. Finally she took a deep breath and started.

'Dad and a friend of his, John Cassidy, are working some kind of fiddle with most of the horses that we have here.'

'This John Cassidy is my so-called manager, 'Harley muttered almost under his breath. He hunched further back in his chair and gazed at her intently.

'I am sorry but whatever it is that they are doing, he is involved in it up to his neck.'

'What exactly are they doing? Do you know?' Victor asked her. The girl shook her head. 'No, but I think that they must be doping the horses somehow. I am not sure. I have noticed several times that some of them are very lethargic when they arrive back from a race. Naturally a hard race takes something out of them, but their eyes seem glazed and there is no spring in their step. If you want to know more about what they are doing, then you will have to talk with my mother. This is the reason that she left here. I heard her and Dad have a blazing row one night. She told him that she was not going to put up with his dirty dealings any more. She said that sooner or later he was going to get caught. She told him that she was not going to be around to take the blame with him. He was in it on his own.'

'Why didn't you go with your mother, Lilly?' Harley asked her gently.

Tears came to her eyes and she started to shake as she said hoarsely. 'He wouldn't let me go. He said that he couldn't stop Mum from going, but he could me.'

'How was he able to do that? Surely you are old enough to be able to go your own way aren't you?' Victor said in a puzzled tone.

'It is because of my brother Jack that I have to stay.' She started sobbing.

'Your brother, does he work here as well?' Harley posed the question.

Lilly was crying quite hard now so the two men just sat and waited. 'He used to work here, although he hated it. Jack was terrified of horses, some people are. He wanted to be a writer. Dad insisted that he worked for him in the stables. He told him that he could waste his own time with his writing. Then one day Dad made him take out one of the horses. His normal boy was sick with the flu. Jack was absolutely petrified with fear. He had never even ridden a horse before, only mucked out in the stalls. They were riding out in the lane and a bird flew out of the hedge. It startled his horse. Jack, of course, did not know how to control it and it threw him. Right in front of a passing car. He was lucky that its driver was one that slowed down for horses. You would be amazed how many don't. Even so it was still going at a fair speed and poor Jack had no chance. He broke his back so it means that now he is a permanent invalid. He needs a full-time nurse to care for him. Mum has to go out to work to support them so she can't look after him. So Dad pays for the nurse just as long as I work for him. If I leave then the money will stop.' She finally managed to get out her story.

Harley and Victor looked at each other. 'The Bastard! Victor we are going to have to do something about this guy. If he treats his family like this how does he treat the horses?' Harley could scarcely contain his anger or disgust.

'I agree, but how do we go about it?'

'I'm not sure at the moment, I will have to think about it for a while.'

'There is one thing that still puzzles me though. What is he hoping to achieve by doping the horses? Surely he can't expect to run them all in races and get good odds? People would start getting suspicious,' Victor said.

'That is where John Cassidy comes in. I know that some owners have got fed up with their horses not doing as well as they expected. Cassidy then steps in and sells them for them. Usually it is to the same guy but the owners are never aware of that. They are just happy to recoup some of their losses. They don't worry as they are happy to have them taken off their hands,' Lilly explained to the two men.

Harley rubbed his chin. 'Hmm, that is very interesting. I wonder who the mystery buyer is? Also what does he do with the animals once he has bought them?'

'I think that he must be a Frenchman. At least it sounds like a French accent when he speaks. I have spoken to him on the phone a couple of times.'

'Well well, a Frenchman eh. That could explain a lot. Very neat in fact.' Victor looked at him. 'I don't quite follow that. You are losing me, Harley. What difference does it make?'

'Just think for a minute. How many people would think of looking for their horses in France once they had sold them? Look what happened to me? Mine won four races and I had absolutely no idea that they were even racing there. He might not stop at France. He could run them in Italy or Germany, who is to know? If the horses that they have stopped here in England have had any real form, they sell them to this French guy. Then Oxford and his cronies are able to buy top class stock at bargain basement prices. They then race them on the continent on their proper capabilities and clean up. This guy seems to have more fiddles than a string band. I am sorry Lilly, I realise that he is your father but . . .'

'He is my father in name only,' the girl shook her head angrily. 'He has never done anything for me. How can you hope to stop him though? If you succeed and put him out of business, what will happen to my brother Jack?'

Victor reached out and gently took her hands in his. 'Don't you worry yourself about Jack. I promise you that if you help us your brother will be well looked after. Harley and I will see to that won't we Harley?'

'You betcha and I think that you will find that the other owners would chip in something also. If we show them where your father is screwing them I am sure that they would show their appreciation to you. Now, if you could just let us have your mother's address, then we will get out of your hair and leave you in peace.' Harley stood up.

'What about your horses?' Lilly asked. 'Don't you want to see them?'

'Not today,' the American shook his head. 'I think that we are better off leaving before someone sees us here. I can check on them another day. Now that address please.'

Lilly went over to the dresser and, taking out a pen and some paper, wrote down her mother's address for them. Silently she handed it to Harley. He glanced at the piece of paper and then stuffed it in his pocket.

Victor turned to the girl. 'There is one thing that you can do for us if you will. Make us up a list of the horses that Cassidy has sold to this Frenchman. Also, if it is at all possible, the names of the original owners. It is just possible that we may have to get in touch with them.'

'That shouldn't be too hard. I have to do all the office paper work for Dad. What do I do with all this when I have it?' Victor took the pen and paper that she had been using and wrote down his address. 'You can send it here. Now don't you worry about Jack, we will take care of him. I give you my word on that. As Harley said, I think that we had better go. Your Dad might come back early.'

Lilly walked the two men to the door. They shook hands with her. As she stepped aside to let them pass she said in a heartfelt voice, 'For once, I feel as if things might go right, for a change. Thank you both.'

As they walked back to the car, Victor asked Harley what he intended to do about Delmore. 'For the time being Jenkins is still looking after him for me. He will do so until we sort this mess out. I laid out too much money on that colt for someone like Oxford to stuff him up. I hope that we might be able to give him a run in a week or two. I will keep you posted on his progress, anyway.' The two friends then got into the car and headed back towards Newbury. Victor dropped Harley off at the inn where he had decided to spend the night. He wanted to get something sorted out with Billy about his proposed database and get that underway. He invited Victor to stay and have dinner with him, but he declined and set off for Cornwall.

The next morning, Victor was up bright and early. Josh had still not finished working on the four-poster. Victor was beginning to think that he had made an error of judgement by asking him in the first place. If it hadn't meant it would have to be broken up to get it out of the bedroom, he might have discarded the idea of renovating it. He had been very tempted merely to buy a new bed. But as he had come this far with it then Josh may as well finish the job. He just hoped that the finished product would be worth the wait.

After eating a light breakfast, Victor started out on the drive to Cheltenham. He was really looking forward to seeing this course. Mary had told him that it was the home of the National Hunt and really quite spectacular. Her father had told him how to get there. All that he had to do was to get on to the M5 and follow it until he reached junction 10. Keeping an eye on the signposts as he drove, he passed 11A. Then to his dismay he discovered that the next was not 10 as he expected but 9. He was later to discover that for some inexplicable reason there was only an outlet 10 on the southbound side of the motorway. Cursing, he pulled off the road and consulted his map. Eventually he was able to find his way to the racecourse and parked the car. He then realised that he had come in from the opposite direction that John had imagined that he would. Consequently, he had to walk up the hill in order to reach the gate where he was supposed to meet the others.

By the time that he had reached the top, he was short of breath and somewhat short tempered. The way that things had gone so far did not augur well for the rest of the day. He pulled his coat tight around him in an effort to protect himself from the bitterly cold wind. It was half way through March, but the country was experiencing a very cold snap. It made him think once more of home. It would be Moomba Week, he thought to himself, and decidedly warmer than this. He used to enjoy watching the water skiing on the Yarra. He went there most years to watch the world stars in action.

'Dreaming of what you are going to do with your winnings, Victor?' A female voice broke into his thoughts. He turned around and found Mary and John were watching him.

'No, actually I was thinking that no one in their right mind would come out in this weather. Especially to watch a horse race. If I was at home right now I would be dressed in shirt and shorts.'

Mary giggled.

'What's so funny may I ask?'

'I am sorry, Victor,' she laid a hand on his arm. 'I was just picturing you in shorts with knobbly knees and all. It would be enough to turn any woman on.' She laughed again and he found that, in spite of himself, he had to smile too. With the smile his good nature also returned and he kissed her on the cheek affectionately.

'I suggest that we make a beeline for the bar and get out of this wind,' John said as he watched this interaction between the two of them. 'I believe that Mick was driving the horse box today so he won't be here for another half hour at least.'

'Yes, the guy that he had hired as his regular driver had some family commitment. Mick gave him the day off,' Victor said. 'As you suggested though, let's talk inside. This wind feels as though it's blowing from the Arctic.'

Minutes later, in the warmth and comfort of the bar, the three of them ordered coffee and sat down at a vacant table. As they settled, Victor turned to Mary and asked, 'What is this jockey like that you got to ride for me? Mick told me that he had never heard of him.'

'I guess that could be right. He is an amateur too of course but I can assure you that he is very good. He is from South Africa and I have raced against him several times at point to points. He was due to ride in Somerset on Saturday but his horse is lame. He was thrilled at the prospect of riding here at Cheltenham. Most of us point to point riders never get a chance like this. He won't let you down. He always rides to win.'

Victor looked her straight in the eye. 'How many times has he beaten you?'

'He has never beaten me, but he has come fairly close. The last time he tried, Dad just managed to grab the whip in time.'

Victor looked at her blankly for a moment. Then he too laughed as the words struck home.

'Neither has he ever ridden a horse past me at the winning post,' she added with a laugh.

'How do you manage to put up with her John?'

'She makes my life a pure misery I can tell you. I can't wait for the day that she meets a man who will marry her and take her out of my life. Do you fancy the job Victor? She is house trained and can cook up a reasonable meal when called on to do so.'

Mary jumped to her feet, flushing a bright red. 'Dad!'

Victor was highly amused to see that she was embarrassed for a change. He reached out and pulled her back down on her chair. 'If Pride jumps as well as that this afternoon, then we have the race in the bag. Wouldn't you agree John?'

'You two are impossible! I am going to see if I can find Mick and Sally. At least the horse can't talk back to me.' Her father reached out a restraining hand to her.

'Calm down, sugar. Anyway they have just walked in the door, so you can relax.' So saying John got to his feet to greet the new arrivals.

They all watched the first two races on the closed circuit monitors as the weather had worsened and now the rain was coming down in buckets. The favourites duly obliged in both cases but none of the party had even bothered to have a bet.

Finally Mick got to his feet. 'Well I suppose that I had better get down there and get this horse saddled up. Why don't you all stay here in the warm and watch the race? There is no point in us all getting soaked to the skin. I will catch up with you after he has won.'

Victor shook his head. 'No way! I have driven all this way so at least I am going to watch him from the stand. How about you, Mary? Are you coming or staying here in the warm?'

'Just you try and keep me away. Anyway, this rain is going to stop for us. You wait and see.' They all made up their minds that they would brave the elements. As they walked out of the door, to everyone's amazement, the rain did indeed stop. 'See, I told you so,' Mary cried. 'Come on Victor, I want to go and have a bet. I am making allowances because I know an owner in this race.' She grabbed his arm and half dragged him off to the bookies. Pride of Tintagel was showing odds of 5–1 on most of the boards that they looked at. 'Gee I thought that we would get better odds than that,' Mary said. The disappointment in her voice showing clearly. 'I mean there are some really good chances in this race.'

'Yes, but don't forget that it was a good run of his at Newton Abbott,' Victor replied. 'I think that I am going to back him on the Tote, he is 9–1 there.' They all decided that they would back the horse on the Tote. Victor also coupled it up with two rank outsiders in the quinella, 'Just for an added interest,' he told them.

Not wanting to be outsmarted Mary followed his example and

backed the same horses. They made their way to the mounting yard. Mary introduced them all to Hans, her South African friend who was going to ride Pride. When the horses started to make their way out on to the course, they wished him luck and left him to receive last minute instructions from Mick. The four of them made their way to the cover and protection of the grandstand.

The rain started to fall lightly again as the horses were pulled into line. The tapes flew up and they jumped off. Pride was slowly away and Victor's heart sank a little. Hans seemed to be having a little trouble getting the horse settled. Eventually he managed to take control just before the first jump. Pride of Tintagel sailed over the first fence and landed a good half a length in front of its nearest rival. The pace was fairly slow and by the time the horses had travelled about a mile, Hans had managed to work his way up into fifth spot. They completed the circuit and by now both the horse and its rider seemed to understand each other better. They appeared to be travelling a lot easier than at the start.

With seven fences left to jump, the favourite, Kindergarten, took the lead. Behind him Pride of Tintagel moved up and drew level with two other horses. At the sixth, he jumped well and landed clear of the other two runners. He then started to drift out towards the grand stand side of the course.

'Hans what are you doing? You are going to let them catch you again,' Mary cried out as she lept to her feet, clutching at Victor's arm.

He shook his head. 'No, I don't think so. I would say that the going is better there and he is giving himself a chance of running down Kindergarten in the straight.' The second last loomed up and Kindergarten sailed over it with Vixen two lengths behind him. Pride was a further length away, third. At the last both Kindergarten and Vixen took off together, landing almost the same way but the favourite faltered and Vixen took the lead. Hans on Pride of Tintagel landed almost half a length away.

'Come on Hans! Come on!' Mary was jumping up and down with great excitement. Victor's palms were sweaty as he silently urged his horse on. John and Sally, too, were on their feet, shouting their encouragement. Slowly but surely Hans drew level with Kindergarten. The jockey on the favourite urged his mount forward. The heavy going was now beginning to take its toll on the top weight and Pride passed him. Vixen looked as though he had the race in his grasp when Hans gave his horse a slight tap with his whip. Pride seemed to find something extra and caught Vixen on the post. The two horses passed the line locked together and a great roar went up from the crowd. 'Oh my God! A photo!' shrieked Mary. 'Dad, did he get there in time or not?'

'I am not sure,' her father replied hoarsely, 'it's as close to a dead heat as you could get. I wouldn't like to say either way. What do you think Victor?'

'I don't know. A length past the post he had it won. I am just keeping my fingers crossed, that's all.'

The PA system spluttered then crackled into life. 'The winner by a short half head, number 5, Pride of Tintagel; second, number 7, Vixen; and third, number 1, Kindergarten.' Mary let out a wild shriek and, grabbing Victor, kissed him full on the mouth. A couple next to them nudged each other, 'Guess who backed the winner?' one said to the other. Mary took no notice but when she eventually released Victor she looked at him and said huskily, 'Grand National, here we come.'

'Before that happens I suggest that we go down and congratulate Hans on winning this one,' her father remarked drily. He looked at Victor and there was the merest hint of a smile about his face as he said, 'It looks as though you have found yourself a winner there, my Boy.' Victor's face coloured and they all laughed. They then started to make their way down to the unsaddling enclosure. As they descended the steps, Victor took Mary's arm and pointed. 'Look, those two outsiders that we took with Pride are just coming in now. So much for a big forecast payout,' and laughed. Mary looked up to see the two horses that he spoke of, both trotting in riderless. 'Well, at least you would have had a good win. How much did you bet on him anyway?'

'Enough to pay for the dinner that I have planned for us tonight at the Llandoger Trow in Bristol. I have us booked in for seven o'clock.'

'The Lan what?' Mary asked him, her face creased in a smile.

'The Llandoger Trow. It is an old inn in the centre of Bristol, near the river. Not far from The Old Vic. They say that it is the inn that Robert Louis Stevenson used in his book, *Treasure Island*. I thought that it would be an appropriate place to celebrate. The food there is very good and it is easy to get to.'

'It has nothing to do with being near The Old Vic then I take it?' Sally teased.

'Arr, Vic me lad, shiver me timbers and all that yo hoing stuff.' Mary almost doubled up with laughter.

Hearing all the noise John called out to them. He had been chatting to an acquaintance and was a little way behind them. 'Just what are you two up to?'

Mary turned and through her giggles managed to tell him what Victor had said about booking dinner.

'I say Victor, you must have been very confident about winning,' Sally remarked solidly.

He shook his head in disagreement. 'I thought that whatever the outcome that we would go. I must admit though I am far happier arriving as a winner. Come on, if we don't hurry Hans will have gone to weigh in,' he urged them.

They finished clambering down the steps and quickly made their way to the unsaddling enclosure. Mick was already there with Hans and was in process of unbuckling the saddle. Victor went up and patted Pride on the muzzle and watched as Mick threw a blanket over the horse's steaming back.

'I had better go and see to him and then I will join the rest of you in the bar, I would imagine?' Mick said briefly. He then flashed a smile at his wife and led the horse off towards the stalls.

Victor went up to Hans and shook him warmly by the hand. After offering his congratulations to the jockey he told him about that evening's arrangements.

'That is very kind of you sir, but I am afraid that I must head off home. I already had my evening mapped out before Mary asked me to ride your horse,' he replied, with an apologetic air. 'Some other time perhaps, no doubt I shall see you again.'

'Well, that is too bad, we would have loved for you to come along. Our success today is mainly due to your good judgement. If you hadn't have pulled over to the better going I am sure that he would have been beaten. Anyway, I will get your address from Mary and there will be a present in the mail for you. Mary says that you are also an amateur rider and I would hate to compromise you here in any way. You never know who is watching you. Once again, thanks indeed. You rode a great race and I am pleased that Mary was able to get you.'

'You have a very good horse there,' Hans said modestly. 'It was a treat to ride such a creature. I wish you luck in the National. Mary

144

told me that he was entered. I think that with a little bit of good fortune he will have a very good chance. He is such a beautiful jumper and with Mary on board, well, anything can happen.'

'Yes indeed, how right you are. With Mary around anything can happen and usually does,' Victor agreed drily. He patted Hans on the shoulder and the jockey strode off to weigh in leaving Victor alone with his thoughts for a brief moment.

John Collins walked over to him and took him to one side. 'Why don't you and Mary just go out on your own tonight? We would all understand. You don't want us lot dragging along and spoiling your fun.'

'No, no,' he protested. 'You have all helped with this and I would much prefer if we were all involved in the celebrations, especially Mick and Sally. Besides that,' his face broke into a broad grin, 'I would feel a whole lot safer with some company around.'

John gave a hearty laugh. 'Yes, I must admit that she can be a shade overpowering at times. Ok then, we shall all go, but right now I am going to collect my winnings. I took your horse in a forecast with Vixen. Whatever you do don't tell Mary. She might think that I am having a go at her, especially after what happened at Cheltenham.'

Later that evening the five of them had finished an excellent dinner and were sitting enjoying their coffee and brandies. The conversation eventually drifted around to Arcadian Steel. 'We gave him a proper trial over a mile and a half yesterday. I am a little surprised that Mary didn't tell you,' John remarked.

'I just thought that you might like the satisfaction of doing so, Dad. After all I had enough to talk about with Pride and today's race,' Mary said coyly, and they all laughed.

'Anyhow, how did he go?' Victor asked anxiously. John did not answer immediately but took a swallow of his cognac. Then looking at Victor said slowly and in a low voice. 'He did it in 2 minutes 25.' Victor absorbed this for a moment and then gave a low whistle.

'That's not too bad is it?'

'Victor! You are the master of understatement. That is bloody good my friend. You have to look at it in perspective though. I mean that Lando won the Japan Cup back in 1996 in 2.24. Bear in mind also that the track there is a lot easier than Epsom. Epsom only has a very short run in and is a very undulating track to boot. If you are racing at Ascot, which is quite a stiff course with an uphill finish, then your horse is most likely going to be several seconds slower over the same distance. All that being true, you still have a very smart colt there my boy.' John sat back and drained his glass.

Victor digested all this for a moment before he spoke. 'Yes I had forgotten that. I suppose it is like comparing the tracks back home. Moonee Valley for instance is a very tight track and a lot of horses aren't suited by it. Yet when they race at Flemington the same horses seem to find an extra leg. Then horses in Sydney race in the opposite direction from Melbourne. That too can upset the horse. Now, how about that jockey that Mary was on about? Has he tried to ride him yet?'

'Jason is coming down tomorrow morning to try him out. Why don't you stay with us tonight and then you can meet him? After all it's a fair drive back to Cornwall.' He hesitated for a minute and he was sure that Mary's eyes suddenly shone. At the same time Mick stood up. 'Well, that was a great meal but Sally and I ought to be making tracks. Some of us have a living to make.'

'Sure, I understand. Wait a minute, I never thought to ask, what happened to the horse? You drove him up here, surely he isn't still at the track?'

'As if I would do a thing like that.' Mick looked pained. 'No, one of our neighbours came up today to watch a friend's horse run. I told him that Pride was a good thing. Apparently he had £500 on him, so he was more than happy to drive him home for me. He will leave him in one of his paddocks tonight and I will pick him up in the morning.'

Sally looked at her husband with her mouth open wide. He saw her look and laughed. 'Yes, he actually took my advice. We must be on the way back love.' His wife got out of her chair and walking round to give her husband a big hug. 'Oh Mick I am so pleased for you. Maybe your luck has changed at last.' She kissed him and then turned to Victor. 'We owe it all to you. We can't thank you enough for bringing Pride to us in the stable and pride back into our lives.'

Victor shook his head. 'You owe me nothing. Mick is the one who is training the horse and I was more than repaid today, I can assure you.'

'As a matter of interest, Victor, exactly how much did you have on him? I asked you earlier but you never gave me an answer,' Mary asked him. But before he was able to reply her father broke in, 'I really think that that is his business, Mary, don't you?'

Chapter Ten

'But I want to know,' his daughter answered a trifle petulantly. 'Go on, please tell us. Don't worry, I shan't be hitting you for a loan or anything.' Victor still hesitated for a short while then said quietly, 'If you really must know, I had £5,000 on him.'

There was a gasp from everybody. They were all silent for a minute and then John said, 'I know that you have a lot of money but you must admit that you took an awful chance. You must have been very confident in both Mick and the horse?'

'I was,' he replied simply.

'Well, seeing as how you won all that money, I am going to have another helping of desert. It was delicious,' Mary piped up and signalled the waitress. Mick looked at Victor in silence for a moment and then said softly, 'As much as I admire your confidence in me, I sincerely hope that you don't bet like that in the National. For one thing, I am not sure if he will last the four and a half miles. It is a very tough race and there is a lot that can go wrong in that distance.'

'With Mary here riding him, he wouldn't dare not to last the distance,' quipped Victor and then had to duck quickly as she swung a punch at him.

It was still dark the next morning when Victor was awakened by a knock on his bedroom door. It opened and Mary came in carrying a cup of tea. 'Come on, sleepy head. It is 5.30 and Jason Carter has already arrived. Dad says that he will be ready to take Samson out at six, so you had better hurry up.' Putting the tea on the bedside table she beamed at him and left the room.

Victor sat up and shook his head in an effort to clear it. He was still a little hazy as to how the previous evening had ended. He remembered Mary driving him back to the house and downing a couple of John's excellent cognacs, but details after that were a trifle blurred. He swung his feet out of the bed and managed to get himself dressed. He gratefully eased his parched throat with the cup of tea. He then found his way to the bathroom and eventually staggered downstairs. As he reached the bottom, he met John coming out of the dining room.

'You look a little bleary-eyed this morning. Did you sleep well? We will have some breakfast after the trial. If you want, I can arrange for a bacon sarni or something to keep you going?'

John's cheerful voice and the offer of a sandwich did nothing to improve Victor's disposition. Giving out a low groan he struggled to put his coat on. With John's laugh ringing in his ears he made his way to the front door thinking that he was in no mood to meet an arrogant jockey. So heaven help him if he got too out of hand.

Once outside, the sharp nip in the air worked wonders for him. By the time that they had reached the stable, his head was almost clear. There were half a dozen horses being prepared for their morning exercise as they arrived. In all his years following the horses nobody as yet had managed to convince him that exercises should start so early. He knew that back in Melbourne a large percentage commenced their day around 4a.m. He could not see Samson among the horses circling around. What he did see, however, was a bright red Maserati parked at the top of the yard. Lounging against its door, smoking what appeared to be a small cheroot, was a thin, blond-haired youth with a sharp, angular face. As Victor approached, the young lad turned towards him. He cast sharp blue eyes insolently over him for a brief moment then his gaze flickered back to the group around the horses.

Taking a deep breath Victor marched up to him and offered him his hand. 'Good morning. You must be Jason Carter I take it?'

The youth did not answer him right away but instead continued to smoke his cheroot. Finally he turned towards Victor and stared at him. 'Maybe, who wants to know?'

Victor understood instantly why John did not like this man and mentally sided with him. 'I am Victor Barnes and I own Arcadian Steel. I must say from the outset that I am not sure that I like your attitude. I am the one who will be paying you to ride my horse so you could at least be polite when you are spoken to.'

'Is that a fact, Victor? Well, from what I have heard, you need me far more than I need you,' the youth drawled, blowing a smoke ring into the crisp morning air.

Victor could feel his anger rising. Taking a deep breath he said icily, 'You still have to prove to us that you can actually stay on the horse Mr Carter. Many have tried.'

'There is not a horse racing that I cannot ride,' boasted Carter.

Victor was spared from making any further comment by the arrival of Mary with her father in tow. 'Well now, if it isn't the delightful Miss Collins? When are you going to let me take you out Mary? You don't know what you are missing.'

Chapter Ten

By now she was at Victor's side and she felt him bristle. She smiled sweetly at Carter and said, 'I am afraid that I am spoken for at the moment Jason.' She took Victor's hand and gave it a squeeze.

'So that's how the land lies is it? Well, don't forget that when you want someone to show you a really good time, you know how to find me. You can't imagine what you are missing Mary, so don't leave it too long.'

'Thank you Jason, I will remember that. Now how about us getting on with the reason that you are here, shall we?'

'I heartily agree, we can't spend all day exchanging niceties, there is work to be done,' John barked. 'Cliff, is Samson saddled yet?' he called out to his head lad. 'If so bring him out so that Jason can have a look at him.' The man nodded and went off to check on the horse in question. He reappeared a few minutes later leading Samson who appeared to be quite docile. As they approached Jason stood up, carefully stubbed his cheroot and ambled over to the horse. Taking the bridle in one hand, he ran the other down the animal's neck, shoulders and withers. He then walked around to face him and, taking its head in both hands, looked it squarely in the eyes. He remained in this position for a few minutes then releasing Samson's head he stepped back.

'This is a fine horse that you have Victor,' he said grudgingly. 'Now where do I get changed?'

Without a word, Cliff pointed to a room at the end of the stalls. Opening the boot of his Maserati, Jason took out a canvas bag and swaggered off to get changed. The others watched him walk off in silence for a moment.

'I wish to hell that we could find somebody else,' John said with a deep sigh. 'He is such an arrogant prig that one. Still, beggars can't be choosers. Right, we had better get on with the rest. You can lead them out Jimmy, just a brisk canter until his majesty deems to join us. We may as well give them all a good gallop over a mile this morning. You can then try and catch Samson over the final four furlongs. Cliff, you can come with us.'

None of the lads seemed very keen to ride off. A couple even dismounted and made the pretence of checking their mounts' girths and surcingle.

Mary watched them with amusement and then had to laugh. 'They are all waiting to see if Jason can ride him. You might as well let them

149

Dad, they won't go until he is aboard Samson.'

'I suppose that you are right. Ok boys, mount up but you can just trot them around until Super Jock is ready,' John called resignedly.

Victor gave Mary a wide grin. 'I can't say that I blame them. Nothing would give me greater pleasure at this moment than to see Samson throw him.' A sudden thought struck him. 'What is this that you were telling him about you being spoken for?'

However, before she was able to answer, Jason strode back into the yard. Even in his work clothes he made an imposing figure. He was dressed all in white, including boots, which Victor surmised correctly were hand made of soft kid. His helmet was a snow white and even his goggles had white frames and straps.

'Good God! He looks like a bloody advert for a soap powder commercial,' Cliff's guttural tones could be heard clearly across the yard and the comment was followed by several stifled laughs from the other boys.

If Jason had heard Cliff, he took no notice but marched over to where Samson was standing. Taking a hold on the reins he then turned to Cliff. 'Give us a leg up old man.' Without a word Cliff placed his hands under Jason's boots and tossed him lightly into the saddle. Everyone held their breath. Nothing happened and a small sigh of disappointment could be heard issuing from Jimmy's lips.

Jason stretched his arm out and patted Samson's crest and then gave him a gentle kick with his heels. The horse reared suddenly and its front hooves thrashed the air. The move was so sudden and unexpected that Jason almost came off but managed to save himself by grabbing at the mane and twisting his fingers through it. The horse settled back on all fours again and stood there. Jason patted his neck and gave the reins a flick. Samson remained immobile. His rider waited a few more seconds and then gave him another gentle kick. The animal started to rear once more but, this time, as he started to lift his front legs, the horse suddenly dropped them again. His head dropped with them and at the same time he turned his body in a vicious sideways twist and bucked Jason clean over his head, to land in a crumpled heap in front of the Maserati. Nobody moved or said a word but watched with bated breath to see what Jason would do next. He got up very slowly and dusted himself off. He then walked over to the horse that was standing quietly, watching him. Jason took hold of the reins and rubbed the animal's nose gently with his knuckles.

Silently, Cliff walked over to them and once again held out his clasped hands. Jason put his foot into them and the other man heaved him back into the saddle. Samson immediately reared again but this time Jason was ready for him. Samson tried to buck again but Jason was prepared and managed to stay on. Samson reared once more and then bolted. He raced out of the yard and down towards the track. Jason lowered himself along the horse's neck and waited patiently for the animal to slow down. He was not prepared for Samson's sudden prop, however, and once again found himself flying over Samson's head. He hit the ground hard and this time was not so quick in getting up. John and Cliff started to run towards the fallen figure.

'Jimmy, you and the others ride on down to the track but go around the back way, we don't want to spook the horse,' Mary shouted with enough authority in her voice for the other riders to obey. Victor, too, started to run towards Jason but then changed his mind and instead grabbed Samson's reins. John reached the crumpled heap first and knelt down anxiously beside him. As he did so Jason stirred, then sat up gingerly.

'Shit that hurt!' he yelled out in anger. He rubbed his shoulder vigorously for a few minutes, swearing under his breath.

'Come on Jason, we had better get you back to the house. That was a nasty fall.' John said.

However, Jason shook off the hand that John had put out to help him and glared at him.

'No way! I came here today to ride a horse and ride him I will.' So saying he scrambled to his feet and this time did not even bother to brush himself down. He strode purposely towards his waiting adversary. The horse eyed him warily but grabbing the reins from out of Victor's hand led the animal down towards the training track. Upon reaching the track he stopped. Taking a tight hold on the reins this time he pulled himself up on to its back.

Once in the saddle Jason leaned forward and patted the animal on the neck. He then stroked Samson's ears and finally, to everyone's amazement, started to sing to him. The horse gave a half–hearted attempt to rear once more, then settled down and started to trot around the track quite peaceably. Everyone watched in astonishment.

'See Dad, I told you that he had away with horses,' Mary whispered to her father.

He looked at her for a moment and then smiled. 'You are right, as usual, my girl. I don't know what I'd do without you.' He kissed her gently on the forehead and then waved to Jason to join them. He cantered over and stopped expectantly. Samson dropped his head and started to chomp on a tuft of grass growing at the side of the track.

'Jason I owe you an apology. I thought that you were an arrogant bastard but you have redeemed yourself in my eyes here today, well and truly. That was a great piece of work. I have never seen anything like it.'

'Thanks but I don't think that you should blame the horse. Obviously it looks as though someone has had him at some time and, when they couldn't ride him, they have beaten him. He was always waiting for me to give him a belt.'

Victor then walked over to him and held out his hand. This time Jason shook it warmly. 'This horse and I are two of a kind,' he said. 'We both have a reputation but it is really a front. With me, you need something that will give you an edge over the other riders. If owners think that you are tough they also tend to think that you possess a killer instinct that will give you extra winners. So they think that they have more of a chance with me riding their horses. That is why I am always in demand and why I freelance.'

'Well, I for one am impressed, Jason. I must admit that when I first met you this morning, I too thought that you were arrogant. To be honest I was more than pleased when Samson threw you the first time. I was concerned that you might have been hurt the second time though. The way that you responded and consequently treated the horse has won my respect. I can't say that I would have blamed you if you had hit him after that second fall. I was more than pleased to see that you didn't. If you can get Samson cleared by the Jockey Club, you have a Derby ride if you want it.'

'The Jockey Club! A piece of cake! Now let's see if this horse of yours can run shall we?' With that he gave Samson a tap with the reins and cantered off back down the track.

Later that morning after the horses had been returned to the stalls and hosed down everyone was sitting in the kitchen having just finished breakfast. The topic of conversation naturally enough centred on that morning's trials. Arcadian Steel had swept past both Blue Bayou and Pepper Pot, leaving them floundering in his wake. He ended up by beating the pair home by a good nine lengths. Jason was in raptures over the horse declaring him one of the best he had ever ridden. He was adamant that it would take a real champion to beat him in the Derby.

In all of this animated discussion, John Collins alone remained quiet and thoughtful. He had not joined in the chatter very much at all. At last Mary could stand it no longer and turned to her father. 'Dad! For goodness sake what is wrong with you? I would have thought that you would have been over the moon with that performance this morning. Most trainers would give their back teeth to have a horse like that running in the Derby. I truly can't understand you. Why are you so glum?'

'Yes John, you are rather quiet,' Victor observed. 'Are you afraid that he won't pass the Jockey Club's trial? If that is the case then don't you worry. If he does by some remote chance fail, well, I knew that was on the cards when I bought him. However, Jason seems to think that he will be fine and get through with flying colours.' The latter nodded his head in agreement and then returned to his own conversation that he was holding with Ginger.

John gave a big sigh. 'No, it's not that at all. I have every faith now in Jason's ability. I am just wondering how I am going to face my friends and tell them that their very expensive thoroughbreds have been made to look like second-rate hacks by your horse. It is bad enough having your horses beaten by a rival stable. When the challenge comes from your own, well, I just don't know what to say.' He somewhat dejectedly poured himself another cup of coffee and slumped further down in his chair.

'Dad you are such a worrier. You know as well as I do that they will only be too happy for you. You have won enough races for them in the past. Besides, they only bought those horses to offset their tax bill. They will most likely back Arcadian Steel and make a killing that way.' Mary winked at Victor and motioned towards the door. Shaking his head he pointed to Jason.

Puzzled, Mary looked at him, so in desperation he tapped Jason on the arm. 'What is going to happen now Jason, any idea?'

'Well, I have to go to Wolverhampton on Saturday but we can most likely tee up an inspection by the Jockey Club for some time next week. When is your horse due to have its first run?' he drawled, forgetting himself for the moment and lapsing slightly back into his alter ego.

Victor looked across at John who thought for a moment and then said, 'I had entered him at Doncaster next week, then Newmarket. I must admit that I hadn't planned too far ahead in case he er, um in case he . . .'

'In case we were unable to get a rider for him,' Victor laughed. 'That's ok John you can say it. I won't be offended.'

'What are you riding at Wolverhampton, Jason? Anything worth us having a flutter on?' Mary asked politely, not wanting to be left out of the discussion.

He didn't answer right away but pulled a notebook from his pocket and riffled through the pages. 'I truly don't know yet. I had a call from this trainer yesterday who said that his regular rider had taken a fall. Apparently the doctor has given him a week off so this guy was looking for a jockey to ride in a couple of races for him. As you know, I am a freelance rider so had no regular stable booking. I was free on Saturday so took the rides.'

'Ok then, who is this trainer so we can look up the form of his horses?'

Jason was busily skipping through the pages of his notebook. 'Ah, here he is, a Colin Oxford. I must admit that I am not familiar with his name. Do you know him John?'

John and Victor looked at each other across the table. Jason was quick to spot the exchange.

'Well, I know of him, never met the man mind you, but I've certainly heard a lot about him. Victor here has actually met with him.'

'Why don't you like him Victor?'

'Well, as John said, I have met the man. Actually, he was hoping that I would place Arcadian Steel with him. You should be on your guard with him, Jason, some of his methods are a trifle suspect to say the least,' Victor commented quietly.

'Well, he needn't think that he can play silly buggers with me. If he is not straight down the line, then I don't ride. I have too much at stake to try anything the least bit dodgy.'

'I shouldn't think that he would try anything with a stranger though. If he is pulling a stroke he should have enough sense to wait until his regular rider is back. A casual jockey would pose too much of a risk.'

'I think that it is about time that I was off.' Jason stood up. 'It was nice meeting you Victor and, more importantly, your horse.'

'You see Victor, your horse rates higher than you with Jason,' Mary laughed and even John had to chuckle.

'I don't have to be told when I am not wanted. I think that I will head home too.' Victor also stood up. 'Thank you for the hospitality John. It has been quite a couple of days.'

'Oh you don't really have to go do you? I was hoping that we might have gone for a drive somewhere,' Mary pouted. 'You are welcome to stay as long as you like, isn't he Dad?' She turned to her father with a pleading look.

'Of course he is, but I am sure that he knows that,' John said in a matter of fact voice.

'Thanks, but I really think that I should be getting back. For one thing, I want to catch this old guy who is supposedly restoring my bed for me.'

'Your bed? What on earth do you mean?' Mary asked, intrigued.

So he explained.

'A genuine four-poster, I should love to see that.'

'Maybe you can if Josh ever manages to finish it. I am sure that Rome was built in a far shorter time than this guy is taking.'

'I have never slept in a four-poster bed,' Mary said rather wistfully. 'I wonder what it would be like?'

'The same as sleeping in an ordinary bed I'd imagine,' her father said drily. 'You cannot see anything different with your eyes closed.'

'Oh Dad, where is your sense of romance?'

'I think that I am getting a little too old for that sort of stuff,' John replied. 'Anyhow, I think that you had better let these boys go if they have to. I am sure that you will get to see Victor's bed at some time or other.'

'Oh, I hope so Dad. I sincerely hope so,' Mary replied with a wicked grin at Victor, who could feel the colour rushing to his cheeks again. She reached up and kissed him on the cheek.

'Mary Collins! Have you no shame girl?' her father asked her in an embarrassed tone.

Jason looked at the three of them. 'I think that I am in the way here. What about you Victor? Are you going to stay a tad longer?' He also was grinning.

'I am out of here. I will see you all later,' Victor said as he strode towards the door with the sound of Mary's laughter ringing loudly in his ears.

Chapter Eleven

Victor was almost home when his mobile phone rang. 'Hey Victor, this is Harley. You are not going to believe this: I have just had a call from Cassidy. He suggests that I have a serious rethink about selling my horses. Apparently the two of them are entered for a couple of good races. The Chester Vase and the Lingfield Derby trial no less. They are also both down to run at Newmarket in mid-April as well.'

'Right, it is going to be interesting to see what happens to them. If Oxford were running true to form, I would not be putting any money on them at Newmarket. How long are you going to stay anyway? I forgot to ask you the other day.'

'I am due to fly back again tomorrow. Have you got that list that his daughter was going to send us?'

'No not yet. It should be there when I get home. I am still on my way back from Cheltenham,' Victor explained. His friend's laugh came ringing through the phone.

'Been celebrating have we? I saw the race on TV. To be perfectly honest I thought that Vixen had you beaten. It was a nice win though. Right now, to get back to this list. I have spoken to a guy at the Jockey Club. He is some kind of investigator for them. He wants you to fax him the list when you get it. He has promised me that he will look into things. He thinks that there is enough evidence to warrant him becoming involved. Also, do you think that you can go and see Oxford's wife?'

Victor thought it over carefully for a moment or two and then said, 'I could most likely get up there tomorrow. I don't know that we will get anything of use out of her though.'

'Just see what you can find out. The more ammo that we have on this guy the better. By the way, the guy at the Jockey Club, his name is Martin Buckingham. He will be expecting you to get in touch with him.'

'Ok, whatever I find out I will pass on to him. Incidentally John Collins asked me about Delmore. When precisely is he due to have a run?'

'That thing!' Harley snorted in disgust. 'You would not read about it! The very first time that Jenkins puts him to a full gallop this morning, the bloody nag goes and breaks down. It will be a while yet before he is fit to race. Who'd be a horse owner?' Victor made sympathetic noises and waited patiently for his friend to continue. 'Another thing, that lad Billy, he is now on my payroll too. He certainly knows his way around a computer. A bright kid that one, he could go a long way. Right, I will touch base with you after I get back to the States. What are you going to do with that horse of yours that won yesterday?'

'Pride of Tintagel will be running in the Grand National,' Victor stated proudly. 'Will you be here to see the race?'

'When is it? A couple of weeks isn't it? I don't really know. Now, what about that other one that you are having all the trouble with? The one that you bought from Ambrose, Arcadian something?'

'Arcadian Steel. We have finally found someone who can stay on him long enough to be able to ride him. That is one super horse Harley. I am going to win the Derby with him.' The American laughed at his friend's obvious enthusiasm. 'That is what I thought about Delmore. Anyway, I hope that you have better luck than I am having at the moment.' He then hung up.

Victor sat there for a few minutes, his imagination fired up. In his mind he could see his horse crossing the line first at Epsom and Mary jumping up and down with excitement.

Mary Collins! She had made it more than obvious that she wanted to go to bed with him. I suppose that a lot of people would think me a fool for refusing, he mused to himself. It still did not feel right with him. Not for the time being anyhow. After all it was only four months since Amanda had died. Still, if Mary was the right kind of girl for him, he knew that she would be prepared to wait. For all that he knew she could be testing him out, trying his loyalty. Maybe if he did agree to go to bed with her, then she might end the relationship. Whatever the outcome, nothing was going to happen as yet as far as he was concerned. He decided that he should get home. Turning the ignition key, the engine sprang into life and he pulled back onto the motorway.

About half an hour later, Victor pulled up outside the house.

Parking the car he went inside and made his way to the kitchen. Seated at the stone table were Josh and Mrs Humber, deep in conversation. They stopped abruptly at his entrance. Mrs Humber was the first to speak. 'Why good morning Sir. Josh and me were just having a nice cup of tea. Just made it is, would you like one or would you prefer coffee? The Victoria sponge is just out of the oven too, can I get you a slice of that?' She got to her feet and bustled over to the range where the teapot was keeping warm.

'I will just have the tea, thank you Mrs Humber,' Victor said then seeing the crestfallen look on his housekeeper's face, corrected himself. 'Well, perhaps just a small slice of your sponge, it smells delicious.' She brightened up at once and proceeded to cut him a fairly large portion.

Taking both the tea and cake from her, he sat down at the table. He swallowed a mouthful of the hot liquid and then looked across at the old man.

'How is that old bed coming along Josh? Is there any sign of it being finished yet?' The other looked at him and his well-lined face creased into a huge grin. Victor was certain that there was another tooth missing from his mouth since the last time that he had seen him. It was a face that only a mother could love as the saying went.

'If ee plaise sur, I axed me dattur to fex some clath an 'tould 'er to fex some ribands from Trura. She worked 'ard all yesterday an' she finishes a lettle afore mednight. Fefteen pound she do pay fer the ribands,' Josh told him. Victor took a couple of moments to figure out what the Cornishman had said to him and then spoke.

'Don't worry, I will make sure that your daughter is not out of pocket. Now let's go and see what you have done to this bed.'

'Do you mind if I come up as well sir? I would love to see it all fixed up proper like.' Mrs Humber asked. Victor nodded and the three of them made their way upstairs to the main bedroom. Victor threw open the door and then stood there in amazement. Instead of the old broken-down piece of furniture that he had left, he found himself gazing at a truly majestic bed. The four posts had been stripped back and now revealed highly polished, intricately carved, mahogany uprights. The headboard too, he discovered, was made of the same magnificent timber. Its cloth centrepiece had been replaced and freshly padded. The six curtains that made up the canopy were of a floral design and tied back by lace ribbons. The old, moth-eaten quilt had been replaced by a new one, the cover of which was made from the same material as the curtains. Four, white, lace-frilled cushions completed the setting and these had been carefully placed along the front of the pillows.

'I simply can't believe that we are looking at the same bed.' Victor was truly astonished. Mrs Humber too held her hands clasped to her ample bosom and gasped.

'If I hadn't seen it myself, I would not have believed it.'

'Josh, how you did this I don't know. It's almost like magic,' Victor said.

'Magic! I worked to a bal weth a man coal'd Jeremiah Fiddick an' 'e knowed everything about magic and witchery. Hes wife, Jinny, she wor a witch right nuff and give'e no paice, that's sortin sure. She used ter feed 'e roots so 'e cudn chow nor cudn clunky. 'e got so bad 'e almost come to commithin susanside. I have no trek with magic, tes naught to do wi' me.' Josh made the sign of the cross across his chest. Even Mrs Humber looked a trifle bemused at this mouthful from the Cornishman.

Victor walked around the bed, prodding the quilt and running his hands up and down the highly polished posts. 'This is really amazing. I am finding it hard to believe that it is actually the same bed. Josh, you are indeed a craftsman and should be proud of yourself. Your daughter too.' He put his hand in his pocket and pulled out his wallet. Taking out five £50 notes, he thrust them into the old man's eager hands. Josh very slowly counted them twice and his face creased into a huge toothy grin once more. Carefully folding the notes in half he then placed them in his pocket and raised a finger to touch his forelock. 'Thank ee kindly sur.'

Victor sat on the bed and bounced on it a couple of times, still trying to come to terms with the almost unbelievable transformation that the old man had wrought in the bedroom.

Josh looked at him and then said, 'If that be all, sur, I thought to be getting down to the kiddlywink fur some starry-gazey pie an taaties fur denar. Then some apple pie with craim an' trikel. Mebbee a bottul or tow o' porter. Thank ee, kindly sur.'

'Mrs Humber, what on earth is "starry-gazey" pie?' The woman gave a hearty laugh and slapped her thigh. 'That's one of my better dishes. It is a pie made from whole pilchards that you cook with their heads pointing out of the crust. I think that it originally came from

Mousehole, which was a pilchard-fishing village. I bake it every Thursday and Friday for the inn. It is very popular amongst the older regulars, I believe,' she said modestly.

Victor could only shake his head in disbelief. It was amazing that he knew so little about the county and its customs. He had only understood about half of what Josh had been saying. He knew that a kiddlywink was the old Cornish name for a pub. He had learnt this from the Poldark books by Winston Graham that he had read. But the longer that Josh spoke, the broader his dialect seemed to become. Standing up once more, he shook hands with the man and asked Mrs Humber to show him out.

After the two of them had left the room, Victor turned his attention once more to the bed. The old man had certainly done a wonderful job and it had been worth the wait. He pulled the quilt back and was pleasantly surprised to find that the bed even had new sheets on it. Well, no more sleeping on the couch for me, he thought to himself. He then remembered that he had not checked for any mail as he came in. He went back downstairs to see if any had arrived. Mrs Humber had evidently collected it and placed it on the small table in the lounge for him. There were a couple of items of junk mail. Amazingly, he had only been here for a short while but already he was being plagued. There was also a thick manila envelope with a Newbury postmark among the letters. He opened this first. Inside the envelope there were half a dozen or so sheets of paper. He unfolded them and started to read.

Lilly had certainly been very thorough. Each page had the names of two horses on it and listed when they had arrived at the stable, when they had raced and finally when they had been sold. In each case the same man, a Henri Duvall, had bought them. In all there were fourteen horses listed and between them they had only won nine races. Victor read the details through again; there were no names that he was familiar with, but then that was not surprising. He had been out of touch with the English racing scene for so long now. He decided that the guy from the Jockey Club that Harley had spoken of would most likely be in a better position than he was to chase up the details. He at least would have access to all the race results from the Continent.

Just then Mrs Humber came back into the room. 'Has Josh left? I must admit that I only understand a fraction of what he was saying.

He really did make an excellent job of that bed though; I'll give him that. I cannot credit that I am looking at the same piece of furniture.'

'In all my time here, I have never seen it looking so grand. His daughter did a good job on the curtains and all. No, a true Cornishman is our Josh. I have lived here some thirty years but even I have trouble in catching all that he says at times. He has a good heart though and would never cheat you.'

'I must say that it will be nice not having to sleep on the couch any more,' said Victor with a laugh. 'Though what I shall do with that bed when I leave here, I have no idea. No doubt I shall think of something.'

'Oh, are you not staying then, sir?' Mrs Humber looked slightly startled. 'I thought that you would be here for quite some time. It does seem a shame to go to all that trouble if you intend to leave.'

'Oh, it won't be for some months yet. In fact, I have no plans at all for the future. I will be here for the Derby for sure and then things are in the lap of the gods. Don't you worry Mrs Humber, you will have a job here for quite some time yet. By the way, I don't know whether you follow the horses, but my fellow looks to have a good chance in the Derby. We now have a jockey for him, a guy called Jason Carter. Do you know of him at all?'

'Jason Carter?' she repeated. 'There's folk around here that think he is a toadman, that one.' The woman crossed herself as she spoke.

'A toadman? What the devil is that, may I ask?' Victor said, grinning.

'He has power over horses because of the toad. Devil's work, that's what it is and all.' By now Victor was truly intrigued and pressed his housekeeper to explain herself. Reluctantly, she finally relented and told him. 'It's said that you get a toad and stake it to an ant hill. You leave it until the ants have stripped the flesh from the bones, then you throw the bones in the river. One bone will break away from the rest and travel upstream. If a man was able to catch this bone then the very possession of it would give him power over horses. They do say in the village that Jason is one such man. Nothing but bad luck can come of doing business with a toadman.'

'I have heard about men called horse whisperers that have a secret language which gives them control over horses, bit I must admit that a toadman is quite a new one on me. Mrs Humber you are truly a mine of information. A strange thing though, apart from Mary, Jason Carter seems to be the only person at present who is able to handle

161

my horse. I suppose that if one had the time to investigate it then Cornwall would be full of old legends and myths like that. Most likely a lot of stories of this nature would have been brought over by the Celts. The next time that I see Jason I must ask him if he has any toad bones in his possession.'

'There's a lot of folk in these parts that put a great store in these old tales. I know of one farmer in the next village who always puts his bull to his cows in front of a white wall. Most of his herd is white,' Mrs Humber said defiantly.

Victor could not control himself at this gem of information and burst out laughing. 'Mrs Humber you are priceless! I only wish that I had more time to stand and chat with you but I must get on and do some work. I think too that I had better pay you now as I am not exactly sure when I shall be back. 'So saying, he pulled out his wallet again and gave her some money.

Mrs Humber did not bother to count it but stuck it in her apron pocket. 'I have a nice piece of baked gammon for your lunch as I thought that you might like cold cuts for your supper. I hope that suits you?'

'You really do spoil me. I have no complaints whatsoever about your cooking. It is always so masterful.' Leaving her flushed at his praise, Victor went into the lounge to read the rest of his mail.

Later that day, he finally tracked down Martin Buckingham and relayed to him what was in the sheets that he had received from Lilly. Promising to chase up the details with his counterpart in France, Buckingham rang off. For a while Victor sat by the fire and tried to figure out his next move. He was not certain what kind of reception he would receive from Mrs Oxford. Lilly had told him that she would willingly help. But he was not so sure. Although she obviously did not agree with what her husband was doing, Mrs Oxford may not feel that she could betray him. Eventually he decided to telephone her. When she answered his call, he asked if he might come and visit her. After explaining the reason she was silent for a moment. Sensing her hesitation and obvious reluctance, Victor repeated what he had told her daughter: if she would help him then he would make certain that Jack was taken care of. That was, if his father was not in a position to do so himself. This guarantee finally persuaded her and she agreed to see him the next day. Securing directions from her as to how to get there, he then hung up. Well Victor old son, maybe Naomi's prediction of him becoming a private eye was not so far fetched after all, he thought to himself. Then, taking a book from the small bookcase, he settled down to have a read before lunch, which he could already smell, thanks to Mrs Humber.

Victor awoke early the next morning and for a brief moment could not remember where he was. Then he realised that he was in the four-poster bed. His sleep that night had been perfect and now he felt relaxed and ready to take on the whole world. He couldn't believe how comfortable the bed was in spite of its age and for a short while he merely lay there enjoying the ambience. After a while he decided somewhat reluctantly that he simply had to get up. He looked out of the window towards the sea. The sky was a pale azure blue with a few puffy, white clouds slowly making their way across it. It looked as though it was going to be one of those glorious spring mornings. He breakfasted heartily on the remains of the gammon and three free-range eggs, washed down by several cups of freshly brewed coffee. After checking his map, nine o'clock saw him heading up the A30 once more to Exeter, where he linked up with the motorway and headed towards Cheltenham yet again.

Victor made excellent time and, as he drove into Bourton-on-the-Water, he discovered that he was too early for his appointment with Mrs Oxford. He parked the car in the car park and set off on foot to have a look around the village. As he strolled down the narrow path that led from the car park to the village itself, Victor wondered how it would compare to the famed Castle Combe. That village's houses were built from honey-coloured Cotswold stone. He had been there as most tourists had after it achieved fame as England's prettiest village and the site for Rex Harrison's movie version of *Doctor Doolittle*. He had been a trifle disappointed with what he had found there.

Mrs Humber had told him that she thought that Bourton was far prettier, when he had mentioned that he was making the trip here today. He was anxious to see if her statement was correct. The path suddenly brought him into the main street and he immediately agreed with his housekeeper. The centre of the village was indeed a postcard picture. The river, which he later learnt was the Windrush, gently flowed beneath two well-weathered stone bridges, right through the middle. The left-hand bank consisted of a broad expanse of grass that separated the river from the road, from which graceful willow trees gently dipped their branches towards the water. He was astonished to find that the river actually flowed alongside the very foundations of the stone cottages. He crossed the bridge to the Old New Inn and discovered that the whole village had been reconstructed in miniature in its gardens. Mrs Humber had also told him that one of the main attractions of the place was Birdland. This had been built in the grounds of a Tudor manor and Victor made a mental note that he would have to visit there when he had more time. The aromatic smell of fish and chips floated through and assailed his nostrils. Realising that it was indeed lunch-time, he went into the shop and bought a portion, which he ate with relish as he made his way back to the car park. Mrs Oxford lived a ten-minute drive out of the village towards Stow-on-the-Wold. Finishing his lunch as reached the car, Victor was soon on his way again.

He found the cottage easily enough and, after pulling off the road and parking on the grass verge, he unlatched the gate and walked up the path. As he approached, the door opened and a tall, willowy blonde stood there looking at him. Victor adjudged her to be in her mid to late forties. He held out his hand. 'Mrs Oxford? I am Victor Barnes.' She gazed at him coolly for a moment and then took his hand and shook it lightly.

'Well then, you had better come in Mr Barnes.' She stepped aside to allow him to enter. 'Go straight ahead into the parlour.'

'My that is a word that I haven't heard in a long time and do please call me Victor. Mr Barnes sounds so formal.'

'Well, you are not exactly here on a social call, now are you Mr Barnes?' Victor looked suitably contrite. 'I am sorry, this cannot be very easy for you.'

'It's not everyday that someone rings you up and asks you to tell them how your husband has been doping horses,' she remarked with a touch of sarcasm.

Victor walked through to the parlour and found himself to be in a room that was small, but tastefully furnished with period reproductions.

Motioning for him to take a seat, Mrs Oxford bent down and turned off the gas fire. 'I like to light it just to take the chill off the room but it is too expensive to keep on too long,' she said. 'It really is quite mild today don't you think?'

He nodded in agreement. 'Would you like some coffee? I am afraid that I have nothing stronger that I can offer you.'

'No, coffee would be most welcome, thank you.' She moved across to a table, on which stood a tray containing cups, a coffee-pot and a milk jug. Pouring out two cups she then picked up the milk jug. 'Drat it, I forgot the cream. I won't be a moment.' Before he could utter a protest she had left the room, returning a few minutes later with another jug and a plate of biscuits. Adding some cream to the coffee she then handed the cup to him. He took it without a word and declined a biscuit with a shake of his head.

'I have just had some fish and chips in the village,' he explained. Taking a mouthful of coffee, he swallowed it and sat back in his chair.

'Mr Barnes, what exactly are you hoping to achieve by your coming here today?'

Victor remained silent for a moment and then looking the woman straight in the eye said quietly, 'I am trying to discover how a friend of mine is being cheated by your husband. Your daughter Lilly said that I should talk to you because you did not approve of the way that he was conducting his business. You did not like the way that he was making money out of people who trusted him. Now, if you are able to help me at all, I shall indeed be very grateful.'

She looked at him for a moment and then said bluntly. 'If what I tell you results in my husband being charged by the police or losing his stable and subsequently his income, how are you going to look after my son? To me he is the most important thing in my life at the moment.'

'Where is Jack by the way?' Victor asked her.

'I asked the nurse to take him for a walk. The weather has not been very good here lately, not good enough for him to go out, anyway. As it was a nice fine day and with you coming here as well, I thought that it would be the ideal time for him to go out. I told the nurse to take her time, it is not easy trying to push a wheelchair along these roads.'

Victor leant forward in his chair and once again looked her straight in the eye. 'Mrs Oxford, if you can help us then I promise you that your son will not suffer. We can either make you a cash payment or, better still, get Jack into some place where he can be looked after properly. If that isn't what you want, then you tell me and I will do whatever it takes.'

'Of course, if my husband does have to give up his stables for whatever reason whatsoever, then Lilly would also be out of a job. We have often talked about setting ourselves up in business; she has a great talent for designing clothes. If you promise me that you will help her set that up, then I will give you all the help that I can.'

'It's a deal. I can't ask fairer than that. You would need to tell what exactly it is that you need in order to do this, of course. I have to be honest, dressmaking is not really my calling. But between us, Harley and I would do whatever is needed. You have my word on that Mrs Oxford.'

The woman gave a delicious, tinkling laugh at his words. 'Ok Victor, I suggest that we start again.' She held out her hand to him. 'My name is Jennifer. Lilly phoned me and told me about the pair of you. She seemed quite happy to trust you but I just wanted to make sure. She can easily be swayed but now that I have met you for myself, I find that I share her assessment of you. I don't know that I can really help you with anything that would stand up in court but I will tell you the little that I know.'

Mrs Oxford then went on to explain that her husband, John Cassidy and Henri Duvall had formed a partnership to race horses on the Continent. Various horses that came through his stable were selected to appear to be of little or no consequence as potential winners. Colin usually picked animals that belonged to owners such as Harley, who spent a lot of their time out of the country, or owners who, only raced as a hobby. The latter usually did not know too much about the racing game. The beasts that he selected were drugged so they did not perform up to expectations. Colin would then approach the owner and suggest that the horse should be sold and would offer to do the deal for them. He used to say that he would not accept a commission for the sale as he felt that he owed the owner something for not being able to train the horse up to expectations.'

'What I don't understand is why people would bring their horses to Colin in the first place? If he had such a poor record, as a trainer I mean?'

'Ah but that is where he was so clever. He is in fact a very good trainer and he manages to produce quite a lot of winners every season. He would never dare try his tricks with the more knowledge-able of his customers. He was very careful indeed in the way that he selected his marks. He used to do a lot of homework on each owner before he attempted anything. Every now and again of course he might stop one of his bigger clients' horses simply to get a better price on it the next time that it ran. With that scam it was merely the old trick of keeping a horse away from water for a couple of days, then letting him drink his fill just before the race. No matter how good the horse is, there is no way it is going to run at its best with a couple of gallons of water sloshing around in its stomach,' Jennifer explained. 'I also know that he was looking at the idea of steroid implants in order to improve a horse's performance but I don't know how far he went with that idea.'

'But he doesn't stop all the other horses just to sell them does he? I have been told that some, like Harley's for instance, he enters for top-class races and then cleans up on the ante-post odds. The trouble is that I don't know how we are going to prove any of this. At the moment all the evidence is circumstantial and hearsay. About the only thing that we can prove for a fact is that Colin ran Harley's two and he has never declared them to him as being winners.'

'Another of his tricks is to inject a horse with vitamins, straight into its bloodstream. That is almost impossible to detect without knowing exactly what it is you are looking for. He did that with a horse called Arson last year at Ascot but again there is no proof. Lilly told me about it because she actually saw him do it.'

'I will pass all this on to the guy at the Jockey Club, he might have some idea what we can do about it.' Victor stood up. 'I want to thank you for all your help, Jennifer. I will give you my mobile number so if you happen to think of anything else, you might give me a ring.' He shook her hand and followed her out to the front door. Thanking her once again he left the cottage and made his way back to the car.

Before he started the engine, Victor tried to get hold of Buckingham but was told by his office that he would not be in till the following day. Hanging up, he started the car and slowly drove off. Just as he rounded the bend he saw a woman pushing a lad in a wheelchair towards him. Obviously it was Jack. For a brief moment he was tempted to stop and make himself known. He then thought better of it, it would achieve nothing, and so once past the couple he accelerated and headed back towards Cheltenham and the motorway home.

Victor had just arrived back at the house when his phone rang. It was Mary. 'I am riding in a point to point at Buckfastleigh tomorrow. I thought that you might like to come and cheer me on.'

'Why, are you in need of moral support then?'

'No, I am not but there is a party after the meet and I have been invited. My invitation also extends to a guest and I thought that you might be interested in going with me. Then on Sunday I thought that you might like to take me on a picnic to Dartmeet. I bet that you haven't been on one since you arrived?'

'The weather has not really been the best for picnics. I take it then that this party must also include accommodation for the night?'

'Why, of course. These things usually go on until the wee small hours of the morning but you don't have to worry about your reputation. I have asked then to put you up in a tent in the garden. See you tomorrow.' Mary hung up leaving Victor with the sound of her mischievous laugh ringing in his ears. With a wry smile he put the phone down and went into the kitchen in search of something to eat.

The next morning Victor awoke to find the weather a complete contrast to the previous day. Rain lashed at his window and the sky was a dull leaden colour. The wind too was strong and as he sat in the kitchen, he could hear the branches of the oak tree thudding against the roof. The day did not improve, either, as Mary came a disappointing sixth in her first race and failed to even complete the course in the next, her horse refusing at the eighth hurdle. So it was a somewhat disconsolate being that joined him in the bar after the race. Without a word, he placed a glass of white wine down in front of her.

'I am glad that Dad wasn't here to see me ride today.' She took a sip of her wine. 'I rode a shit of a race in the first and then to really finish me off, that bugger refused to jump. Now I am cold and miserable.'

'Well then, the party should cheer you up,' Victor said.

'Would you mind very much if we didn't go? I just don't feel in the party mood any more. Judging by the look of the weather, our picnic is going to be off tomorrow too. It is no fun sitting on soggy grass.'

'Maybe it is just as well seeing the mood that you are in.' He smiled at her. 'I was talking to a guy while I was waiting for you to get changed. He told me that the River Dart has something of a grisly reputation. Apparently at least one person is drowned in it every year. The people living near it cannot settle properly until they hear the news that the river has claimed its annual victim.'

Mary stared at him for a while and then said slowly, 'You must be a great person to have on side at a trivia night. You seem to come up with the strangest information.'

Chapter Eleven

'I will take that as a compliment. Now if you don't want to go to the party would you like to go out to dinner somewhere? We could go into Plymouth or Exeter. They are both about the same distance from here I think.'

She was quiet for a while and then looking at him said softly. 'How about going to your place? You keep telling us all what a great house it is but, as yet, I haven't been invited to see it.'

'If that is really what you want to do. I suppose that I could whip up a beef stroganoff or something, that is if the shops are still open.'

'Don't tell me that you cook as well?'

'I have done my fair share of dabbling in the kitchen, although since Mrs Humber started working for me, I haven't needed to,' he replied somewhat modestly.

Mary finished her drink in one gulp and grabbed him by the arm. 'Let's go Mr Epicure, I have suddenly developed a huge appetite.'

Later that evening they were both seated in the lounge in front of a huge log fire. The wind had dropped but it was still pouring with rain. However, they both felt warm and snug in the protection of the lounge. Victor got up and poured them another cognac each. As she took hers, Mary looked at him. 'You know, that really was a wonderful meal, I am impressed. That baked Alaska was superb. That is one thing that I have never been able to figure out. I mean, whoever heard of cooking ice cream in the oven and it not melting? You are very lucky that it is not a leap year this year. After a meal like that it would be almost impossible to refrain from proposing.'

'Even if it was, there is no guarantee that you would hear the answer that you were hoping for,' he said to her gently.

'Maybe not, but I can be very patient when I want to be. If there is enough at stake.'

'I will have to make a note of that,' he replied with a laugh.

'I am glad that we decided not to go to that party, it is so very much nicer here on our own.' Mary took the brandy balloon from his hand and placed it on the table with her own. Reaching out, she put her arms around his neck and pulled him towards her. Their lips met.

Five minutes later he struggled to his feet again after gently unlocking their arms. 'I think that I had better go and get your room ready young lady,' he said a little huskily. 'I will make your day for you. You can have the four-poster tonight.'

'I would far rather have you,' she said, smiling at him coyly.

169

'Not tonight, Mary Collins. Not tonight.'

The next morning Victor was awoken by the arrival of Mrs Humber. She came marching into the lounge and let out an exclamation of surprise at seeing him lying on the couch. 'Why, Mr Barnes, I thought that I would find you sleeping in your nice new bed. Is there something amiss with it? I will get that Josh Penhalon back here right smartly, I can tell you. You paid him good money to fix it.'

He explained quickly that there was no need and no cause for alarm. 'Miss Collins spent the night here as it was too late and too wet to drive back to Milverton last night. I think that I have mentioned her before, haven't I? She is the lady who rode my horse.'

'You do not have to explain to me sir, 'tis none of my business what you do in your own house. Would you like me to take the young lady up a nice cup of tea? I am sure that she would like one.'

Victor smiled to himself; evidently Mrs Humber could not wait to have a look at his houseguest. 'That is very kind of you Mrs Humber. I am sure that she will appreciate it.'

'Right then, I'll take it up directly. So there will be two for breakfast then this morning then? 'Tis nice to see you have some company. This is a big house and it can get lonely when you are on your own. I know that when Mr Humber, God rest his soul, passed away, it took a long time to get used to being here on my own. But look at me chattering away. I will be off and see to your breakfasts.' She then bustled out of the room, leaving Victor alone with his thoughts. He lay on the couch for another five minutes then decided that he should get up and dressed quickly.

Some twenty minutes later he was at the kitchen table with Mary. Mrs Humber had taken no notice of her request for toast and coffee but placed before her a full English breakfast. She gaped at the eggs, bacon, sausage mushrooms and tomatoes. 'Good God Victor! Do you eat like this every day?' she exclaimed.

He shook his head and indicated his housekeeper. 'Only on days when she is here. She says that you should start the day right and then it doesn't matter if you happen to miss a meal,' he whispered.

Having served them their coffee, Mrs Humber said the she would make a start upstairs. After collecting her mop and duster, she left them to finish their meal. They tucked into their food with a relish. Finishing his off, Victor was about to pour himself another cup of coffee, when he stopped. He looked at Mary. 'What is that noise? Can you hear it?' She nodded and listened for a minute and then went out into the passage. She returned a few seconds later giggling into her hands. 'It is your housekeeper. Believe it or not but she is singing!'

Victor too went out into the passage and listened intently. Upon his return he looked at Mary and laughed. 'Do you know what it is she is singing Mary? You certainly must have made a huge impression on her.'

She shook her head.

'"Love Is In the Air".'

They both looked at each other for a moment and then simultaneously burst into fits of laughter. Eventually they got control of themselves once more.

Mary put her arms around his waist and said quietly, 'You see, even your housekeeper thinks that we are meant for each other.'

He waited for a moment and then gently took her arms away and said, 'Let's not rush things, eh? Now where would you like to go today? It looks as though the rain has cleared up and we could be in for a fine day.'

'You certainly know how to make a girl feel wanted,' she said petulantly. 'Ok, ok' I promise that I won't say any more. I tell you what, let's go to Land's End and then I can throw myself off the cliffs.'

Victor laughed and gave her a hug. 'We don't have to drive all the way to Land's End for you to do that, we are about a twenty-minute walk to the cliffs here. But seriously, though, Lands End sounds like a great idea. I believe that there is a spectacular sound and light show that has been built there since I was there last. You had better give your father a ring though and let him know where you are. He will be getting worried about you.'

Mary looked at him coyly and gave him a playful poke in the ribs. 'He already knows where I am. I told him that I was going to beard the lion in his den. You should give him a ring and see if Jason has sorted anything out with the Jockey Club yet.'

'Ah yes, Jason. With everything else going on I had forgotten about him. I wonder how he did at Wolverhampton last night. What did your father say when you told him that you were coming here?'

'What could he say? In case you haven't noticed, Victor, I am a big girl now. Anyway, he seems to have some notion that you are related to someone call Galahad.'

Victor was about to come back with some sharp retort but thought better of it and instead picked up his phone and dialled. He spoke for a few minutes and then offered the phone to Mary but she shook her head. He spoke into the phone for a short while longer and then rang off. He turned to her excitedly. 'Apparently Jason has arranged a trial for Tuesday at Bath. Then, depending on the outcome of that, Samson runs in a maiden at Doncaster on Thursday. Well, after this week I should know whether or not I have a possible runner in the Derby. Come on Mary, let's go to Land's End.'

By the time that they reached their destination, the morning had turned into another perfect spring day. In spite of this, they were both amazed at the strength of the wind that blew across the tops of the cliffs. They stood there at the very edge of the country and stared out at the sea. The wind was so strong that they had to cling to each other for support as they stood and watched the huge breakers crash over the jagged rocks below. Showers of spray were sent dancing skyward causing an unusual effect of multiple rainbows reflecting in the sun's rays.

'I suppose that it would be nice here when it is calm, but I think that it is far more majestic when the sea is like this, don't you?' Mary had to shout for him to hear above the roar of the wind. He looked down at the boiling white cauldrons of foam and nodded. They stood there for a few minutes longer admiring the view, then Victor pointed to the cluster of buildings that housed the Last Labyrinth, the electronic theatre that depicted the growth of Cornwall, the legends and the history that they had travelled to see. With one last look at the signpost that showed Australia to be a mere 12,000 miles away, they managed to make their way to the protective calm of the resort's attractions.

The two of them spent a good couple of hours exploring the varied exhibits that were housed there. They then decided that they would have dinner in Polperro. So for the rest of the afternoon they became a couple of tourists. They drove to Mousehole, Penzance, Falmouth and St Austell before making their way to Polperro. Victor had forgotten that cars were banned from the village, apart from those of the residents, so he had to do a sudden U-turn into the car park as he came to the no vehicle zone.

Parking the car they made their way down to the quay, stopping every few yards to watch the stream that flowed through the village splashing its way past the many guesthouses that lined the main street. After lazily drifting around the many souvenir shops, mostly deserted now but always a hive of activity in the holiday season, they finally settled on the Nelson for their final meal of the day. Later on that evening, having eaten their fill of another wonderful meal, they slowly made their way back up the hill to the car park. As they got back in the car they sat for a moment looking at the star-filled sky.

Mary turned to Victor. 'You know, Victor, with all that money that you won, do you realise that you could spend the rest of your life doing things like we did today?'

'Ah yes, but where would the challenge be if I settled for that?'

'Marry me and you would have all the challenge that you would ever need.'

'I see, so it is just my money that you are after?'

'Of course. Surely you didn't think that it was you that I was interested in did you?' she replied and gave him another of her wicked grins. 'Once we were married for say six months I'd ask you for a divorce and marry a much younger man.'

'I think that we had better get off home don't you?'

Early on Tuesday morning, the two of them, Mary having stayed with Victor, saying that there was no point in him driving her up there twice, left the house and made their way to Bath. When they arrived at the racecourse they found that John had beaten them there. He was waiting for Jason to arrive so that they could start the trial. He made no comment about Mary having stayed with Victor beyond asking her whether having curtains around the bed made her sleep better. 'Who slept?' she said much to Victor's dismay but her father just laughed. 'Don't you worry now Victor, I left my shotgun at home.'

'You two are as bad as each other,' Victor muttered. He was spared any more embarrassment by the deep-throated roar of a powerful engine and Samson's jockey drove up in his Maserati. Jason went off to change into his riding silks. Victor did not think that really necessary as he only had to prove to the officials present that Arcadian Steel was a changed horse and able to race. John had brought another box with two of his other horses with him so that they could simulate a genuine race. Eventually Jason appeared and, quickly mounting Samson, rode him around to the back of the stalls. Urging him forward, the horse trotted into his stall without any fuss at all. They released the gates and let the horses canter a couple of furlongs before bringing them back. They repeated the manoeuvre three times before the Jockey Club officials finally gave their approval for the horse to race. Victor hugged Mary and shook both John and Jason's hand vigorously before finally going up and patting his horse on the neck. He then gave the horse a couple of carrots and turned to face the others. 'People, we have a Derby runner, now all that we have to do is to win the race.'

'Victor, you are like a little boy who has just discovered Father Christmas for the very first time,' Mary said laughingly.

'Oh come now, Mary. That is hardly fair. It is not everyone that can own a horse that is good enough to run in the Derby. He has every right to feel proud. I know that I would were I in his shoes,' her father protested strongly.

'I agree with John here, Victor has every right to feel that way. There is just one thing though, what have you done to upset Colin Oxford? My, but he hates you, man,' Jason drawled lazily.

Startled, Victor looked at him as though seeing him for the first time. 'I am so sorry Jason but with all the excitement here I forgot to ask. How did you get on on Saturday night at Wolverhampton? Did you ride any winners?'

'No, it wasn't a good night at all I am afraid to admit. Neither of the two horses appeared to have any real go in them. But to get back to Oxford, he says that I shouldn't trust you, that you were a man that I should be wary of. A troublemaker in fact.'

'So you told him that you were going to ride Samson for me, did you?'

'I mentioned it. I am sorry, was it supposed to be a secret?'

'It doesn't matter. He is most likely upset because he thought that he had a chance of training it. I never got back to him about it.'

'Well, I have to go and get changed.' Jason shook his hand again and said, 'See you at Doncaster then. At least I know that I shall have a better ride than I did at Wolverhampton.' He then strode off in the direction of the changing rooms.

Mary turned to her father. 'Are you going home Dad?' Her father looked at her a trifle warily not knowing what to expect. 'I had intended to, why, where do you want to go?'

'Well I thought that as long as we were in Bath, we could have lunch at Sally Lunn's. You know how much I love those buns.'

'You and Victor go. I think that I had better get home with the horses.'

Victor looked at her, puzzled. 'Where or what is Sally Lunn's?'

She stared at him in amazement, as though she couldn't believe her ears. 'I thought that you said you lived in Bristol?'

'So I did but that doesn't mean that I know Bath,' he answered.

'Sally Lunn's is the oldest house in Bath and they make these marvellous buns which you can have either as a sweet or savoury dish. They have been making them since the time of Beau Nash.'

'In that case then, I would imagine that they might have some ready,' Victor stated with a completely straight face.

Chapter Twelve

On the Thursday morning, Victor was awake by five o'clock. His stomach felt a churned-up mess and, deciding that nothing further could be achieved by his staying in bed any longer, he dressed and went downstairs to make some coffee. This was going to be the big test. He had felt nervous when Pride of Tintagel had raced but this was a lot different. He had picked out the horse himself. He had been through the difficult period of trying to find a rider for him and had in fact seen far more of the horse than Pride. Samson had been a real challenge and now, at last, he hoped that he was going to see some rewards for his efforts. If by a fluke he did happen to win the Derby, well, his own financial future was assured anyway but if he won, well... He paced up and down the kitchen sipping his coffee. His whole body felt tense and on edge. He could have done with some of those Valium that his doctor had prescribed after the accident.

Victor suddenly decided to ring Dan and Naomi. It would be around four in the afternoon in Melbourne, he thought as he dialled. It was Naomi who answered his call. Her surprise and pleasure at hearing his voice came through even at that distance. Very briefly he told her what had transpired since the last time that they had spoken. He explained that today was a big day as far as the horse was concerned. Everything hinged on how Samson performed that day. He also told her that Pride was going to run in the National. His exuberance painted quite a vivid picture for Naomi and she promised that she would tell Dan to watch out for the race on cable TV. He said that it was due to run at the beginning of next month. Naomi hesitated slightly before she asked the next question, as she was a little afraid of the answer that she might receive. Taking a deep breath she plunged in, 'When are you thinking of coming home, Victor?'

Although Victor had been expecting and lightly dreading it, the question cut like a knife. His hesitation and obvious reluctance to answer was reply enough for her.

'Well, just as long as you are happy, that is the main thing. I do realise that England is your natural home, but don't forget that you still have a family here who love and cares about you.'

'I haven't forgotten, Naomi, I promise. It is just that things are a little hectic over here at the moment. I have the two horses and then am trying to sort out the mess with Harley as well. At least I seem to be making some headway with that part of things.' His voice became husky and he had to stop talking for a while. He did not want to make a fool of himself.

'Your house is being well looked after. I was over there the other day and the kids are taking real good care of everything. Naturally they asked me if I had heard from you. You must admit that it is a little unsettling for them not knowing when you are likely to be wanting it back.'

'It won't be for at least another three months, Naomi. Even if I were to come back suddenly they would have plenty of time to find something before I moved back in. I owe them that much at least. I suppose that they are hoping that I remain away for some time yet so that they can save more for a deposit on their own place.'

'You can't blame them for that. Now do take care of yourself and let us know if you win today.'

Promising faithfully that he would keep in touch, he hung up. He knew that he should try and eat something but his stomach felt so tied up in knots that he couldn't bring himself even to look at food.

Wrapping himself up warmly, Victor decided that he would take a walk to the cliff tops and try and calm his nerves that way. It was still dark as he made his way past the giant oak trees towards the cliff tops. As he got nearer he could hear the sound of the sea crashing in on the rocks below. With somewhat of a shock he realised that in all the time that he had spent there, he had not yet ventured down to the beach. He had almost taken it for granted but this was not the time to be doing that today. He contented himself with just taking in deep, gulping breaths of the fresh air. He remained there listening to the power of the huge waves as they pounded an invisible shoreline. He stood there for about thirty minutes then slowly made his way back to the house. As he reached it, he found to his surprise that he was a lot calmer. Also, all the fresh air that he had inhaled had sharpened his appetite to the extent that he went in and cooked himself breakfast, which he devoured hungrily. His craving for food now appeased he wrote out a cheque for Mrs Humber and leaving it on the kitchen table went out, locking the door behind him.

Victor had made up his mind earlier that it was too far to drive to Doncaster so he had arranged for a charter plane to fly him from St Mawgan at Newquay to Humberside. He was aware that many race-courses allowed light aircraft to land, but did not want to make an entrance like that so he had picked Humberside. The staff there had told him that they would arrange for a hire car to be waiting for him when he landed.

He was early arriving at St Mawgan airport and was forced to wait while the plane was fuelled and the pilot did his safety check. Eventually he was allowed to board and after getting their clearance from the tower, the plane taxied out onto the runway. As they began to pick up speed, he was beginning to think that this had not been such a great idea. He had never flown in anything smaller than a 727 before and to say that he was a little nervous was an understatement. However, as the plane took off and began its steady climb into the morning sky, his fear quickly evaporated. The pilot circled over Newquay's beautiful beach and followed Watergate Bay before turning inland across Bodmin Moor. The flight across England was uneventful and they made good time, arriving at Humberside some fifteen minutes ahead of schedule. As they landed, Victor arranged with the pilot that he would be leaving around 5.30 and most likely he would have a passenger with him. He had already planned to invite Mary to fly back with him regardless of the outcome of the race. Arcadian Steel was due to run at two o'clock so he reckoned that they should be back at the airport by five easily. The airport staff had been as good as their word and the hire car was waiting for him outside the terminal buildings. Quickly dealing with the formalities, he was soon speeding along the motorway towards Doncaster.

The Doncaster course was a left-handed, flat galloping track ideal for horses such as Arcadian Steel with his big long strides, which was why John had entered him there. He would get a real workout and they could better adjudge his potential.

'Not a track for the faint-hearted. Your horse needs courage and stamina to run there. It will be an ideal hit out for the testing track at Epsom,' John had told him when he had queried why they should come all the way up to Doncaster.

Chapter Twelve

Reaching the course, Victor parked the car and then went in search of the others. They had arranged to 'meet in the bar as usual', 'ideal place for celebrating' Mary had said. When he got there, however, he only saw Jason. Buying two orange juices Victor carried them over to where Jason was already seated. He raised his eyebrows at Victor's choice of drink but asked no questions. The two men sat quietly sipping their drinks, both of them caught up in their own thoughts. Eventually Jason was the first to break the silence.

'Victor, do you mind if I ask you a rather personal question?'

'Not at all, fire away,' he replied though he was not quite prepared for the inquiry that the other fired at him.

'Are you and Mary Collins an item?'

Victor hesitated for a moment trying to come up with an appropriate answer that would satisfy the other.

'You could say that we are good friends.'

'Yes, but you must have had her in the sack a time or two?' Jason persisted. 'I mean after all, a good looking girl like that?'

'Why? Are you interested in her that way, Jason?'

'I just thought that she might be good for a spot of fun but I don't want to come between two if you are serious about her.'

'Mary is a free agent and able to make her own choices,' Victor chose his words carefully. 'Ah, there she is now.' He stood up and waved as she came through the door.

She made her way across the room and then stood looking at the two men. 'You two seem very deep in conversation. What were you doing, discussing your chances today?'

Jason looked across at Victor and then said with a laugh, 'I suppose that you could say that, eh, Victor?'

Victor did not reply but merely grunted.

Mary sat down at the table. 'Isn't anyone going to offer a poor girl a drink then?'

Jason got to his feet. 'My turn I think, what'll it be Mary?' She told him and he wandered off to the bar.

Mary took Victor's hand in hers and gave it a squeeze a couple of times. 'This is it, Victor, the big day. Are you nervous?'

'Why should I be nervous with Super Jock on board?'

Mary looked at him quizzically for a moment.

'Is there something wrong between the pair of you?'

He shook his head.

'No, it's just me being a little stupid I guess.'

'I thought that we were going to be late getting here. The Land Rover got a puncture near Nottingham but luckily Dad was able to fix it pretty quickly. Just as well that he brought Ginger with him, because he kept the horse company while Dad and I fixed the tyre.'

'Ginger? I thought that it was Jimmy who usually accompanied your Dad?'

Mary nodded. 'That's right he usually does but Ginger has been a little morose lately so Dad thought that it might perk him up by coming up here today.'

'What would he have to be unhappy about for goodness sake? From what I have seen of your stable, your dad is a great bloke to work for. He certainly appears to look after his boys well. He treats them like family most of the time.'

'That he does,' Mary agreed, 'but Ginger has been having some problems at home lately and his work has been suffering. Dad has had to pull him over the coals on more than one occasion lately. One day he received a phone call just as he came back from morning exercise and he rushed off without attending to his horse first. That is a cardinal sin as far as my father is concerned, the animals must always come first. So when he did eventually get back to the house, Dad read him the riot act. It is a shame I know but he has to learn. That is one of the reasons that he is an apprentice. Ah here are our drinks.'

Jason arrived back and set two glasses on the table. He looked at his watch and said, 'I had better be off and get changed. I have a ride in the first as well today. There was no point in coming all this way just for one ride.' Bidding them both farewell, he picked up his bag and swaggered off.

Mary and Victor sipped at their drinks and then when they had finished they got up and made their way, arm in arm, down to the stables to see Samson.

Having got as far as the entrance to the stables they had to wait until the security guard had checked with John Collins before they were allowed to proceed any further. The horse was looking absolutely magnificent, his black coat shone like coal and he showed no signs of sweating up. His bright eyes viewed them warily, then he brought his head down and nuzzled Mary's neck. She in turn reached up and fondled his ears. The runners for the first race were being led out and Samson snorted as they filed past.

'Impatient to be out there are we?' Victor laughed. 'Well, your turn will come soon enough, old boy.' He turned to John who was lounging against the door watching them. 'Do you really think that he has a chance of winning today? I can't but help thinking that he is already past the post.'

The older man looked at him and then smiled at his high spirits.

'He has as good a chance as any of them out there today. None of them have raced since last season and there are also a couple, like Samson, who have never raced before. They are unknown quantities of course. The favourite, Village Lad, was a fairly good two-year-old, plenty of placings but never actually winning a race.'

'I am going to watch Jason ride in the first race. Are you coming or can't you bear to be parted from your precious horse?' Mary teased him.

'I suppose that there is not a lot that I can do here. Ok, we will go and watch him ride.' He turned to John. 'We will see you in the mounting yard in about twenty minutes then.'

'That is fine by me but you had better go if you want to see the first race. It is only a five-furlong affair.' So the two of them waved to Ginger who was coming out of the stall and left John with the horse.

They had almost reached the grandstand when Victor decided that he wanted a race book, a souvenir of his first flat runner. So, telling Mary that he would catch her up, he detoured to buy his formbook.

'Victor Barnes!' A voice boomed out. He turned in surprise at hearing his name called and saw Ambrose lumbering towards him. Highly delighted at seeing the man again, Victor marched up to him and shook his hand warmly. 'Hey Ambrose, how nice it is to see you.'

'When I happened to see that Arcadian Steel was entered here today, I thought to myself that I must see this race. I will be honest with you. I never thought that the day would come when I would ever see him on a racecourse. How are you getting on with him?'

'Ambrose, that horse is going to win the Derby!'

'Well, I must say that it is nice to see you so confident. I still have tinges of conscience that I ever let myself be talked into selling him to you.' The other man smiled. 'So you must have found a jockey that can actually stay aboard him then?'

'I have found two of them. Jason Carter who is riding him today and also Mary Collins, the trainer's daughter. She rides him in track work.'

Silks and Saddlecloths

'Not John Collins? Is that old reprobate still training horses? I would have thought that he would have retired years ago.'

'Oh, so you know him then?'

'Yes,' the other man lowered his head briefly. 'He and I have know each other for years. So his daughter is a rider too is she? She used to ride my knee when she was a young tot. So she has graduated to real horses has she? I have not seen Mary for years, I bet that she has grown into a striking woman. She always had good looks, that one, even at a very early age. I bet that she has the fellers lining up eh?'

'She is in the stand; why don't you come and say hello?' Victor tugged at the other man's sleeve and pulled him towards the stand.

'I think that I might just do that. It will be good catching up with her and John. Especially now he is training my old horse.' The two of them marched towards the stand and finally found Mary sitting with a pair of field glasses trained on the horses that were milling around the starting stalls.

'Hey, Mary, look who I ran into,' Victor said. She glanced up, said hello then went back to watching the horses. 'I do apologise for her, Ambrose. It looks as though we are going to have to wait until the race is over before we get any sense out of her.'

Just then, the course PA system crackled into life. 'They are under starter's orders and they are off.' Jason's mount had drawn the inside barrier and as the horses came out of the stalls he leapt to the lead and was never headed. He came home half a length clear of the runner up.

Mary jumped up excitedly. 'I won £50 and I am going to put it all on yours, Victor. Just a moment, don't I know you?' she said peering at Ambrose as though seeing him for the first time.

The big man chuckled. 'I think that you are a little too big to be riding my knee now Mary and you have filled very nicely too, I see.'

She blushed and gave him a kiss on the cheek.

'So your Dad ended up with my horse, did he? Well, it looks as though he has had far better luck with it than I did. Victor here tells me that you ride him as well.'

'Ambrose, it really is nice to see you after all this time. I didn't realise that Samson used to be your horse.'

'Changed his name and all I see. I must admit that the one that the lads chose for him did not sit too well with me but he was the very devil even to approach.'

182

'Would you like to come down to the mounting yard with us?' Victor inquired of the big man. He would have been surprised if the invitation were refused.

'Yeah, why not? It will be good to see John again any way.'

'Well, first, I am going to collect my winnings and put it all on Samson.' Mary said. 'I will see you two down there.' The clerk of the course was leading Jason's mount in as they made their way back down the steps, so they stood and watched them into the winner's enclosure before they continued on their way.

They had a short wait before the horses for the next race started to come out. Mary joined them as the first of the bunch were led into the mounting yard. Her cheeks were flushed with excitement. I managed to get 100–8 on him. That means over six hundred pounds when he wins.'

'If he wins, don't you mean Mary?' Victor remarked casually.

'You are more certain of his winning than I am,' Mary retorted sharply. 'Oh look, here comes Dad now.' The others saw John walking towards them, followed by Ginger leading the horse with some trepidation. John's pace quickened as he caught sight of them and he shook Ambrose's hand warmly.

'How very nice to see you again Ambrose, it's been a long time. I understand that Victor bought Arcadian Steel from you. He looks all right don't you think?'

Ambrose stared as Ginger led the horse into the ring. 'God! He looks terrific John! You haven't lost your touch I see. I don't think that I have ever seen him looking so well.'

'Are you sorry now that you sold him to me?' Victor said with a grin patting the horse.

The American shook his head vehemently. 'No. As far as I am concerned a deal is a deal. I thought that I was coming out on top. You were the one who was taking a chance. I couldn't do anything with him anyway. I sincerely hope that he wins for you. Now, after seeing him, I am off to lay a small wager on him. Perhaps we can meet up after the race?'

'Right, we will see you in the bar then.'

'Where else?' said Mary with a smile. 'We seem to spend most of our time in one bar or another. Ah here comes Jason now.'

'I am off. I will see you all later.' Ambrose heaved his bulk in the direction of the bookies as Jason strode into the ring, grinning from ear to ear.

John grabbed his hand. 'Nice win Jason, now let's go for the double.'

'It might even be a treble. I just got offered another ride as a jockey hasn't turned up.'

'Let's try and win this race first shall we? You have time for any others afterwards. First things first,' John said slightly impatiently.

'Right boss, I am all ears. How do you want me to ride him?'

'The draw isn't really going to help you, but you have a good run in of five furlongs. See if you can manage to be in the leading group by the halfway stage. He should be fresh enough to run anything down if you are close enough in the last couple of furlongs.'

Jason listened intently to what John was saying. His arms were folded across his chest but he had stuck his whip in his boot and not under his arm as the other riders did. The call came for them to mount up and John offered cupped hands.

As Jason slid into the saddle, Samson reared wildly, knocking Ginger, who only had a slack rein on him to the ground.

'For God's sake, Ginger! I told you to keep a firm hold on him. Can't you do anything right boy?' John yelled at him in exasperation.

Meanwhile Mary had made a grab for the reins and at the same time put up an arm towards the horse's bridle.

'Don't you worry, Mary, I have him,' called Jason who had almost been unseated by the episode. Grabbing the bridle he leaned forward and spoke into the horse's ear. He then tapped him lightly on the withers and, taking the reins from Mary, shortened them until his clenched fist rested on the animal's neck. He then lightly ran his whip down the black mane several times until the horse became calm once more.

'There's folk around here that reckon he's a toadman, that one,' Victor heard Mrs Humber's words once again. Looking at the man perched up there, high in the saddle, in complete command, he began to wonder whether or not there might be a grain of truth in what they said.

Seeing that the horse was now perfectly at ease once again, John told Ginger to take the animal's rug back to the stable. The boy picked it up and sullenly slouched off back to the stable. Everybody heaved a sigh of relief as the runners started out onto the track and Samson followed.

Chapter Twelve

'Good luck Jason,' Mary called as he trotted past them.

'With me on board, who needs luck?' he called and blew her a kiss.

John and Victor looked at each other. 'He might be able to ride but he's still an arrogant little sod, isn't he? But, to give him his due, he can handle that horse,' John muttered as the man in question guided his mount out onto the track.

While the rest of the field cantered down onto the track, Victor's party moved back into the grandstand. He knew that he was entitled to enter the owners' enclosure but force of habit made him head for the stand. Ambrose was already there, his huge hands clasped around his field glasses. He trained them on each horse in turn as it trotted down to the start.

'Well, if looks are anything to go by, then your horse is already past the post. He looks a real picture and that's for sure,' Ambrose stated with just a slight touch of envy in his voice.

'If it makes you feel any better, I will waive any stud fee for you after he wins the Derby,' Victor said, and the big man turned slowly and looked at him.

'Now that is an offer that I shall have no hesitation in taking you up on.'

'Keep your fingers crossed, he is about to go into the stalls,' John said.

They all raised their glasses and focused them on the starting stalls. Victor watched Jason trot up and approach Samson's stall. Suddenly the horse dug in his heels and would not enter the narrow confine of the stall. The attendants raced up and tried to lead him in, but he refused to budge. 'Just Arcadian Steel to move in now, but they seem to be experiencing some difficulty with him' the cold, metallic voice of the PA system drifted across the course.

'If they don't get him in soon, then the stewards will be forced to withdraw him from the race,' John's hoarse tones echoed all their fears. Mary's hand found Victor's and squeezed it tightly.

'Come on Samson, please go in,' she whispered to herself.

Victor's heart was now racing wildly and he felt an icy chill slowly start to creep up his back. He was beginning to fear that all his dreams were about to be shattered when Ambrose's voice boomed out.

'Wait a minute, your jockey has dismounted and, what in Hades? He seems to be talking to the animal. He has both its ears in his hands and he is talking to it!' he said incredulously.

Victor watched Jason with bated breath. 'Come on toadman, do your stuff!' he cried out suddenly.

The others turned and looked at him in amazement. 'What did you say Victor?' Mary asked him in an amused voice.

'I will explain to you later,' he muttered. 'It won't make any difference anyway if he can't get the horse to go in.'

'Well, Jason is trying to lead him in now,' John growled. 'This will be his last chance. They won't hold up the race any longer for him. Oh thank God, he is in!' They watched as the attendants closed the gate behind the horse and then helped Jason to climb the stall and remount.

'Arcadian Steel, the last of the runners, is locked away. They are under starter's orders,' the inanimate voice crackled once again. They held their breath. 'And they are off. Arcadian Steel missed the start by a good half-length. Village Lad has taken the lead, closely followed by Fringe Benefit and Metung Bay. Coming up to the Milepost and it is still the favourite Village Lad that leads the way from Corinth Star and Metung Bay. The others are closely bunched with Arcadian Steel bringing up the rear. The leaders are coming into the straight now and it's still Village Lad by a long neck to Fringe Benefit. Several horses are starting to make their moves now. Arcadian Steel has been pulled to the outside. Two furlongs to race and the favourite has gone. It is Fringe Benefit and Arcadian Steel coming with a withering run right down the outside.' The commentator's voice seemed to go up an octave in pitch, 'Arcadian Steel is absolutely flying and with a furlong to go has taken the lead. He is now drawing away from them. Coming from last, it's Arcadian Steel the winner by three lengths. Second is Fringe Benefit and a photo for third place.'

'He did it! He did it! He won!' Mary cried, tears of joy running down her cheeks. She hugged Victor. Ambrose held out his hand. 'Let me be the first to congratulate you, my boy. That was a great run, he just destroyed them. I always knew that the horse had it in him but I wasn't the lucky one to find it.'

Victor grasped his hand warmly. 'It is John and Mary that you should be congratulating, not me. Mary was the first one to ride him and John has done a fine job in training him.'

'You shouldn't forget Jason, either, Victor. It was he who got the horse into the stalls after all. For all his boastful ways, he is one heck of a horseman. Now what was that you called him, toadman? Why would you call him that?' John was curious but as he spoke his chest filled with a sense of pride for what he had achieved.

'Yes, tell us Victor. I don't believe that I have heard that expression before. Is it Australian?' Ambrose looked at him in amusement. Somewhat sheepishly, Victor related to them what he had been told by Mrs Humber. As he spoke about it, he realised himself how absurd it all sounded. He had to admit though that something happened out there between Jason and the horse.

The American slapped a huge paw on his shoulder. 'If that don't beat all Victor. I shall have to try and remember that when I get back home to the States. Bones that swim upstream! Now I reckon that I have heard everything.'

His whole body shook again as it was enveloped in waves of laughter, causing passers by to stare at the group of them. 'All that I can say is, whatever he did to that horse, it worked and he has made me ten thousand pounds richer. I reckon that I owe that guy a drink. Him and his toads!'

'Ten thousand! I thought that I was doing well winning my £600.' Mary yelped. 'How much did you win Victor?'

'I think that the prize money was a little over £4,000.'

'I am not talking about the prize money, stupid, how much did you bet on the horse itself?' Victor didn't answer for a moment and then mumbled something.

'I am sorry but I didn't hear you and I don't think that anyone else did either.'

Victor gave a big sigh and with a slightly embarrassed look repeated, 'If you must know, I didn't have a bet on him. I did not want to jinx him. I am more than happy with the prize money and the fact that he won.'

John roared with laughter and slapped him heartily on the back. 'I just can not work you out. You bet £5,000 on a horse over the jumps. A far riskier bet and more likely to lose and yet you put nothing on a super horse on the flat. Come on, let's get down and meet Jason. You have to lead the winner in. The only black spot to this whole afternoon is that where we thought Jason arrogant before, he is going to be utterly impossible now.'

Later that afternoon, Jason again saluted the judge and after changing met them back at the bar. Ambrose had insisted on buying them all drinks and they had watched the race in comfort. When he finally joined them Jason had even agreed to a glass of champagne. He sat at a table with John and Mary, while Victor and Ambrose were at an adjoining one. Having missed out on lunch they were all enjoying a snack of fried chicken with their drinks. Ginger had declined to join them, instead settling for sitting in the Land Rover to wait for them. Victor had felt guilty about leaving him there but both John and Mary had assured him that the boy would be far happier on his own.

'He would feel out of his depth with Ambrose here,' Mary had told him. So Victor pacified his conscience by having some of the fried chicken sent down to the boy.

'So, what have you got planned next for the horse?' Ambrose asked John as he poured the trainer another glass. 'I am not really sure, but I thought that I might try him in the Arlington at Newbury. He certainly is up to the class.'

'If he runs as well there as he did here today then he should walk it in,' the big man stated emphatically. 'Once Jason managed to get him settled, he appeared as though he was loving the exercise. He seemed as arrogant as his jockey did and treated those other horses with contempt.'

Jason must have overheard their conversation because he leaned across the table towards them. 'If you have got it, flaunt it, I always say,' the jockey drawled.

'Well, I can't argue with you today, Jason. You certainly proved your point.' John said. 'Where are you going Victor?'

Victor had got to his feet and was about to walk away.

'John, I feel guilty about leaving Ginger on his own for all this time. I think that I will just pop down and make sure that the lad is ok.'

'Suit yourself but he is used to being on his own. He doesn't mix much with the other lads, even at home,' John stated dourly.

'I will be back in a few minutes.' Victor turned and left the bar.

He was wondering what to say to Ginger as he walked around until he spotted the Land Rover in the car park. He was about to make his way over to it when he saw someone open the driver's door and get out. The man had a familiar look about him but for the moment he could not place him. 'No doubt it will come back to me', he thought. He watched as the man hurried off and got in the passenger side of a dark blue Jaguar. As the car drove off Victor tried to see who was driving but the car had tinted windows, which made it impossible to identify the occupants. As he approached the Land Rover, Ginger climbed out. Seeing Victor coming towards him, the lad hurriedly shoved something in his pocket.

'Hi there, Ginger, I thought that you might like something to drink. I can look after the horse while you go and have something if you like. The others are still in the bar and Ambrose is buying.'

'No thanks I am just fine,' the boy answered. 'I don't suppose you know when the boss will be ready to leave do you?'

Victor felt a tinge of sympathy for the lad. It must be boring just sitting there with no one but a horse to keep you company. 'I shouldn't think that they will be much longer. If you are certain that you are all right I will get back there. I may be able to speed them up a little.' He then pulled out his wallet and extracted two £50 notes from it. These he handed to the boy. 'Here this for doing such a good job looking after Samson for me today. I am very grateful.'

Ginger took the proffered cash eagerly and stuffed it in his jeans. 'Thank you very much, sir. Do you want to check the horse?'

He shook his head and said that he should be getting back to the others. 'The longer that I am down here, the longer it will be before any of them make a move. Incidentally, who was that man I saw getting out of here when I arrived?'

The boy flushed a deep red and kicked the ground self-consciously. He was quiet for a minute and then he pleaded, 'Oh please don't tell the boss. I know that we are not supposed to talk to anyone about the horses. The guy said that he had backed it this afternoon and he wanted to know when it was going to run again. I told him that I didn't know, so he left.'

Victor could sense the boy's panic and did not want to cause him any more trouble. 'There's been no harm done so I won't mention it.' Then telling Ginger that he shouldn't have too much longer to wait retraced his steps to the bar.

He arrived back to find Ambrose on his feet and making his farewells. He came up to Victor and clapped a hand on his shoulder. 'Good luck with the horse, my boy. Now that it has had its first run I shall be following it with a great deal of interest. I mean to hold you to that stud fee offer also.' He shook hands with them all and then ambled off.

Mary came up to Victor and took him by the arm. 'Victor, Jason has invited me out to dinner to celebrate his treble today. I have never ridden in a Maserati before, it should be fun. You don't mind if I go, do you?' He felt the green god of jealousy taking a hold of him and he tried in vain to shake it off. 'Why should I mind? I have no claims on you Mary,' he said testily.

'I just didn't want to upset you. I can always tell him that I have changed my mind. I will say that you had dinner booked as you expected to be celebrating.'

'No, go. We can always go out another time. Anyway I don't own a Maserati. I hope that you have a good time. I shall see you at Aintree anyway. I presume that you are still going to ride Pride for me aren't you? I am counting on you.'

'Just you try and stop me. I would never speak to you again if you pulled me off that ride.' He looked at her for a moment and then gave her a peck on the cheek. 'Go and enjoy your dinner and your ride in that red monster of his.'

Mary then kissed her father and Victor watched as she and Jason walked towards the door. Her father watched them go in silence. Then, after the door had closed behind them, he turned to Victor. 'I would have been far happier if she had have been going out with you. In spite of being an excellent rider, I still maintain that he is a jumped-up braggart. As for that car of his . . . You know what they say about men and their fancy cars. Don't you worry though, Mary is quite capable of looking after herself.' John laid a consoling hand on the other man's shoulder.

'I hope so. I truly hope so.'

The flight back from Humberside was anything but the pleasure trip that Victor had envisaged. He had seen Jason, with Mary at his side, drive off in his flash car as he was getting into the little Seat that he had hired. When he arrived back at the airport the pilot had inquired about the extra passenger that he was supposed to be carrying. Victor told him tersely that Mary had changed her mind. Having notified the tower of the change, the pilot taxied the plane out onto the runway. He was given clearance and took off. They had not been in the air for long when they ran into a violent storm that sprung up out of nowhere. The small charter plane was tossed about like straw in the wind. Eventually the pilot was forced to land at the East Midlands airport. Victor had wanted to fly on but the pilot had refused saying that the wind was far too strong. Also, visibility was almost down to zero. So they were forced to sit out the storm on the tarmac. When they did finally land back at St Mawgan, Victor was tired and irritable. Collecting his car from the airport car park he drove home at a slightly faster speed than the law allowed. Fortunately for him, he arrived back at the house without any mishap.

Eventually around ten o'clock Victor was back in the warmth and comfort of his lounge. He had poured himself a large Jack Daniels and was sitting in front of the fire, brooding. Finishing his drink he decided to go to bed but found that he was unable to get to sleep. As soon as he closed his eyes all that he could see was Mary in Jason's arms. Angry with himself for this bout of jealousy he got up again. Going downstairs to the kitchen he made himself a pot of coffee. He then sat on the settle drinking it and staring at the trunk of the oak tree. Over the years, the smoke from the fire had caused the gnarled bark to become covered with layers of black in varying thickness. As he stared at it he remembered what Mrs Humber had told him of seeing faces and scenes, carved into the blackened surface. The longer that he stared at it, the more vivid his imagination became. He was able to see all kinds of pictures forming amongst the sooty timber. He was able to see faces staring out at him, faces of old men with long greying beards, countenances creased with the lines of old age. He walked among the stone chimneys of decaying tin mines, jagged cliffs and deep mysterious valleys. He began to think of the trunk as a prison for tortured souls who had lived hundreds of years ago. His gaze shifted to another part of the massive stem just before it disappeared into the roof. As he watched, he visualised a pair of arms that reached out to him, beseeching him for help. He could see them as they struggled to free themselves from the tangled mess that bound them to the tree. The sudden searing pain of hot coffee spilling over his knee brought him back to his senses with a jolt.

'Shit! I have had too much to drink,' he cried aloud. 'I will be seeing Mrs Humber's toads next if I am not careful.' He cleaned up the mess on the floor and, after fetching himself another cup, filled it with black coffee. Moving from the settle to the table he sat down again and sipped his drink.

He was about to go to bed for the second time when his phone rang. 'Hey, it is almost midnight. I wonder who this can be, unless it is Dan,' he spoke aloud to himself as he picked up the phone.

'Victor, I hope that I didn't get you out of bed,' Mary's voice came over the line. It was obvious from her tone that she had been crying.

Pulling a chair toward him, he sat down. 'Mary, what is the matter? Are you all right? What has happened? You sound really upset,' Victor replied his voice full of concern.

'I am fine, really. I just needed to talk to you, to hear your voice. I am so sorry, Victor. Dad told me that you were going to ask me to fly back with you today. You should have asked me, I would have come.'

'I didn't want you to have to choose between me and your dinner date with Jason,' he replied with a tinge of regret. 'You wouldn't have enjoyed the flight anyway. We hit a hell of a storm and had to be diverted.'

Then to his dismay he heard her start to cry. 'Mary what is the matter? Something must be wrong, why are you crying?'

'Oh, I have been such a fool. I should have known what he wanted from the beginning. Silly me, I just thought that he wanted some company to help him celebrate his treble. If I had realised that there was going to be more to it than that, I would not have gone with him.'

'You are not making much sense. What are you saying? Didn't you go out to dinner?'

'Yes the dinner was fine. Afterwards he invited me back to his flat for coffee. At first I said no, that I should be getting home. So he said we would just have a cup of coffee and then he promised that he would drive me home.'

Victor began to feel an icy knot forming in his stomach and fear began to well in his throat. 'Mary what happened?'

Her sobbing became much louder and more violent.

'Oh Victor, it was awful. Jason tried to rape me!'

Chapter Thirteen

Victor scarcely remembered the drive to Hill Top Stud. He was just conscious of passing traffic on the motorway as though they were standing still. Pulling up outside the house he saw that most of the lights were burning. He hammered on the front door and after a short wait it opened and John stood there framed against the light.

'Victor! Well I can't say that I am surprised, but I certainly am grateful for you coming. Come in, she's in her room at the moment.'

'How is she? Is she hurt at all?' he asked frantically.

The older man took him gently by the arm and pulled him inside. He then shut the door. 'I don't think that she has been physically hurt but emotionally she is in a hell of a mess. Now that you are here you might be able to talk some sense into her. She won't let me phone for the police, says that she doesn't want them involved. She has some fool notion that if she does contact the police, then you won't have a jockey for the Derby.'

'What? I don't believe it! Surely she doesn't think that I am going to have that wretched ingrate within a mile of her, let alone ride my horse.'

'Just don't be too hasty at the moment and let your heart rule your head,' cautioned the other man. 'You must realise that the chances of you finding another jockey for Samson are pretty remote?' John warned him.

Victor faced the other man and looked him squarely in the eyes. 'If that is the case, then so be it. The horse will not run. There is no way that I am going to allow Jason Carter to come anywhere near Mary. Now let's go and see how she is shall we?'

In spite of the anxiety that he felt over his daughter, Victor's words sent a warm glow and a feeling of pride through John. Taking a deep breath he led him upstairs to his daughter's bedroom. Tapping lightly on the door, he slowly opened it. Mary was lying in the bed simply

193

staring at the ceiling. She turned her head as her father opened the door. Seeing Victor standing there she let out a cry and scrambled to her feet. Flinging her arms around him, she burst into loud, uncontrollable tears again. He held her to him gently until her sobbing subsided. Taking a hanky from his pocket, he wiped her face with tender but deft strokes.

'Oh Victor, I have been such a fool. I should have seen through him. Dad was right about him all the time.'

He did not reply but merely cradled her in his arms.

Just then the telephone rang. Excusing himself, John left them and went downstairs to answer it. A couple of minutes later he re-appeared at the doorway.

'Mary love, it's your mother. She would like to speak to you.'

'Mum? But why would she be ringing at this time of night? There is nothing wrong with Gran is there?'

Her father shook his head.

'I don't think that I can talk to her right now Dad. Tell her that I will ring her in the morning.'

However her father wouldn't take a no for an answer but asked Victor to take her downstairs. He did just that and led her to the phone. As she picked it up, John signalled to Victor that they should leave the room. Outside the lounge he explained, 'I rang my wife as I thought that Mary needed another woman to talk to.'

'How about a doctor, don't you think that you should call one?'

'I wanted to but she said that she didn't need one. To be perfectly honest, the fact that you are here is probably the best medicine that she could have right now. You do know that she worships you, don't you?'

Victor squirmed and looked embarrassed. John laughed. 'I am sorry. I did not mean to put any more pressure on you. I know that you have enough on your plate as it is.'

Victor thought for a moment and then faced the other man. 'Look, I don't know quite how to say this. You have to remember that it is only a short time since I lost my whole family. I have tried to explain this to Mary. It is just that I don't feel comfortable starting up a deep relationship. Not right at this time anyway. Maybe in the future that might be a possibility. Right now I am more concerned about her as a close friend would be. If I disappoint you I am sorry but that is just the way that things are.'

Chapter Thirteen

'Don't worry, I understand and respect you for it. Mary knows it too as she has told me several times that she needs the patience of Job where you are concerned. Just for the moment go in there and be that friend, please?'

Victor looked at the elder man, saw the torture and the pleading in his eyes. His daughter was hurting and she needed something that he as a father could not give her. He was desperately praying that Victor could.

For a brief moment Victor was taken back to that hospital in Melbourne. Once again he experienced the pain and anguish over which he had no control. He had been alone then and nothing could change that. This was different, he was in a position where he could help. He squeezed John's hand then, slowly opening the lounge door, he went in. Mary was sitting at the table, weeping softly. He went over to her and knelt down by her side. He gently took her hands in his. She looked at him with tear-filled eyes.

'Mary you have to phone the police. This guy cannot be allowed to get away with what he tried to do to you tonight. He has to be punished.'

'But if I phone the police what is going to happen to you and Samson?'

'Sod the bloody horse! You mean more to me than a thousand horses. A horse can be replaced, you can't.'

She looked at him and the tears poured down her face. Her mascara had run and made thin, wavy black lines across her otherwise pale face. 'Do you really mean that?' She gazed at him with awe-struck wonderment.

'It looks as though there is only one way that I can convince you Mary Collins.' He moved across to the telephone, picked it up and dialed. 'Police? I would like to report an attempted rape.'

By the time that the two constables had finished asking their questions and making copious notes, it was almost 3a.m. Victor looked at the clock and said, 'I know that I am getting a little tired but I missed how you got home, Mary. Jason lives somewhere in Oxford doesn't he? How did you manage to get all the way down here?'

'Well, as you know, I won £600 on Samson today. So I just went to the end of the street and hailed a passing taxi. You should have seen the driver's face when I told him that I wanted him to drive me to Taunton.' For the first time in several hours she managed a small giggle. 'Then when I reached Taunton I phoned dad and he came and picked me up and brought me home.'

'I wonder what will happen to Jason. The police said that they would contact Oxford didn't they? They should send someone round to his place from there.'

'Even if nothing happens to him, he is going to have an almighty headache this morning. I really clouted him with that photo frame. Trust him to have a silver-framed photograph of himself and that car of his, in the lounge. He certainly paid for his vanity,' Mary said disgustedly'.

'I am still surprised that you were able to fend him off.'

'Don't forget he is a jockey so he is fairly light. Also he was only holding me with one hand, while the other one was trying to undo his trousers.'

'But didn't he try and chase you?' Victor queried her. She looked at him with an amused smile playing around her lips. 'Have you ever tried to chase someone with your trousers flapping around your ankles?' She tried to laugh again but the memory of what had happened made her burst into tears again. Taking her in his arms once more, Victor held her until her crying subsided. Just then there was a light tap at the door. Her father entered followed by a grey-haired man carrying a small black case.

'Dad, I told you that I didn't need a doctor.'

'He is just here to give you a sedative to help you to sleep that is all,' her father said firmly.

The doctor motioned for Mary to sit on the couch and took her wrist to check her pulse. 'I think that as long as I am here, I might as well check you over properly young lady. Now if you two gentlemen would leave us alone for a short while?' With that the doctor ushered them both out of the door.

Victor followed John into the kitchen. 'How about some early breakfast? I have to be up in a couple of hours anyway.'

'No thanks. I don't feel as though I could eat anything anyway.'

'Nonsense. You will feel far better with something solid inside you. We will wait until the doctor has finished with Mary and then get her to bed. Susan, her mother, is catching the first train back from York this morning. She should be here by lunch time. She will ring me when she gets to Taunton and I will go and pick her up.' He hesitated for a brief instant before he continued. 'I don't think that I really have to ask you, but would you stay here with Mary until I get back? I realise that you most likely have plans, but I don't like the idea of leaving her on her own. If you . . .'

'Of course I will stay. I don't have to go home for anything. I promised to ring Buckingham at the Jockey Club, but I can do that from here. Besides I am anxious to meet your wife. I just wish that it was in better circumstances than this.' Just then the door of the lounge opened and the doctor joined them in the kitchen.

'How is she, doctor?' John's voice showed his concern

'She seems to be fine. Her blood pressure is way up, of course, but that is only to be expected. I have given her some sedatives; just make sure that she takes them. She seems to be rather a stubborn young lady. I want her to go to bed but she says that she has to ride one of your horses in track work this morning. That, of course, is out of the question. She has been badly shaken up and delayed shock is likely to set in shortly. Just try and persuade her to go to bed. Any problems at all, feel free to give me a call.'

'Thanks, doctor. We will make sure that she takes those sedatives. Would you like to stay and have some breakfast? I am just about to cook it,' John said, but the doctor declined.

John walked him to the front door and saw him off. As he came back into the kitchen Mary joined them. 'Ok my girl, take those tablets that the doctor gave you and off you go to bed,' her father said firmly.

'I can't go to bed, you need someone to ride Samson,' she protested.

Victor stood up and took her by the arm. 'That horse had enough exercise by winning yesterday. Now if you don't do as your father says, then I am leaving.'

'But Victor . . .'

'No buts,' he said authoritatively. 'You either go to bed right this instant or else I am out of that door and on my way home.'

'Oh, you are so masterful. How could a poor girl like me disobey you?' she said coyly. 'Right, I will go up for a couple of hours but then you have to wake me up.' Her father took her other arm and they gently but firmly propelled her out of the door in the direction of the staircase. 'What do you think will happen to Jason, Dad?'

'I don't know, love and frankly I don't care. All that I do know is that he is going to find it a lot harder to get rides after I make a few phone calls. Now, for the last time, get on upstairs and to bed.' Her father kissed her and watched as she made her way up the stairs to her room. After he had seen her go in and close the door behind her, he then relaxed.

Some time later, John and Victor made their way down to the stables for the morning track work. As they approached the group of waiting apprentices, John said to his companion, 'I would appreciate it if you didn't tell any of the lads what has happened. They will hear about it soon enough of that I am sure. We can just say that Mary is feeling a bit off colour this morning, agreed?' Victor nodded. The two men then joined the waiting boys and John explained the reason for his daughter's absence.

Jimmy looked at him for a moment and then said shyly, 'What about Samson, Boss? Who is going to ride him?'

'He will just have to miss a gallop today. He has probably earned a rest after yesterday's run anyway.'

The boy stood there, uncertain of himself. He then plucked up enough courage to speak again. 'I would like a try at riding him, boss. I have been watching Miss Mary very closely and I think that I can handle him.'

John and Victor looked at each other in amazement. John then looked back at Jimmy standing there with his helmet clutched in front of him. 'So Jimmy, you think that you can handle the beast do you? What do you have to say Victor?'

'If he is willing to give it a try, I don't see why we should stand in his way. You do know what you will be letting yourself in for don't you Jimmy? He is a hard horse to handle and I would hate to see you hurt in any way.' Victor cast his eyes over the snippet of a lad that stood there before them. 'You had to admire his courage at least.'

The trainer thought about it for a few minutes, mulling things over in his mind then said slowly, 'Right then Jimmy. You can give him a try but just take it easy. No heroics, do you hear me?'

The look that came over the boy's face was one of pure joy. 'Thanks boss, you will not be disappointed, that I promise you.'

'Nor will I say that I told you so if he throws you,' John laughed as Jimmy ran off to fetch the horse from his stall. 'Come on Victor, we had better follow him just in case he finds him too difficult to handle.' So the two men also made their way down to the stall.

The other lads had mounted up and were walking their charges around the yard, waiting for instructions. John and Victor reached there just as Jimmy was leading the black colt out of his stall. Tying the reins loosely to the rail he patted the horse on the neck a couple of times and then put his hand in his pocket. Pulling it out he offered something to the horse. As quick as a flash, John moved in and grabbed the boy's arm. The horse gave a snort and threw up his head. The reins prevented him from moving too far.

'What the hell are you giving him Jimmy? You know the rules as well as anybody else here. You know that none of you lads are allowed to give the horses anything without clearing it with me first. Now show me what you have got there.'

Jimmy slowly opened his hand to reveal a now somewhat crushed hard-boiled egg. 'He loves them boss, honest he does. Miss Mary often has one in her pocket to give him. I just thought that he might treat me right if I gave him one before we started.' The boy looked crest-fallen. 'I just wanted him to let me ride him. I didn't mean any harm, honest. I was trying to make friends with him.'

'Well, I suppose that if you have seen Mary do it, I can't really blame you. I shall have to have a serious word with that daughter of mine though. Eggs are regarded as a luxury for a horse's feed. If she is giving them to him without my knowledge then it can upset his diet.'

Whilst they were talking, the animal must have smelt the egg in Jimmy's hand. He suddenly lowered his head and gulped down the mess before anyone could stop him. Jimmy then let him lick the remains off his hand and then gave him another pat.

'Go on Jimmy, you had better mount up. In future you must check with me before you give the horses anything, understand? That goes for the rest of you as well, do you hear me?' he yelled at the other riders who had witnessed the proceedings. They nodded their heads in acknowledgement.

Victor walked over to the boy. 'Come on Jimmy, let me give you a leg up.' The apprentice flashed him a grateful glance, put a foot in Victor's hand and climbed onto Samson's back

Everybody waited in anticipation but the horse merely trotted out to join the others. John went up to each rider in turn and issued him with instructions, leaving Jimmy to the last.

'Now lad, as long as you can stay on the horse, you can give him a gentle workout. Just trot him around the track to let him get used to you. We do not need to push him hard after his race yesterday.' Jimmy nodded and cantered off after the other riders. 'Come on Victor, I think that a brisk walk will do us both good. We should get down there in time to see them workout. So we won't bother with the car this morning unless you don't feel up to the walk.'

'No, that is fine by me, the walk is just what I need.' So the two men set off at a fair pace down to the track.

It was still quite dark and the drumming of the horses' hooves echoed eerily through the morning mist that covered the track. The horses were merely shadows in the gloom and it was hard to tell which one was which with the naked eye. Suddenly John let out a shout. 'What does that boy think that he is doing? I told him a gentle trot and now just look at him.' As he spoke Victor saw one animal break away from the pack and race towards them at full gallop. In spite of the poor light the horse was so dark that Victor knew with a sinking heart that it was Samson. As he neared then, the two men could see that Jimmy was pulling back on the reins for all he was worth. 'The damned horse has bolted and the boy can't hold him. Now what are we going to do?'

'How about using the other horses? Can they try and cut him off?' Victor asked anxiously. John shook his head and started to run towards the track. 'They will never catch up with him, he is too fast. We can try sending them around in the opposite direction and see if he will slow up when they all meet up together.'

'I don't think that you can really afford to take a chance doing that. If you do then someone might get hurt or one of the other horses could be injured. I think that you might just have to let him run his course. He will have to stop eventually. Let's hope that Jimmy can hang on until he does.'

'So much for giving him a gentle workout. He is going to be well and truly buggered by the time that he does stop,' John slapped his thigh in annoyance

As the horse and rider thundered past them, Victor realised that Jimmy had stopped pulling on the reins but in fact had given the horse its head. He was now crouched down along the animal's neck and riding him as though he was in a race. Samson careered around the track and, as he came up to the other horses, his pace began to slacken. Jimmy let him catch the main group and then started to pull back on the reins once more. Samson passed through the bunch of riders and without warning began to slow right down. Jimmy at last managed to rein him in. Pepper Pot and Blue Bayou ranged up on either side of him and their riders each put a hand on his bridle.

Tom, who was astride Blue Bayou, began to lead the horse to the side of the track. 'I think that he is okay now, Mr Collins, he seems to have quietened down,' he called out.

John walked over to meet them and taking the reins from Jimmy's hands tied then to the rail. 'Well Jimmy, do you still think that you can handle him?'

'It wasn't Jimmy's fault Mr Collins. A rabbit ran out right under the horse's nose and startled it. That is why he bolted like he did,' Tom was quick to explain.

'Well, I myself thought that you did very well Jimmy,' Victor remarked. 'If you had panicked at all then things could have been very different. Anyway, he did prove one thing and that is he is fast.'

'I will drink to that,' John said thickly. 'I managed to clock him over six furlongs: 1.06. Now if he can produce that speed for a mile and a half then nothing will be able to catch him.' John untied the reins and handed them back to the boy. 'I think that he has had more than enough exercise for this morning. Take him back Jimmy,' the boy started to trot away, 'and Jimmy, well done my boy. You certainly proved to me that you are indeed quite capable of riding him.'

Mary was still asleep when John drove off to pick up Susan from Taunton, so Victor tried ringing Martin Buckingham again. After a lengthy delay he was finally connected to him. The man had certainly been busy. He had discovered that Duval had bought every horse on the list that Victor had given him. He had also found that all these horses had won either in France, Germany or Italy. There was nothing that he could do though to implicate Oxford in any shady dealings. 'It could just be the wildest coincidence that the horses started to win well, after leaving his stable. It isn't, of course, but I don't see as how I can prove that he is actually concerned in fixing them prior to leaving his stable,' Buckingham said philosophically.

'It just doesn't seem right to me that he is able to do this and get away with it. Surely there must be something that we can do?'

'The only thing that I can do at this stage is the next time that friend Harley's horses run, I can order a dope test. Then we just have to hope that he has actually done something to them. If he decided to let them run on their merits then we won't have a case.'

'I suppose that that is better than nothing but it seems so bizarre that he can get away with a fraud like this.' Victor spoke gloomily.

Silks and Saddlecloths

'The main problem is that we have to prove that there is actually a fraud being committed. In some respects he has been seen as helping some people who unhappily have dud horses. He has managed to sell them at a reasonable price. No mean feat if your horse is a donkey. The fact that another trainer manages to find a way of getting them to win is neither here nor there. Oxford has been seen as being very helpful. In most cases he has been able to sell a dud horse.'

'He has sold them all right but usually to himself although of course his name never appears as a buyer,' Victor retorted.

'I am afraid that is about all I can do at this stage. My hands are tied until he actually makes a mistake. So for the time being we shall just have to bide our time and see what happens. I will keep in touch.'

Victor hung up in disgust. He then crept upstairs and looked in on Mary. She was still sound asleep, so evidently the sedative that the doctor had given her was doing its job well. Hell, if he ever met that Jason Carter again, he would leave him something to remember him by. 'There must be something that I can do to make him pay for what he has done?' Victor thought to himself. 'The question is what? It was like Oxford, you knew what he had done but there was nothing that anybody could do to prove it.' He slowly wandered back into the lounge, sat down on the settee and within minutes was himself fast asleep.

He did not stir until he felt someone shaking him gently by the shoulder. He opened his eyes and blinked several times. When at last he managed to focus properly he saw John standing there with an attractive looking brunette at his side. He struggled to his feet. 'I am sorry, John, I must have dozed off for a minute.'

'More like ninety minutes I would say,' John laughed. 'Still that is not a problem, I know that you got virtually no sleep last night. Victor, I would like you to meet my wife Susan.' The woman held out her hand. As he took it, he found it to be cool but firm.

'So you are the latest man in my daughter's life?'

'Is that what she told you?' Victor asked warily.

'She doesn't have to tell me. She never stops talking about you,' Susan replied with a warm smile. 'Every time that she phoned me in York, all I ever heard was that Victor did this. Victor did that. If it wasn't you that she talked about it was your horses. I tell you no lie, she is quite smitten with you, to use the vernacular popular with the young ones at the moment.'

'Whatever happened to cool? I thought that was all the rage, at least in America. I am very sorry, it must have made the conversation pretty boring if my name kept cropping up all the time.' Victor groaned.

'On the contrary, it is a relief to see her so happy for a change,' Susan reassured him warmly. 'It has been quite some time since we have seen her like this.'

'I promise you, Mrs Collins, I do nothing to encourage her. In fact quite often it is the opposite. I gather she has told you all about my situation.'

'She hasn't mentioned anything but John has filled me in and please call me Susan. After all, from what I can gather, you are almost family. Though from the way that she talks sometimes I am not sure if it is you or your horse that interests her the most,' she said with a laugh. By now he was fully awake and in control of all his faculties. 'Have you decided what you are going to do about Jason Carter? Are you going to press charges?'

'I am against the idea,' Susan said. 'I know that he deserves to be punished but we don't know what it will do to Mary. She will have to get up in that witness box and have to relive it all over again. You can bet that his lawyers will try and make out that she was agreeable and then changed her mind. Or else they could say that she led him on – she did accept his invitation to go back to his flat. This is where the system stinks. The woman instead of being the victim is often made out to be the instigator. I would rather that we left things as they are.'

John and Victor looked at each other. 'But he shouldn't be allowed to get off scot free which is what is going to happen unless Mary presses charges. Something should be done to make him pay for what he has put her through,' Victor said adamantly.

'As I said earlier, I have a lot of friends who will ban him from riding for them again. That will really hurt him as he is freelance and not tied to a stable. He is going to find that rides are very hard to come by. I don't see what else we can do though, outside of going to court,' John said with more than a tinge of regret in his voice.

'I am not going to let him off that lightly. Just leave it to me, I will find some way of paying him back,' Victor stated forcefully.

'For the moment we can forget about Jason Carter. I am starving. I came away this morning without even having breakfast. I presume that you will be staying for lunch?' Susan asked him and then without waiting for an answer, she left the room.

John went over to the bar and poured himself a drink. 'I know that it is still a little early in the day but, after being up all night, I feel as though I have earned it. Would you like one?'

Victor thought about it for a moment and then declined the offer. 'No, I shouldn't. When Mary wakes up I shall have to get off home.'

Just then his mobile rang. He answered it and for the next couple of minutes merely listened to what the caller had to say. When he finally spoke all that he said was, 'Right, thanks a lot. I will be seeing you.'

He snapped his phone shut and then turned to John. 'That was Martin, the Jockey Club investigator. He has had someone checking on Harley's horses. Apparently, Oxford has them both entered in races for next month. Alaskan Jack is down to run on the Thursday at Newmarket and Cash Crisis on the Saturday at Newbury. It would be ironical, would it not, if it turned out that he was running in the same race as Arcadian Steel?'

'You do realise of course that there is every chance that Jason might still be riding for Oxford?' John said glumly. 'Which means that we shall have to try and keep Mary away from the meeting, and that will be no easy task.'

'We shall just have to hope that he has his own jockey back. The doctor only gave him a week off, so he should be. Besides, if Oxford is pulling a stroke I am sure that he would want his own jockey riding for him and not a relative stranger.' Just then Susan came in to tell them that lunch was ready.

It was well into the afternoon before Victor finally took his leave of the Collin's. Mary had come down and joined then for lunch although she had only picked at her food. They had taken their time with the meal with Susan trying to catch up with what had been going on while she was away. Mary and John too were just as eager for news about Mary's grandmother. Eventually he had to insist that they let him go. After he promised to ring Mary in the morning they had somewhat reluctantly bid him farewell.

Victor took his time driving back as the lack of a proper night's sleep, coupled with all the excitement of the past few days, was beginning to take its toll. He was not prepared to drive fast on this occasion. He finally arrived home around dusk and after parking the car made his way into the house. As he walked into the lounge the sight of the cold, grey ashes in the fireplace suddenly made him feel in need of some company. So, after taking a quick shower and changing, he took the short walk down to the inn for his evening meal. Glancing through the menu, he was pleasantly surprised at the wide variety that it offered. He remember Mrs Humber telling him that since the strict drink driving laws had come into force, they had changed the whole aspect of the village pub. Now, in order to attract custom, most publicans were relying more and more on food to make a decent living. Consequently this had resulted in the humble village pub rapidly becoming a gourmet's delight.

Victor ordered a lamb curry and was amazed to find that his meal was served with a huge range of condiments, far more in fact than he ever remembered being served in Indian restaurants in Melbourne. The meal was delicious and he thoroughly enjoyed it. Being a Friday night the local team had a darts match there and they were one player short. The landlord, knowing Victor to be a tenant of Seven Oaks and thus technically a resident, asked him if he would like to play. Despite protesting that it was literally many years since he had even picked up a dart, he was persuaded to play. He had a great evening, more so because his team won. So it was a very contented man who left the inn and made his way back up the hill after closing time. The clock was striking eleven when he finally made his way up to his bedroom. By now he was comfortably tired and, having undressed and got into bed, he was soon in a deep sleep.

He was rudely awoken by the shrill sound of his phone ringing. Bemused, he rubbed his eyes and looked at his watch. There was just enough moonlight coming through the window to make out the time. It was twenty to four. 'Who the hell is ringing me at this hour?' he muttered to himself. He reached over to the bedside table and picked up the phone. 'Hello Victor here. Do you realise what time it is? Is that you Dan?'

'Victor, I am so sorry to wake you so early. This is John Collins.' He sat up in bed immediately, his heart pounding. 'John! Is Mary ok? What's happened?'

'No, she is fine. I think that you had better get up here right away. There's, um, there's been an accident,' John's voice faltered.

'What kind of accident? It must be Samson; you wouldn't call me about anything else. Has something happened to the horse?'

'It's kinda hard to talk on the phone. Can you come up here right away? I would appreciate it. We have a problem here at the moment.'

'Sure. I will leave at once. I will be there just as soon as I am able.' Victor hung up the phone and began to dress quickly. 'What can have happened now?' he exclaimed out loud. 'Whoever said that Cornwall was a nice peaceful place to retire to did not know what they were talking about. There is never a dull moment here.'

Again he made record speed to Milverton. He was well aware that he had greatly exceeded the speed limit but very glad now that he had only been drinking orange juice during the darts match. Speeding through the village he reached the Collins's house without incident. Knocking on the door, he waited. No one came to answer his summons, so fearing the worst he made his way round to the stable yard.

As he rounded the corner he pulled up short. He could not believe what he was seeing. The entire yard's spotlights were blazing, lighting up the whole area. He could see an ambulance and a police car parked near one of the stalls. To his horror he realised that it belonged to Samson. He ran across the yard and nearly collided with John as he came out of the stall. 'John, what is going on for goodness sake? What is with all the emergency vehicles?'

Before John was able to answer him two ambulance officers came out of Samson's stall carrying a stretcher. They carefully placed it in the waiting vehicle.

'Who is that on the stretcher and what was he doing in Samson's stall at this time of the morning? Surely it is too early to start track work? What the hell is going on here?'

By now, Victor was becoming quite agitated. John took him gently but firmly by the arm and led him away from the stall. He took him to the centre of the yard and then stopped and faced him. 'It looks as though someone wanted to put your horse out of the Derby. That was Ginger that they just carried out. We had to wait almost ninety minutes for the ambulance to arrive. There has been a very bad multi-car pile up on the motorway. Then, apart from the fact that nothing could get through the mess, all the available ambulances were needed to ferry the injured to hospital. This one had to come all the way from Exeter. What I don't understand is why Ginger? If it had been one of the other horses that he tried to get at I could comprehend it. I would have said that he was taking it out on me because I have been giving him a bit of a hard time lately. But the boy is terrified of Samson although he hates to admit it. This means of course that he must have had a real good reason to try to nobble him. Someone must have paid him and paid him well for him even to attempt what he tried to do.'

Victor felt as though a thunderbolt had hit him. He punched his hand, hard. 'John Cassidy! That's who it was! I knew that I should have recognised that face. I just couldn't put a name to it at the time.' He grabbed the other man's arm. 'When we were at Doncaster, you remember that I went down to see Ginger in the car park? Well as I arrived I saw a man getting out of the Land Rover. I couldn't place who it was and asked Ginger. He said that it was someone who wanted to know our plans for the horse. It was John Cassidy. Why would he want to have a go at Samson though? I don't understand it.'

'Didn't you say that Oxford wanted you to place the horse with him?' Victor nodded.

'I reckon that they must have seen his run that day and felt that it was a severe threat to anything that they had entered. They must have decided that if they couldn't race it, then nobody would. Yes that all makes some kind of sense now.'

'What did Ginger try to do? You haven't told me yet what happened.'

'When we found him there was an iron bar lying in the straw,' John said grimly. 'I think that he meant to try and smash Samson's leg with it.'

'Surely the horse would not have let him near enough to try anything like that? You said that Ginger was afraid of him but you would need to be close to hit him hard enough to smash his leg. He wouldn't dare go that near would he?'

'He might if the animal was doped and docile enough. We also found five hard boiled-eggs stuffed with some kind of tablets. Evidently he must have thought that as the horse became calm for Jimmy with the egg then he could get him to swallow the pills in the eggs that he had. Once he had him calm enough it would be easy to get right up to him.'

'So what happened? Why didn't Samson eat the eggs?' Victor asked.

John scratched his chin. 'I am not really sure. That animal of yours is pretty smart. Maybe he smelt the fear on the boy, I don't know. Whatever happened he smashed Ginger to the ground. It looks as though he has at least half a dozen broken ribs and most likely a busted arm too. We won't know the full extent of his injuries until they get him to the hospital. We will have to wait for the X-ray results I guess.'

'Oh my God, this is shocking! I will pay his hospital expenses of course.'

John looked at him in astonishment. 'He has just tried to smash your horse's leg. If he had succeeded most likely it would have had to be put down. Yet you say that you will pay for his hospital treatment. I don't understand you at all. If it were my horse I would want to throttle him.'

'You must admit though he must have been pretty desperate to even try anything like this. Particularly as you said he is afraid of the horse. Then, regardless of what he tried to do, it was my horse that caused him the injuries.'

'Purely in self-defence don't forget. You may not be so keen to help him after you see what he done to your horse. I have rung the vet and he is on his way now,' John said grimly. Before Victor was able to ask what state the horse was in, the conversation was interrupted by the arrival of a policeman.

'Mr Collins have you any idea why the boy would try and harm the horse? I mean he does work for you, doesn't he?' the officer asked.

John looked at Victor who gave the merest shake of his head. 'Not at this stage, officer. When do you think that we might be able to talk to him?'

'I would say that it will be quite some time before anybody will be able to get anything out of him. He looked in a pretty bad way when they carried him out. He was unconscious of course,' the policeman said. 'How did you come to find him, Mr Collins?'

'His screams set the dogs off. They didn't bark when he first went into the stables, most likely because they knew him. We have the dogs there in case of prowlers. When he started to scream he must have upset them. Their barking and the noise that he was making woke us up at the house. I raced down here and found him lying in the stall. I dragged him outside to stop the horse from causing him any more harm,' John explained briefly and tersely.

The policeman made a note of it all and then looked up again. 'The blood on the straw, Mr Collins, where do you think that came from?' John looked at Victor as he answered slowly. 'At this stage it appears to come from the horse. We haven't been able to get close enough to examine him yet. He is still very distraught. We are waiting for the vet to arrive. He should be here at any time.'

Victor's mouth had dropped on hearing this piece of information. 'Blood! Blood! Then Samson is injured too? What the hell has he done to him? I thought that you said he had some tablets to give him? So where did the blood come from?'

'As I said, we don't really know as we can't get close enough to examine him. Once the vet arrives he will give him a tranquilliser and then we can have a proper look at him. Until then we would only be guessing.'

'Ah yes, that is another thing Mr Collins, do you have any of those tablets that you spoke about? We can send them away for analysis,' the officer asked politely. John hesitated for a minute, then put his hand in his pocket and drew out some tablets. He silently handed them to him. The policeman placed them in a plastic bag and carefully put them in his pocket. John continued, 'They look like ACP to me but I can't be absolutely sure of course.'

'Do you have any on the premises Mr Collins?' he was asked. He shook his head. 'No, if we ever have a use for any, I ring the vet.'

'In that case then you would have no idea where the boy could have got them?'

'No, not really. You can have a look in his locker if you like.'

'That might be a good idea. Perhaps you can show us where it is?'

Just then another car drove into the yard and a young man carrying a black case got out. 'Ah, here is the vet right now. I will have to go with him to check the horse. If you would like to go up to the house, my wife can show you where the boy's locker is,' John said. The policeman walked off towards the house and the other two men went to meet the vet.

'Hi John, what appears to be the trouble?' the young man asked. 'You were pretty vague about things on the phone.'

'We are as much in the dark as you are, Peter. We won't know until we can get into the stall and have a proper look at him. This is Victor by the way, he owns the horse. Victor meet Peter Jarvis, the vet.'

The two men exchanged handshakes and then the three of them walked over to Samson's stall. John quietly unlocked the top half of the door and peered in. 'He appears to be pretty docile at the moment. Hold on, I'll undo the rest of the door.' The door was opened and the vet entered first, followed by the other two. The horse stood there quietly, gazing at them with disinterested eyes.

Peter turned to John. 'Are you sure that you haven't given him anything? He seems to be very placid, not at all as you described him.'

The trainer shook his head, puzzled by the animal's quiet demeanour. Then an idea struck him and he dropped to his knees and began scrabbling around in the straw. The other two watched him without a word. Eventually he stood up and brushing the scraps of straw from his clothes turned and faced them. 'He has eaten them, he has eaten the rest of the eggs with the pills in them. No wonder he appears to be dopey. Whatever it was that Ginger had in those eggs to give him, he's eaten and sedated himself.'

'Well, I had better have a look at him while he is nice and quiet then,' the vet said with a laugh. 'He certainly is going to make my job a lot easier.' Approaching the horse, he patted him on the neck and began to examine him. After a few minutes he had finished checking him over and both the other two men gave a start when they saw that his hands were covered in blood.

'Don't worry, I don't think that it is as bad as it looks right now. He has an incised wound here on his chest. It looks to me as though a knife or very sharp piece of metal might have caused it. The lacerations above the ribs and along the flanks look like the result of him knocking himself along the side of the stall. There are still fragments and splinters of wood still in the wounds. He also has a small puncture just above the rib but it doesn't look too serious. I will give him a tetanus shot and some anti-toxin just in case. The wound on his chest should heal fairly quickly. We will have to get a poultice strapped to his side to draw out any contaminating material that might have got into the wound. I have some animalintex in the car, which should do for the puncture as well. The lacerations look as though they might cause some necrosis at a later stage. Apart from all that he looks fine. I know that it is hard to believe at the moment.'

'Necrosis, what exactly is that and is it serious?' Victor asked him anxiously. The vet shook his head. 'No, it just means that the blood supply is compromised slightly, resulting in flaps of dead skin. It should heal fine but you won't be able to enter him in any beauty contests I am afraid. No, he should be fine, no permanent damage.' He went out to the car to get the poultice.

Victor looked at John. 'What are we going to do about Cassidy? We know that he is involved in all of this.'

'Until we are able to talk to Ginger there is not really much that we can do. We need some solid proof before we can go to the police with any of this,' John said bitterly.

'What about that iron bar that you spoke of, do you think that that could have caused the cut? I suppose that the police have taken that though?' John nodded his head slowly.

'Yes, they took that away. I don't think that it would have been sharp enough to cause a wound like that though. Perhaps we should have a look around and see if we can find anything else. I don't think that the police searched through here after finding that iron bar.'

The two men started to hunt around in the straw of the stall whilst the horse stood idly by and watched them. 'He must have eaten a hell of a lot of those pills, whatever they were. I have never seen him looking so docile before,' John said.

Victor was rummaging through a pile of straw in one corner of Samson's stall when he let out a yell. 'Shit! I reckon that I have found it.' With blood pouring from his fingers he held up a broken wineglass.

John took it from Victor carefully and looked at it. 'This looks like one of our glasses.' He put what remained of the glass to his nose and smelt it. 'I think that it has had vodka in it. I'd say that our Ginger needed a shot of Dutch courage. Somehow when the horse reared it must have broken the glass. Or else Ginger himself may have used it to try and protect himself. Is there any more glass there?'

Victor carefully pulled the straw back. 'Not that I can see but with all this blood dripping from my fingers, it is a little hard to see anything on the floor.'

Just then the vet re-entered and started to tend to the horse's wounds. Looking at the blood still pouring from Victor's fingers he inquired with a grin, 'Do you want me to have a look at you after I have seen to the horse?'

'I will take him up to the house and get Mary to fix him up. She and Susan will be going frantic with worry because I wouldn't let either of them come down here. I didn't know what we would find and so I told them to stay put. Come on with me Victor, Nurse Collins awaits you. Do you need a hand there Peter? I can get one of the lads to come down if you like.'

The vet shook his head and yawned. 'No, I can manage as long as I can stay awake. I will come up when I have finished though and scrounge a cup of coffee off you, if I may?'

The two men left the vet to continue with his work and made their way back to the house. Victor was curious to know why nobody had answered him when he had knocked on the door on his arrival. John laughed heartily. 'I don't believe it, they actually did as they were told for once. I said that on no account were they to open the door to anyone except me. We did not know what was going on or how many people were involved. I am sorry Victor.'

'Does that mean that they wouldn't have let the policeman in either? You know, the one that you sent up to the house.'

John looked startled for a minute and then said, 'No, he should have been ok. They would have seen his helmet through the glass. At least I hope so or else the poor sod is still going to be standing there.'

As they came in sight of the house they found that it was clear. John took out his key and unlocked the front door. As soon as they walked through the door, Mary came rushing out. She gave a startled cry at seeing Victor with bloodstained hands. She rushed him off to the kitchen to wash them under the tap while John went into the lounge. He found Susan in there with the policeman. On the table he could see a small jar and a pile of bank notes. They both looked up as he entered.

'Five hundred pounds, Mr Collins,' the policeman indicated the pile of money. 'You must pay your stable lads well.'

John looked at the notes and then at his wife. 'We pay them a reasonable wage but the lads never have any spare cash that we know of. Where would Ginger get that kind of money? He would never have saved it, I am sure,' John said slowly.

His wife opened her mouth to ask a question but he silenced her with a shake of his head.

'I agree. The obvious answer is that in view of what happened in your stables there tonight, somebody has evidently paid your lad a lot of money to put one of your horses out of action, Mr Collins. You wouldn't have any idea of who could be behind all this?' The policeman's apparently casual tone did not fool John. He looked the man straight in the face. 'No, I know of no one. However, if we do discover anything I will be sure and let you know, officer. We are as keen as you are to get to the bottom of this. Until we are able to talk to Ginger, though, I don't think that there is much chance of discovering anything.'

The policeman nodded in agreement and then added, 'Will you be pressing charges against the lad, Sir?'

'I think that will be up to Mr Barnes, the owner of the horse. Personally, I don't think that any punishment than can be meted out will be worse than the pain that lad is going to go through for quite some time. I shall not be doing anything but Mr Barnes of course is quite at liberty and within his rights to do so if he wishes. What will happen to the money, if we can not establish its source?'

The policeman picked it up and placed it in a bag. 'We will look after it for the time being. I have already given your wife a receipt for it. Of course if the boy can prove that he came by it honestly, then naturally it will be returned to him. As for these pills, whatever they are, we will have to take them away to get them analysed.'

'May I see them for a moment?' a voice asked and they turned to see that Peter Jarvis had entered the room. Without a word the constable handed them over to him. Peter opened the jar, shook a couple of the pills into his hand, and looked at them. 'They certainly look like ACP to me.' Then tipping them back into the jar, he handed it back to the policeman.

'But where would Ginger be able to lay his hands on ACP John? I mean, we don't even keep them here ourselves.' Susan said in a puzzled tone. She was still in a state of shock that someone who lived under the same roof as them could be capable of such a thing.

'I assume from the same place that he got the £500 from,' her husband replied.

Just then Mary and Victor also returned to the room. Victor, his fingers bandaged, waved a hand at them. 'Look at all this lot for a couple of small cuts. I hate to think what she would do to me if I had a really serious injury.'

They all laughed. The policeman closed his notebook and slipped it into his tunic pocket. 'I am afraid that I can't do anything more until I am able to interview the lad. That won't be for some time I would imagine. So I will bid you all goodnight or at least good morning. I shall be in touch,' he promised. John went with him to see him to the door.

Peter turned to Susan. 'John promised me a cup of coffee if is not too much trouble.' She nodded and left the room.

Peter sat himself at the table and looked at Victor for a short while before he spoke. 'I'd say that your horse should be physically fine in a few days. The injuries look a lot worse than they actually are. I will drop in on Monday and just check him over to make sure. That is a very fine animal that you have there. John tells me that he is very valuable and he certainly looks it.'

'He is going to win the Derby!' Mary burst out excitedly, but Victor looked at the vet with some concern. 'He will be able to run, won't he?'

'Oh yes, his wounds are not so serious that they would prevent him from racing. What concerns me more is his attitude. John has explained how much trouble you have had getting someone who was able to ride him. This attack, however, may have some dire side effects. Horses are very temperamental beasts at the best of times and this one may never trust a man again. I hate to put a dampener on things but you are going to have a devil of a job to get him to trust anybody again.'

Chapter Fourteen

First thing on Monday morning, Victor was on the phone to Martin Buckingham. Briefly he brought him up to date on what had happened. He also told him that he had contacted Harley in the States and his friend had told him to take his horses away from Colin Oxford.

Victor had offered the pair to John Collins but John had refused them. He said that he really was semi-retired and didn't have the staff to look after two extra charges, especially now that he had lost Ginger. Mick too had refused them saying that he would rather concentrate on getting Pride of Tintagel fit and ready for the Grand National for the moment. He then thought of Ambrose's trainer Jenkins, who already had Delmore, although it looked as though it would be some time yet before he would be fit to race. He telephoned the man who said that he would be only too happy to take a couple more horses. He then arranged for a horsebox to meet him at Oxford's stable that afternoon to collect them.

Anticipating some strong opposition from the trainer, Victor asked whether Martin was free to go with him. On Harley's last visit they had arranged for Victor to be given power of attorney to act on the American's behalf. Ginger was in no state yet to be questioned so there was still no proof that it was Cassidy who had arranged the episode with Samson. However, he was no longer prepared to let the matter rest and had suggested to Martin that they confront Oxford over the French races and find out what he had to say for himself.

'If he thinks that the Jockey Club are now investigating then he might panic and do something rash,' Victor explained to Martin, who was not so certain. 'I feel that we may be jumping the gun a little. I need far more concrete evidence than I have at the moment in order to build a case against him.'

'I don't think that we can afford to wait any longer and run the risk of someone getting hurt. I think that we have to make our move and Harley is of the same opinion. He would rather put a stop to things now, even if it means Oxford getting away. He has said that he will go along with anything that I want to do.'

'You seem to be forgetting one thing. This latest episode was directed against you and not Harley,' Martin reminded him.

'Yes, that is because he saw the colt as a threat to his chances in the Derby. I have checked and he has a horse called Clearview jointly owned by him and Cassidy. It is a definite starter in the race. Jason Carter must have told him the times that Arcadian Steel has been doing. My main concern at the moment is that he may try again to get at the horse when he finds out that this attempt was unsuccessful. Now, if we were to confront him and let him know that we are aware of his little games, he is far less likely to try again. He would know that he would be a prime suspect for certain,' Victor argued.

'Yes, you may have a point there,' Martin admitted rather grudgingly. 'Right then, I will see you at Oxford's place at two o'clock.'

'He should be there, I couldn't find any of his horses entered in either race meeting to day,' Victor said and then hung up.

Victor made up his mind that he would leave right away so that he could call in and see either Becky or Billy at Newbury before going on to Palladian Lodge. As he drove into town he passed a string of horses trotting back from their morning gallop on the downs. He wondered idly what stable they were from and if there a future champion among their midst. As he passed the lead horse he accelerated once again and within a few minutes was pulling into the car park of the pub. The bar was deserted as he entered and he had to wait a few minutes before the landlord appeared.

'Sorry to keep you waiting. I am a bit short handed and of course the brewery had to make an early delivery. Now what will it be? Just a minute, it is Mr Barnes, isn't it?' he asked as he suddenly recognised Victor.

'You have a good memory,' Victor smiled.

The other man laughed and poured a shot of whisky into a glass. 'You need to have one in this game. The drink is on the house Mr Barnes. Actually it is because of you that I am short of staff today.' Victor looked at him stupidly and the publican laughed again. 'Yes, it was because of your help and influence that Billy landed that job with your American friend. He has gone up to London for two weeks to organise his office computers for him. He has also finally finished that computer game that he was working on. Once again through your American friend he has sold it to a big concern in the States. It is because of all this and that now Billy has a job with some excellent prospects, he and Becky are getting married earlier than planned. So this morning she and my wife have gone up to London to buy some new clothes and look at wedding dresses. They owe all of this to you and I think that they may be going to invite you to the wedding Mr Barnes.'

'Victor, please, I never feel really comfortable with Mr Barnes. I am glad that something good has come out of all this. Please tell them that I may not be around for the wedding but that I wish them both a happy and successful life together,' Victor said with genuine emotion. It made him feel good that he was able to contribute to the young couple's happiness. 'I had hoped for a spot of lunch or is it not on today?'

'It should be ready in about half an hour. I have a girl coming in to help me then. If you are really pushed for time I could rustle you up a chicken salad if you like. It would only take a few minutes.'

'That would be fine, I can't really wait another thirty minutes. I have to go and collect some horses and I should be there before the float arrives.'

Some twenty minutes later with both his hunger and thirst satisfied, Victor was on his way to Burghclere. He had arranged with Martin Buckingham that they would meet at the turn off to Palladian Lodge and then drive down together. Victor thought that it would be better if he actually came face to face with the investigator before they arrived at Oxford's place. He was nearing the lane that turned off to the stables when he spotted a large horsebox ahead of him. 'This could be for me I reckon,' he said to himself. He flashed his headlights at the truck and, thinking that he wanted to pass him, obligingly pulled over tight to the left-hand side of the road. Victor overtook him and then drew up some fifty yards ahead and, getting out of his car, he waved the other vehicle down. The driver wound down his cab window. 'Are you going to Palladian Lodge to collect two horses to go to Newmarket?' Victor asked him. The driver nodded assent and consulting a clipboard on the seat beside him said, 'I am supposed to meet some geezer named Barnes, are you the one?'

'Yes, I am Barnes. Look we may have a bit of trouble when we get there. The trainer doesn't know as yet that we are collecting the horses.'

'Look 'ere, this is nothing dodgy like is it? If so I am out of 'ere smartish.'

'No. I can assure you that it is all above board. I can show you the papers if you like and besides there will be a fellow from the Jockey Club there to meet us. So you needn't worry, it is all legal and above board. It's just that I suspect that the trainer will not be very happy when he finds out that he is losing them.'

Just then a small, blue Fiat drove past them and then came to a halt. The car reversed back and came to rest just in front of Victor's car. A young, rather muscular looking youth with blond hair cut in a crew cut got out.

'Are you Victor?' A trifle surprised Victor told him that he was and shook his outstretched hand. The youth's grip was firm and powerful. 'I am Martin Buckingham and, before you say it, you were expecting someone older. Well, I will let you into a little secret, I am older than I look. Quite often though it is an advantage to look young as people don't look at you twice. Plus the fact that people underestimate the amount of clout that I can bring to bear when needed,' he laughed. 'Don't look so worried, I am good at my job.' Martin then put his hand in his pocket and pulled out his wallet. Opening it he showed both Victor and the driver his credentials. Having satisfied the driver that they had every right to move the horses, Martin and Victor got back into their respective cars. The three vehicles then slowly made their way down the lane that led to Palladian Lodge.

They drove into the yard and parked. Oxford could not help but see them as he looked out into the yard from behind his desk. Telling the driver of the horsebox to wait, the other two men marched over to the office door. Oxford had moved and stood in the doorway watching them as they approached. He made no attempt to come out to meet them but waited until they reached the door.

'Well now, I was not expecting any horses today. What is the idea of the horse float? Wait a minute, I know you. You are Victor Barnes, aren't you?'

'That's right,' Victor agreed. 'I am glad that you remember me, that should make things a little easier. I have come to collect Mr Klugman's two horses. I would appreciate it if you can get one of your lads to load them into the box for me.'

Oxford made no move to comply with the request but merely stared at the two men. 'What does John Cassidy have to say about all this? I believe that he is Mr Klugman's manager and not you. I have received no notification from him and therefore the horses stay where they are.'

'John Cassidy has no say in the matter.' Victor put his hand in his jacket pocket and pulled out a sheet of paper. Here is my power of attorney to act on Mr Klugman's behalf.' He offered the paper to Oxford who made no attempt to take it but simply stood in the doorway of his office with his arms folded across his chest in an act of defiance.

'I take my orders from John Cassidy. I don't care what piece of paper you have in your hand. Now clear off, I've got work to do.'

'I don't know what you think that you are going to achieve by adopting this attitude Mr Oxford. This paper gives me the legal right to do what I think is best for Mr Klugman. Now I am not leaving here without those horses,' Victor said calmly.

Oxford stared at him for a moment and then said thickly, 'You either leave this yard right now or I will call the police and have you thrown out.'

Victor looked at Martin who gave a nod. 'Then I suggest that you give them a call. I think that there is a slight matter of embezzlement that they might be interested in. Here, I will save you the cost of a phone call and ring them myself.' Victor pulled out his mobile and held it up to Oxford's face.

'Embezzlement! What the hell are you talking about?' Oxford glared at Victor who smiled as he saw the man's face give a nervous twitch.

'The simple matter of what happened to the winnings from Mr Klugman's horses when they raced in France.' For the first time Martin Buckingham joined in.

'Who the hell are you? His body guard? Why is he afraid to face me on his own with these wild accusations?'

Martin slowly pulled out his card and showed it to him.

The trainer first went white and then he began to sweat profusely. 'You will have to ask Cassidy about that,' he blustered, 'he dealt with all the money side of things. He was his manager after all. I just trained the horses. As far as I am concerned Mr Klugman has always received whatever prize money that he was due. I had nothing to do with the financial dealings. You will have to see Cassidy.'

'How about your winning fee for the French races? Were you ever paid?' Martin asked him. 'You see, Mr Klugman has never been given any notification that his horses even raced in France, let alone won any races. Now I have been given to understand that you used to send him a report every month detailing the races that they were entered for. So why is there no mention of France? Also, if he had known that his horses had done so well in France why would he be wanting to get rid of them?'

'I used to give the report to Cassidy to send off. It is nothing to do with me if he withheld certain information. As I said, I am just his trainer. Cassidy is his manager.'

Martin eyed him silently for a few seconds and then said, 'You still haven't told us whether or not you received your fee for the French races?'

'Yes, of course I got my usual percentage. Cassidy would have sent cheques to me and the jockey as normal. As I am tired of telling you. Cassidy dealt with all the money matters from Mr Klugman's account. Look, I don't know what you are trying to imply here but I resent the insinuation that I have done anything at all that is underhand. If there has been any kind of fraud committed, which I don't believe for a minute, I have had no part in it. Cassidy is the one who signs all the cheques so I strongly suggest that you go and talk to him.'

'Oh, but we intend to Mr Oxford,' Victor said with a smile. 'By the way, they must have been some major races that those two horses won in France. That is judging by the size of your commission cheque.'

Oxford's mouth dropped open and he gaped at Victor, who continued slowly, 'You see Mr Klugman hired someone to go through his financial affairs and do you know what he found?'

'I have no idea. My daughter would have banked any cheques that came in.'

'Including cheques totalling over £50,000? You see, Mr Oxford, when we checked Mr Klugman's bank we found a second account of which he had no knowledge. Imagine our surprise when we found that cheques from a French bank had been deposited there and that the amount was the same as the prize money from the races that horses won in France. Then we were even more astonished to find that half of that money had been paid to you, Mr Oxford. Perhaps you are able to explain this also.'

By now Oxford was beginning to look quite sick. 'I always have cheques for large amounts coming in here. I buy and sell horses as well as just train them. As I said, it is my daughter who does all the banking. I doubt whether I have even set eyes on that particular cheque,' he muttered. 'I have already told you that if there is some kind of fraud going on, then I am completely innocent. Now just take your horses and get the hell out of here.'

'That was always our intention Mr Oxford.' Victor smiled at him again. 'By the way, how is your friend Monsieur Duval? Has he managed to purchase any cheap racehorses lately? I believe that he has quite a flair for picking up real cheap bargains from you?' Oxford staggered under the weight of this last verbal attack.

'Get your horses and get out. I don't want to see you here again.'

'I betcha don't. I promise you though, Mr Oxford, we shall be back.'

'Get out!' he hissed through clenched teeth. He then turned and stormed back into the office. Picking up the phone he barked something into it and then slammed it down again. Martin and Victor walked across the yard towards the stables. A man appeared from around the back of the building. 'Your two are in six and eight,' he said but made no attempt to bring the horses out.

They were just securing the second horse in the box when another car pulled into the yard. A man got out and started walking towards the office. 'This is going to be very interesting,' Victor said to Martin. 'That is Cassidy who has just arrived.' They finished checking the horses into the box and after locking the doors told the driver to get on his way. The man shrugged his shoulders, climbed into his cab and slowly made his way out of the yard. Victor and Martin watched the van safely out of the yard and then walked back towards the office. Through the glass wall they could see the two men were in the middle of a somewhat violent argument, with both shouting and waving their arms about wildly.

'Do we leave them to get on with it or what?' Martin asked Victor. 'We have already told Oxford far more than I intended to.'

Victor thought about it for a minute and then shook his head. 'I think that we might as well let them know where we stand. It might be safer if we give them something to worry about for a change. Up to now they have thought that they have gotten away with it all.'

'Ok, you are the boss,' Martin replied.

Victor marched into the office closely followed by the investigator.

Cassidy turned and faced them, his face red with anger. 'What do you mean by taking those horses out of here? I am Klugman's manager not you,' Cassidy positively yelled at Victor who looked him squarely in the face before replying.

'You used to be his manager but not any more I am afraid. As of this moment Harley Klugman no longer employs you. A severance cheque will be forwarded to you but, seeing as how you have stolen money from him, I shouldn't bother to try and cash it if I were you.' Victor announced all this quite calmly although his heart was beating wildly and his palms were beginning to sweat.

Cassidy whirled round on Oxford. 'What the hell have you been saying to them?'

'Oh, we have had a very enlightening conversation with Mr Oxford.' Victor said. 'He has been very helpful and cleared up one or two points that we were uncertain about. There is one more thing you should know, Mr Cassidy. Your attempt to get at Arcadian Steel was unsuccessful. All that you managed to do was to put Ginger in hospital. As soon as he is fit he will have no problem identifying you as the one who paid him to put the horse out of action.'

This time it was Oxford who turned on Cassidy. 'You utter fool!' he raged. 'You just couldn't wait, could you? I told you that I would look after that horse. You are on your own in this.'

'Thank you gentlemen, I think that I have heard enough. We will be in touch with you in due course once I have figured what charges will be brought against you.' Martin then caught Victor's arm. 'Come on Victor, I think that it is high time that we left and let these two sort out their problems.'

Once outside he rounded on Victor sharply. 'You can't go around saying things like that. You have no proof.'

'Not yet, maybe, but they good as confessed to it didn't they?' Victor laughed loudly.

As the two men were walking back to their cars, Lilly came around the corner. 'Hi there Lilly, it's nice to see you again.' Victor greeted her. 'This is Martin and he works for the Jockey Club.'

Lilly returned his greeting and then pointed to the office. 'What's going on in there today? All that shouting I could hear. I have just seen a horsebox going up the lane as well. Have you taken your friend's horses away? Dad will be furious if you have.'

'I don't think that now is a good time to stop and talk Lilly,' Victor answered. 'Your father is not a happy man and yes we have taken the horses.' He then pulled out his wallet and took out several £50 notes. Pushing them into her hand he said, 'If I were you I'd pack your bags and get over to your mother's. This should help a bit. You can tell your mother that I will be in touch with you both about your new dressmaking business.'

Lilly stared at him for a minute and then it slowly dawned on her what must have happened. 'You mean that Dad has finally been caught out?'

'You could say that, but we had better go before he catches us talking to you. I will be in touch and, Lilly, thank you for all your help.'

'Oh Mr Barnes, thank you,' she cried and hugged him.

'Very touching I am sure, all this, Victor, but I suggest that we get out of here before Cassidy comes gunning for you. Believe you me he is not the sort of man to take this lying down. I will ring you when I find out what action the committee wants to take. Tell me, is this the way that you usually do business in Australia?' So saying, Martin shook his hand and with a huge grin on his face drove off down the lane. Victor too, got into his car and started the engine. With a final wave to Lilly he followed the Fiat, feeling well satisfied with his day's work.

Victor had reached Andover before he decided that he should call John to see if there was any change to Ginger. He was also concerned about how his horse was doing. Pulling into the car park of a coffee shop, he dialled the number. Mary answered the phone and informed him that there was no change in Ginger's condition. The police still had not been able to interview him. As for Samson, she told him that the horse seemed to be coming back to his old self but was very ill-tempered.

Victor then told her what had transpired at Oxford's place. 'I wish that I could have been there to see his face,' Mary said, 'he must have got an awful shock when he found out that you knew about France and the horses.'

'I imagine that he did,' Victor said drily. 'We were lucky that Billy was able to find that other account with his computer. We would not have had a case without it. Oh yes, he and Becky are going to get married earlier because Harley got a company to buy one of his video games. I believe that I am going to be invited to the wedding as well.'

'I should love to see you at my wedding, Victor,' Mary said with a chuckle in her voice.

'Your wedding?' Victor was startled. 'Are you getting married too?'

'I wish! That Becky is a lucky girl though. It must be exciting for her looking forward to becoming a bride. To think that she has you to thank for it too.' There was an awkward pause for a moment, then she continued. 'Where are you now? Why don't you come here for dinner? It would save you the long drive to Cornwall and you could see Samson in the morning.'

'I should really be getting home. It seems to me that I have spent more time away from the place than I have been there lately.'

'Oh, I suppose that you are right. It would have been nice to see you though.'

He could sense the disappointment in her voice so after thinking about it for less than a minute, he replied. 'Right, I will come to dinner but I will have to leave first thing in the morning. Perhaps by then we might have some news about Ginger, too. Ok, I will see you soon.' He hung up and then started off for Taunton.

By the time that he reached the Collins's house it had got very dark and it looked as though a storm was brewing. Indeed, as he was walking up to the door the sky was lit with a jagged flash of lightning and he was almost deafened by the loud crash of thunder. Perhaps it's just as well that I am not driving home in this, he thought to himself as he knocked on the door.

John opened it and said, 'Hi there, Victor. Mary told me that she had persuaded you to come for dinner.'

'I hope that you don't mind. If it is a problem then I can leave.'

'Don't be silly. For a start it looks as though we are in for a very dirty night and you wouldn't want to be driving in it. Anyway, you are just what she needs at the moment. She hasn't said much but it is obvious that she is still upset over Carter. She has spent most of the day in her room and that is not like her at all.'

'What did the police have to say? Have they seen him yet?' Victor asked as he took off his coat and handed it to the other man.

'He denies everything, of course. The police told Mary that they would charge him if she wants to take it further but at the moment I get the impression that she just wants to forget about it. It would be a different matter if he had actually raped her but, thank God, he didn't get that far. I think that she will just let things go. I am still trying to think of something that we can do but, as yet, I haven't had a single idea that is within the law. I have thought of a number of things that aren't lawful but that would not help matters.' John was very perturbed and decidedly unhappy about the whole business, Victor could see.

Victor felt a trifle awkward about having to broach a new topic but took a deep breath. 'Before we go in, I think that it would pay you to employ a security guard for the stables for the next couple of weeks, just in case there is any trouble. I will foot the bill of course. I can't see either Oxford or Cassidy trying anything but you never know. I think that it is better to be safe than sorry,' Victor had dropped his voice so that only John could hear him.

'A good idea. I had thought about it myself actually and in fact I might even go and arrange it now. You go on in and talk to Mary. Susan is in the kitchen. We will join you shortly.' So saying John hung Victor's coat in the cupboard and went to join his wife in the kitchen, leaving Victor to go into the lounge.

Mary was sitting by the fire but, seeing him enter, jumped to her feet. 'I am so glad to see you Victor,' she said hugging him tightly. 'Thank you for coming. I know that you wanted to go home but I am really glad that you are here.'

'I have to look after my jockey now don't I?' he teased.

The next morning they were all up early. The storm, although violent, had blown itself out during the night. Everything smelt fresh and clean as they made their way down to the stables. Cliff, John's head lad, met them in the yard with a long face. 'That Samson is playing up a bit again this morning, boss. I have tried several times to change his dressing but I can't get near him. That thunder last night didn't help either, he is very skittish this morning,' the man said concernedly.

'How about his feed? Is he eating better?'

'I rolled his oats myself this morning and we added palm kernel as you said, plus there is a good mix of nuts as well. He seemed to eat well enough, there's not a lot wrong with his appetite as far as I can see.'

Victor approached Samson's stall with some trepidation. The top half of the door was hooked back and, as he neared the doorway, Samson's head appeared and he snorted. Victor reached up to pat him but the horse veered away.

Mary came up to his side and gently pushed him away. 'Here let me try,' she said softly. He is most likely still a bit wary.' She took a couple of carrots from her pocket and held them up. The black head appeared once more and, after a moment's hesitation, chomped on the carrots. Mary spoke softly to the horse and fondled his ears.

John arrived carrying two bottles of beer. 'Let's see if he will let us give him these,' he said to his daughter.

Victor looked shocked. 'Beer! You give him beer?'

The older man laughed at the expression on the other's face. 'Horses regard beer as a luxury, like eggs. Do you want to go and pour it in his bucket while Mary here holds him?'

Victor hesitated for a second and then took the two bottles.

Mary continued to pat the horse as Victor opened the lower half of the door and cautiously entered the stall. 'Don't make any sudden moves, just take your time and move slowly,' she told him.

He edged his way over to the bucket and poured the beer into it. The horse must have smelt it, because he immediately retreated back into the stall and started to gulp the amber liquid down as Victor was pouring it out. The bottles empty, he slowly made his way back out of the stall.

'He seems calm enough now,' John said. 'Cliff, see if he will let you change his dressing now.'

'I will do it,' Mary cried and took the clean dressing from Cliff's hands. Cliff gave it up quite readily and with a sigh of relief. Within minutes Mary had changed the dressing and was back outside again.

Her father was pleased. 'I think that he looks well enough for a gentle canter. Do you want to take him Mary?'

'Surely no one can ride him with those dressings on?' Victor looked quite aghast.

Mary roared with laughter at his expression. 'I am not going to ride him, silly. I will put a halter on him and then lead him from one of the other horses. Victor, I am surprised at you.'

He looked somewhat abashed and coloured up slightly. 'I am sorry. I should have realised, it was stupid of me.' Even John had to smile.

By now the other lads had their horses saddled and ready to go. Cliff brought over Pepper Pot for Mary to ride and her father gave her a leg up. Just take him around the track a couple of times and see how he goes. Are you sure that you can handle two horses?'

Mary smiled at her father and gathered up the reins. 'Just you watch me, Dad.' The horses trotted off towards the track.

John watched them go and then turned to Victor. 'At least this seems to take her mind off Jason Carter. I sincerely hope that it doesn't take too long for the horse to be healed enough to ride. At the moment he is fighting fit and we need to keep him that way, if he is to have any chance at the Derby.'

'Yes, but even if he is fit, we are going to be back with the same old problem again. We have to find somebody who can ride him,' Victor said gloomily. He kicked at a clump of grass angrily. John put a comforting arm around the other man's shoulder. 'Don't look so glum. We may find now that the horse has become used to someone riding him. He may not be the problem that he has been in the past. Young Jimmy handled him ok and we might be able to use him. I admit that this episode with Ginger might, and I repeat might, be an issue but we won't know that until the horse is fit to ride. The vet said yesterday that he thought his wounds should be cleared up in a couple of days.'

'I never realised that there could be so many problems associated with owning a racehorse,' Victor said rather morosely. 'There is this trouble with Samson, then this other business with Oxford and Cassidy. On top of that we have had Carter trying his best to rape Mary. I used to think that the only difficulty that owners used to have is whether their horse might break down or get a touch of colic. This gets more like a Dick Francis novel every day.' Victor gave a big sigh and the older man looked at him.

'Now, firstly, Carter is a problem that could have happened anywhere, it is just a coincidence that the man is a jockey. Oxford and Cassidy, well fraud can happen anywhere and is not confined to racing. The last thing is as long as you have top-class horses racing for big money, there will always be someone trying to stop them. It is a fact of life in this game, whether they are bookies, punters or the stables themselves. However, you cannot blame the industry. These are hassles that we all run into somewhere along the line, no matter what kind of business that we are in. You have to look on the bright side of things. You have had the thrill and excitement of your horses running and winning. Also, you must have got a kick out of solving your friend Harley's dilemma with his manager.'

John smiled at him. 'There is one more thing that has come out of all this. Whether or not it is a comfort or a curse, I am not quite sure of at the moment.'

'What are you talking about now?' Victor asked bewilderedly.

'You have met my daughter Mary,' John replied and burst into roars of laughter and slapped him on the back. Even Victor had to grin at that.

Later that morning Victor received a phone call from Martin Buckingham that cheered him no end. The Jockey Club had decided that there was a case to answer and had set up an inquiry into all Oxford's transactions and methods. The police too had been notified about the winnings from France not being paid to Harley. They were only waiting for confirmation from Victor and then Cassidy would be charged with embezzlement.

'I am not sure how the word got around so quickly but most of the other owners are also pulling their horses out of his stable. The switchboard at the club has been flat out with people ringing to confirm what was going on. At this rate he will be lucky to have a horse left tomorrow,' Martin told him briefly. 'You had better watch yourself, you have made yourself an enemy there.'

'It was most likely someone from Jenkins's stable. He must have told someone in the pub about Harley's horses arriving. Nobody at the stable had been told why we had the horses pulled out. I guess when an owner like Harley suddenly withdraws his horses from a successful trainer, then rumours start to fly. I will get in touch with him and get him to fax you about the illegality of that second account. I don't think that he is due back in the UK for some time.' Victor then hung up and went to find the others and bring them up to date. Mary was upstairs changing so he made a mental note to tell her later what Martin had said.

John listened with great interest to what Victor had to say but was clearly worried by the time that he relayed Martin's conversation.

'I am afraid that Martin is correct. You will have to watch yourself. If Oxford has lost all his horses, he is not going to take it lying down. I mean, you have almost single-handedly destroyed his business. I think that to be on the safe side I had better double the security at least until the inquiry is over. We can't afford for anyone to have another go at Samson.'

'But surely he wouldn't be stupid enough to try anything? He would have to know that he would be the first one blamed if anything did happen.'

'Victor, if the man has just lost his business then he may not be thinking rationally. All he would want to do is to extract his revenge on you.'

'Well, I really must get on home. It is far later then I intended staying.' Victor, got up. 'Don't forget it is the National on Saturday and I have several things to attend to beforehand. I just hope that Lilly has managed to move away from her father. I promised that I would help her and her mother set up their dressmaking business. Also Harley has agreed to pay for the nurse for Jack Oxford until they can get on their feet. So I have phone calls to make and cheques to write; I feel as though I need a secretary.' He laughed. 'On top of all that I must get some proper sleep. I seem to have spent all my time lately driving all over the countryside.'

Just then Mary came in and her face fell as she realised that Victor was about to leave. Before she could say anything he held up his hand. 'I am very sorry Mary, but I simply must go. The National is only days away and I have so much to do. The most important thing at the moment is for me to contact the estate agent in Truro. I need to confirm that I want the house for at least another three months.'

'Only another three months? Have you decided that you are going back to Australia then?' Mary said unhappily.

'I have to confirm before he tries to let it for the summer season. No, I haven't any plans at the moment for going back home.'

'Are you sure about that Victor?'

'Mary,' he looked her straight in the eye, 'hasn't your father ever told you that in life, as in racing, there is no such thing as a sure thing?'

Chapter Fifteen

The day before the Grand National Victor drove up to Hill Top Stud early in the morning to collect Mary and take her down to St Mawley. Mick had decided that she should take Pride out for a short gallop just to get the horse used to her again, as she had not ridden him for a while. He had told Victor that he always considered it important for the horse to be familiar with his rider if it were at all possible. He also wanted to go through the rest of the field in detail with her before the race. The traffic was light and they made good time.

By ten o'clock the car was pulling up outside the cottage. Hearing them arrive Sally came to the door. 'Hey you two, you must have smelt it, the coffee's just perked.' They made their way indoors and were soon seated at the dining-room table drinking their coffee. At one end Mick had copies of *Racing Post* and *Sporting Life* strewn out among scraps of other papers with all sorts of notes scribbled on them.

Victor was impressed. 'You seem to have gone to an awful lot of trouble over this race, Mick.'

'There is prize money for the first six horses. With a race of this length and the number of entries that are engaged, anything can happen and usually does.'

'How many runners are there this year?' Mary asked.

'At present there are thirty-nine but Prince Sharman is a doubtful starter.'

'How many do you reckon will finish?' Mick asked curiously.

'You might as well ask me who is going to win,' Mick said, laughing. 'It's impossible to say or to even have a guess. I think that it was in 1928 that only two horses finished. In 1994, six out of thirty-six came in, while back in 1980 only four lasted the course. It is surprising, too, how many horses come down at the first fence. It can completely alter the outcome of the race, that first jump.'

'Imagine going through all the drama of getting your horse just right for the biggest race of its career only to fall at the first, it would be heartbreaking. Why is it so hard then Mick? Is it such a high fence or what?' Victor inquired with interest.

'No, it's not really big, only 4ft 6in high. The problem lies in the fact that there are so many horses and it is 420 yards from the start. This means that by the time they reach it they have built up quite a bit of speed. The safest way to avoid trouble is to head for the outside, but then it is the longest way round. The ideal position for the good jumpers is the inside but most horses head for the centre making it really crowded. That is why so many come down there, they are cramped for room.'

'Which way do you want me to go, Mick?' Mary asked quietly. He hesitated for a minute before replying slowly. 'Pride is a good enough jumper to take the inside but it is a lot harder. I will leave that up to you.'

'Right then, we will take the inside route,' Mary said defiantly. Victor looked at her anxiously. 'I don't want you to take any unnecessary risks now Mary.'

'Faint hearts never won fair ladies,' she said with a smile.

'I see, so what we want then is for half the field to fall at the first fence and our Mary to come galloping through on the inside,' Sally came into the conversation, laughing.

'Anything is possible in this race,' her husband repeated. 'One year twelve runners came down at the first.'

'Just as long as I am not one of them,' Mary said. 'How do you want me to ride, Mick? That is assuming, of course, that I get over the first jump,' she said with a chuckle.

Mick looked at her across the table. 'I am quite happy for you to ride your own race. You have enough experience in point to points. After all the race is four and a half miles long and things can change quite dramatically out there. It is really too hard to give you concrete instructions.'

'Who are the main chances as far as the bookies are concerned? Also, while we are on odds, what price is Pride?' Victor asked him.

Mick checked one of the papers that he had in front of him. 'Hills and Ladbrokes both have him at 35s and Corals at 25–1. The favourite with them all is US Male at tens. Then Another Day Gone, Fool's Moon and Cathay High Road are all at twelves.'

'What about that grey that came fifth in the Cheltenham Gold Cup?'

'Chevy Blue Eyes? He is 20–1 but history is against him. There has not been a grey win the National for nearly fifty years,' Mick replied in answer to his wife's question.

She looked at him grimly. 'Suny Bay came second in 97,' she retorted sharply.

Her husband looked at her and grinned. 'He still didn't win it though, did he?'

Mary finished her coffee then stood up and made for the door. 'I am going to get changed while you lot fight it out among yourselves. I have got a horse to ride.'

Mick too drained his cup. 'Yes, we can talk about the others after we have seen to Pride. I am going to get changed too. I will ride Emma seeing as how we are only going for a gentle gallop and keep you company. Will you two be OK?' he asked Sally and Victor. They both nodded so he followed Mary out of the room.

'Would you like another cup of coffee?' Sally asked. Victor pushed his cup towards her. She filled it and passed it back. She then sat down and faced him. 'Mick wants me to ask you something,' she said slowly.

'This sounds serious,' he said, 'what's the problem?'

Sally looked at him steadily for a few moments before she asked quietly, 'How badly do you want to win this race?'

'I don't quite understand. I mean that the race is worth nearly £180,000 to the winner. I mean that everybody would love to win that.'

'This is not going to be easy, that's why Mick asked me to ask you instead of doing it himself, the coward.'

'I think that you had better get to the point Sally.' She gave a big sigh and then said. 'Winning this race would mean everything to Mick. As you know we have had a tough time of it lately but now, thanks to you, he has a chance to prove to everybody that he has what it takes. To be a good trainer I mean.'

Victor shot her a puzzled look. 'I understand that. He has managed to get the horse ready for the race, so I don't really see what his problem is.' This train of thought mystified him.

'No woman has ever won the Grand National. In fact as far as we know only a couple have ever completed the course.'

'So this means that Mary could be the first, I don't see . . .Wait a minute, are you saying what I think that you are saying?' He got to his feet, his face blazing with anger. 'There is no way that is going to happen Sally! For one thing it would break her heart and I will not have any part of it.'

'But Victor, with a male jockey Mick thinks that you will have a much better chance of winning. Don't forget this is far harder than a point to point. You really need to be strong to even last the distance. Now Mick has found someone who can ride the horse and all that he needs is . . .'

'You can tell that cowardly husband of yours, if Mary doesn't ride the horse then I will withdraw it. How could you do this to your own cousin?' He turned to leave but Sally grabbed his arm.

'I know that you are angry but if you stop and think for a minute, it does make a lot of sense. The race is hard enough on a man and I know Mary. If she thought that you had more chance of winning by her not riding, then she would accept it. She would be unhappy, of course. She would see it gives the horse a far better chance and that is what counts in the end. Just say that you will think it over.'

Victor slowly turned and looked her straight in the eye. In an icy tone he spoke slowly and distinctly. 'Sally, I shall say this one more time. If Mary doesn't ride then I will scratch the horse. Have I made myself clear enough for you?'

Then, to his amazement, Sally grabbed him and kissed him warmly. 'Mary has told me what a great guy you are and she is right. I told Mick that there was no chance of you taking her off Pride and I was right. To be honest, Victor, if you had gone along with Mick, then you would not have been the man that I thought you were. Now shall we go and see if we can find the others?'

They had to wait a full twenty minutes before the riders came into sight. Mary reined in ahead of Mick and dismounted, her cheeks full of colour and her eyes ablaze with excitement.

'Oh Victor, he is just fine. He is fit and raring to go. I am just so excited about tomorrow. Well, I had better go and hose him off.' So saying she led the horse off in the direction of the stables.

As she left, Mick rode up on the mare. 'Either Emma is getting old or that one is getting faster,' he said pointing to the rear of the other horse. 'She just could not keep pace with him. Victor, did, er, Sally, um, talk to you about tomorrow at all?'

'Yes, she did and the answer is an emphatic no!'

Mick merely shrugged his shoulders and avoided his wife's glare. 'Ok, if that is how you feel, you are the boss after all. I will see you both back at the cottage after I have finished with Emma here.'

Back in the cottage, they were all seated around the table once more. Mick shuffled through the papers and pulling out a sheet handed it to Mary. 'I have compiled a list of who, in my opinion, are going to be your main opponents and consequently the most trouble. Manx Warrior will try to lead from start to finish so try and keep in touch with him if you can. Multi Purpose is suspect over fences; to my mind he is a far better hurdler, so try and stay clear of him. The same thing applies to Swallow's Nest. He has run in the race three times and has yet to complete a circuit. However, on his day he can get the distance without any trouble. Myself, apart from Pride of course, I reckon that the one with the best chance of winning is Highgate. He will stay all day and has won the Foxhunters' Chase, so he knows the course well, to boot. Well, I guess that it is all up to you now Mary.'

'I can't believe that I am going to ride in the Grand National. I will most likely wake up tomorrow and find that all this is a dream,' Mary sighed gently. 'I have never raced with so many people watching me before either.'

Victor leaned across the table and patted her hand. 'Don't worry you will be fine. Your Mum and Dad will be there to cheer you on as well. We will be up there in the stands and . . .'

'Dad won't drive all the way to Liverpool and back. He has to get up too early in the morning. He and Mum will watch it on the telly.'

'He won't have to. I have chartered a plane again and we will be flying up. You need to be nice and fresh when you get there, so we are flying high.'

'Oh yeah, what is it that they say about a fool and his money?' Mary said in mock criticism, but inside her heart was racing. She simply could not believe that this was happening to her. Not only was she going to ride in the greatest steeplechase in the world but also she was being flown there to do it.

'While you lot are gallivanting about the skies, Mick and I will have to leave at 5a.m. to drive up there. You wouldn't have room for us on the plane, as well, would you Victor? Oh yes and the horse of course, we couldn't very well leave him behind now could we?'

They all laughed and then Victor turned to Mick. 'Unless you have anything else to say to Mary, we might get going. I don't want to be late getting back.'

'No, I guess there is not much more that I can do now. You are quite welcome to take all these form sheets with you but they may confuse you even more. I guess that everything is now in the lap of the gods,' Mick stated with far more enthusiasm than he felt. He still considered that they would have a better chance with a stronger jockey. 'Right then, we will see you tomorrow at Aintree.

Mary and Victor drove off towards the village. 'Are you going to drive me home Victor or had you something else in mind?'

'I can drive you home if that is what you want, but I thought that we might drive into Perranporth. Did you know that in all the time that I have been living here, I have never been there? Yet it is only about six miles from the house. The beach there is supposed to be marvelous. I have got champagne in the boot and we can pick up some fried chicken. What do you say to a picnic on the beach?'

'That sounds great but I had better ring Dad. He will be expecting me home, what with the race being tomorrow.'

'No, he won't. I have already told him that you will be staying at my place tonight. I said that we would pick him and your mum up tomorrow. I have arranged with the pilot that we call at Exeter airport on the way to Liverpool. I thought that it would be easier for your folks to get there than to St Mawgam.'

'You seem to have thought of everything, so let's get on down to the beach. Eat, drink and be merry, for tomorrow we die,' she quoted forcefully. Victor laughed heartily.

'I sincerely hope not, for tomorrow you have a horse race to win Miss Collins.'

The next morning, Victor again woke early. He got up from the couch and stretched himself lengthily. 'God, I am going to have to do something about this arrangement soon if Mary is going to keep coming here to sleep. My back is killing me, kipping on this couch all the time. Hell, what am I talking about? I cannot marry her yet and there is no way that I am going to bed with her unless we are. I could never live with myself if I did. Anyway, let's forget about sex for the moment we have a horse race to win. There will be time to think about things like that after we are past the post.'

As he mumbled to himself he made his way upstairs and rapped sharply on the bedroom door. 'Come on, Miss Collins, wakey wakey. You have an appointment with destiny today.' Hearing a muffled grunt, he assumed that she was awake and went back downstairs to start the breakfast.

By the time that Victor had managed to get Mary to eat some toast and drink two cups of coffee, she was almost fully awake. He then managed to bundle her into the car. He drove to St Mawgam where their plane was fuelled and waiting for them. The cold air as they walked across the tarmac worked wonders. As they clambered into the plane Mary was her usual bright and cheerful self. Taxiing out onto the runway, the pilot received his clearance from the tower. Taking off, the pilot laid in a course for the short trip to Exeter. Upon landing, Victor told Mary to stay put and he got out and went in search of her parents. They were soon back in the air and heading for Liverpool.

When they arrived at their destination and after promising to back Pride of Tintagel the pilot dropped them off. He then taxied the aircraft into a hangar to await their return. Victor had arranged with the airport to have a taxi waiting for them and they were soon on their way to Aintree. Arriving at the course, John and Susan said that they were going to have an early lunch while the other two went in search of Mick and Sally. Having found them Victor invited them to join the others for lunch. They both declined saying that there was too much riding on the race for them to have any appetite. 'OK, I will tell what I will do. Whatever the outcome of the race today, I propose that we all meet in Truro for a celebration next week. How about it you two, does that sound better?'

'That suits me fine. There is no way that I could sit down and enjoy a meal right at this moment. I already have too many butterflies in my stomach to find any room for food,' Mick said gruffly and Sally agreed.

'If we are not going to eat, I may as well go and get changed. I have to do something to take my mind off the race.' Mary's voice was husky. She could feel her pulse starting to go into overdrive.

'In that case you and I may as well go and sit in the stand, Victor, and watch some of the racing. Mick has to stay with Mary and the horse of course but at least we shall be out of their way,' said Sally pulling at his arm.

As Mick marched off to check on the horse, Mary started to follow him but then turned back to Victor. 'Sally here told me what you said to Mick when he suggested replacing me with a male jockey. I can't thank you enough. But don't you worry, I promise that I won't let you down.'

'I have no doubts on that score. Whatever happens in the race I know that I couldn't have a better jockey riding Pride.'

'If you two have finished your mutual admiration society meeting, there is a horse that I want to back in the next race,' Sally said with a laugh. Victor lightly kissed Mary on the cheek, then, wishing her good luck, gave her a gentle push in the direction of the changing rooms.

The clock was striking 3.15 as Mick was making a few last-minute adjustments to Pride's saddle. The whitewashed walls behind the horse seemed clean and pure compared with the green of the sides. The heavy shower of rain that had fallen just before three o'clock had now subsided, leaving only a few drops to fall on the corrugated iron roof. Mick had tied Pride's tongue down to help with his breathing and gave him a few reassuring pats. Finally satisfied that everything was as it should be, he led him out of the saddling stalls and down to the paddock. Victor had agreed with Mick beforehand that he would not be in the paddock along with the connections of the other horses. He felt that as he could not add any new thoughts to Pride's case that it was better to leave Mick and Mary alone. He knew that there was far more riding on the outcome of this race for Mick than just winning. He was more than happy therefore to give them both some free space.

After what seemed an interminable delay, the bell sounded and Mary mounted her horse. The mounted police led the parade down the long path past the blue and white hospitality tents until they reached the course. As the horses rode out onto the course, they seemed almost indefinably to split into two groups and form two circles. Eventually they made their way to the course proper in the numerical order of their saddlecloths. The various riders tested their girths or sneaked a look at themselves astride their mounts on the huge video screen. Some of them broke away to ride down and inspect the all-important first jump. Mary pumped Pride with her knees and cantered down for her view of the somewhat imposing first obstacle. 'This doesn't look so bad,' she said to herself. 'I reckon that I can hold my own here.'

The starter was beginning to call them in. Mary could hear him telling them not to get on the tape. She could also hear pleas from some of the riders to keep the more sketchy jumpers out of the way. She could see Swallow's Nest moving up on her outside and, conscious of Mick's warning, tried to move away. 'Off the tape there please,' the starter called again. By now Mary was not aware of her stomach, just a huge lump of stone that lay about her midriff, threatening to drag her off her horse. Her goggles became misty and she hurriedly wiped them across her silks. As she replaced them another huge bay backed onto her again. Half a dozen of the jockeys hooted down her objections. Quips like 'if you can't stand the heat' and 'a woman's place' she let fly over her head. The jockey on the bay backed onto her once again.

'Right my lad, I will remember you,' she said. She squinted at the saddlecloth, number nine, the favourite, US Male. She dropped her hold on the reins and her horse ambled towards the starting tape. The adrenaline was at full flow now and she tensed herself as she saw the starter's hand begin to fall.

Manx Warrior bounded away as the tapes rose and Mary, giving Pride a firm kick, followed him. The horses thundered towards the first fence some four hundred yards away. Even as they went Mary sensed that they were indeed splitting into three groups. Manx Warrior stuck to the inside and Mary stayed with him. Seconds later she had cleared the first but heard the muffled swearing of someone not quite so lucky.

Up in the stand, Victor had his radio tuned to the race. Mick had said that it would not seem the same without Peter O'Sullevan calling, but as this was the first National that he had heard for years, he personally did not miss the famous commentator.

'The third fence is a big open ditch but all the leaders clear it with ease. Mission Blue makes a bad mistake at that one, in fact he's gone,' the course commentator cried. There was a loud moan from some of the huge crowd as the horse was well fancied.

Back on the course, Mary was still tracking Manx Warrior. Her heart was beating so fast now that she thought that it would burst. But to her joy she was still there with them. Beneath her thighs she could feel the pounding as Pride's hooves dug deep into the turf. She came up fast to Becher's Brook, once the most awesome obstacle on the whole course. Since the drop on the landing side had been altered, it was no longer the terror that it used to be in the past. She felt Pride's haunches tense and the next second she was sailing over the spruce and the two-foot wide ditch on the other side.

'Still very little change at the front but Bechers has claimed two more victims this year. Cathy High Road and Castle Park are gone,' the radio blared out in Victor's ear. But Mary was still there, coming to the Canal Turn, which has a sharp left-hand turn after it; for the first time the leaders cleared it with ease. Two of the other horses unseated their riders and then galloped on after the pack. Mary could not see what had happened to the jockeys but kept a wary eye on the two riderless mounts. Back in the stand, Victor and his group, their sweaty hands grasping their binoculars, heard the course commentator reveal that all the remaining horses had negotiated the Chair, the largest obstacle in the field, without mishap.

'Come on Mary, you can do it,' Victor whispered hoarsely, his mouth beginning to dry up.

'Now just the water jump to go,' Mary said to herself, 'and then I have completed the first circuit. Only another fourteen jumps to go.' Pride stretched out and cleared the water jump with ease.

'Fool's Moon has completely misjudged the water and has brought down Another Day Gone and Swallow's Nest with him. Swallow's Nest has scrambled to his feet but has veered off to the right in front of Avon's Glory and has brought him down also. The other horses are jumping but are getting caught up with the riderless ones. Oh my God, this is Foinavon all over again. There are horses and riders everywhere.' The commentator gasped for breath. 'There are at least eight or nine down, maybe even more. The ambulance attendants are rushing in. Two of the riders are lying motionless on the ground. This is a real tragedy, we will try and keep you up to date as to who is still in the race and the fate of the fallen jockeys as soon as we can.'

The next voice took up the commentary. 'Still very little change at the front. Manx Warrior has made most of the running closely followed by Highgate and Morning Dew. Tuesday's Girl is fourth, Multi Purpose is right off the pace. Pride of Tintagel is hugging the rails with Chevy Blue Eyes still wide of the field. The favourite, US Male, is still there and the back markers are Mother's Ruin and Hey Girl.'

They crossed the Melling Road and Mary sensed that the big bay was about to pass her. She gave Pride a slight kick and he managed to keep pace. The horses came up to Becher's Brook for the second time. By now Pride and the bay were almost neck and neck. They reached the jump together and Pride soared over it. US Male managed to land half a length ahead of him. As he landed, the bay's hooves began to slip but recovered. However, his jockey was not so lucky and started to slide out of the saddle. Without thinking, Mary urged her mount forward and, reaching out her right arm, grabbed the jockey by his silks and literally hauled him back into the saddle. His head turned in surprise and Mary yelled at him. 'A good job that I'm not in the kitchen eh!' The jockey blew her a kiss and raised his whip in gratitude.

By now every bone in her body was aching. The fences were beginning to become a blur and she had to lean forward along the horse's neck for support. 'Come on now boy, don't you let me down.' Her goggles were caked with mud making it almost impossible to see. She raised a hand and carved a viewing point through the grime. With partial sight restored, she plunged onward.

On Victor's radio, the broadcaster's voice boomed out, 'It's still Manx Warrior by three lengths as they approach the Canal Turn for the last time. He is closely followed by Morning Dew and US Male. They reach the Canal Turn and the favourite ploughs through the top but is still on his feet. There is a gap of ten lengths to High Gate and Multi Purpose. They are followed by Pride of Tintagel, ridden by the only female jockey in the field and what a splendid job she has done. Her connections must be proud of her. Chevy Blue Eyes and Tipsy Dame are just behind him. Then a long way back is Hanson's Dilemma, in fact he has been pulled up.'

They crossed the Melling Road for the second time and Mary had gone through the pain barrier. In fact, she felt as though she and the horse were joined. Her vision had become blurred and she was relying on the horse to take them home.

'Just two fences left to jump and US Male has taken the lead followed by Morning Dew and High Gate. Manx Warrior is going backwards, he has run out of steam. Coming to the second last and the favourite clears it first, followed by Morning Dew and High Gate. Multi Purpose is fourth and now Manx Warrior now dropped back to fifth. He jumps but crashes into the fence, his legs are gone. He manages to scramble over but stumbles and falls. His jockey is thrown to the ground. He is just lying there motionless. Pride of Tintagel jumps but his feet connect with the fallen horse. His jockey is catapulted out of the saddle, right into the path of Tipsy Dame. That horse's jockey has no chance, the horse trips and oh, good heavens, it has landed right on the jockey from Pride of Tintagel. The last horse manages to avoid the fallen figures and ploughs on. This looks

serious, a very nasty fall for the jockey of Pride of Tintagel. This race
really is going to be the survival of the fittest with only five runners
left in the race.'

'Meanwhile US Male is over the last,' the broadcaster's voice
boomed out breathlessly. 'He is holding off a strong challenge from
Morning Dew and High Gate in the run home. Just fifty yards to go
in this year's National. Twenty yards and the favourite US Male has
won the Grand National. High Gate is coming in second followed by
Morning Dew, Multi Purpose and Chevy Blue Eyes last to finish. Only
five horses have finished this year's epic Grand National. Five out of
a total of thirty-eight runners. Wait a minute, the rider of Pride of
Tintagel has got to his feet, sorry her feet. It is the lady jockey Mary
Collins, what a magnificent performance she put up. However, she
looks in a very bad way but . . . I don't believe this: she is waving away
the ambulance attendants that have rushed to help her. Yes I can't
quite believe this but she is waving the attendants back, even though
her right arm appears to be broken, or maybe it is her collarbone.
Whatever it is she is badly hurt, her arm is just lying at her side. She
is trying to remount her horse! I simply do not believe what I am
seeing! There is of course prize money for sixth place plus the honour
of finishing this great race. But no one can mount a horse with a
broken arm. This is incredible and I can't accept that I am saying it,
but the horse seems to know what she is trying to do. He is nudging
her with his head as though giving her support. Never in all my years
of race calling have I ever seen anything like this. She has a leg in the
stirrup, an attendant has come up to give her a helping hand but she
waves him away also. She seems determined to do this on her own.
What is she doing now? She is leading the horse over to the rails. She
has climbed on to the rails and LADIES AND GENTLEMEN, SHE
HAS REMOUNTED! With just one hand on the reins she is going to
try and finish the race. Never have I seen such a display of guts and
courage. This is what makes this the greatest race in the world. She
still has one jump to go. Never in all my years can I remember such a
large crowd so absolutely silent. We are witnessing history being made
here today, ladies and gentlemen. The horse has started to trot
towards this last jump. Has this courageous young lady got enough
strength left to hang on and jump that final fence and finish the
National? We shall very soon know.'

Suddenly up in the stand, Victor, with tears streaming down his face stood up and started to clap. John and Susan looked at him in amazement, and then Susan started clapping too. A couple in front of them took it up and within seconds eighty-thousand pairs of hands were clapping as Mary and Pride approached the last fence. As the horse's pace picked up speed, the clapping became faster and faster. The fence loomed and Pride leapt. For what seemed an eternity to Victor, the horse sailed through the air, Mary clinging desperately to his neck. He landed, stumbled and recovered to gallop on towards the winning post. As the horse and rider passed the post, the whole racetrack erupted. People stood unashamed as tears streamed down their cheeks as Mary Collins, riding Pride of Tintagel, passed the post in sixth place.

Victor and his companions battled their way through the ecstatic crowd to reach the track. Security guards tried to hold them back but stood aside as John yelled, 'We are family.' The clerk of the course had caught the horse and held him while the ambulance attendants gently placed Mary on a stretcher. Victor raced to her side before they could carry her off to weigh in. 'I am sorry Victor, only managed sixth place, but don't worry there is always next year.'

'Oh, I don't know, there is so much that can happen in twelve months,' the tears were still streaming down his face as he held her hand. She looked up at him through pain-filled blue eyes. With her good arm, she gently wiped them from his face and said softly, 'Can't it just so?'

Chapter Sixteen

The media had a field day with the result of the Grand National. Always a newsworthy item, this year's race, with Mary's heroic ride, captivated the imagination of Britain's racing public. To make it even more of a sensation, when the triumphant jockey of US Male was interviewed about his win, he dropped his bombshell. He told startled reporters that he owed his placing to the fact that it was Mary Collins who had prevented him from falling from his mount.

The winning owner, Property Tycoon Dave Charles, promised to donate twenty-five per cent of his winnings to any charity that Mary cared to nominate. Victor had refused an offer of a similar sum saying that the winner deserved the prize. Mary's hospital bed was surrounded with flowers and cards sent in by well-wishers from all over the country. Victor had great difficulty in clearing her room of the TV cameras and reporters trying to question her. John and Susan, after much protesting, had flown back to Exeter in the hired plane. The hospital had assured them that Mary would most likely only be kept in for observation, her fractured collarbone, they were told, being one of the easier breaks to heal. She would be very sore for several days with her badly bruised ribs. X-rays had revealed that luckily none were broken.

It was mainly the fact that she was a woman that prompted the media attention. It was this fact that had Mary more than a little annoyed. 'I can ride as well as most of the men and I proved it,' she complained to Victor. 'So why do they have to make so much fuss over me?'

He simply could not believe that she was playing down her heroic achievement so much. 'Mary the fact is that you are only the third woman to even finish the race. Not only that you finished in the money and you rode with a broken collarbone to boot. None of the other jockeys would have even attempted what you did. On top of that, of course, you are a young, attractive desirable who is a top class horsewoman. You, lady, are a news director's dream.'

She raised her good arm and grabbed his hand. Giving it a squeeze she looked up at him with a mischievous glint in her eyes. 'So you finally had to admit it, you think that I am attractive. Can I quote you on that? That makes it all worthwhile simply to hear you say that.'

He looked down at her, her right arm strapped across her chest, her face still pale and her blonde hair uncombed. He could feel the warm waves of emotion start to sweep through his body once more. 'I think that I had better leave you to get some rest, don't you?' His husky voice betrayed the emotions that he was so desperately trying to keep under control.

'Oh no, please don't leave me Victor, at least not until I am asleep,' she pleaded. 'Where are you going to stay the night anyway?'

'I shall most likely sleep in this chair here. If the doctor clears you in the morning then I will go and hire a car to get us home. Now just you try and get some rest, you must be exhausted. The race itself is tiring enough but with all that you have been through plus all those reporters. . . if it were me I would just want to crash.'

'OK, I must admit that I do feel a bit tired. Those tablets that they gave me for the pain are starting to work. Victor tell me that we did all right out there today. You must be a little disappointed that I didn't win.'

'Mary don't be so silly. I could not have asked for anything more. You did more than I had a right to expect. You did just great, honestly.'

Smiling as she closed her eyes Victor watched her medication take affect and she was soon sound asleep. Leaning over her, he kissed her lightly on the lips. She stirred slightly and gave out a small whimper.

The next morning Victor awoke stiff and cold. He looked across the room and saw that Mary was still asleep. Getting to his feet, he stretched and then quietly left the room in search of a coffee machine. The liquid that he got from the machine was hot but virtually tasteless. He managed to drink about half of it and tipped the rest down a handbasin that he found set into the wall. As he re-entered the room, Mary stirred and then woke up.

. 'Good morning and how do we feel this morning?' he asked her, smiling.

'I don't know about you but I ache all over. I have had falls before but I don't remember feeling quite as stiff and sore as this,' she answered with a weak grin.

'I don't suppose that too many horses have landed on you before?'

'Oh, it was only a horse was it? I feel as though I have been run over by a train or at the very least a herd of elephants.' She groaned and tried to sit up but he laid a restraining hand on her, gently but firmly holding her down. 'You can just lie there until a nurse comes in. Now, never having been run over by either a train or a herd of elephants, I can only imagine how you must feel. However, I don't need to be a doctor to say that you are going to find it very hard to move today. Walking is out of the question I would say.'

'Well, I can tell you that I am not going to stop in here any longer. I wanna go home.' She pursed her lips in a pout just as the door opened and a nurse came in carrying a newspaper. 'Good morning and how is our heroine this morning? Look you have made the front page,' she said as she handed Mary the paper.

'Didn't anything else make news yesterday?' she asked as she took the paper. Sure enough, there on the front page was a photograph of Mary clinging to the horse's neck as he made that last jump. The headline read 'Mary Collins Leaps into History'. Mary gave a startled gasp. 'That is hardly fair to the winner now is it?'

'If it hadn't been for you, Mary, he would never have won,' Victor reminded her. 'I am quite sure that he doesn't begrudge you one little bit of the limelight.'

'I thought that you were wonderful,' the nurse gushed. 'I watched the race on television and I was astounded when you got back on that horse. I know that I couldn't have done it. I would have been finished for certain.'

'When can I get out of here, that is what I want to know?' Mary snapped.

'The doctor should be here about nine o'clock and he will tell you then. Now, if your husband doesn't mind, he can wait outside while I check you over.' The nurse waved Victor to the door as she took down a thermometer.

'I am not her husband nurse.' he said as he left.

'Not yet anyway,' Mary whispered to the nurse, who giggled.

By 10.30, they had left the hospital and were heading for the M6. The doctor had suggested that Mary ought to stay there another day but she wouldn't hear of it. Seeing the determined look on her face, he knew that he would be fighting a lost battle. Reluctantly he signed the release forms for her to go. Victor drove steadily and they soon joined the M5 at Birmingham. Mary slept fitfully and did not really wake up until they reached Weston-super-Mare. By the time that they hit the Taunton turn-off, she was wide awake and chattering quite cheerfully. It was obvious to Victor though that she was still in a great deal of pain. As they pulled up outside the house, the front door flew open and Susan came rushing out. Mary had just managed to open the car door before her mother got there.

'Hi Mum, I'm home.' She swung her legs out of the car and stood up. Her mother hugged her, tears streaming down her face. 'Hey Mum, steady on. Why all the tears?'

'Because I have had time to stop and think about that crazy thing that you did. Mary, don't you realise that you could have broken your neck if you had fallen at that last jump? Oh you silly girl! Whatever possessed you to attempt such a foolhardy thing as that?'

'Mum, I run the risk of breaking my neck every time I race. Yesterday's race was no different from any other and besides I wanted to finish the race. I didn't want to be known as the girl who almost completed the National. Now where is Dad? I want to know how Samson is doing.' Mary looked around as she spoke.

'That horse is far fitter than you are my girl. As for your father, he is down at the stables with the vet. He supposedly called in to see the horse but he was far more interested in how you were doing. And the phone, it hasn't stopped ringing since we got home. I had to take the damned thing off the hook. Please Mary the next time that you want to do something stupid like that, don't do it in front of the whole country!' Her mother hugged her again. 'We are so proud of you, pet. The whole stable is.'

Mary tried to wriggle out of her mother's embrace. 'Steady on Mum, I am just a trifle sore you know.'

Susan dropped her arms immediately, her face full of concern. 'I am sorry, I wasn't thinking.'

'That's OK. Now are we going to stand outside here all day or can we go inside?'

Her mother laughed and taking her daughter's arm led her towards the house.

'Victor aren't you going to come in?' Susan asked him as he started the engine. He shook his head. 'No thanks, I have to get the car into Truro and Mary needs to go to bed and rest. I am sure that she won't do that if I am here. No, I think that it's best if I get going now.'

'Please stay for a bite because I am sure that you haven't eaten, have you? Will you come in if she promises to go to bed as soon as we have finished?'

He looked at Mary who, after a lengthy pause and a couple of exaggerated sighs, agreed. He got out of the car and the three of them went inside.

Finally Victor did manage to get away and after dropping the hire car off at the Truro depot he grabbed a taxi to take him home. When he got there he was surprised to find lights on in the house. Opening the front door he found Mrs Humber busy in the kitchen. 'Mrs Humber, what on earth are you still doing here?'

'I am sorry, Mr Barnes, but I simply could not leave until I found out how that young lady of yours was. I watched the race yesterday and couldn't sleep for thinking of what she did. The whole village is talking about it and I am afraid that I was late getting here this morning. It is the first time that we have had a celebrity in the village. I just thought that I might do a spot of baking while I waited for you to come home. Is she very badly hurt? We all saw her taken off in the ambulance. The vicar even said a special prayer for her in church this morning. You must be so proud of her Mr Barnes, so very proud.'

'You are so right, I am very proud of her. Although when you think about it, it was a very silly thing to do. She might have been very badly hurt. I hope that you didn't lose too much money on the horse though.'

'It was worth every penny to see such a race.' His housekeeper was almost in tears but quickly pulled herself together. 'The lass is all right though, isn't she?' she asked, her voice full of concern.

'Well, she should be after a few days' rest. She will not be riding any horses for a while, that's for sure,' Victor replied with more assurance than he felt. He just hoped that she would soon mend, as riding meant the world to her, he knew. For a moment he stood there reliving the end of the race over and over again. By God! Mrs Humber was right; he did feel proud of her! He could not fathom the depth of emotion that he was feeling for her at that moment. Suddenly he was aware that he was being spoken to. 'I am very sorry Mrs Humber, I was miles away then. What was it that you said?'

'That other jockey that she helped, he was very lucky that one. There's not too many as would have done what she did and no mistake. Did it upset you, her helping him like that? She would have finished in fifth place if she hadn't.'

'No, as far as I am concerned she did exactly the right thing. The horse was better than mine anyway.'

Later that evening, Victor was in the lounge watching the fire burn when the phone rang. It was Harley.

'What a great race that National was . . . It even made the news over here. That jockey of yours, well she really is something else. You want to hang on to her, girls like that are very rare indeed, bold and beautiful! Now to transgress to a far more serious note. I have faxed the Jockey Club the information that they needed on Cassidy and my accounts. That was a great job that you did for me Victor. I shan't forget it. Maybe my horses will stand a better chance now. I think that they are racing some time next week. I hope that I will be able to get over there to see them run. Has anything else happened that you think that I should know about?'

Victor thought about it for a moment and then told him about Lilly and Jack. 'There is no problem there, we will get it sorted out the next time that I see you. Anything else? though you do seem to have had quite a busy time there as it is?'

Victor hesitated momentarily before he decided to tell him what Jason Carter had tried to do to Mary.

'The son of a bitch! We will have to do something about him.'

Victor explained that both he and John had racked their brains for a solution but neither of then could come up with anything that was legal.

'Let me have a think about it and I will see what I can do. There is no way that we are going to let him get away with something like that. That is the trouble with you Limeys, you are too soft hearted and always want to do everything by the book. Life doesn't operate that way. You of all people should know that. Now can you pick me up at the airport again, say Wednesday?' Victor agreed and Harley rang off.

By now the excitement and drama of the past couple of days was beginning to catch up with him. Suddenly he felt very tired. Finishing his drink, he doused the fire and made his way up to bed. Within minutes of getting under the covers he was sound asleep.

The next few days saw Victor moping about the house. The weather had turned quite nasty again. The wind howled through the oak trees and the rain beat upon the windows with such ferocity that at times he thought that the glass would break. He telephoned the Collins's house each day and was told that Mary was still in bed and very sore. By now most of the bruises had come out and Susan said that her daughter looked like a patchwork quilt. In fact she looked such a mess that when Victor suggested driving up to see her, Mary had begged her mother to dissuade him. Most of the times that he rang she was asleep and he told Susan not to disturb her.

He had telephoned Dan and brought him up to date with everything that was going on. The race had been shown in Australia on cable TV and Naomi had taped it. 'At least we got to see something of you although it might have been in better circumstances,' Dan said. 'We also saw a close up of your jockey being carried to the ambulance with you walking beside her. How is she anyway? That looked a very nasty fall she had. Then when that horse fell on her, well all that I can say is that I am glad that it wasn't me.'

'She won't be doing any riding for a while but she is very resilient.'

'She must think an awful lot of you even to attempt what she did. Is there anything that we should know?'

'She is just one of those people who like to finish what they start, so don't go reading things into this that aren't there Dan.'

'So you say but Naomi thinks that the two of you are involved.'

'We are just good friends Dan, after all her father is training Arcadian Steel.'

'How many times have I heard that expression?' Dan laughed. 'Well, we are both very glad that you are being well looked after over there.'

'I think that we should leave it there, Dan. Goodbye for now.' Victor hung up.

By midweek, the weather had cleared and he decided to drive down to St Mawley. He had only spoken to Mick on the phone to tell him how Mary was, so he thought that it was time to pay him and Sally a visit. When he arrived at the stables he found that Sally was there on her own. She gave him a hug as he got out of the car.

'Hi there Victor. Mick had to go into Truro but he should be back soon. You would not believe the change in him. Since the National, he has had four people ring him who want him to take their horses. He has gone to the bank to see if he can raise enough money to do this place up. He wants to get the barn repaired and the entrance cleaned up. He realises now that some people could be turned off by the rundown appearance of things. Just as well for him that you weren't eh?' He followed her into the cottage and accepted her invitation to stay for lunch. 'We really are very grateful to you. Mick seems to have taken on a new lease of life since you brought Pride here. There is another thing that I am indebted to you for.' Sally paused and coloured slightly. 'Things between Mick and I, well, shall I say that we were on rocky ground. We were up to our eyes in debt; nothing seemed to be going right for us. We spent most of our time fighting. Your arrival in our lives has been a godsend. We have managed to patch up our differences and things are back on track as far as our marriage is concerned.'

Victor could see the tears starting to well up in her eyes and he felt uncomfortable. 'You brought Pride into our lives in more ways than one, Victor. You will never know how grateful I am to you.'

'I am happy that Mick was able to do such a good job with him.'

'You know what? He wants to run him in the Scottish Grand National at Ayr next week. He thinks that on last week's show he should walk it in.'

Victor looked at her in concern. 'But there is no way that Mary will be fit to ride him.'

Sally took him by the arm and said reluctantly, 'We all understand that. Mick has a jockey lined up to ride him. He knew that Mary would not be fit enough. I told him that you would not be happy about it, but it would mean an awful lot of prestige to Mick and the stable if he were to win it. Coming after his great showing in the race last week, please say that at least you will think about it. I know that you are a little different from a lot of the owners in that you race just for the fun of it. I also know how you feel about Mary and that horse. Particularly after what she did for you it would be hard for you to run Pride without her riding. I will be honest with you, I have already spoken to her and she says that you should let Pride run.'

'It looks as though I don't have much to say in the matter, doesn't it?' Victor spoke a little testily. 'All right I will think about it and I will let you know after I have spoken with Mary. But, I am going to talk to her first, do you hear?'

Chapter Sixteen

'Oh thank you, Victor, Mick will be absolutely thrilled.' Sally jumped up and kissed him. 'You cannot believe what a difference you have made to our lives.'

'I only said that I would think about it' Victor warned. 'I am making no promises, mind. Mick must be fairly sure of himself to drive the horse all the way to Ayr. I wouldn't want to do it I can assure you.'

'What's a thousand miles among friends?' Sally asked and Victor had to laugh. When Mick did arrive back from his trip to the bank, Victor promised him that he would let him know about running the horse, after he had spoken with Mary, the next day. The three of them then went down to inspect the topic of their conversation. Victor was pleased to see how well the horse had pulled up after his big race. He looked fighting fit and Victor was already half convinced that he should run at Ayr.

'He certainly is a credit to you Mick, he is in fine fettle and there is no doubt about it.'

The young trainer looked pleased at the praise and patted the horse affectionately. 'You would never know that he had such a hard race on Saturday. He seems to thrive on hard work this one, he is a pleasure to train.'

'Sally tells me that you have had people wanting to place their horses with you again. That must make you feel good?'

'Yes. Since he won at Cheltenham and then his great run in the National, people have started to show an interest in me again. I have you to thank for that and I know that Sally feels the same way too.'

'No, I don't agree. If you haven't got the knowledge and the skill, then it doesn't matter how many horses you have or how much money. People want results and at the moment you are getting them. So it speaks for itself. Anyway, I have to be getting back home. I will ring you tomorrow about Ayr.' So saying Victor shook Mick's hand, lightly planted a kiss on Sally's cheek, and made his way back to the car.

The next morning he phoned Mary and after some discussion with her made up his mind that Pride should run in the Scottish National. He personally thought that it was too far to travel for just one race but everybody seemed to agree that the horse had an excellent chance of taking out the race. Victor would rather have tried for the Whitbread Gold Cup at Sandown but Mick was the trainer, so he should really accept his decision, he supposed. After all, part of the trainer's job was to place his charges in order to achieve the best results for them. He then asked Mary how Samson was doing and she said that he seemed to be OK. The lacerations were healing nicely, the poultice was off and he was eating well. Peter, the vet, was of the opinion that the horse should be fit and well enough to run at Newbury. He then arranged that he would pick Mary up and take her to Bourton-on-the-Water on Saturday to see Lilly and her mother. After arranging to meet her in Taunton, he hung up.

At a bit of a loose end, he decided that a walk around the garden might be on the cards. He had never really examined it since he had rented the house. Mrs Humber had told him that 'it was a real picture in the summer. I just wish that I had more time to spend there.' Most of the daffodils had long since died off but he was pleasantly surprised to find that all the climbing roses were in bud. What a picture they would make when they were all in bloom, he thought. The azaleas and the rhododendron bushes showed promise of a mass of flowers too. The huge oak trees were already covered with new growth and he was fascinated by the many twists and turns the trunks made. The result of perpetual poundings by the West Coast winds. As he strolled through the garden discovering plants and shrubs that he did not know that he even had growing there, Victor began to realise just how attached he was becoming to the house. He felt comfortable there, the place was beginning to feel like a home rather than a house and he felt as though he belonged there.

As he stood looking at the outline of the house against the sky, something that his mother had said to him many years ago came rushing back into his memory: 'You will never go far wrong if you put your money into bricks and mortar.' It was then that he reached a major decision. If Pride of Tintagel won at Ayr, then he would put in an offer for the house. He knew that Dan and Naomi would be horrified but he could tell them that he had bought it as an investment. This was sound common sense when you thought about it. Even if he did not live in it himself, during the summer months he would have no trouble in renting it out. So it would all depend on the horse. Victor was a firm believer in fate. If things were meant to happen, then they would, although his faith had been sorely tried with the wiping out of his family, something that as yet he had not completely come to terms with. That was really pushing things a little too hard.

Chapter Sixteen

Saturday dawned bright and clear and shortly after eight o'clock saw Victor well on his way to Taunton. John Collins had arranged to drop Mary off there as he had business in town. They met up in the car park of a Safeway supermarket. In spite of the weather being fairly mild, Victor was glad to see that she was well wrapped up. He knew that she still must be very stiff and sore but she made no mention of any discomfort. Her arm was still strapped up but she seemed quite bright and cheerful. He helped her with her seat belt and, having made sure that she was comfortable, started the engine.

They made good time and before they realised it they had reached the Cheltenham turn-off. Seeing as they had plenty of time to spare, Victor decided on a detour that he knew. It took them through the charming villages of Upper and Lower Slaughter with the River Exe running through them. Their name belied the rustic charm that exuded from the sixteenth and seventeenth-century buildings that they drove by.

Mary gave a big sigh. 'It must be wonderful to live in a place like this. Life here is so much more leisurely than the way that we live.'

Victor looked at her and then laughed heartily. 'You live a life of leisure? I cannot imagine that. I don't think that I have ever met anyone who is so full of life as you are.' He slowed right down so that she could admire the view until they had cleared the villages. A short drive further on brought them to the cottage where the Oxfords lived.

Victor tapped lightly at the door and it was opened by Lilly. 'Hello Lilly. I am glad to see that you arrived here safely. Is your mother home? We have come to see about setting you up in business.'

'You had better come in Mr Barnes.' The girl stood aside to allow them to enter. Victor introduced Mary to both women and she and Jennifer shook hands. Lilly looked at Mary closely. 'I say, aren't you the lady who rode in the National? We watched the race on television. I don't think that I could have done what you did. In fact I know that I couldn't. You must be very brave.'

'Very foolhardy more like it, but we are very proud of her,' Victor said with a laugh. He looked at Jennifer and sensed that there was an air of tension about her. 'Is there something wrong Jennifer? You don't seem overjoyed at seeing us.'

She looked at him thoughtfully and then sighed. 'I am sorry. I am sure that it is not your fault. Er, Victor wasn't it?' He nodded and waited for her to continue. 'As I said, I don't think for a minute that it is your fault but I have just had my husband on the phone.'

'I suppose that he is blaming me for everyone taking their horses away from him. Well, he only has himself to blame for that I am afraid.'

'There is more to it than that I fear. The Jockey Club has threatened to revoke his licence to train. On top of that, last night someone set fire to the stables.'

Victor looked at her in astonishment. 'Someone set fire to the stables?' he repeated.

'Yes, late last night apparently. There were only a couple of horses left there. Luckily, whoever did it set them loose first. They then poured petrol into the first couple of stalls and set them alight. By the time the fire brigade got there, they were almost completely destroyed. Colin wasn't there and he knew nothing about it until he arrived home to find the police waiting for him.'

'Good heavens! Have the police any idea who would do such a thing?'

'John Cassidy is quite a strong suspect as far as the police are concerned. Or so Colin tells me. He has been charged with embezzlement and at the moment he is out on bail. Evidently he blames my husband for the mess that he is in. Colin has denied any knowledge of any fraud. He has given a statement to the police that Cassidy was in charge of all the financial side of things. Nobody believes him, of course, but there is no love lost between them at the moment. Each one is trying to lay the blame at the other's feet.'

'Oh well when thieves fall out you have to expect . . . I am sorry Jennifer, I didn't mean . . . I was forgetting that he is your husband for the minute.'

She smiled at him and laid a hand on his arm. 'Colin deserves everything that he has coming to him. I don't know how many times I told him that one day he would get caught. You cannot repeatedly cheat on people and not expect to be found out. I never thought that someone would set the place on fire though. We were lucky that Lilly had already moved here. She might have been hurt if she had stumbled on the arsonist.'

'Dad was absolutely livid when he found out that I had gone. I was too frightened to leave while he was there but the minute that he went out I phoned for a taxi and left. I was already packed and just waiting for a chance. He phoned Mum last night and asked if I was here but she said no. Then he phoned again this morning to tell Mum about the fire and unfortunately I answered the phone.'

'What has happened to the two horses? Were they hurt at all?' Mary asked.

'No, they both ended up in the paddock. Whoever torched the stables only wanted to get at Dad. The evidently didn't want to harm the horses. The only thing is that Dad's horse, Clearview, hurt his leg when he jumped a fence. This means, of course, that he will not run in the Derby. That pissed Dad off too, I can tell you. I am not sorry that the stables burnt down though. I hated the way that he forced me to stay there, threatening to stop paying for Jack's nurse if I left. He deserves all that he gets. It is a pity that he wasn't in the fire too. Then at least Mum could have claimed on his life insurance!' Lilly spoke quite vehemently and both Mary and Victor looked at her in amazement. Even Jennifer looked a little embarrassed at her daughter's outburst.

After a rather pregnant pause, Victor decided that he should get on with the reason for their visit. 'Why I came today was to see about finding you a shop. Or at least somewhere where you could set up your business as I promised you. Also I want to give you a cheque to cover the wages for Jack's nurse for twelve months.'

Jennifer gazed at him quite thoughtfully before she spoke. 'What I can't understand is why you would do all this for someone that you hardly know? What are you getting out of this? There must be something.'

'I made you a promise that if you helped me sort out things with the horses we would look after you. We don't want to cause you any suffering. I am merely living up to my part of the bargain.'

'I know what you said, but what do you get out of all this?' Jennifer was most insistent.

Victor looked quite ill at ease for a moment and then he answered her. 'Look, without going into a lot of detail, I have plenty of money and I would truly like to help you and your family. Consider it wages for a job well done. I got what I wanted and it is only fair that you don't suffer by it. I am not a philanthropist by any stretch of the imagination. I do however have money and it gives me great pleasure to be able to help people like yourselves.'

Jennifer just looked at him blankly and then turned to Mary and asked. 'Is he for real?'

'I sometimes wonder that myself,' she said with a deep chuckle, 'but I can assure you that he has no ulterior motive. He is also in a position financially to do what he says and more. In fact the poor guy has got so much money that he is finding it hard to spend. The more that he spends the more he seems to make.' She then roared with laughter and soon everyone joined in.

The tension now well and truly broken they were all soon in earnest conversation about suitable premises for Lilly's new dressmaking venture. The three women had quite an animated discussion until Victor came to the conclusion that nothing concrete was going to be achieved that day. He wrote out a cheque to cover the nurse's wages and handed it to Jennifer.

'I think that the easiest thing to do is for you and Lilly to set your-selves up and just send me the bills. That way you can take your time and do things properly.'

'We really can't thank you enough. I still find it a little hard to accept that you are prepared to do all this for us. To be perfectly frank with you, you sound too good to be true,' Jennifer said clasping his hands.

Victor's face coloured slightly. 'Believe me, I am more than happy that I can do something to help. You and Lilly are going to be a lot happier living together and I set great store on family values. What is the point of having a lot of money if you can't do some good with it from time to time? I am going to win it all back the next time that my horse races, so what have I got to lose?' he said, grinning broadly. Jennifer smiled.

Finally Victor and Mary made their good-byes and, after promising to come and visit soon, got into the car and drove off. As Mary waved to the two women she looked at Victor. 'Do you know what I think?'

'The same thing as me, I expect. It wasn't Cassidy who started that fire. He would never have bothered about letting the horses out first.'

'That's right. I reckon that Lilly did it just before she left.'

'I don't suppose that we will ever discover the real truth. Rather ironical though if you think about it. All the things that man has done wrong and got away with, he could be blamed for something that he didn't do. As they say, what goes around comes around. He could go to jail for arson and he might be innocent.'

'Lilly certainly had the opportunity and the motive. Did you see her face when she spoke about her father? She was deadly serious when she said that she wished that he had been caught in the fire. He must have given her a hard time working there. The only thing is he really will have it in for you now. With Clearview being hurt, he hasn't a runner in the Derby. Though I don't suppose that he would have been allowed to race him anyway.'

'Let's forget about both Oxford and Cassidy for the time being,' he said to her. 'How about me taking you out to dinner?'

'Do you think that you can afford it after all that money you have spent today?' Mary smiled at him.

'As long as you don't mind somewhere that's not too expensive. I know, how about that McDonald's that we passed on the way here?'

'Don't you dare! I want a very large steak and some champagne. Don't forget that I am still convalescing and I need to build up my strength.'

'You need building up like I need a hole in the head. Still, steak and champagne does sound nice. Ok you win . . . again.'

Chapter Seventeen

Victor could not get the thought of Mick and Sally having to drive almost a thousand miles to take Pride to Ayr and back, out of his mind all weekend. He still felt that Mick was wrong by racing him there but had resigned himself to the fact that he would go along with the idea.

'This year the prize money for the race is the most that it ever has been. The going up there is generally good and as a rule there are usually at least sixteen runners in the race. This means, of course, that even if he only manages to finish fourth then you can still win money on him with the bookies. The last ten favourites have averaged 5–1 so you should be able to get a good price about the horse. We know that he can run the distance and he is fit. So what have you got to lose?' Mick had put up quite a convincing argument, even Victor had to admit. Evidently the trainer had put a lot of thought into the idea of running him. Plus if he was prepared to drive him all that way himself then he must be pretty confident of taking out the race.

Finally, after a great deal of soul searching, Victor phoned Mick. 'Right then Mick, I have decided to bow to your arguments and let him run on one condition.'

'Exactly what is the condition?' Mick asked warily.

'I insist that we charter a plane and fly you and the horse to Prestwick. That is about three miles from the course so we can arrange for a float to meet you there. It is too far to drive from Cornwall up to Scotland.'

'But why spend all that money on a plane? Sally and I can take turns with the driving. We will be all right. A charter plane is too expensive.'

'Mick I have won nearly £50,000 on him so far, I think that I can afford a plane. You either fly or you don't go, it is as simple as that.'

So Mick agreed and secretly he was pleased. He hadn't been too keen on the idea of having to drive almost the entire length of the country and back in a horsebox.

Early the next day, Victor phoned the airport and booked the plane. Sally rang him later in the day and asked him what time they should pick him up.

'I won't be going this time,' he said. 'You and Mick can go and then you will be able to lead him in when he wins. I am not sure of my plans for the day as yet so I may have to watch it on TV.'

Once Victor had organised both the plane and the float he felt a lot better. He had told Mrs Humber on the previous day that the horse had a better chance of wining at Ayr than he did at Aintree. She then promised him some jugged hare for lunch. His main reason for not wanting to go to Ayr was that he was still hoping that Arcadian Steel was going to be fit to run at Newbury. Harley's horse, Cash Crisis, was also due to run in the Levy Board Handicap. Jenkins had told him that he had no idea how Cash Crisis would perform as he had not had him long enough to judge.

He had scratched Alaskan Jack, who had been due to race at Newmarket on the Thursday. 'The horse is only half fit and we would achieve nothing by running him' he had told Victor. He knew that Harley would be disappointed but would accept the trainer's decision. But now the only real topic of concern was whether or not the vet would pass Samson as fit to race. John had felt confident that he would be ready but agreed with Victor. They would accept the vet's recommendation, whichever way it went. 'After all that is why we pay him,' John had said. The only other problem that they then had was whether or not the horse would let Jimmy ride him. Again, John was very optimistic.

The next couple of nights were fairly sleepless ones for Victor. By the time that he got up on Wednesday morning to go and fetch Harley from Heathrow he was feeling tired and irritable. The plane from Los Angeles was not due in until late in the afternoon, so he lay in bed far longer than was his norm. As he lay there, he went over in his mind all that had happened to him since the beginning of November. He could scarcely credit exactly what he had been through and done in the space of only a few months.

Eventually he got out of bed and stood looking out of the window. From this distance, the sea looked as calm as a duck pond but he knew that the huge Atlantic rollers would be crashing in at the base of the cliffs. At this particular time Melbourne seemed to be part of another world. He wasn't even sure if he wanted to return there or not. He felt that the city held too many memories for him, memories that he would prefer to forget. He knew that he was in the fortunate position of being able to live wherever his mind took a fancy. The thing that kept bugging him, however, was whether he would be able to be truly happy anywhere without his Amanda. He knew that she would never have agreed to live in England, even though she knew that he had dreamed of retiring there. 'Your family is dead and gone Victor, mine is here living in Melbourne,' she had once told him when he had broached the subject. How events can change one's life so dramatically when one least expects it. 'Enough of this,' he said to himself, 'you are becoming maudlin again. Get dressed, you have to pick up Harley.'

There were major roadworks on the motorway outside Swindon and the traffic was reduced to one lane for several miles. Consequently the delay meant that it took him a lot longer than expected to reach Heathrow. The plane had already landed when he arrived so he went looking for Harley. He found his friend waiting in the lounge for him and talking to a pair of identical twins. They were in their early twenties with long black hair and figures that made men weep for joy and women weep with envy. 'I see that you have managed to keep yourself occupied while you waited for me. Are you going to introduce your friends or are you keeping them for yourself?'

'Hey, Victor, old buddy, how are you? I should like you to meet two gals that I met on the plane. They are from LA and are over here for a short holiday. The one on the left is Patsy and the one on the right is Peggy. Girls, this is Victor, the guy that I was telling you about.' The twins smiled at Victor and Patsy waved a hand at him also. 'The girls have promised to come and see our horses race. Their father has a stud farm so they know all about horses.'

'I am not sure if they will see both of ours run but it should be a good day anyway judging by the calibre of the fields.'

'Well gals, I had better go seeing as how my ride has arrived.' Harley struggled to his feet. 'Can we give you a lift anywhere?' The two girls shook their heads. 'No? What a shame, we will see you on Saturday then.' The two brunettes blew them a kiss. Picking up his suitcase Harley said, 'Come on Victor, let's go and get a meal somewhere, I am starving.' Victor turned back to the girls. 'It was nice meeting you. We will most likely see you at the races on Saturday then?'

'Bye, now Victor,' they said in unison.

Victor had to hurry to catch up with his friend who was striding towards the exit. Taking hold of his arm, Victor steered the American in the direction of the car. 'Trust you to meet up with two bimbos like that Harley.'

'Bimbos! Don't you be deceived by their looks,' Harley chuckled. 'I can tell you that those girls are two very tough ladies. You wouldn't want to meet them on a dark night. Back in LA they run a martial arts school for women. Hey now! I have just had a brilliant idea. Yes, yes, I don't see why it wouldn't work.' Victor looked at him mystified and waited for him to explain what he meant. 'I will tell you later. There are a few details to work out and some facts to check first.'

Harley started laughing and a big grin split his face. Victor just shook his head.

'I don't know what the hell you are talking about.'

'You will, my boy. You will, when the time is right. Now come on, let's eat.'

Having satisfied Harley's hunger pangs, Victor dropped him off at the inn in Newbury. He had offered to put him up at his house but the American had declined. 'I have to be here on Saturday anyhow, plus I want to talk to Billy. It is just as easy for me to stay here. The rooms are pretty comfortable and the food is good,' he had said.

By the time that Victor got back to Cornwall it was pretty late, so he decided that he would wait until morning to ring John Collins. Instead he telephoned Dan and told him about Pride running in the Scottish National.

'My, you are becoming quite another Robert Sangster aren't you?' his brother-in-law remarked in an amused tone of voice. However, he was not quite so thrilled when Victor told him of his plans should the horse win. 'Tell me straight Victor, are you planning on staying over there for good, because that's what it sounds like to me?'

'I honestly don't know what I am going to do at this stage. This house is a good investment no matter what I decide about the future. I have to put some of my money to work, so what is wrong in buying a little real estate?' Victor asked.

'There is plenty of that here in Melbourne you know. You don't have to buy something on the other side of the world. I mean it is not as though you just have to pop down the road to collect your rent when it's due. I am sure that Naomi is going to be very disappointed when I tell her your news,' Dan chided him.

'I told you, I haven't made up my mind what I am going to do at the moment,' Victor replied angrily.

Dan realised that it was futile to argue with him so he let the matter drop. 'Well, good luck with your horse.'

After replacing the phone Victor poured himself a large Jack Daniels and sat down in front of the fire to drink it. He suddenly felt very much alone. He slowly got to his feet and walked outside into the garden. The night sky was clear and the stars shone like diamonds. There was a slight breeze and he could smell the honeysuckle. Looking up he noticed there was a new moon and without thinking he took some money from his pocket and turned it over beneath the pale crescent. When he realised what he had done he laughed to himself. There are some habits that never die, he thought. Who would have credited that he would still turn his money over under a new moon in an effort to double it? What the action did, however, was to raise his spirits. He went back into the house and up to bed feeling far brighter.

He was awoken the next morning by the telephone ringing. He struggled to reach it on his bedside table. 'Hello, who is it?'

'I am sorry Victor, did I wake you?' John Collins's voice boomed in his ear. 'I don't think that you will mind though when you hear my news. Jimmy rode Samson this morning at exercise. He had no problems getting on him and he fairly sizzled over a mile. Everything looks fine for Saturday. Peter the vet is coming up here tomorrow but I am sure that he will give Samson a clean bill of health. Just a minute, I think Mary wants to talk to you.'

Before Victor had time to answer him, Mary's voice came swimming over the line. He could sense her excitement as she said breathlessly, 'Oh Victor, you should have seen him. It was as though he knew that he was born to run. He literally made the other horses eat his dust. Oh, what a shame that you weren't there, you would have been thrilled.'

Victor had to laugh at her enthusiasm, she was bubbling over with joy. 'So you think that he is worth going to watch on Saturday then?' he asked her smiling to himself.

'Victor, I am shocked! How could you even consider not coming?'

she demanded.

'I do have another horse racing up in Scotland don't forget. I thought that you might have wanted to see Pride run.'

'Not when I have the chance of seeing a real champion race. Don't you dare go to Scotland. Mick is quite capable of looking after that one for you. You and I are going to Newbury and that is all there is to be said.'

'I think that you had better put your father back on so as I can talk to him.'

When John eventually managed to rescue the phone from his excited offspring, he invited Victor to come and stay with them for the next couple of days so they could all leave together on the Saturday.

'Was this your idea or Mary's?'

The other man gave a hearty laugh. 'Whose do you think? But seriously, though, if you would like to come up, please do. You can be here when the vet arrives then.'

'I will have to see. I seem to be spending far more time up at your place than my own lately. Mrs Humber is beginning to complain that she is getting her money under false pretences because there is never any work for her to do.'

'Tell her that she can come up here then. I can always find plenty of things to keep her occupied and out of mischief.'

Victor laughed and, after promising that he would drive up later in the day, rang off. It now looked as though he would have two horses running for him on Saturday. His next task was to ring Mick to inform him that he would be going to Newbury to watch Arcadian Steel do his stuff. 'You will have to ring me and let me know how Pride does in the National.'

'They will most likely have the race on the video screens at Newbury so you should be able to watch it there. But I will ring you anyway whatever the result,' Mick promised him. Victor then got up and dressed. He was making his way downstairs when the front door opened and Mrs Humber came in. She was honestly pleased to see him and told him that she would have his breakfast ready for him 'in a flash'.

It was just on two o'clock as Victor drove up to Hill Top. He was a little surprised to see a police car parked there and it was with some apprehension that he went up to the front door and knocked. He had to wait a short while before Susan came and opened the door. 'Hi there Victor. You have come at the right time I think. The police have finally got a statement from Ginger and they have come to talk to John about it.'

He followed her into the lounge, where he found Mary and her father talking to two police officers. John looked up as they entered. 'You are just in time to hear the news,' he said grimly. 'It certainly looks as though it was Cassidy who paid Ginger to try to put your horse out of action. He has told the police that a man approached him at Doncaster and asked him if he would like to earn a lot of money. You said that you saw Cassidy get out of the Land Rover in the car park, didn't you? You are sure that it was him?'

'Yes, I am sure. As I said I couldn't place him at the time, but I remembered later who it was. I suppose that I should have asked Ginger why he actually got in if he just wanted directions as he said.'

'Apparently, according to Ginger, they promised him £1,000 to fix the horse. Five hundred they gave him and the promise of another five after he had done the job. They really must have been afraid of your horse, Victor. That's an awful lot of money to lay out.' John looked upset at the thought that one of his boys would even think about doing such a thing.

'It would take a lot of money to persuade the boy to do it. Particularly, as you said, because he was terrified of the animal,' one of the officers told them. 'The lad told us that he was supposed to dope the animal first and then to break its leg. It was not going to be an easy job, even with the horse tranquilised.'

'They deserve to be shot, wanting to maim a magnificent animal like that,' Mary said hotly. 'Of course then we would have had no option but to have him put down. I don't know how Ginger could even contemplate such a thing.'

'Yes, but a sum of money like that would seem like a fortune to a young lad like him. Also he apparently thought that Mr Collins here had been picking on him lately. So in his mind it was his way at hitting back,' the policeman said.

'As soon as he is released from hospital, we will pick up this fellow Cassidy and see if the boy can pick him out in a line up.' The other officer spoke this time.

'I don't suppose that there is any chance that he will not identify him in the hope of picking up the other £500 is there?' Victor said thoughtfully.

The officer laughed. 'There is no danger of that, I can assure you. The boy thinks that he will go to prison if we don't catch the people concerned. At the moment, unless either of you wants to press charges against him, technically he hasn't committed a crime. Naturally, he is not going to get off without a severe lecture. Under the circumstances, though, we feel that his injuries alone are punishment enough. He is not going to forget them in a hurry. Mind you, it is entirely up to you. We can charge him with malicious damage if you like.'

'No, I see no value in that. As you say he has suffered enough already, I think. No, as long as he is prepared to identify Cassidy then I am content to leave it at that. How do you feel John? It is your stables after all.'

Victor looked at him. John did not answer right away but stood there stroking his chin thoughtfully for several minutes, then nodded his head in agreement. 'I think that Ginger will have learnt his lesson. He is going to find it hard to get another job as it is. Not too many stables will be prepared to take him after pulling a stunt like this. I don't know quite what he will do.'

'Oh you needn't worry on that score. The lad has decided that he wants to join the army, though whether he will be able to pass the medical I don't know,' the policeman cut in. 'Now, unless there is anything else, we will be on our way.'

Susan got up to show them out. 'Well, as soon as Ginger is ok and picks out Cassidy from the line up, then my job for Harley should just about be over. Both Oxford and Cassidy will be behind bars and his horses should start to perform.' Victor gave a huge sigh of relief and sat down. John looked at him and then roared with laughter. Getting to his feet he went and poured some whisky into a glass and handed it to him. 'Didn't you tell me that Harley had made you his manager? Then my lad, your problems are only just beginning. Now you will have to keep a check on when his horses are running, make sure that all the bills are paid, get a vet to them when they are sick etc, etc, etc.'

'Never mind, it will give you something to do in your quiet times,' Mary said with a beaming smile. 'Now come on, drink your drink and then we can go and see your horse. I bet that you have missed him?'

'For goodness sake, Mary, can't you leave the man alone for five minutes to enjoy his whisky? The horse will still be there later,' her father said in an exasperated tone. 'Now just give him a break and let him relax.'

'Besides I think that I would rather go for a drive up on the moors,' Victor told her. 'There are so many places around here that I have always wanted to see.'

'All right then, in that case you can take me to dinner at the Rising Sun in Lynmouth. I have been told that the food is very good and the pub is famous.'

'The Rising Sun? Why, what is so special about that?'

'Don't you know anything? I thought that you were a trivia buff. That's where Blackmore stayed when he was writing *Lorna Doone* or are you going to tell me that you have never heard of that Mr Barnes?' Mary looked at him with an impish grin.

'Actually I have the book at home. But of course we shall have to go to the Rising Sun. What would people think of me if I neglected that famous spot?' Victor chuckled and John joined in too.

Mary glared at them. 'Why is it that you men have no feeling of romance? The whole countryside around here is full of literary history. People like Coleridge, Kingsley, Du Maurier, Graham, Quiller-Couch; they are all associated with this part of England. They say that 'a prophet is never recognised in his own country'; well it certainly seems to apply here.' She sat back in her chair with a defiant air.

'My, I would love to have you on my side in a fight, Mary. Does she always get so het up about a subject, John?'

'Oh she can get a bee in her bonnet and no mistake,' John said, grinning.

'Ooh, you men! Stick together as usual.'

'Steady on Mary, look I am sorry,' Victor said to her. 'I'll tell you what, if either of my horses wins on Saturday, I will take you on a tour of all the romantic places that you can find in both Devon and Cornwall. How's that suit you?'

'Ok, you are on and you are a witness to this, Mother,' she said as Susan came back into the room. Her mother looked at her warily. 'I am a witness to what?' she queried. Mary walked up to her and putting an arm around her broke into a mischievous grin. 'Victor here has promised to take me on a romantic tour of Devon and Cornwall if his horse wins on Saturday. Now wasn't that nice of him?'

'I said no such thing,' protested Victor. 'You have to help me out on this John. She has completely twisted my words.'

'I am afraid that Mary here thinks that a tour of romantic places and a romantic tour mean exactly the same thing,' her father said in between laughs. 'I think that you had better go and see your horse. It is a far safer bet.'

'I think that Samson is far easier to control than your daughter.'

'We can all drink to that, I reckon,' John said raising his glass.

The next day Victor was very much on edge and kept pacing up and down the yard until the vet finally arrived. He took his time and examined the horse thoroughly until he finally gave it his stamp of approval. 'Everything seems to be fine with him and he has healed up well. Any problems at all, don't hesitate to give me a call.'

Victor thanked him and gave him a cheque. 'I might take a chance and put this on your horse on Saturday. I don't usually bet on the horses except on Derby Day but I think that this fellow of yours might prove to be an exception.' The vet then pocketed the cheque, wished him luck and drove away.

John told Jimmy to get the horse saddled up and to take him out for a light canter. Most of the yard had gathered round to watch Jimmy put the horse through his paces and eventually John called him in. 'Victor, as far as I'm concerned that horse is as fit as he is ever likely to be.'

Dinner was served early that evening. Victor, though not having much of an appetite, forced himself to eat so as not to upset Susan, then, feigning a headache, he went up to bed soon after finishing his meal. He had found too that being around Mary all the time was something that he was becoming accustomed to a little too much. He thought about it and wondered whether or not it was such a good thing.

He spent a restless night tossing and turning and was the first one up in the morning. Eventually the remainder of the household wandered in for breakfast. Once finished they started to work out who was to travel with whom. Finally they decided that John and Susan would take one car with Jimmy, while Cliff would drive the Land Rover with the float. This of course left Mary and Victor to go together.

'We are going to need our own transport for when Victor takes me on this romantic tour that he has promised me,' Mary said with a chuckle, but he just gave a groan.

Samson was engaged in the first race, so John did not want to leave their departure too late.

As Mary climbed into the car, Victor thought that she looked more vibrant and alive than at any time that he could remember. She showed no signs of the injuries that she had sustained. In fact she looked a picture of health. By nine o'clock the three vehicles had left the house and were heading up the motorway towards Bristol.

They turned off the M4 at Junction 12 and proceeded to the race-course. The traffic by now was almost at a crawl and John was glad that he had insisted on an early departure. They parked their cars and made their way to the Tattersall's ring. Victor had scarcely had time to find a seat before he heard Harley's raucous voice hailing him. The various introductions were made and then John had to leave them to give his final instructions to Jimmy. Victor had rejected an invitation to go along with him, saying that his presence would achieve nothing. He and Harley then compared notes on Oxford and Cassidy.

The American confirmed that Victor was now in charge of his three horses and would take over everything that Cassidy had been doing. 'Except robbing me blind of course! I think that I have had enough of that for the time being. I should like to see these nags start showing a profit.'

'As far as I can remember that part was not in the job description when I read it,' Victor said with a laugh. The conversation then turned to the chances of their two respective runners that afternoon.

'I will be lucky if Cash Crisis even manages to complete the course,' moaned Harley. 'I shouldn't even be running him but I didn't want Jenkins to think that I didn't trust him. I know that he feels bad about what happened to Delmore, although of course it wasn't his fault.'

'Jenkins is well aware of what has been going on with your two. I can assure you that you would have no trouble from him if you did decide to scratch the horse,' Victor said quite emphatically.

'No, he is here now, so we might as well give him a run. You never know he might surprise us all, though I tend to doubt it. By the way have you seen those twins yet? They told me that they would be here today.'

'Harley! You are old enough to be their father,' Victor exclaimed.

'Haven't you ever heard that saying, the older the violin?' he retorted with a grin. 'Anyway, I have something else in mind for those two beauties.'

'Can't you men think of anything else?' Mary said disgustedly.

'Mary, I can assure you, you have not the slightest idea of what I'm thinking of,' Harley smiled at her. 'If you did then I am sure that you would thoroughly approve of it my dear.' Harley's grin became even broader.

'I could not imagine that for one minute.'

'I will tell you what, I will have a little wager with you. When you find out what I have in mind, you will be so pleased that you will buy me dinner. If you are not happy with the result, then I will buy your whole party dinner. Is it a deal?'

'Right, you are on, but I had better warn you, I have very expensive tastes. Especially when someone else is doing the buying,' she replied with a delightful laugh and gave him a poke in the ribs.

Before they could get any further involved John and Susan rejoined them. They both sat down and John let out a big sigh. 'Well, it is all up to Madame Fortune now.' he said. 'Young Jimmy has as much chance as any of them.' He turned to Victor. 'There are two late scratchings but I don't feel as though that is going to help us. The draw has little advantage in this race. There is a nice run in of five furlongs so as long as he is near the lead at the final turn, then he has that burst of speed that he should catch anything that is in front of him.'

John's words turned out to be fairly prophetic as Arcadian Steel was lying second as they rounded the final bend. Jimmy gave him one tap with the whip and his stride lengthened appreciably. He then stormed past the leader to win by three lengths. Victor was ecstatic and hugged Mary heartily, almost lifting her off her feet. Then grabbing her by the hand he almost dragged her down to the winner's enclosure to meet Jimmy who was trotting in, his face split in a wide grin. 'He ran just right for us, Boss and he still had plenty in reserve. He is a great horse.' Jimmy was almost beside himself with glee. He jumped off, unbuckled the saddle and was striding towards the weighing-in room almost before John and Susan had reached them.

Victor turned to Harley who had followed them down at a more leisurely pace and grabbed his hand. 'I hope that yours does as well, my friend.'

The American shook his head despondently, shrugged his shoulders and held his hands skyward in the Jewish manner, 'My son, I think that you have a champion there. My fella could not come within yards of him.'

Hardly hearing what Harley was saying to him, Victor pulled Mary towards the presentation area. The American watched them go and smiled to himself. 'You don't look anything like the guy that I saw in Melbourne just three short months ago, Victor. You deserve a bit of happiness, my friend.'

After the presentation, John and Susan decided to head back home with the horse. They left Mary and Victor to try their luck at picking a few winners while they waited for Cash Crisis to race. It was not due to be run until five o'clock so they arranged to meet after the race. Harley suggested to Victor that they might be better off watching the rest of the afternoon's programme from the comfort of the bar. He was about to protest when Harley tapped the form guide from the morning paper several times.

At first he did not understand what he was trying to say until he saw Jason Carter's name printed alongside horses that were due to run in the third and fifth. Nodding his approval, Victor then escorted Mary to the warmth of the bar just stopping long enough to buy her a form book. Sitting down they went through the book together making their selections. Victor then offered to go down to the bookies and place their bets while she stayed in the sanctuary of the bar.

Neither of them had any luck until Mary picked the winner of the fourth race. Victor got up to go and collect her winnings for her. He was on his way back when he spotted Harley in the crowd. He was about to go and join his friend when he saw the twins approach and wave to their fellow countryman. Soon the three of them were in earnest conversation. Victor saw Harley point to the runners that were just coming into the parade ring. He pulled something from his pocket and gave it to Patsy or was it Peggy? Both of the girls laughed, then made off into the crowd.

By now Victor was truly intrigued and hurried over to catch his friend before he too made off. 'Aren't the girls going to join us?' he asked when he finally caught up with Harley.

'Girls? What girls, Victor?' Harley said, his face a picture of innocence.

'The twins, of course. I just saw you talking to them.'

'The twins? I haven't seen them all day. They must have changed their minds about coming. Hey, don't tell me that you have left the lovely Mary on her own?'

'But Harley, I saw you talking to them, you can't deny it.'

'It must have been someone who looks like me,' Harley closed an eye in an exaggerated wink.

Victor shook his head. 'I don't know what kind of game you are playing, but I know what I saw.'

'Come on, I think that you can afford to buy me a drink out of your winnings,' Harley said as he took the other man's arm and gently but firmly pushed him towards the bar. Victor bought another round for the three of them. He was setting them down on the table and was about to ask his friend what was going on when his mobile rang. When he answered it, he let out such a yell that everyone in the crowded room turned to stare at him.

'He did it! He only went and did it!'

Harley looked at him then back at Mary, a bewildered look on his face.

'What is he on? Whatever it is it must be pretty potent stuff. Do you know what he is on about Mary?' She shook her head.

Victor spoke for a short while longer then he put his phone away, his eyes blazing with excitement. He sat down and just looked at the two of them. 'Come on Victor don't keep us in suspense. What has got you so worked up?' Mary asked him and then a look of understanding crept into her eyes. 'I had forgotten all about it. You don't mean that . . . ?'

'Yes, he did it Mary. Pride of Tintagel won the Scottish Grand National by five lengths! I honestly thought that Mick was out of his mind going all that way just for one race, but he's done it. My horse won the National!'

'It's true what they say then, Mary,' Harley spoke emphatically. 'Money does go to money.'

She looked at Victor sitting there with a look of disbelief on his face. 'I would say that dinner is definitely on Victor Barnes tonight wouldn't you Harley?'

'Why, how much was the prize money on this race then?'

'I don't really know. I don't think that Victor mentioned it.'

'A house in the country,' Victor interjected with a laugh.

'What on earth do you mean?' Mary asked him, a puzzled look on her face. He looked at the pair of them for a moment before replying. 'I think that the prize money would cover the cost of buying that house that I am renting. I collect about £65,000 for winning the race, plus I had £5,000 on the horse with the bookies up there. Mick said that he got odds of 15–2 for me on the course. Pride of Tintagel has earned me over £100,000 today. Not bad for a day's work I would say.'

'One hundred thousand pounds!' Mary gasped. 'Victor, that is incredible!'

'You shouldn't forget the winnings from Arcadian Steel either, my boy,' Harley reminded him. 'Your luck is certainly running for you today.'

Mary was still sitting in her chair trying to get over the shock when suddenly something Victor had said sunk in. She looked at him slyly. 'Why would you want to buy that house? Aren't you going back to Melbourne?'

'I haven't said that. Property is always a sound investment. Wouldn't you agree Harley?' His friend nodded in agreement. 'You see Harley agrees with me.'

'Yes and, knowing your luck, you are just as likely to be digging in the garden and you will be striking oil,' Harley pounded his fists on the table as he spoke.

'Not in Cornwall, my friend, but still what is the point of winning all this money if I don't do something with it? Besides, think of all the money that I will save in rent.' Victor got to his feet and went to get them another round of drinks. While he was away Mary was reading through the form of the horses in the next race. As he returned she said to him, 'Here you are Victor, you should have a bet on Luck's a Fortune. That's you to a T today.'

'No thank you. I reckon that I have had my share of fortune for today. I will go and back him for you if you want it.'

'Right but you can pay for the bet for me as well I think. I will have ten pounds on him, thank you very much.'

'Just as long as I get my ten pounds back if he wins,' he demanded.

The horse duly obliged at 10–1. Mary was thrilled and ordered Victor to go and collect her winnings for her right away. 'I will collect them after we have watched Harley's horse run,' he assured her. He wondered what she was going to say when she discovered that he had not bet £10 but £100 on the winner.

Harley had told them both not to back Cash Crisis as they would be wasting their money. The horses were milling around in the parade ring and Victor had his fieldglasses trained on them, trying to spot Cash Crisis. As he scanned the ring he caught sight of the twins. He was about to tell the others when he saw them saunter up to a man and start chatting. There was something familiar about the man that caught his attention. He focused the glasses on him and then realised with a start that it was Jason Carter. As he watched, the three of them started to move away, Jason having an arm around the waist of each girl. Silently he gave the glasses to Harley and pointed them at their retreating backs. Harley watched them for a while, then handed the glasses back to him with a grin.

'What exactly is going on Harley?' Victor asked him quietly.

He merely put a finger to his lips to indicate that he should be quiet.

Highly intrigued by now with his friend's antics, Victor remained silent for a moment and then asked, 'Are we going down to watch the race or are we going to stay here?'

'We may as well stay here I guess. I don't think that I shall be called upon to escort the winner in,' Harley said with a rueful smile.

True to his word, Harley's services were not required, Cash Crisis finishing a creditable fifth. The three of them then went to pick up Mary's winnings from the bookie. Victor gave her the betting slip and then stood back to watch her face as she collected the money.

'Nice one lady. I am glad that I don't have too many like you each race,' the bookie said in a good-hearted manner as he counted out £1,100 into her astounded hands. She turned round to Victor with a glazed look in her eyes.

'How much did you put on for me?' she gasped, still looking with disbelief at the wad of notes in her hand.

'Only a hundred I am afraid,' he replied.

'Only a hundred! But what if he had lost?'

'I thought that you told me he couldn't lose. Anyway I would still have been streets ahead on the day. But I will take my stake back if you don't mind,' he said grinning from ear to ear.

'No, I insist that you take half this lot;' she began counting the notes out.

Victor shook his head and taking two £50 notes from her, closed her fist around the rest. 'You take it Mary, it's yours. You were the one who picked the horse after all.'

'Well, I think that I might be off,' Harley said to them.

'Aren't you going to stay for the last race?'

The American shook his head 'No, it's only a maiden, so anything could win. I have an errand to run. I need to hire a car. Do you think that they would bring one out to the track for me?'

'You don't need to hire a car. I can drive you wherever you want to go. How did you get to the course this afternoon anyway?'

'Some guy that I met in the pub gave me a lift. No, thanks for the offer but I think that I have to do this trip on my own. I am heading off towards Oxford, there are a couple of things that I promised to collect.'

'I am not fussy about staying for the last either. I think that I have won more than enough for one afternoon thanks to you. The least that we can do is drive Harley back to town. He can pick up a car there,' Mary stated firmly.

Having settled things the three of them walked back to the car park. After dropping the American off at a car hire firm, Mary and Victor decided to head for home rather than go out that evening. 'I think that I have had too much excitement today to do justice to a meal. I would rather do it another time when my stomach has stopped its heaving,' Mary said lightly.

Later on that evening they were all seated around the blazing fire in the lounge drinking champagne that Victor had bought on the way. Mary was still excited about her win; even though her father was a trainer she had never been a big gambler. One thing that she could not understand was how Victor could remain so calm about the amount of money that he had collected that day.

Her father laughed at her. 'Don't forget my love that he is a multi-millionaire. Today's cheques and winnings will only seem like pin money to him.'

'It's a bit obscene to have all that money when you think about it.'

'Mary! You have no right saying a thing like that,' her mother scolded her in a shocked tone.

Victor merely laughed. 'She does have a point though,' he said. 'It is a lot of money for one person to have but as far as remaining calm about the amount that I won today, I don't think that the reality of that has sunk in yet.'

'Well, for my part, I would far rather be that way than wondering where my next meal was coming from,' her father stated.

Just then Victor's mobile phone rang. It was Harley at the other end. 'Turn on ITV's News. There is something on there that might interest you all.' Before he had a chance to ask any questions, Harley hung up on him.

Victor turned to John. 'That was Harley. He said that we should watch the ITV news.'

John looked at the clock on the mantlepiece. 'It should be coming on about now. Turn the set on will you love and let's see what all this is about?'

His wife got up and switched on the TV and they all sat back in anticipation. The announcer sat behind his desk looking very composed until the theme music faded out.

'Jason Carter, the well-known jockey, will want to forget this day as soon as possible. Not only did he not ride a winner at this afternoon's Newbury meeting but this evening he was discovered in what can only be described as a bizarre and very compromising situation. A farmer, out looking for a cow that had strayed away from the rest of his herd, discovered Carter in one of his paddocks on the A34 to Oxford. Mr Carter was completely nude and stretched out over the bonnet of his red Maserati. His hands and feet were securely tied to the car door and bumper bars.

'There was also a message written in lipstick on the windscreen of his car. The message read, and I quote; "I am Jason Carter and I enjoy molesting defenseless women." The message was signed, "The Avenging Angels". Police are investigating the incident but Carter has not co-operated with them. He was seen late this afternoon leaving the Newbury racecourse in the company of two young women in his car. Oxford police later confirmed that a charge of attempted rape had been made against the jockey but it had been withdrawn for lack of evidence. It seems today though that Mr Carter met his match, in tandem as it were. No doubt his next appearance at a racetrack will be interesting to say the least.'

Victor looked at Mary who was staring at the television screen, her mouth agape. 'Harley you old rascal. So that is what you were up to with the girls.'

'Who on earth managed to get the better of him like that?' Susan queried.

'Shall we say a set of twins from the City Of Angels.' Victor then roared with laughter as he pictured the sight in his mind. 'I would say that not only will Jason find it hard to get rides now, but he will have his work cut out finding anybody that will go out with him.'

'That is what I call poetic justice. No way is Carter going to bring charges against those two girls even if the police do manage to find them. He would be the laughing stock of the country.' John looked at his daughter. 'Well, my love, do you feel avenged now?'

Mary looked at her father for a few moments and then burst into a fit of giggles that continued into waves of laughter. Soon they were all laughing and, with tears streaming down her cheeks, Mary burst out, 'That poor old farmer, he went out looking for a stray cow and found a naked rat.'

Chapter Eighteen

Over the next couple of weeks the weather really improved and it reminded Victor of a Melbourne autumn. After the excitement of both his horses winning, he found it hard to settle in the house on his own. He began to act like a tourist, travelling to the many little fishing villages that were to be found dotted around the Cornish coast. He spent his days wandering around the many small shops and sandy beaches. Though quiet at the moment in a few weeks they would be packed with throngs of holidaymakers. For his meals, he sought out ancient inns and historic coachhouses.

Mary had gone up to York with her mother to see her grandmother, who sadly had been taken ill again. In a way Victor was glad that she was gone, because he felt that he needed a break away from her for a while. He had to get things sorted out in his mind. It was obvious to him that he had become so used to Mary's company that he felt somewhat depleted when she was not with him. On the other hand, he felt that things were moving at a slightly faster pace than he was comfortable with or desired.

On one of his many trips through Truro, he had stopped at the estate agents to inquire what price the building society had placed on the house. The rep he had originally dealt with had been transferred to the Plymouth office. His replacement, a young chap called Matt Perkins, was not even aware that the property was on their books.

'Does this mean that I no longer have to pay you rent?' Victor had joked. The jest had fallen on deaf ears, however. Matt had then promised to get in touch with head office and get back to Victor with a price.

Some time had gone by without Victor hearing from the agent. He was beginning to despair of ever being given a figure, when one morning there was a knock at the door. Victor opened it to find Matt standing on the doorstep. 'Mr Barnes, I am very sorry about the delay but the valuer had to come out and value the place. Apparently he had great difficulty in even finding it. He then told them at the office that if anyone was fool enough to want to buy this house in the middle of nowhere, then they shouldn't lose him.'

Victor smiled faintly.

'I am sorry Mr Barnes, his words not mine. The upshot is that you can have the house for £55,000.'

Victor looked at him for a moment and quietly digested this information. He then replied, 'I will give you £50,000, cash. Take it or leave it.'

Matt accepted his offer so quickly that Victor had a nagging feeling that he most likely could have got it far cheaper. Matt had obviously been prepared to haggle over the price. However, Victor was happy with the offer that he had made and gave Matt a cheque for the ten per cent deposit required to seal the sale. The agent promised to have all the papers drawn up in a week for Victor to sign.

Closing the door behind the agent, Victor slowly made his way into the kitchen. He walked around it and then made his way through every other room in the house. In his bedroom he stopped by the window and gazed down on the remains of the old tin mines. 'Seven Oaks. A Cornish Residence,' he spoke out loud reading from the brochure that Becky had given him when she had first told him about the house. 'Well, Amanda, my love, I now own my own little piece of Cornwall. My only regret is that you are not here to share it with me.'

Victor was about to go down to the village when his phone rang. It was John Collins. 'I have just had a call from the police. Ginger has identified Cassidy in a line up as the man who paid him. When he was told that the boy had picked him out, he apparently sang like a bird. He said that he was not going to take the blame all on his own. It looks as though it will be an open and shut case. The Jockey Club has been notified and they have confirmed that Oxford's licence has been revoked. The police say that unfortunately they cannot make a case against the Frenchman Duval, but the other two will be charged. Oxford with doping and several other minor irregularities and Cassidy has already been charged with embezzlement. Now on top of that he has this nonsense with Ginger to face. They will both be warned off the race tracks for life.'

'I must say that this news is not entirely unexpected. Still, it is nice to hear it confirmed, just the same. Also it finally clears things up as far as Harley is concerned. Now to the important things, how is Samson doing?'

'That horse of yours is eating me out of house and home at the present time,' John laughed. 'If he keeps on like this I am going to have to charge you extra for his feed. I think that I might run him at Newmarket. Don't bother backing him though, he won't win. It is just a race to keep his mind on the job; the distance will be too short for him. I have also entered him for Newbury but the same thing applies there too. Six furlongs is too short for him, so keep your money in your pocket until the Derby. Any news from your end of the world?'

'Harley has got Alaskan Jack running in the Chester Vase. Jenkins reckons that he has improved several lengths since he has had him. He rates him a good chance for the race.' Victor paused for a moment and then asked quietly, 'Have you heard from Mary at all lately John? It seems ages since I last saw her.'

'She thinks that she will be home at the end of the week. Her grand-mother is a lot better again, so both Susan and she should be back.'

'My only other piece of news is that I have bought this house.' There was silence on the other end of the line. 'It really is a good investment John. As far as I am concerned, I got a bargain.'

'I believe you. After all, what is the point of having money if you don't make it work for you? Besides a man needs to put down roots of some kind.'

'I will catch up with you later. I promised Mick and Sally that I would go down and see them. Today seems to be as good a day as any.' Victor then said goodbye and closed up his phone. He made himself a cup of coffee and while he sat there drinking it decided that he would drive down to St Mawley while he was in the mood.

When Sally opened the door to him it was obvious that she had been crying. Victor looked at her for an instant, uncertain what to do. He did not want to muscle in on a family argument, if that was what had been going on. Sally, however, solved his dilemma for him. 'Victor, how nice to see you. We could do with some cheering up right now. You had better come in and have a talk to Mick. I should warn you, he is not in the best of moods right this instant.'

'What is the matter? I thought that things were going fine with you both at the moment. Mick should be on top of the world after that Ayr result.' Sally led him into the kitchen. He found her husband slumped over the table, holding his head in his hands.

'Hey, Mick, what is wrong buddy? Is there anything that I can do to help at all?' Victor asked him. He was a little dismayed to see the expression of absolute gloom on the other's face.

At the sound of his voice, Mick looked up. 'Hi there, Victor,' he replied wearily. 'No, you have already done more than enough to help us. Actually, that is a major part of the problem. Since Pride did so well, I have been offered another six chasers to train. The facilities here are not really adequate, at the moment anyway, to look after them properly. Then on top of that I need to hire someone to help out. It is getting too much to cope with on my own.'

'I can understand all that. I mean, that is why you approached the bank for a loan in the first place wasn't it? So what has changed to make you so despondent?'

'That's just it. I haven't got the loan. There is a new manager just taken over at the bank. To say that he is a bit of a Puritan is putting it mildly. He doesn't believe in gambling. Training horses constitutes gambling as far as he is concerned. If I want to open a pizza parlour then I can have as much money as I need. However, to improve my property so that I can train racehorses is out of the question. There is too much risk for the bank to get involved. Even though they would hold title over the stables.'

'But yours is a business venture too, surely he is able to see that?'

'No matter. I even told him that the previous manager had approved the loan. He has vetoed it and won't even listen to argument. I can't take on all this new work without expanding the way that I want. Damn! I simply do not believe that this is happening. After all this hard work and then some prick at the bank tells me that my profession leads to families being left destitute.'

Victor pulled up a chair and sat down at the table. He was silent for a while and then looked at Mick. 'How much money do you need Mick? I mean to do things properly and not skimp or take short cuts?'

'Well, with these six new horses, I was budgeting on between £20,000 and £25,000. I need to be able to guarantee the wages plus make quite a few repairs and improvements to the place. Also I should have a new float; it is cheaper than having to hire one all the time.'

Victor looked at him and then at Sally, whose eyes were still red from crying. Taking a deep breath he asked, 'Have you ever thought of taking in a partner?'

'A partner?' Clearly the question had taken the other man by surprise.

'I would think that would be one solution to your immediate problem. I am willing to buy into the stables right now. Or, if you prefer to keep it just between you and Sally, I'll understand and I will just lend you the money. Now, just let's get one thing clear from the outset. If I became a partner, I should be a silent one only. I know absolutely zero about running a stable and I intend to keep it that way. I would put up the money in return for a small percentage of the profits.'

'I truly don't know what to say.' Mick was stunned.

Victor pulled out his chequebook and wrote in it. Tearing out the cheque he pushed it across the table. 'For a start, take the money. There is a cheque there for £30,000. You and Sally can talk it over which way you want to go. Either way I won't mind. Neither will I be the least upset if you don't want me involved as a partner. After all, it is you and Sally who have done all the hard work here so far. The only thing that I do insist on is that you bank the cheque and, as soon as it has been cleared, close the account and take it elsewhere. You need to show this guy that someone is willing to back you and that he has lost a good account. We have the same trouble with a lot of the banks in Australia. They want your money but in most cases seem to throw every obstacle at you that they can find. Their fees too are outrageous, they charge for everything. They tend to forget that it is having the use of our money that keeps them in business. Now have we a deal?'

Mick looked across the table at his wife who had tears in her eyes again. This time, however, they were tears of joy. She nodded happily. Mick stood up and held out his hand to Victor. Without hesitation he said, 'We have a deal, partner. Yippee!'

Sally came round and hugged Victor. 'Oh Victor, I thank you from the bottom of my heart. You cannot imagine what this means to us.'

'Oh I think that I have a pretty fair idea of what all this means. For one thing, I am now involved in a business as well as owning horses.'

'Lady Luck must have been in a really good mood the day that she brought you to our door. They say that every cloud has a silver . . . Oh my God Victor, I am so sorry I . . .' Sally stopped in horror when she realised what she was saying.

Victor put a hand on her shoulder and gave it a gentle squeeze. 'That's ok Sally, don't let's spoil things.'

Mick who was a lot slower to pick up what was going on suddenly realised the implications of his wife's words. He quickly decided that he should change the subject. 'What are we going to do about Pride of Tintagel Victor? I mean that I think that he deserves a spell after what he has achieved.' He brought the conversation back to business. His wife flashed him a grateful look.

Victor thought about for a while and then said, 'I would be inclined to give him a break say until October. That way it would give you more time to spend with your new charges. Anyway, if he never raced again, I reckon that he has done me proud. I couldn't ask for anything more from him.'

'Well, if you decide to sell him before you go back to Australia, I would be grateful if you would give me first refusal on him. I realise that he will cost me a lot more now but if things improve the way that I hope then . . .'

Victor held up his hand to stop the man from going on any longer. 'Mick I give you my promise that if, and I repeat if and when, I go back to Melbourne, you can have the horse for what he cost me. That is a promise. At the present time, however, I have no idea what my future plans might be. You never know, if Arcadian Steel does well in the Derby, I just might let him have a crack at the Melbourne Cup.'

'What does Mary think about all this?' asked Sally with a grin.

'To be perfectly frank with you, I have only just thought of the idea. You two are the only people who know about it.'

'The Melbourne Cup, I wouldn't mind seeing that,' Sally said.

'The premier, if not the richest handicap in the world. It is a fraction under two miles and it takes a good horse to win it,' Victor said with a touch of pride and Mick looked at him. 'Well that is a few wins away I think, plus you have a business here to consider.'

After telling Mick to get his solicitor to draw up the papers for the partnership, they all went down to have a look at Pride. Victor was pleased to see that the horse was none the worse for his couple of hard races. He then took his leave and made for home.

By the time that he had reached the house it was almost dark. He parked the car and moved towards the front door. He was about to go in when his mobile rang. He propped himself against one of the tubs on the front porch and pulled the phone from his belt. It was Mary. 'Hi there Victor. I have missed you. How are you and what have you been doing with yourself since I saw you last?'

He didn't answer for a while but leaned back against the elder bush and stared up into the sky. It was now a dark blue that was just becoming illuminated with several thousand twinkling stars.

'Victor, are you there?' Mary's voice came crackling over the phone.

'Yes, I am right here.'

'What are you doing? You sound kind of strange tonight. Is there something wrong? You don't sound as though you have been drinking. What are you doing?'

'Oh, I am just standing here outside the house looking up at the stars. They seem to be different somehow. I know that it sounds silly but there seems to be something missing.' His eyes raked the heavens. Then it hit him. There was no Southern Cross. 'Mary, the Southern Cross is gone. It's simply not there any more.'

For a few seconds there was complete silence on the line. Then Mary's voice came soft and low. 'Victor, you can only see that in the southern hemisphere. What's wrong? Are you feeling homesick?'

'Homesick? No, I don't think so. It's just that Amanda and I, when we used to go away for a weekend, used to love to just sit and look at the stars. It is so hard to see them in Melbourne because the lights of the city were so bright. But when we were able to get out into the bush, the skies were clear and bright. Millions of stars just hanging there.'

'Victor, I think that I may have called you at an awkward time. It is probably best if I hang up now and I will ring you again tomorrow. Just remember this one thing, Victor,' and she spoke softly into his ear. Then wishing him goodnight, she hung up. He stood there staring at the night sky for a while. Finally he opened the front door and went inside.

The day of the Chester Vase dawned bright and clear. Victor did not really feel like driving all the way up there but he felt that he owed it to Harley to attend. So he caught a plane at St Mawgam once again and flew to Liverpool. By now most of the airline staff had come to know him and the pilot gave him a cheery good morning as he boarded. When he landed at Liverpool, the taxi driver that he hailed, however, was not nearly as friendly. He demanded £20 before he would even drive off. The Vase was the third race on the card. When Victor offered the cab driver £50 to have a bet when they arrived at the course, his attitude changed completely. He even promised to wait for Victor until four o'clock and drive him back to catch his plane.

The one thing that Alaskan Jack had in his favour was that Chester was a very tight track, similar to Moonee Valley in Melbourne. This meant that form shown at Chester was not indicative of any form shown at most other tracks. The course itself was only a mile round with most of the racing being done on the turn.

Harley had told him that he would not be too disappointed if the horse did not fare too well. Another of his string of thoroughbreds in the States, Blackjack Charlie, had won the Kentucky Derby at Churchill Downs, three days earlier. 'You never know though, Victor, I could be on a roll. A winner at home and one in England in the same week,' Harley had exclaimed.

There were only seven runners in the Vase and after a slow start Alaskan Jack flew home to pinch the race by the narrowest of margins. Harley picked up just over £28,000 for the win, which made Victor very happy for his friend. The fact too that he had backed the horse at the very good odds of 100–8 helped to make the day a very successful one for both of them. The errant cab driver could not believe his luck as Victor gave him a £100 note on arriving back at the airport after the race. He tried to apologise for his demand for money at the beginning of the trip. Victor waved his apologies aside saying that he understood the man's initial reluctance. So, when the plane landed back at St Mawgam, Victor was in a far happier frame of mind then when he had left that morning.

He did not bother to go to Newmarket to back Samson when John ran him there. Also, true to his prediction, the horse didn't win but did finish a game third. Consequently they decided to scratch him from Newbury as they both felt that another run before the Derby would achieve nothing beneficial. Victor then started to count down the days before the big race. He telephoned Dan and told him with great exuberance how the horse was progressing. When his brother-in-law asked him what he had been doing since his last phone call to Melbourne, Victor told him what had transpired with Oxford and Cassidy. He told him all about the charges that had been brought against them and the likely outcome. He also gave him details of Alaskan Jack's win and related Jason Carter's encounter with the twins with relish.

The two items of news that Victor somehow managed to avoid revealing during the conversation were the big ones. The fact that he

Chapter Eighteen

had gone ahead with his stated intentions. He had bought Seven Oaks and had become a partner in Mick's stables. He had a nagging feeling that neither Dan nor Naomi would be exactly overjoyed at these snippets of information. He knew that he would have to disclose the news at some time, but wanted to put it off as long as possible.

Mary and Susan returned home from York and Mary invited him up for the weekend. 'It seems like an eternity since we last saw each other. Please say that you will come,' she had pleaded with him when she phoned him. After agreeing that he would drive up there on the Friday night and stay until the Monday morning, Victor sat on his bed. His mind and active imagination were working overtime. If Arcadian Steel were fortunate enough to win the Derby, should he take him over to France for the Arc d' Triomphe? Would he be strong enough to take him home and run him in the Melbourne Cup? He knew that Samson was a trifle young to compete in the great race but the horse had a heart as big as Phar Lap. He knew that he would give a good account of itself. If he did go to Melbourne, would he be forced to stay once he had felt the effects of home once again, or would he have the courage to return to England? He thought about those pop stars who spent part of the year in England and the USA and the rest of the time in Oz. Was he able to live like that or indeed did he really want to? After all he was still English, but then what family he still had lived in Melbourne. His mind in a complete turmoil, Victor downed several large brandies and eventually managed to drag himself off to bed. There, after some time, he drifted off into an uneasy sleep.

Victor's dreams were wild and crazy ones that night. He found that he was on a ship heading for the cliffs. He could see the savage seas crashing over the jagged rocks, just waiting for his vessel to be driven onto their hungry teeth. Then suddenly he saw Amanda appear on top of the cliff. She was waving a lantern wildly, trying frantically to attract his attention to steer him towards the safety of a channel that she was pointing the way to. Then, just as he was about to swing the rudder over to bring the ship in line with her, Mary appeared on the other side. She was carrying a torch in either hand. She flashed it on and off in what he thought was a message in Morse code. He tried desperately to remember what he had learnt in his youth of this form of signal. His memory failed him and he was unable to decipher this obviously urgent message. Then, suddenly, from behind him and with a deafening roar, a huge sea monster shot up from the murky depths of the ocean. It reared high above the ship. Foam-flecked water cascaded off its scaly body and flashes of fire shot from its malevolent eyes. Victor stared in abject terror. Its long neck supported two gargantuan heads. He realised to his horror that one possessed the face of Colin Oxford, the other that of John Cassidy. The monster was poised about to strike when a jagged flash of cobalt blue lightning split the fiery heavens. Victor felt himself being picked up as though by a giant hand. He flew through the air to the relevant safety of a pair of arms.

Victor awoke in fright, sweat pouring down his face. He was shaking like a leaf and felt as cold as ice. He pushed the tangled duvet aside and swung his legs out of bed. He looked at the clock bathed in moonlight. It showed 3.30a.m. Dragging on his trousers he stumbled downstairs. He then made himself a cup of strong black coffee and sat at the red stone table to drink it. His pulse was still racing as he sat there and tried to recover his wits. In all of his life he had never experienced so vivid a nightmare. Was this the result of a guilty conscience, he wondered? Was he betraying Amanda by even thinking about Mary? The longer that he thought about it the more muddled his thoughts became. He felt that he was incapable of making a rational decision. He was familiar with post traumatic stress syndrome, maybe this was what he was experiencing. Then a terrible thought came into his mind. In all his memories of Amanda he had never really given the twins much thought. He missed them of course but he didn't devote his time to them like he did Amanda. He felt ashamed. Finally, he decided that he would put his coat on and go and sit in the garden for a while.

The shaking had stopped and he felt a little calmer. The moon was almost full and its silvery light lit up the whole of the house. A tawny owl hooted from the branches of one of the oak trees. He jumped, almost spilling his coffee. He sat there on the porch sipping his coffee. The almost boiling liquid warmed his hands as he clasped the mug tightly. The time was rapidly approaching when he would have to make up his mind one way or the other. Did he really want to live here or was his place back in Melbourne? If he went back what was it that he was going back to? If he did return he knew that he would have to sell the house. It held too many memories for him ever to live there again. Maybe it was best to make a fresh start here in England.

Evidently it was his conscience that was the main cause of his nightmare. 'Once the Derby is over then I have to make a choice one way or the other,' he said to the moon. 'I simply cannot go on living like this.'

On Friday morning Victor had just finished his breakfast when the phone rang. It was Matt Perkins from the estate agents. 'I have got all the papers for you to sign, Mr Barnes. Would you be able to go to the building society's offices in Exeter instead of coming here to Truro? As you know, we arranged for their solicitor to handle all the transfer work to expedite matters, as you did not have anyone who could act for you. Well, he will be there this morning. So if you could meet up with him then we can get everything settled for you today.' Victor agreed that this was a good idea and arranged to be there at 11.30.

As he had plenty of time Victor thought that he might take the scenic route across the moors to Exeter. Leaving Okehampton, he took the Newton Abbott road and consequently drove right through the Dartmoor National Park. The sun was shining and there was hardly a cloud in the sky. The gorse-spotted moors, criss-crossed by numerous tiny streams, stretched as far as the eye could see. The many clusters of granite boulders, interspersed with Bronze Age remains, gave the moor the life and character that artists loved to paint. Up ahead, Victor could see what appeared to be a kestrel. It was hovering against the breeze, poised waiting to swoop on some small, unsuspecting mammal for its lunch. Victor experienced both a feeling of desolation and grandeur as he drove along the narrow road. He turned off the A38 and continued into Exeter.

After finalising all his business with the solicitor, Victor was told that he was now officially the new owner of Seven Oaks. He decided to take a walk around the town itself. As with everything else, it had changed a lot since he used to visit it in his youth. In the centre of the town as in so many nowadays, only buses were allowed to drive along the main street. The wide pavements were now home to a large collection of stalls displaying a multitude of different wares for sale. As he wandered slowly along, Victor's stomach reminded him that it was lunch time. He suddenly found himself outside an attractive looking pub. 'The Black Horse, I guess that this will do as well as any,' he said to himself and, pushing open the door, he stepped inside.

Some seventy minutes later, feeling fully nourished, Victor retraced his steps to the town centre until he found a florist. He had purchased a large bunch of flowers that he had intended to give to Susan and was about to leave the shop when a thought struck him. He then bought a second bunch for Mary. Next, he went in search of an off licence. He had to try a couple before he found what he was looking for: a bottle of Wolfe Blass Black Label. His wallet now considerably lighter it took him a good twenty minutes to find where he had parked the car. By the time that he was on his way again to Taunton, the clock in the car showed the time to be a little past three o'clock.

When Victor finally arrived at the Collins's house, Mary greeted him as though he was a long lost brother. He had to hold the flowers away from his body or else she would have crushed them. Luckily Susan came to his rescue and he managed to disentangle himself from Mary's clinging embrace. Her mother was delighted with her flowers but Mary scarcely glanced at her bunch. She shoved them into Susan's arms to go and put into vases along with her own.

'Come and sit down, Victor. It seems like a lifetime since I saw you last.' She caught him by the arm and dragged him into the lounge. Her father was seated in his armchair and he rose to his feet as they entered. 'Good God, Mary, you are like a cat with a ball of wool that it has found. For goodness sake, leave the poor fellow alone for a minute to catch his breath.'

Victor managed to pull the bottle of wine out of his coat pocket and thrust it towards John.

'Here John, you had better take care of this before it gets broken in the fray,' he said with a laugh.

John took it and studied the label carefully before setting the bottle down on the sideboard. 'I see that it is another of your Australian wines. You know I had never tasted any wine from that part of the world before I met you. To be honest I don't know whether I even realised that Australia made wine. It is very good though, somewhat softer than the French reds that we are used to, but a nice drop all the same.'

'That one there I was surprised to find. It is hard to find it in Melbourne.'

Mary looked at him, her lips turned up in a petulant pout. 'I thought that you might be pleased to see me, it has been some time. All you can do is talk about some old crushed grapes.' He gave her a peck on the cheek.

'I am pleased to see you Mary, but you might let me walk in under my own steam. I am not going to run out on you, not yet anyway.'

'He is more likely to leave if you don't stop being so possessive, girl. The man is under no obligation to you remember,' her father said rather sternly.

'I am not being possessive at all,' she retorted. 'Hey Mum, Dad says that I am being too possessive where Victor is concerned, please tell him that he is wrong,' Mary appealed to her mother, who had just entered carrying two vases with the flowers that Victor had brought with him.

Susan laughed. 'I am not going to get caught up in this argument. Victor knows that he is always welcome here but that is as far as it goes.' She put the vases down, one at each end of the sideboard, and then stood back to admire them.

Mary flounced down in one of the armchairs. 'OK, I will leave him alone if he promises me one little thing.'

'What little thing might that be I wonder,' Victor said. 'I am almost afraid to ask. I didn't think that the term "little thing" came into your vocabulary Mary.'

She looked at the three of them and then grinned wickedly. 'Well, since I had to come back from Aintree in a car, I reckon that you still owe me a plane flight Victor.'

'Mary!' Both her parents spoke in unison. 'Mary, I am shocked at you,' her mother cried. 'That is no way to behave, young lady! That is really hitting below the belt.' Her father looked decidedly angry at his daughter's cheek.

Victor, on the other hand, looked really amused at the suggestion. 'Actually, I think that is a splendid idea. I will tell you what. As long as we can have a nice quiet evening here tonight, tomorrow we can drive up to Bristol. Then we can fly across to Ireland to watch the Irish Guineas. The 1000 is being run tomorrow and the 2000 on Sunday. In fact, I insist on it, but not just Mary. We shall all go.'

'No, no that is not right,' John protested strongly.

Mary grabbed at his arm. 'Oh please, Dad, say yes. I have never been to Ireland and the racing should be top class. Please say that we can go.'

'What do you think about the idea, Susan?' Victor asked her.

She hesitated a moment before answering him. 'I will be honest with you Victor. If I were to fly anywhere, I would rather go to France. I have enough of horses day after day here. It would be nice to go away somewhere for a change where they played no part in the day's proceedings. But don't let that stop you three from going.'

Victor looked at her in amazement, as did her husband. 'I had no idea that you ever wanted to go to France,' John said with a bewildered look at his wife.

'You have never asked me, John. A couple of times when you were off gallivanting around the countryside with your horses, I have been very tempted to go. You know, one of those day trips that go through the Tunnel.'

'Mum, that is a marvelous idea,' Mary exclaimed. 'Victor, if you really want to take us out somewhere, why don't we do just that? I can ring Bristol and see if there are any trips going this weekend. If so, we can all go to France for the day.'

John started to protest very loudly that this was not at all fair on Victor but Victor held up his hand and said, 'What is the point of having plenty of money if you can't spend it on your friends?' He was quite excited by the idea now, also. 'I will tell you what. We will ring Bristol and if we can get seats then we will go. If we are not meant to go, there will be no seats left. That will easily solve the problem.'

'Oh, I hope that you don't think that I was asking you to take us to France. I never meant that you . . . ,' Susan was quite upset.

'Nonsense. I think that it is a wonderful idea. Mary is right and it looks as though she is already making enquiries about it.' They all turned round and sure enough Mary was on the phone. After getting the number that she wanted from the operator, she then dialled Bristol. A few minutes later she replaced the receiver and announced, 'We are all going to France in the morning. Thank you Victor, you may now give me a kiss.' Her parents both threw up their hands in mock horror.

The next day all four of then thoroughly enjoyed themselves. After a somewhat eerie drive through the vast tunnel that had been carved from under the English Channel, they arrived in France. The two women spent most of their time shopping whilst John and Victor sampled the many wines available. In fact, when they got back to Bristol on the coach, neither of them was fit to drive. Mary was forced to take the wheel on the drive back home. Nevertheless, both men were up early the next day for the morning gallops. Samson was looking absolutely magnificent. Jimmy informed Victor that he and the horse had become good friends and he was no longer any trouble to ride. Victor had heard from Jenkins that they had decided to run Alaskan Jack in the Diomed Stakes on the day before the Derby. After some discussion John agreed that they could all travel up to Epsom on the Friday morning. After all, Victor was paying all their accommodation bills. On the Monday morning he left Hill Top about mid-morning to travel back to Cornwall. He drove home feeling very contented with the way that the weekend had gone. He had a couple of duty free bottles in the car and he felt nice and relaxed.

The next few days seemed to drag by very slowly indeed. Victor was somewhat at a loss as to what he could do with himself. On Wednesday morning he was feeling so bored that he hopped in the car and drove down to Penzance. There he caught the helicopter across to the Scilly Isles. He spent the day pottering around the beaches and shops of St Mary's. He wasn't even able to get away from her down here, he thought. The weather though was very mild and he enjoyed the quiet solitude of the place. Flying back to Penzance, Victor decided that he would spend the night there. 'This is crazy,' he said to himself, 'I am like a schoolboy the day before his exams.' He found a small boarding house and booked in there for bed and breakfast. He then went back to the town centre and found a small restaurant for his evening meal. His hunger appeased, for a while at least, Victor knew that he would find it difficult to get to sleep, so went for a walk along the sea front. The wind was starting to blow a little stronger as the tide came in. He soon found that he had to cross to the other side of the road to avoid being soaked. The waves broke upon the beach with such force that the resulting spray was hurled twenty feet into the air. The pavement was soon awash as the salty water cascaded down. Eventually he found that he had walked in a complete circle and that he was back at his boarding house. Finally, he fell asleep, lying on the bed watching television.

Friday morning dawned and Victor was up and about very early. He had arranged with John Collins that he would meet the family at the race track. When he arrived he began to think that he had made an error in not travelling up with the rest of them. He had not anticipated any problem in finding them. He was not prepared, however, for the number of people who were already there. He had been to Flemington on Melbourne Cup Day with a crowd close to 100,000 but he had not expected the scene of apparent utter confusion that met his eyes. The Downs were literally packed with vehicles and caravans of every description. He had no idea that they stretched so far. The huge fun fair was being moved into its allotted place. There were several of the highly decorated open buses taking up vantage points near the running rail. The crowd was already large but by this time tomorrow would have swollen to ten, twenty times the number. John had told him that the stables were situated at the back of the stands. He knew that he had no hope of getting in to see his horse until John was there to sign him in. Alaskan Jack was due to run in the third race, so he had plenty of time to find the others.

The world-famous track, based on chalk, looked in perfect condition. Jenkins had told him that it would most certainly be firm going. As Victor pushed his way through the jostling crowd, a tout came sidling up to him. 'I've got a horse for the big one tomorrer Guv'nor, only a fiver and it's yours.'

Victor laughed and pushed him away. 'I already have my own horse and I don't need to be told that it is going to win.'

Once he had managed to push his way into the bar, Victor looked around for any of the Collins family. He could not see any of them but he did spot Ambrose at the counter. Threading his way through the crowded tables, he reached the bar and clapped his hand on Ambrose's shoulder.

The big man turned around slowly, then, recognising Victor, grabbed his hand and almost crushed it. 'Well, my boy, I see that he has at least made it to the form book then,' his voice boomed out above the discordant noise of the throng that surrounded him.

'Yes, and he has an excellent chance of winning tomorrow. His times have been remarkable, or so John tells me.'

'Thought that he won well that day at Newbury, backed him too,' Ambrose stated in a matter-of-fact voice. 'Now, how about this one of Harley's today? Do you reckon that he will put up much of a show? He has some strong opposition.'

'As much of a chance as any of the others. Harley couldn't get here today. Some crisis meeting at the last minute in LA so I am here to represent him. His other horse Cash Crisis has a leg injury and won't race for at least six or seven weeks. He is not having an awful lot of luck with this year's purchases.'

'These things happen in racing and quite often too. The better the horse is then the more prone he is to injury. You can take an old hack and it can run for ever. These thoroughbreds, however, have to be kept wrapped up in cotton wool almost. I say, is that young lady waving at me or you, Victor?' Ambrose gave a throaty laugh and Victor turned around to see Mary waving frantically, trying to attract his attention.

'I think that I am being summoned, Ambrose, I had better go.' The two men shook hands and Victor started to make his way over to where Mary was standing.

'The best of luck tomorrow, my boy. I will be watching him.' Ambrose called after him and Victor raised his hand in acknowledgement.

'We are in the other bar, Victor. Dad thought that this one was too crowded. Mr Jenkins is in there with us too.' As they were leaving Victor looked around at the mass of people.

'If it is as busy as this today, what is it going to be like tomorrow?'

'Dad said that the officials are saying that it looks as though it is going to be a record attendance for the Friday. But, come on, they are all waiting for us.' When they arrived Victor was dismayed to see that John was far from being in a good mood. 'What's wrong there John? Nothing has happened to the horse has it?'

'Not yet anyway, but I have had some bad news all the same. The rider of Bixby Lad was thrown from a horse this morning and he broke his leg.'

'Bixby Lad? But in the paper this morning he was quoted as being a 150–1 shot; why would that affect us? I don't understand,' Victor said.

'It's not the horse that I'm worried about, it's his replacement jockey.'

Victor stared at him. 'You don't mean that . . .?'

'Yes I do,' John said grimly. 'It's Jason Carter! Now if he were riding a horse that stood a chance of winning I would not be too bothered. But for him to climb aboard a no-hoper like that, well, it can only mean one thing as far as I'm concerned. He will be doing his level best to see that Arcadian Steel does not win.'

Victor stared at him aghast. Silenced by his thoughts, he then came back to reality. 'Is there nothing that we can do?'

'I have already been to the stewards and alerted them. Unfortunately their hands are tied unless they actually catch him doing anything to stop the horse. For all we know this might be Jason's last ride. He won't care if he is caught as long as he can put our fellow out of the race.'

'What if he tries to dope the horse?' Mary asked.

Her father looked at her. 'Mary you of all people should know how well those stables are guarded. The horseflesh that is stabled here is worth literally millions of pounds. Not even a mouse can get through this security. No, if he is going to try anything it will be on the track. You can bet your life on it.'

'Where is Jimmy by the way? I don't see him anywhere,' Victor said looking around for his jockey. 'I let him go to the West End to the pictures. He is not really needed here today, so he might as well try and relax.'

'I suppose that nothing can be accomplished by us thinking about it anymore today. I suggest that we try to forget about Jason Carter for the moment and enjoy the racing. Look, the runners are coming out for the first race,' Susan said.

However, none of them felt like having a bet so they decided to go in the stands and watch the race. The favourite duly obliged in the first and again in the second. As the time came close to the third race, Alaskan Jack was showing 7–2 with most of the bookies after his win in the Cheater Vase. Mary managed to find one bookie that was prepared to offer 4–1 against him winning, so they all made their wagers with him. Victor only put £100 on the horse but Mary was far more adventurous and laid out £200 to win. 'It's not really my money anyway,' she said.

The favourite, Hi-Fi, jumped first, closely followed by Alaskan Jack. The field was pretty well bunched throughout the race with a lot of bumping and jostling for position. Hi-Fi maintained his lead with Alaskan Jack close on his heels. As they passed the final furlong post Harley's horse made his move, but the favourite began to run off the track and the jockey on Alaskan Jack had to check his mount momentarily. Hi-Fi passed the winning post a long neck ahead of Alaskan Jack and Victor threw down his race book in disgust.

'Steady on there, if your jockey doesn't lodge a protest against the winner then he shouldn't be riding.' John put a hand on Victor's arm as he spoke. Sure enough a couple of minutes later the warning siren sounded. The course commentator announced that a protest had

been lodged by the rider of the second horse against Hi-Fi for inter-
ference in the last half furlong. A further ten minutes elapsed before
the siren sounded again. The commentator then declared that the
protest had been upheld and Alaskan Jack was declared the winner.

'Well, Harley should be very pleased with that run I should say
Victor,' John said.

'Not to mention the £29,000 that he has picked up as prize money,'
Victor said drily as he started to make his way down to the winner's
enclosure.

They all ate a hearty meal at the restaurant in their hotel that
evening. After enjoying some coffee and a couple of rounds of drinks,
John suggested that it might be prudent if they all got an early night.
'We should get some sleep as it is going to be a big day for everyone
tomorrow.'

'You can say that again,' Victor said huskily. Then he added under
his breath, 'You don't realise how big John.' He wished them all good
night and started for the door. Mary walked up the stairs with him. As
he stopped to say good night, he saw to his dismay that there were
tears in her eyes.

'Hey, what is this all about? What is wrong Mary?' He was becoming
concerned.

'If anything goes wrong tomorrow it will be my fault.' She started to
cry harder.

'What are you talking about?'

'I know how much this race means to you and if Jason does
anything to stop Samson then it will be my fault. My fault.'

'How can you talk such bloody nonsense Mary Collins? You
really do amaze me at times.' He took her in his arms and gently
kissed her on the forehead. 'Now do as your father suggested and
go to bed. If Samson loses tomorrow because of Carter, well, it
won't be the end of the world. For all we know Oxford and Cassidy
could have paid him to try. They have got it in for me far more
than he has.'

She looked at him, her eyes still full of tears. Suddenly she grabbed
him and kissed him hungrily. She finally released him and whispered
softly, 'I love you Victor Barnes.'

Before he had chance to voice a reply, she opened the door of her
room and swiftly entered, closing the door behind her. For a moment
he just stood there, his mind in a whirl. He had known for some time

that she was attracted to him. She had made that fairly obvious all along. This time she had thrown down the gauntlet. The question was, did he want to, or indeed was he able to, pick it up? As he made his way slowly to his room, all that he could see in his mind was Amanda's face looking at him.

The following morning at breakfast, neither Mary nor Victor made mention of the previous night's conversation. Both John and Susan could sense that something had happened but neither was sure what. John made a point of not saying anything to Jimmy until Mary had left the table. He then warned the lad to be on his guard. Nobody had an inkling of what Jason might try, but they were all certain that he would attempt something during the race.

They arrived at the track reasonably early but, as early as they were, a huge crowd was there before them. The track looked terrific, a deep, rich green. The flower boxes around the winning post were a mass of red and white blooms. The owners's car park was already half full as they drove in. The scene reminded Victor of the car parks on Melbourne Cup days. A large number of people parked there with their baskets of champagne, smoked salmon and caviar, never even making it to the races. The difference was of course that at Flemington a lot of them arrived via the river. There was always a large variety of craft moored alongside the track. But the people here were the same as those in Melbourne, they just drove Rolls Royces and Daimlers instead of Statesmen and LTDs.

Jimmy had never ridden at Epsom before and John tried to explain to him how much the ground undulated. He told him to take particular note of the last three and a half furlongs from Tattenham Corner to the winning post. That final climb nearly always sorted out the champions from the rest of the field.

Victor looked across at him, the poor kid was a bundle of nerves. Whatever Victor was feeling it would be nothing compared to how the lad was. He would be riding in one of the world's greatest races and the eyes of millions of people would be on him. If he were to make one mistake, one small error, the whole world would know it. Victor knew that he had to say something to the boy. He went over and grabbed his hand.

'Jimmy, I just want you to know, whatever happens out there today, that we wouldn't be here if it wasn't for you. Even if you were to finish last, which I am sure will not happen, you will have made a dream come true for me. I am really proud of what you have achieved with this horse. You have done your best and that is all anyone could ask of you. Thanks to you, I have a runner in the Derby. I could not have done this without you Jimmy. I thank you most sincerely.'

Victor could see the lad swelling with pride. He shook his hand once more and left him with John. Rejoining Mary and Susan he saw to his chagrin that they both had tears in their eyes. Susan stepped forward and gave him a hug. 'What you just said to Jimmy was wonderful, Victor. It was exactly what he needed. He has been terrified that he was going to let you down and that would have affected his riding, I'm sure.'

'I am sorry Mary, I wasn't trying to dismiss what you have done for that horse or belittle you in any way, but I felt that I had to try to tell Jimmy what a great job he is doing.'

Mary wiped her eyes and smiled. 'I have to be honest with you Victor, it is Jimmy who has done most of the hard work. He surely deserves your praise. In fact, I would have been annoyed at you if you hadn't given him credit for what he has done.'

There was a sudden fanfare that blasted over the PA system. 'What did they go and do that for? It is nowhere near the time for the race to start,' Victor asked them in a puzzled tone. Both Mary and Susan looked at him and shook their heads.

'Really Victor, even you should know that the Queen has arrived. She will drive down the course before going to the royal box. That's it there, above where the winner and the place getters in the Derby parade after the race. She has come a little earlier than usual today because she has a runner in the first race.'

As Victor watched he saw a procession making its way down the centre of the course and the huge crowd waving wildly. 'Does she come into the paddock before the Derby?' he asked them.

'Yes, so you will most likely meet her. But I thought that all those people in Australia wanted the country to become a republic, so why would you want to meet her anyway?' Mary giggled and even Susan had to smile.

'I have told you before and you know it. I was born here in England. Apart from that, it is mainly the younger crowd and the politicians who want a republic. Believe you me, there is still a lot of support for the monarchy down under,' he replied rather haughtily.

By now the crowd had grown considerably. The tic tac men, their arms flying in all directions were becoming more and more frantic. The bookies were shovelling money into their bags and writing tickets as fast as they were able. The queues at the many takeaway food stalls seemed to stretch for ever. Everywhere that you looked was a mass of people, pushing, shoving and always queuing. Some were smiling, some scowling but most of them were adding to the noise. Victor saw several bands of gypsies elbowing their way through the dense crowds. Some were trying to offload tiny bunches of lucky heather, while others were trying to sell their tips to the many gullible punters. Policemen patrolled in pairs, their sharp eyes alert for pickpockets. They scanned the heaving mass of humanity that had taken over the Downs for this special day.

'I am a part of all this, this year,' Victor said to himself. He felt someone tugging at his sleeve. 'If you want to back your horse then I suggest that you do it now. You will never get near the bookies close to the race.'

'I am not going to back him,' Victor said shaking his head. 'If he happens to win or even just run a place, I shall be more than happy with the prize money. I am not greedy.'

There was a huge roar from the crowd. The runners were coming out for the first race. They made their way down to the starting stalls and the crowd waited in anticipation. Another roar as the starter let them go in a thundering of flying hooves. Evidently it was well worth Her Majesty arriving early because her horse was the first to salute the judge. A loud cheer went up from the crowd as the winner was announced. A very popular win.

As the time for the main race edged closer, the knots in Victor's stomach became tighter and tighter. He had watched the other races but if anybody had questioned him he could not name one winner. Most of the afternoon was merely a blur but not from any alcohol that he had consumed. Indeed, he had had only one glass of white wine, but the immensity of the occasion had finally gotten to him. No longer was he a $10 punter. He was an owner with a horse that was about to run in one of the most prestigious races in the world. He really was in the big time now, like it or not.

'Victor it is nearly two o'clock. I think that you should be getting down to the paddock. Jimmy needs to see you there.' He felt someone tugging on his arm again. It was Mary. 'You are certainly looking after me this afternoon,' he said to her.

'Well, someone needs to, you are miles away. Both Mum and I have been talking to you and all that we get in return is a glazed look in your eyes.'

Victor and the two women made their way down to the paddock. The security guards checked their passes carefully and then allowed them through. The Queen was already moving among the owners and trainers, stopping to chat with some of them. She drew level with Samson and looked him over with a professional eye. 'That is a magnificent animal that you have there. Good luck with him.'

'Thank you, Your Majesty,' John just managed to blurt out the words. She then passed on to the next group.

Jimmy was ecstatic. 'She spoke to us. The Queen actually spoke to us,' he cried.

'If you win the Derby then she will speak with you again,' Mary said to him.

John gave Jimmy a leg up into the saddle and they all stood back and watched as he started the long trip down to the start. As he trotted off John turned to Victor. 'Win, lose or draw, Victor, that horse has been the makings of young Jimmy. So, even if he achieves nothing else, Samson has turned a young, hopeful kid into a jockey.'

'We should be getting up into the stand John or we won't be able to see a thing,' Susan said to her husband.

John and Victor both laughed. 'We have a box, darling. You don't think that Victor would be content to watch this race from the stands do you? Come on, though, we had better make a move all the same. The horses are crossing the road so it won't be long before they are off.'

The four of them made their box in good time, however, and watched anxiously as the attendants tried to get their charges into their respective stalls.

The PA system crackled into life. 'The horses are moving in for the start of this year's Derby. Most of the field has gone in but a couple are sweating up badly. Arcadian Steel is one and Blue Rinse another. The attendants are in a spot of bother with Owen Season, no, he is going in now. Just a couple left to move in now. They are all in and the red light is flashing. They are under starter's orders and they are off in this year's Derby.'

'And the first away is Steven's Curse closely followed by Code of the

West. The outsider of the field, Bixby Lad, is prominent although his jockey has to work on him to keep his place. Running up to the hill now and it's Steven's Curse followed by Bixby Lad and Arcadian Steel. The leaders have reached the top of the hill and are coming into the left-hand turn. It is still Steven's Curse, followed closely by Bixby Lad and Arcadian Steel. The filly, Blue Rinse, is coming out of the pack. A filly has not won the Derby for over eighty years, could this be the year? Five furlongs out and they are beginning to come down Tattenham Hill. It is still Steven's Curse leading in the Derby from Bixby Lad, the outsider being urged on by his jockey. Arcadian Steel is third, then follows Milestone. Behind Milestone it is Vocal Trio from Ireland. Dropping back now is Family Star and All Washed Up is unfortunately living up to its name and is now last of all. Owen Season too is gone and the favourite Chocolate Box is pulled to the outside and he is four lengths behind the leaders. Coming to Tattenham Corner and it is the rank outsider Bixby Lad in the lead. Are we in for an upset in this year's Derby?'

'It is Bixby Lad closely followed by Arcadian Steel. Steven's Curse is gone and Blue Rinse appears to be going backward through the field. Ranger's Son has made up considerable ground and is closing rapidly on the leaders. Right on his tail is Chocolate Box.'

'Swinging around Tattenham Corner with just over three furlongs left to run. The jockey on Bixby Lad has pulled the whip on him and appears to be thrashing him hard in an effort to maintain the lead. Arcadian Steel has pulled out and has started to make his run. The jockey on Bixby Lad is still using the whip on the horse. He must have more than exceeded the allowed strokes. Arcadian Steel has almost caught Bixby Lad but the horse has swung right across his path. Arcadian Steel has received a very severe check indeed, in fact his jockey was almost unseated in the process. He would have to be out of the race.'

'You bastard Jason Carter! You utter bastard!' Mary yelled at him and then burst into tears. Her mother tried to comfort her but her distraught daughter shrugged her off.

'Just two furlongs now to run in this year's Derby,' the resonant sound of the course broadcaster's voice echoed around the box. 'Just two furlongs to go and the favourite Chocolate Box takes up the running being pressured by Ranger's Son. But look at this, Arcadian Steel has been switched to the outside and he is flying. A furlong to go and it is Ranger's Son with Arcadian Steel catching him with every stride. Less than half a furlong to go and it's Ranger's Son with Arcadian Steel just half a length behind. This is an absolutely incredible run by Arcadian Steel. He was completely out of the running after that very bad check he received but he is flying. Thirty yards to go and Ranger's Son is only a neck in front. Arcadian Steel lunges as they cross the line. It is a photo! I cannot separate the two horses. There is no doubt in my mind that had he not received that check then Arcadian Steel would have won with ease. Here is the result of the photo on this year's Derby. And the winner is, by a nose . . . Ranger's Son. Second is Arcadian Steel and third Chocolate Box.'

Mary turned to the rest of them in the box. 'I don't care what they say out there, to me Arcadian Steel won that race without a doubt,' she said miserably. As she spoke she wiped the tears from her eyes with the back of her hand, sniffing fiercely as she did.

'I agree and all that I can say, Victor, is that in spite of the official result, your horse was not beaten. That was one of the most courageous runs that I have ever seen,' John said forcefully.

Victor looked at them all in turn. 'I suggest that we go down and meet Jimmy because as far as I'm concerned he has just ridden the race of his young life.'

They all started to make their way down to the winner's enclosure and Victor's chest swelled with pride at the reception that Jimmy and Samson received from the vast crowd as the pair trotted in. The PA system sparked into life again. 'The stewards have made it known that there will be an inquiry on the running of this race. It will not affect the outcome nor the placings. The result will stand.' The system went dead.

John looked at Victor and said, 'I know that it is not much of a consolation but you can rest assured that Jason Carter is finished as far as racing is concerned. Even if he hadn't tried to knock your horse out of the race, the stewards would have crucified him for that blatant excessive use of the whip. That is one thing that they are dynamite on because it shows racing in a very bad light.'

They reached the enclosure at almost the same time as Jimmy on the horse. He leapt from the saddle and, as he landed, he turned to face Victor. 'We may have just been pipped in the Derby, boss, but we will kill them in the Arc!'

It was Sunday evening before Victor managed to get home. As he drove up he saw that the house had a light on in one of the downstairs rooms. Going in, he found that Mrs Humber had left him some supper on the table with a note: 'Dear Mr Barnes, the whole village is proud of you and your horse. We want to thank you for putting us on the map.'

Victor looked at the cold lamb pie and chutney that she had left for him and laughed. 'Well, at least I made someone happy.' Picking up the pie he took a mouthful as he slowly made his way up the stairs to his bedroom. After the race, Mary had broken down again, big wracking sobs that had torn at his heart. She still blamed herself for what Carter had done. Despite assurances from Victor and both her parents that she was in no way to blame, she had gone to her room in tears and locked the door. As he had driven away he was not sure but he thought that he had seen her at her window. He had stopped the car and, getting out, looked up but saw nothing.

Entering his room Victor slowly made his way across the floor and sat down on the four-poster bed. His mind was in a turmoil going over the events of the past couple of days. He was uncertain of what he should do next. He had achieved so much in such a short time that he should be feeling on top of the world. There still seemed to be something lacking that he could not quite put his finger on. He picked up the photo of Amanda that he always kept on the small chest beside his bed and gazed at it in silence. Suddenly he heard again in his mind something that Mary had whispered to him on the phone the other night. But this time he could swear that it was Amanda's voice and not Mary's that was speaking to him, softly, but with a gentle firmness and authority. He felt a shiver run through his body but it was one of love and not fear that caressed him.

'There are some memories that time can never destroy. You do not have to erase and forget the past to find true happiness in the future.'

He gazed at Amanda's photo for a while as his emotions waged a war within him. He must have sat there for a full ten minutes staring at the picture before raising it to his lips and gently kissing it. Then, just as gently, he placed it in the drawer and closed it. As he did so a warm sense of calmness and contentment swept over him. He picked up the phone and slowly dialled Mary's number. It began to ring and a quivering voice answered, 'Hello.'

Taking a deep breath, he said softly, 'Hello Mary, it's me.'